Winning the Highlander's Heart

The Highlanders
Book 1

TERRY SPEAR

Winning the Highlander's Heart
Published by Terry Spear

DEDICATION

To Joan LeMonte for sharing and caring about my books. Hope you fall in love with the fun-loving Highlanders!

CHAPTER 1

WEST SUSSEX, REIGN OF HENRY I

"My lady!"

The Countess of Brecken's lady-in-waiting, Mai, threw the door open to Anice's guest chambers at Arundel Castle, then quickly slammed it shut. Two gray curls fell loose from the older woman's plaited hair; her ivory cheeks flushed. She breathed in rapid, shortened breaths, and her gray eyes were rounder than the full moon. "His Grace is headed this way. Lady Anice, ye must hide."

'Twas folly for Anice to think she could avoid the king's unwanted solicitations for long. And she, his wife's cousin.

"I am no' hiding, Mai," Anice scolded, "like I said before. I am making myself unavailable to his...charms."

She tied the rope to the bed leg, then ran to the nearest window and tossed the other end out. If the English ladies of her cousin's court had not treated her with contempt because of her Scottish heritage, she would be visiting with the queen right now and could save herself the trouble of fleeing from the king's attempted seduction, *again*.

"Och, my lady, you cannot mean to—"

"Aye, Mai, I mean to. Just delay His Grace if he should come knocking at the door before I have vanished. Moreover, for heaven's sakes be sure to hide the rope. Tell him I am with Her Grace sewing in her solar."

Anice lifted the full skirt of her bliaut and chemise underneath and scrambled atop the embroidered cushion resting on the stone window seat.

With heart pounding, she peered below. 'Twas a shame it opened on the inner bailey of Arundel Castle where women washed garments in large wooden barrels, the blacksmith pounded on an anvil, sending sparks flying, and beyond, noblemen's sons thrust and parried wooden swords on the warm summer day. Still, with everyone a goodly distance across the bailey from where she attempted escape and very much preoccupied, mayhap no one would notice a lady slipping down a rope from the second story window.

Mai wrung her hands. "My lady, what if ye should fall?"

"You are not helping me, Mai. Hush. I have done this many times before as a wee lass. You know that."

But this time was entirely different from her many escapades of the past. 'Twas difficult enough to find a husband who would live long enough to give her wedded bliss, but she was not about to be tupped by a lusty king who already had a wife.

Anice tugged on the rope and when it held, she climbed onto the stone sill. Grasping the rope, she swung over the edge and held on tight. Her arms strained while she wrapped her legs around the rope and began to shimmy down.

A pounding on her chamber door produced a rash of chill bumps to trail along her arms.

Across the courtyard a man shouted, "My lady!"

A streak of panic shot into her bones as she clambered down the rope.

Couldn't a lady take a walk in the kitchen gardens—

even if she got there by extraordinary means—without causing an uproar in the king's staff?

The thud of hooves galloped on the grassy earth in her direction. She cursed under her breath. She needed no horseman's help to descend a rope. Her hands slipped on the coarse hemp and her heartbeat quickened. She was a wee bit out of practice.

"Drop to me! I'll catch you!" the man's deep, sexy voice shouted with a distinctive Scottish burr, as he guided his horse beneath her.

She gave a lady-like snort. If she dropped to whoever was below her, no doubt her skirts would fly up around her ears. "'Tis no concern of yours. Move away." She meant to speak her words harshly, commanding the man to do her bidding at once, but her voice sounded way too soft and overmuch like pleading to her ears.

She glanced down at him, sitting astride his roan destrier. Belted at the waist, a pleated saffron wool tunic rose to mid-thigh, exposing his brawny muscular legs. The narrow tunic sleeves stretched down his arms, widening at the wrist, revealing large hands that clutched his horse's reins with a fierce grip.

Her gaze drew up his massive chest to his dark brown hair, highlighted with reddish strands hanging loose about his broad shoulders, framing and at the same time softening the harsh angles of his face. He had the kind of manly nose that befit Scottish royalty, a sturdy square chin that tilted up toward the heavens, and the kind of lips women begged to kiss. Not a Norman or a Saxon, but a handsome devil of a Highlander. 'Twas not his broad shoulders and chest that gave her pause, but his furrowed brow and darkened brown eyes that compelled a longer look.

Her fingers slid again, and her heart leapt into her throat. To her surprise, the man quickly stood in his stirrups, his hands outstretched, ready to catch her.

"Jump, lass, and I shall catch ye."

A sprinkle of perspiration trickled between her breasts. 'Twas not too far to fall, only one more story now. If she landed on the gentleman, he'd no doubt break her tumble nicely. She continued to slide down the rope, her arms quickly wearying. At twenty summers, she was getting much too old for this.

The rough rope tore at her tender flesh. Her fingers burned. Trying to ignore the pain, she clenched her teeth, and lowered herself further.

"My lady!" The man grabbed at her.

When he caught her foot, she nearly fell and gasped in surprise. She kicked his hand away. "I do no' need your help." Not unless the hand belonged to a Highland laird who wished to take her away from here and back to her home without delay.

His hands slid up her hose-covered leg and rose to her naked thigh. She screamed out in shock. What in heaven's name were his hands doing up her chemise?

"Sorry, if you would quit your squirming—"

"You are no' a gentleman," she snapped, and let go of the rope before the rider manhandled her much more, landing squarely in his lap. He groaned as if she'd caused him pain. Here she thought he looked strong enough to wage the toughest battles without concern.

His large, capable hands curved around her waist with a possessiveness she should be resenting, though she couldn't help wish he'd carry her away home again, and free her from the king's advances. The Highlander smelled of horse, leather, and man—incredibly intriguing—but way too close for comfort, yet she breathed him in like it was the last breath she would ever take. Huskily, he retorted next to her ear, "And ye, lass, are no' a—"

Before he could utter another word, she hopped from his horse, catching the hem of her bliaut on his stirrup. Mortified, she nearly ripped the fabric to get it loose. How many courtiers watched her antics now? She worked on her gown, too busy to find out. Perspiration freckled her brow and her skin grew as hot as the armorer's fire.

"If you would allow me, lass, to free it, you would not show off your chemise or other more remarkable qualities." He smiled broadly and tugged to release her hem. His dark brown eyes now nearly black smiled back at her. Dimples punctuated his bronzed cheeks, but it was the raw look of lust that shook her to the core.

Humiliated, she jerked her gown loose and landed unceremoniously on her bottom on the grassy ground. Horror of horrors her gowns were hiked to her knees. She yanked the hem down with a scowl. His heated gaze shifted from her legs to her eyes and again, his lips curved up at the corners.

Bolting from the ground, she wished she could disappear like a dewdrop evaporated on a sunny day. She darted around the backside of the circular keep. Concerned about who might have watched her jester-like antics, she avoided looking altogether.

Her breath quickened and heart beat as fast as if she'd run a mile through the heather in the middle of summer. Only 'twas not her run that sent her heart soaring, but the man's heated hands that had touched her naked skin and his roguish smile that burned her through and through.

Gently rubbing her hands together, she attempted to soften the sting. 'Twas not the way she planned to spend her days at Arundel. Somehow, she had to convince her cousin to speak with the king on her behalf and allow her to return home before things got out of hand. Well, more so than they were already.

The whole court was sure to know of her escapade by the time she broke her fast.

Reaching the side of the motte that faced the River Arun, she spied Queen Matilda seated upon a stone bench surrounded by her ladies-in-waiting. 'Twas not good.

If Mai told the king Anice was visiting with her cousin

in her chambers, he'd know she lied. Mayhap not. He might have no idea where his wife sat at the moment. Then again, Anice was certain he'd be apprised of her window escape now, too. Would he have a good laugh? Or be angry with her?

She lifted her chin in obstinacy. She refused to be one of his mistresses.

"Lady Anice," Matilda called out near the corner of the garden, enjoying a bit of sun on the warm day.

"Your Grace," Anice curtsied and hurried to join her. "May I have a word with my lady alone?"

The queen's hair, like her ladies', hung in long plaits free of the veils she had hated to wear when she lived with the Black Nuns of Romsey. Even now, Anice could envision Matilda yanking off her veil and stomping on it in defiance of her Aunt Christina who was abbess, and the subsequent beating and scolding she'd received from her. The words Matilda had spoken in her defense before the Archbishop of Anselm of Canterbury before she was allowed to marry King Henry echoed in Anice's mind. Matilda had not taken the holy vows, and her Aunt Christina had veiled her to keep her from the lust of the Normans. She'd been much sought after as a bride, having turned down both William de Warenne, 2nd Earl of Surrey and Alan Rufus, Lord of Richmond. 'Twas rumored even Henry's older brother, William Rufus, king until his untimely death during the hunting accident, considered marrying her. Despite Henry's other more recent love interests, he had espoused he'd been long attached to Matilda, and had long adored her character.

Now, colorful silken cases elongated Matilda's tresses while metal tassels extended them even further. 'Twas every lady's desire to have the thickest, longest hair. Yet, Anice still hid hers under a veil and wimple. Teased mercilessly by the other ladies about her wild red hair and fiery temper, she chose to keep her tresses hidden until she returned to Brecken Castle.

Her cousin tilted her chin down, her eyes worried. "What ails you, Anice? Your cheeks are as red as Elizabeth's gown."

'Twas the man's hands that had clutched Anice's bare thigh that forced the blush in her cheeks. Not to mention exposing her legs and...och, she wouldn't be able to forget the look on the Highlander's face—a scoundrel's fascination and unbridled amusement—all at her expense.

But the queen wouldn't want to hear about that. Nor that the king had propositioned Anice thrice already. He would populate the English countryside with the greatest number of illegitimate children of any of their kings, if he had his way.

"Please, you must speak to His Grace and convince him I need return to my people, Your Grace."

Matilda motioned for her ladies to leave them. Her ladies quit the garden, standing out of their hearing, but waiting still to serve her. Matilda spoke softly. "You know His Grace wishes you to marry a Norman gentleman."

"*I dinna* want that!" Anice scowled. "You were born in Fifeshire yourself, Your Grace. You were..."

Anice fell silent. She wanted to remind her cousin that to an extent Matilda had been forced to marry to make an alliance of sorts to quell the unrest along the Scottish border. Not only that, but to tie the Norman bloodline into the queen's royal Saxon line. Though they were cousins, Anice still had to choose her words carefully.

"What is wrong, Anice?" Her cousin's words were spoken calmly, but she appeared more than concerned.

Your husband tried to interest me in joining him in his chamber earlier this morn while you were at chapel. That's what Anice wanted to tell her, but she could not. She knew very well Henry's philandering hurt Matilda more than she would admit, but the queen would not show how much Henry upset her and Anice would not reveal she was his latest target, if she could avoid it.

Anice bit her lip. How could she convince Matilda she must leave Arundel without telling her of the king's amorous advances? Did the man not stock enough fillies in his stable already? She blew out her breath. "'Tis naught, Your Grace. I am only homesick."

She knew Matilda wanted to return to Westminster where she mainly held court, though like now, she often accompanied Henry on his travels across England, but she hoped her cousin would understand her need to return home.

Wordlessly Matilda studied her, and Anice wondered if her cousin knew the truth of her distress.

Taking a deep, exasperated breath, Anice considered her dilemma. She wished no part of any Norman laird the king wanted her to marry either, who would wed her for her properties and not care one whit about a woman whose Scottish heritage they scorned. Yet, another concern plagued her. Would any marriage she attempted be truly cursed? She quashed the worrisome notion down into the pit of her stomach. For now, avoiding the king proved tantamount.

Not only that, the most dreadful feeling something awful would befall her people at Brecken Castle continued to plague her. Early on, she'd learned to hide from others these strange premonitions that oft came true, but she couldn't contain the dark foreboding that filled her with dread now, forcing her to seek any means necessary to return home where she might do some good.

How could she leave Arundel without the king's permission though? She could not. Not unless her cousin convinced him to allow Anice to return home.

Squinting to get a better look at the inner bailey, she watched as the man—who'd touched her so inappropriately—rode toward the stables with three others. His broad shoulders and the way he held himself erect commanded respect. Impressive. He wore a claymore at his back and a dagger at his hip. And his clothes were of quality fabric. He rode a nobleman's horse, not a common mount, so she assumed he was a man of some import.

"Who is that?" Anice enquired.

"Earl of Pembrinton, but you would do well to avoid the man."

Anice raised a brow, genuinely intrigued. "Why?"

"He seeks audience with His Grace as he is in search of an English bride. It matters not whether she is young and pretty, or that he loves her. He desires what most men crave. Power and money. He is a titled lord without properties."

Anice's heart fluttered. "Mayhap I should meet this Highlander." Though she had already met him, *way* too intimately. But perhaps he would agree to return her home, *if* she could obtain the king's permission.

Matilda shook her head quickly. "He is not for you, cousin. From what I have heard, he had some difficulty with a couple of Scottish families and marriage alliances. Marrying an English woman would end the strife."

Anice's blood heated like a blade of steel grew white hot over an open flame. To think he would prefer an Englishwoman to a bonnie Scottish lass. "But if he seeks property and—"

"I am certain he also believes marrying an English lady will afford him greater...entitlements."

"Then he is no' a true Highlander, but a...a blackguard."

"Watch what you say, Anice. I know how strongly you feel about the English, but I am married to His Grace and this is my rightful place now." She took a deep, steadying breath. "Not only that, but the English educated King Malcolm, after all. My father loved my mother, though he was a Scotsman and she, a Wessex-born princess. Now Prince David has taken a fancy to a Norman lady here, while receiving his education with us. I am sure if King Henry is agreeable, my brother will marry her. 'Tis just the way of things."

Anice groaned deep inside.

The Scottish kings were bought and paid for by the

English. Even Matilda's brother, King Alexander, was considering taking King Henry's illegitimate daughter, Sybilla, for his wife. *That* was why her cousin Alexander, had given her to King Henry as his ward, rather than her being a ward of the Scottish king when her uncle died so suddenly.

Exasperated, Anice sighed deeply.

Matilda patted her arm. "Marry whom His Grace presents to you. You will learn to embrace the changes as I have done. Marriages are partnerships after all. Marrying for love...well, you will grow to love whomever you wed. As for Lord McNeill, 'tis folly to think you will change his mind about an English bride. Let him well enough alone, dear cousin."

Anice curtseyed to Matilda as her cousin motioned for her ladies to return to her.

But Anice would not be thwarted. If the Highlander needed a bride and she needed a husband, the match seemed perfect. Well, almost. Mayhap she would not like his temperament so very much. Though the notion he would touch more than her naked thigh with his large, gentle hands certainly appealed. What would they feel like holding her close? And what would it be like to kiss his smiling lips? There was only one way to find out.

With her heart beating hard, she hastened for the keep where the Highlanders had disappeared. She entered the great hall and ignored the roving eyes of two English knights who glanced her way.

Then she spied the great man and his equally large companions. Her heart skittered.

Laird MacNeill stood between the other two, taller by an inch or so, his hair a richer brown, his eyes the same earthy dark color. The fourth man, a blond with a beard, was nowhere in sight. She turned her attention back to Laird MacNeill. A sensuous smile curved his mouth, forming dimples in his cheeks. But his gaze wasn't focused on her.

Instead, he eyed another lady, an *English* lady, standing near the entrance to the hall. The woman's dark tresses were plaited down her front, but her hair wasn't half as thick or long as Anice's. Anice smiled at the thought. On the other hand, she wanted sorely to scream at the Highlander who made a fool of himself over the Englishwoman.

Rogue.

The other two Highlanders were fairer, their long hair fastened back. She folded her arms. Mayhap if Laird MacNeill were not interested in her, one of the other gentlemen would be.

As if the youngest one had heard her thoughts, he turned and smiled at her. Well-built despite his youth, his hair was the lightest brown of the three men, and a slight scar marred his otherwise smooth cheek. Before she could consider the other gentleman, the youngest quirked a brow to see her gawking at him. Instantly, her cheeks heated. She quickly unfolded her arms and smoothed down her wool gown. The slightest of smiles curved the corners of his mouth, then he tugged on Laird MacNeill's sleeve.

In no way did she act appropriately. She had neither her lady-in-waiting nor a maid attending her, nor was anyone nearby with proper authority, who could formerly introduce her to these gentlemen. Yet, she remained rooted to the stone floor like an oak, unwilling to yield while she contemplated how to approach the Highlanders.

They seemed as reluctant to breech protocol and stood their ground, though they commented freely to one another, smiling with undisguised admiration while she stood ogling them impolitely.

She lowered her lashes and considered the rushes littering the floor. Mayhap this wasn't a good idea after all. Would they think her a brazen woman to...to wish to make their acquaintance in such a fashion? Aye, they would imagine her nothing but a common leman.

Then, too, what did they think of her actions when

she'd climbed out the window?

She wrung her hands suddenly conscious they were cold and clammy. Then she turned, intent on taking a walk...anywhere but here where she was making a fool of herself.

Anice hoped the Highlanders, well one of them at least, would follow her outside so that she could convince him to speak to the king on her behalf and solicit his agreement to return her home. But she heard no footsteps echoing her own and knew then her folly. She was dressed as a lady in exquisite garments, the blue wool the finest of cloth. So they would not think her a serving girl. But these men wanted more than just power and money, or at least the tallest of the three...Laird MacNeill did.

He wanted a lady of quality, but she had to be an English lady.

And that, Anice would never be.

She stomped down the path to the herbal and vegetable garden outside of the kitchen. Hedge walls surrounded the rectangular outdoor room. In seclusion, she walked along the stone walkways, each separating sections of the garden for easier cutting of the plants for meals, medicine, and other uses. Lavender scented the air in the sweetest floral fragrance. She nearly forgot her annoyance when she breathed in the heady scent. But as she continued along the stone path, she fumed about the Highlander again.

Laird MacNeill had a Scottish accent like her. Why should he not like hearing the sound of his countrymen's burr? 'Twas not so bad a sound to her ear.

Footsteps reverberated behind her, and she whipped around, not sure what to expect. Hoping to find the handsome laird following her. Wishing he'd ask her name and want her, just like she wanted him...well, any Highlander to take her away from all this...to return her to her own lands where she'd take on the role of lady of Brecken Castle.

What she found made her heart sink like a stone thrown into the loch. The cook curtseyed to her, then reached down and snipped basil, chive, and red valerian for the meal.

Mayhap, Anice had to find some other Highlander laird if not one of the three were brave enough to attempt to seek audience with her. These did not impress her well enough.

She greeted the cook, then stalked out of the gardens and across the courtyard. She would find some other knights to take her home.

***

Malcolm MacNeill and his youngest brother, Angus, watched the defiant young woman stride toward the stables, while their brother, Dougald, remained behind in the keep trying to find out who she was. Her bearing and dress were impeccable and of the finest fabrics. Definitely a lady. Though he'd never seen one climb out a castle window before to escape from...well, he wasn't sure from what and he still intended to find out.

The interest she'd shown in them just now in the great hall...

Malcolm smiled. He could tell she was intrigued with him by the way her cheeks colored so beautifully, and her perky breasts lifted when her heartbeat quickened. Her green eyes had darkened, just enough to fascinate him further. Had she wanted him to run his hands over more than just her naked thigh?

He sighed deeply. 'Twas an English lady he was bound to wed. Yet, the lass captivated him like no other. But having an English wife...well, he knew he and his brothers would be more accepted by the king and other nobles if Malcolm and his kin married English ladies. Besides, after the trouble he'd had with Brenna, then Catherine...

He shook his head. No more fiery-tempered Scottish lasses.

Was she here looking for a husband like so many of the ladies on the queen's staff? At least he assumed she was on the queen's coterie. More importantly, did the lass hold properties? Or was she like him? Having title, but no land? He had no need of a beautiful, young, titled, and penniless woman. He could offer her nothing in return. Then he chided himself. She was Scottish.

Serving as a steward for his older brother, James, had satisfied him for a while, but now, it was time to settle down. To have lands to call his own. That would remain his sole focus for the time being, he reminded himself.

Malcolm crossed his arms. "What is taking Dougald so long?"

Angus shook his head. "I imagine he is still trying to discover who the young woman is." He glanced at Malcolm. "Think you she is the one for you?"

"She appeared interested, but she is Scottish."

"Mayhap she is already betrothed anyway." Angus drew taller. "Mayhap she was only interested in seeing Highland warriors up close."

Malcolm smiled. "Aye."

"She is a bonny lass. If you dinna please her, mayhap I might have a go."

"She pleases *me*. I do not know about the other way around." Malcolm studied the wiggle of her narrow hips as her blue gown flowed over her backside. Soft curves and all woman. Touching every part of her came to mind, her full pouty lips, her nervous hands, the swell of her fine breasts, and more of her satiny, naked thighs. "She pleases me."

Dougald stepped outside to join them.

"Well?" Malcolm asked, but seeing the look on his brother's stern face, knew he'd found out nothing. "You did not find out anything."

"Nay, but we have an audience with the king."

"I want to know about that woman," Malcolm nodded in the direction of the lady, who was arguing vehemently with some well-dressed gentleman. Malcolm squinted in an attempt to recognize the man. Ah, the marshal in charge of the stables. Twice she wiggled her finger at the marshal to punctuate her statement, though Malcolm stood too far away to hear her words.

Dougald chuckled. "She appears to be a handful." His brother should know, as much as he'd always gotten caught up with that kind of wench in the past, Malcolm thought.

The woman turned and stormed back toward the castle, but as soon as she caught sight of the MacNeill brothers watching her, she stopped dead as if she'd reached the edge of a cliff and stood in peril of falling to her death.

Malcolm's gaze dropped to her bodice, snuggly fitting her breasts, the newer form of gown meant to show off ladies' curves rather than hide them. A girdle of pale blue silk rope wound above her waist, crossed behind, then knotted in front with metal tassels hanging down from them. Certainly for this lady, the girdle accentuated all of the right curves. His attention switched to her hair hidden beneath white cloth. Why, when all the other ladies of the queen's staff showed off their lovely tresses, did this lady not wear her hair unveiled?

"Either she is afraid of us," Angus remarked, placing his hands on his hips, "or she is interested in us, as you have said."

For a moment, she wrung her hands as her gaze focused on Malcolm's, then she strode straight toward them. Rather, toward the entrance to the keep. Her cheeks were positively cherry, and a wisp of hair the color of spun gold, tinted red, fluttered loose from her wimple. Though there were no freckles to bridge her nose, Malcolm thought she resembled a distant cousin on his mother's side. He curbed the notion that twisted his insides. She wasn't a relative certainly, but she was Scottish.

'Twas the end of any interest he had in the vixen. He breathed deeply, trying to rein in his feelings for the woman. He reminded himself any woman he'd touched so intimately would have the same effect on him. Even now, his shaft sprang to life when the image came to mind of spreading her silky thighs and burying himself deep inside her. He'd not been with a woman in far too long.

She tilted her chin even higher and avoided looking at them when she stormed past. Though he caught the look of her eyes as green as the sea and angry as if whipped into a frenzy on a stormy day. Just like his cousin's would be when he and his brothers riled her. He twisted his mouth in annoyance. The woman could intrigue him all she wanted, but he could have no part of her.

He shook his head, wondering how he could have left his native land only to end up in the English castle, lusting after a Scottish lady.

Once she disappeared within the keep, Dougald said, "You dinna think she is Scottish, do you?"

Malcolm ground his teeth in silence and nodded. "Aye, that she is."

His little brother laughed. "Here, Malcolm has convinced each of us to select an English bride and what are we losing our heads over? A Scottish lass?"

"Think you she is here," Dougald asked, ever the man of reason, "looking for an English laird to be her husband?

"Mayhap." Malcolm attempted to appear as though the thought didn't disconcert him, but it did, though why the devil he should care shook him up. Finding a wife to wed was a matter of necessity. 'Twas time to put his title to use, granted to him for having saved King Henry's brother's life, Robert Curthose, during the Crusades. 'Twas time to have a castle, lands, his own people to command, and a bairn to leave his title to. Too bad he had to suffer a wife to make it happen. "If the lady is the king's ward, he may be considering a suitable contract for her hand in marriage."

"Possibly she thought we were some of her kinsman, then finding we were not, she quickly dismissed that notion," Dougald said, rubbing his two-day growth of beard.

"You have a good point." Malcolm motioned to the

keep. "Come, we shall see the king." Though he had to take care of more important business, his thoughts shifted to the feel of the woman's naked skin in his grasp and the sight of her curvaceous legs when she fell on her arse on the grassy ground, her gown resting at her knees, exposing her for his pleasure. Instantly, the blood rushed to his groin again. A bonny lass indeed and one to stay well away from. The rope-climbing incident from the keep tower should have warned him he'd do well to avoid her.

He glanced back at the gate. Had she been trying to leave the castle grounds without escort? Why in heaven's name would she attempt such a dangerous thing?

He shook his head and hastened into the keep, intent on finding out everything he could about the lass...but only for curiosity sake. 'Twas for no other reason he wished to concern himself with the lass. Not because he couldn't shake the vision of her cat-like eyes that held him in contempt, nor the way her cheeks burned with embarrassment, nor the passionate manner in which she expressed herself with the marshal. 'Twas not because he felt obligated from rescuing her from the tower, nor because the feel of her silky skin sent a pleasure-seeking desire coursing through his body.

Simply curiosity overwhelmed him, and he had to investigate her further to satisfy this need. 'Twas no other reason for his interest in her.

"Malcolm," Dougald whispered to him. "You are headed the wrong way. What are you thinking about that has you headed in the direction of the ladies' chambers?"

CHAPTER 2

Anice paced across the bedchamber, still fuming about the marshal not allowing her to remove her horse from the stable. Three knights had said they'd escort her home since they were headed in her direction. So what was the trouble?

The king. He had not approved her leaving, the marshal had reminded her.

Stewing further, she welcomed the solitude in the room, the only sound, her leather shoes crunching on the rushes littering the floor, while the six women she shared the room with sewed with Queen Matilda in her solar that afternoon.

She glanced at the bed that filled a good portion of the large room. How long before the king tried to sequester her to his chambers again?

She lifted the lid of her trunk sitting against the stone wall opposite the door, thinking to change her gown. A purple bliaut hanging on a hook above this tickled her cheek. A gust of wind swept through a crack in the mortar between the thick stone walls. A tapestry, depicting women sewing in a garden, stirred.

Her lady-in-waiting stepped into the room, her blue eyes hot with annoyance. "My lady, Her Grace scolded me for not being with you earlier. She said she glimpsed you in the great hall without me by your side and...and that while you were unaccompanied, you came upon three Highlanders. You did as you pleased back home, my lady, as it was your privilege and you were safe there, too. But here in the English castle, you need to—"

Anice waved for the gray-haired woman's silence. Having attended Anice since her birth, Mai oft shared her words of wisdom. But right now, Anice needed them not.

It did not matter to her lady-in-waiting though, and again, she spoke her mind. "One of the English knights said that one of the Highlanders asked who you were, but he wouldna say, as the Highlander did not belong here anyway."

The knight's highhanded remark stoked Anice's ire. "The knight did not like it that a Highlander laird would be interested in a Scottish-born lady?" Then the notion occurred to her that at least one of the Highlanders was intrigued with her after all. There was hope for her yet.

"Several Norman lairds have asked the king to grant them favor in seeking your hand, my lady, I overheard Her Grace say to one of her ladies-in-waiting."

Anice wondered why the king delayed telling her this. Was it because he wished to have a taste of her first? "Aye, the lairds wish me for my land and money. No' because they are interested in me for myself."

"'Tis the way of the world, my lady. You will be the lady of the castle no matter who you see fit to wed. You need no' marry some stubborn Scotsman. You would be better off without, I say."

But Anice had her heart set on marrying one of her own kind, someone she could understand. She had no understanding of the ways of the English. And no use for them either. "Would the king wish a Scotsman to marry me?" That brought a fresh worry to mind. What if King Henry did not want her to marry one? No, he would not want that. He'd want her to marry an Englishman, actually a Norman most likely, who'd swear fealty to his rule. In that way, the king would control her properties. Could he trust the Scottish warriors to be as loyal to him? She didn't think so.

Mai avoided answering her question. "Are you ready to break your fast, my lady?"

"Aye. I have been ready since I missed morning meal."

"You are not accustomed to the English rules yet, my lady. Mayhap in a couple of more days you shall be well adjusted."

Anice would not be staying at Arundel to grow accustomed to the king's rules. One way or another she intended to be on her way.

With her stomach rumbling, she walked down the massive stairs to the great hall beside her lady-in-waiting. Inside, tables had been erected for the meal like the fingers of a comb. The head table, the spine of the comb, sat slightly elevated and centered against the wall. The smell of burning tallow, of fresh baked bread and venison scented the air, while conversation continued before the king and queen made their appearance.

Anice had no intention of searching for MacNeill or his companions. Nay. She would sit at the table she normally did without any thought to where the Highlanders perched themselves. Why should she care where they sat, or what they ate, or how they conducted themselves? Why should she care when they were so determined to find *English* brides?

Well, at least the tallest one.

She had no interest in them at all.

Not in their warrior bodies, their broad shoulders and backs and tall statures. No interest in their dark eyes, especially the tallest one. The one with the dimples when he smiled at another lady that gave him a roguish, mischievous look.

Did the lady return the smile? Most likely. Too busy ogling the youngest Highlander, Anice hadn't noticed the lady's response to Laird MacNeill's obvious interest in her.

Anice groaned. It mattered not to her whom he attempted to charm. She took a deep breath and glanced around the room. Was there no other Highlander she could solicit to return her home?

"My lady," Mai said, directing her to her usual table. "Queen Matilda wishes to speak with you after the meal."

"I just spoke with her before—"

"Something must be discussed, she said, but spoke no further on the subject."

Anice quashed the worry that plagued her. Had the king decided whom she should wed?

To think some man had to be bribed to marry her. Och, the notion incensed her, and her blood quickly heated with irritation. Had she been a man, she could have married whom she pleased, and the castle and lands would have been her own.

When she stood beside the bench where she would sit, her gaze searched for...not for the Highlanders as she truly didn't care if they went straight to the devil, but for...the king and her cousin's arrival. She straightened her back, readying herself to greet them like all the other courtiers would when the royal couple walked into the hall. The place grew quiet and she took a deep breath, expecting to see them.

Instead, the three Highlanders entered.

Her heart skipped a beat. Annoyed, she attempted to quiet her unwelcome reaction to their presence.

For a moment, they surveyed the room for empty seats.

She held her breath when the youngest pointed in her direction. Two empty spots were situated beside her. Where were the knight and his lady who usually sat there?

MacNeill nodded, then motioned to a vacant place at another long table.

She narrowed her eyes at him. He would take the seat at

the other table to avoid her because she wasn't English?

Her breath caught as he and the youngest strode across the great hall and soon stood beside her while the remaining Highlander took his place before the other trestle table.

Once the king and queen sat, the courtiers followed suit. After the wine was served, and the bread cut, the younger of the two Highlanders began to speak. "I have heard talk of a bonny lass who tried to leave the grounds today without escort *or* His Grace's permission."

"Aye, my little brother. How could a lady be so foolish as to do such a thing?" Laird MacNeill asked. "I have heard tell she displeased the king with her actions. She should be taken across a man's knee and paddled like a da would his unruly bairn."

Anice fumed. They knew it was she they spoke about. How dare they talk about her behind her back, to her face? How dare they say she should be punished...in such...such an arrogant manner? How dare the brigands!

As they crunched on their bread, she fingered her goblet, wanting to get back at them, but not knowing what to say. She considered their words further. So the two men were brothers. Was the other also? What happened to the fourth?

"I cannot believe we came here seeking brides and instead have been given a job...by order of our most illustrious king," the younger brother said.

"Aye. And to think, Angus, we must give up the notion of having a sweet wife hanging on our every word so that we can protect the virtue of one who is..."

Anice waited for the older MacNeill, who couldn't have been any older than his mid-twenties, to finish his statement. He caught her eye and smiled. Her body instantly warmed with embarrassment to be caught listening in on their private conversation, though she had no doubt they spoke loudly enough for her benefit.

When Malcolm didn't finish his words, Angus spoke.

"Be careful what you say, Malcolm. We will have to live by the lady's rule."

"Aye." Malcolm picked up a wedge of cheese. "To think now we have to run the lass's castle while the Norman fop pursues her."

Anice stayed the rim of the cup at her lips. They weren't talking about her. They had to be discussing some other woman now. She stared at the two of them, but both seemed content to shove venison into their mouths and say no more.

"The English ladies," she remarked as if she were speaking to herself, but with an attempt to make her words sound more...English, "willna..." She paused, chiding herself for the mistake. "Will no doubt miss the attentions of three fine lairds..." She cleared her throat. Trying to slip her tongue around the English version of her words proved more difficult than she thought. "*Lords* of the MacNeill clan."

Seemingly dumbfounded, Malcolm and his brother stared at her, then both burst out laughing.

The hair stood on her arms as her blood heated with chagrin. She didn't think what she said funny in the least.

"Aye, that they will," Angus said, still chuckling.

A smile simmered on Malcolm's lips, and his dark eyes watched Anice as if she were a bird and he the hawk who chased her. Yet, he said nothing in reply.

She fingered a piece of cheese. "Why, I wonder, would a Highlander want an Englishwoman for a bride?" She spoke with a modicum of disbelief.

His eyes sparkling, Malcolm asked, "Why no'?"

"A Highland lady oft has no choice, so it seems." She glanced at the king and his wife sitting at the high table, irritated how women had so very little say in whom they might marry. "But a Highland laird..." She shrugged a shoulder.

"You mean to tell me you dinna want a Norman for a husband?"

She glowered at him.

Angus smiled. "Hmm, it seems she was not checking us out to see if we were kin of hers after all, but looked us over as husbandly prospects, Malcolm."

Mai grumbled under her breath. For being an older woman, she had the hearing of a feral cat.

Anice retorted, "Why in heaven's name would I do that? I was looking for...someone else who was not there."

"And the incident at the stable?" Malcolm asked, his voice hardened as if he were her father, who'd she'd lost some years ago, about to give a lecture on something she ought not have done.

"The business is no' yours." She sipped some more of her wine, trying to reduce her annoyance, which immediately brought a heated blush to her skin.

"As a matter of fact, the king has made it my business, if you are Lady Anice, Countess of Brecken of Glen Affric." He bowed his head slightly. "We have not been properly introduced, but I am Malcolm MacNeill, Earl of Pembrinton, and this is my youngest brother, Angus. O'er yonder is our brother, Dougald. We have each been given positions on your staff at Brecken."

"What?" The Highlander was daft. Had he been nipping at the wine cask before the meal? Her steward made the selections for her staff while she was away. Not the king.

"I have been given the job to oversee your properties until you have taken a husband. For now I am your humble steward, my lady." Again, he bowed his head in reverence to her.

She stared at him, wondering if the king had taken leave of his senses. Matilda had said nothing to her about any of this. Yet, a trickle of dread wormed its way into her stomach. Was this what Matilda had needed to talk to her about following the meal?

Nay, the MacNeill was mistaken. "I have a steward, Laird MacNeill, thank you verra much. So you'd best tell the king you are back in the market for an English bride."

Malcolm set his knife down, a look of concern reflecting in his dark eyes. "Seems, my lady, there has been a wee bit o' a scandal at Brecken. I thought you might have been apprised of the situation already, ergo your reason for trying to leave the grounds before the meal. Your steward, chamberlain, and treasurer have all vanished without a trace."

Anice struggled to make sense of the news. The blood rapidly drained from her face, forcing a dizziness to wash over her. She grabbed the oak table to steady herself.

Malcolm's hand seized her arm before the great hall grew dark, as if the day had turned to night without tallow to light the way.

CHAPTER 3

Malcolm paced across the grassy bailey, his head pounding with gusto, furious with himself for breaking the news to Lady Anice in such a forthright manner. It mattered not that he had not known she was unaware of the problems at her estate. Truly, he thought her trip to the stables and subsequent tongue-lashing of the marshal, evidence she wished to return home at once and take matters in hand.

But he should have ensured she had already learned of the situation beforehand. Beyond that, he should have realized the lady was of delicate temperament. Though determining she was Scottish born gave him the false impression she would have more fortitude than that. Still, she was a lady, and he should have taken that into account.

No way had he wanted to cause the scene that followed during the meal.

His brothers now watched him nearby as he crossed the grass back and forth, trying to settle his discomfiture. Worry etched across Angus's wrinkled brow. Dougald's lips, on the other hand, curved upward in a devilish smirk. Dougald was the one who usually got himself into dilemmas with the ladies like this. Malcolm preferred the battlefield, fighting man-to-man, not dealing with women and their highly emotional states, which could lead any man to an early grave.

Malcolm shook his head.

Now what would happen? Everything that had occurred ran through his mind over and over again. The look of utter horror on Lady Anice's face and that of her lady-in-waiting's. The fading of color from Anice's cheeks until she was paler than the moon. Her lower lip had trembled and at once, he'd wanted to take every word he'd spoken back. How could he have hurt her so? But it did not stop there. Her green eyes could not have widened any further, then tears had clouded them, though she had managed to keep the tears in check with some difficulty. There was no sight, no battle, nothing that could bring him to his knees like the tears of a woman.

Particularly, when he'd brought them about.

"Think you the king will change his mind about us taking the lady's vacant staff positions?" Angus asked. Anxiety threaded his words, always the worrier of the three, though despite his youth, Malcolm's youngest brother had seen enough bloodshed for two lifetimes.

"If so we can pursue our previous intentions." When his brothers raised their brows in question, Malcolm clarified, "Find English brides." Though at the moment, the thought did not appeal.

Dougald chuckled. "Think you the king will let us near his Englishwomen after distressing the Scottish lass?"

Malcolm paused and glanced at the location of the sun, ignoring his brother's jibe. "The king wished us to leave as soon as possible. With the lady so indisposed, mayhap we should wait until the morrow."

"Mayhap we should leave her here to recover a wee bit longer," Dougald suggested, his tone deadly serious. "It would be better to set accounts right at her castle if we dinna have to worry about the lady's health, dinna you agree?"

"Aye." Malcolm took a ragged breath, trying to settle the concern that plagued him. Ever since he'd seen the woman, he'd done everything wrong. First, they'd never been properly introduced. No, before that. He'd run his hands up her naked leg. He smiled. That he hadn't minded.

Then he had to tell her horrors that caused her to faint dead away. Worse than that because of his having done so, he had deemed it his place to carry her to the bedchamber, which consequently caused quite a stir. He'd hurt her when he ought not have, and he had to make it up to her in some small way. At least, that's what he told himself.

When he had returned to the meal, he'd overheard the snickering from the English nobles speaking about him as if he were a buffoon. Some of the ladies seemed shocked...others, well, he wasn't certain.

Dougald cleared his throat. "I thought Queen Matilda was going to faint, too, when you carried Lady Anice out of the hall."

"I'm afraid I had not been thinking quite clearly."

"Oh, I dinna know, Malcolm," Dougald said with his typical teasing tone. "The lady sitting next to me told another how heroic the Highlander was. The Englishmen did not like it because you showed them up. They would have had their servants take care of an indisposed lady. But for a laird to make the effort...I think your actions sparked some attention amongst some of the more eligible English ladies. Quite a brilliant plan, really, Malcolm. Wish I had thought of it."

Malcolm groaned. The notion he'd aided Anice just to make an impression on Englishwomen of the king's court didn't sit well with him. If he could, he'd take every action and word he'd committed back and begin all over again...steering clear of the Scottish lass entirely.

Dougald continued with his teasing banter. "I heard tell her lady-in-waiting ordered you out of the bedchamber."

Had they not been at Arundel while King Henry was in temporary residence, Malcolm would have walloped

Dougald good. Though he hadn't meant to explain himself to his brother, the words slipped out before he could stop them. "I offered my further assistance. Truthfully, I wished a chance to express my apologies to the lady."

"Aye." The sparkle in Dougald's eye showed he didn't believe Malcolm at all.

Malcolm bit his tongue, not wishing to further Dougald's subtle ribbing by adding timber to the flame.

"The king's physician saw to her?" Dougald asked, his tone changing to concern, but whether for the lady, or worried that Malcolm might haul off and hit him despite his wanting to keep up appearances, he wasn't certain.

"Aye," Malcolm said, still bothered by what he had done to the lady.

"Then all we need do is find out if His Grace has changed his mind about us working for Lady Anice."

What did the king think about them? That they were boorish, bullheaded Scotsmen with no sensitivities?

His stomach clenched with worrying how Anice had taken the news. He glanced up at the window to the shared chambers. Was she conscious yet?

The king's redheaded steward joined them, his blue eyes narrowed, and his jaw set. "Lord MacNeill, His Grace wishes you to depart as soon as you can for Brecken Castle. But because of Lady Anice's delicate condition, he suggests you leave on the morrow."

"We wondered if perhaps the lady should stay here longer to rest. We can return for her in a fortnight," Malcolm offered, hoping they could leave the lady behind so he could get on with the business at hand. Would not she be safer with her king and cousin Matilda? Particularly when they had no idea what had happened to Anice's staff members.

"She wishes to leave at once, but His Grace says no. She will leave on the morrow with you as His Grace has said."

"Aye."

The steward scuttled back inside the keep. Malcolm glanced at his brothers, who both smiled at him.

Dougald shook his head, the knowing look on his face, annoying Malcolm. "I have told you, the lady is a handful."

"Aye, that she is." A soft, warm, curvaceous handful all right. When he'd had his arms wrapped around her soft body, all he could think of was how fortunate the laird would be who gained her hand in marriage. His neck muscles strained with tension. So why did this thought stir him into wanting to do battle when he desired instead an English bride?

***

Anice stared out the window, watching Laird MacNeill pace across the inner bailey. Was he bothered that he had upset her so? Or did he worry he'd lost favor with the king?

Mai placed her hand on her shoulder, her touch warm and comforting like her mother's had been when she was just a child. "My lady, the king's physician bade you stay in bed until the morrow."

"I am fine, Mai. I dinna need to rest."

Mai peeked out the window. "I told ye to leave the Highlander well enough alone. Look what he did to you! Frightened you half to death. Me, too, if anybody has a care."

Swallowing hard, Anice rubbed her chilled skin. "Did my staff run off because they have stolen my funds? That is what I have to know. Or have they been disposed of for some sinister reason? I will not be able to sleep a wink all night. I must know what happened to them and why. Their families must be overcome with grief. Why cannot His Grace let me leave now?"

Queen Matilda cleared her throat as she walked into the chambers. "Because the king's physician says you shall stay. Why are you up and about? You are to be resting in bed."

Anice quickly curtsied. "I am no' tired, beg your pardon, Your Grace. Why did you no' tell me what happened already?"

"I did not know until right before the meal."

"Was everything he said true? Laird MacNeill, I mean. That he and his brothers will replace my staff?"

"Until you are wed, aye."

Anice narrowed her eyes. "And who is to be chosen for me? An English laird?"

"A Norman lord. Baron Harold de Fontenot will be visiting you once you return. He is the king's most fervent choice."

"Why?"

Queen Matilda raised her chin a notch. "He is loyal to His Grace. He hopes that you will look on the gentleman favorably."

Had Anice any choice? She doubted it.

"I have to say, my cousin, I spoke to His Grace about permitting you to return to your castle because of how homesick you are. You should not have tried to leave here on your own. English nobles will think you are a wild Scotswoman, unruly and unmanageable. Rumors are circulating you even climbed out the keep window. Of course, you would not have done anything so foolish as that. 'Tis a wonder what stories idle tongues will forge next."

Anice fought speaking in her defense, pursed her lips, and kept her mouth closed.

"Then there is this matter of the curse, but of course only the truly superstitious believe in it."

Did her cousin have to bring *that* up? Even though she fought believing it herself, she sometimes wondered—

"I must admit, Anice, I admire you for not succumbing to the charms of my husband. Any woman in your place would not have done so. For that reason, I spoke on your behalf."

Anice smiled, grateful for her assistance, and glad to know that Henry's actions had not gone unnoticed by Matilda. "Thanks be to thee, Your Grace." She curtseyed deeply. "I appreciate all Your Grace has done for me."

Matilda poked her nose out the window. "His Grace is sending the MacNeill brothers to fill your staff in the interim and escort you home."

"Why? Should I no' make this decision about my staff?" Anice couldn't help the dismay coating her words. Though she was pleased the Highlanders would return her home, there were others on her staff she wished to promote because of their loyalty to her and giving the positions to outsiders wouldn't be appreciated by most, she feared.

"His Grace wishes it so. Though, I suspect it has something to do with him not wanting the Highlanders to court the English ladies here."

Anice's mouth dropped open, and she couldn't help being angered that Henry would be so deceitful. "Do the MacNeills realize this?"

"I would think not. These positions are the highest in your staff. They no doubt are proud of their assignment."

"For how long?"

"Until the baron has your hand in marriage. He will then hire his own staff."

"And the MacNeills?"

Matilda shrugged a shoulder. "'Tis not for me to say. As to another matter, His Grace intends to do battle with his brother again, and he wishes this marriage of yours decided soon."

Anice stared at her cousin. "Robert Curthose received the Duchy of Normandy upon his father's death. Cannot he be satisfied? His Grace only received five-thousand pounds of silver when the king died, for heaven's sakes."

"Robert has always maintained that after their older brother died in the hunting accident, he should have been next in line."

As by rights of succession he should have been. But Henry acted as fair handed as kings go, and she'd only heard ill tidings about Robert, who was not liked by many of the

Norman nobles. His being away fighting in the Crusades at the time of William's untimely death left the throne free to Henry, the youngest son of William I. Though many hadn't thought he'd ever have had a chance at the throne, and was educated instead, mayhap to become a bishop. Being one of the first literate kings, who also spoke English, Henry's training was sure to have pleased Matilda.

Matilda took a deep breath, her shoulders sagging, and said, "Uncle Edgar Atheling, is siding with Robert."

"Nay, he cannot do that! What does His Grace think?"

"Edgar would have been king of England had William of Normandy not invaded. Edgar had been too young to fight back at the time."

"Aye." How different would things have been had the Normans not taken over? But if Robert were able to wrest power away from Henry, then what would happen? To Matilda? To her? To any of those who were loyal to Henry?

Matilda motioned to the bed. "The king's physician says you must rest, and I insist you obey his orders."

Anice wrinkled her brow, curtsied, then climbed into bed.

"I will visit with you later."

"Your Grace," Anice said.

A servant closed the door after the queen's exodus. Mai fussed with Anice's bedcovers, the top...a blue cotton quilt brought back from the Middle East by one of the knights during the Crusades and given as a gift to the royal family, had kept Anice warm on the cool nights.

Mai pulled the quilt beneath Anice's chin. "I told you that you should have stayed in bed. Here Her Grace has to go and tell you, too."

"I am fine."

"I could not believe that Laird MacNeill had the bullheadedness to carry you up to the chambers like he did."

Anice clenched the quilt in her fists. "You have told me this repeatedly, Mai. Please dinna bring it up again."

"He wouldna leave either. I thought I would have to call the guard. Black-hearted knave."

Anice stared at Mai. "You said it was because he wished to see if I needed anything more." She unclenched her hands and smoothed out the quilt resting at her breast. "'Twas a kind gesture, naught more."

"Och. The laird himself should not have carried you to your room, then stared at you like that."

Anice frowned, not liking the implication. Was he thinking what it would be like to bed the Scotswoman? The very idea. Yet, the notion forced a flood of warmth to invade her body. He'd already had his hands upon her naked skin where they should never have been. What would it be like to lay with such a brawny figure naked under the linens, making love, though she could only imagine what that would be like.

"He stared like what?" Anice asked, gruffly.

"I should not say."

"You have already said quite enough about the matter when I have warned you to say no more. What are you no' saying this time?"

"Well, 'tis just that he wouldna let any servant carry you up and so it gave the impression that..." Mai plumped her pillows but didn't finish her sentence.

"That *what*?" Anice's blood began to stir. The gentleman had felt terrible for upsetting her. For causing her to faint, nothing else. Why would anyone make anything more of his concern than that?

"Well, others say—no' me, mind you—but others say he has taken a fancy to you."

"That is absurd. He wishes an English lady."

"Aye, but you heard Queen Matilda. His Grace does not want the MacNeills to wed English ladies on the queen's staff. Now he is having the Highlanders work for you. Tongues wag, my lady. Many are wagering one of the brothers will ask you for your hand in marriage once the

34

Highlanders realize they have no chance to wed an Englishwoman of nobility."

To think Anice had even considered the possibility of charming one of the Highlanders to whisk her away to her castle and keep her safe. The very idea that one of the MacNeills would marry her as second choice when they could not have their first. She folded her arms. "They should have bet whether I would take the gentleman up on his offer."

Mai's cheeks reddened.

Anice shook her head, infuriated that the courtiers had nothing better to do than place wagers on her marital status. "And? You are no' usually like this, Mai...careful about what you say. Come out with it."

Mai cleared her throat, then fussed some more with the bed linens. "Many say you shall jump at the chance to marry one of the men, my lady. The rumor you wish to marry a Highlander is well known. I believe many are betting that should one of the MacNeills offer a proposal of marriage, you would accept. Of course, His Grace will still have to approve, and this will most likely be the biggest mountain the two of you will have to traverse."

"That is saying that I do indeed want any of these Highlander scoundrels. Further that any of them would stoop so low as to wish a Scottish bride." She gritted her teeth and again clenched her fists, trying to curb her annoyance. "I willna miss the evening meal. Wake me in plenty of time to prepare myself."

"But, my lady, the queen said—"

"Both His Grace and the queen will be pleased to see I have made such a miraculous recovery. Wake me, Mai, after I have had this no' needed sleep I am being forced to take."

***

The padding of leather crunching on rushes woke Anice some hours later. She sat up in bed, not believing she could really have slept all that time, let alone even a moment.

Mai quirked a brow at her.

Anice shrugged. "My eyes wearied. I rested them a moment."

"Aye, 'tis nearly sunset, my lady." The woman's lips lifted slightly.

"It must have been close to this when I lay down then." Anice knew it hadn't been. Still, she couldn't give her lady-in-waiting satisfaction in saying she told her so.

Though the king's physician had told Anice to stay in her chambers for the evening meal, she merely took his words as a kindly gesture. She intended to eat with the rest of the courtiers to prove that she was fit to travel on the morrow. Furthermore, she had no intention of letting the English think she wilted like a rose plucked from the soil at the first hint of ill news. Nor would the word about her staff deter her from facing her problems just as the lady of the castle should.

With her head held high, she and Mai returned to the great hall. When she spied the same two MacNeill brothers standing beside her usual seat, her resolve plummeted.

Mai whispered to her, "I see the Highlanders have taken up residence next to where you always sit, my lady. Would you prefer some other arrangement?"

The two brothers watched her as if they'd spotted a deer on the hunt for the taking. Her whole body heated. Though she'd have preferred sitting anywhere else this eve, how would she be able to assume her role as their mistress if she couldn't even sit beside them at a meal?

Even now, her hesitation at moving to any bench caused a stir. Several watched her, the room grew hushed, and whispered words, small smiles and nods of heads, greeted her.

Mai, normally not bothered by much at all, seemed to notice the tension and said, "My lady, where do you wish to sit?" She spoke more urgently now, designed to nudge Anice into making a decision, quickly.

Anice straightened her shoulders and headed straight for Laird MacNeill. "We shall sit where we always do, Mai."

"Aye, my lady," her maid muttered under her breath, her voice not entirely pleased.

Across the hall, Laird MacNeill spoke to his younger brother, who responded with a smile and a nod.

She wished she could have heard his words. Did he tell his brother how he knew the lady would want his company at the meal? That she still sought being near them, as she wished having a Scottish laird for a husband?

She harrumphed under her breath. Mai glanced at her, but Anice wouldn't let on what she was thinking.

***

"My lady." Malcolm bowed most courteously when she approached him, attempting to rectify his status with her. The Lady Anice was uncommonly beautiful, with her full pink lips pursed in a pout, and her green eyes now downcast, watching her feet, not him. 'Twas the reaction she had in drawing nearer to him that fascinated him most. Her pert breasts rose with her quickened breath, and her peach-colored cheeks turned rosy. She avoided his gaze, concentrating instead on the seat she would take. Her choice to sit beside him gladdened him, though he'd noticed her hesitation in sitting so close to him again. Now, he could apologize to her and make amends. After all, if he were to work for her, he wished to take care of business in an amenable way.

"Laird MacNeill." Anice's eyes caught his for just an instant, and she curtsied. Then she turned to his brother and they greeted each other in the same fashion.

Before Malcolm could say anything further, the king and queen walked into the great hall. Conversation ceased as the courtiers showed their respect.

Once all were seated, Malcolm faced the lass. "Lady Anice, I beg your forgiveness for having upset you."

"I accept your apology, my laird," she quickly said, as if

another word of the matter would undo her fragile composure.

Wishing to air his concern, Malcolm wanted to reassure her he'd had no intention of upsetting her earlier. "I would have you know I did not realize you knew naught about the happenings at your castle."

She turned away from him.

He took a deep breath, not sure how to handle the situation any better than he was. On the battlefield, he had no difficulty. The lady proved to be more than he had bargained for, however. If he were to work for her, he had to learn how to manage the willful lass better. "I am sorry if I have again upset you."

"Nay, the matter is upsetting, but no' because of you. 'Tis a situation I will have to rectify quickly however."

Her words were spoken softly without malice, but it was the content of her conversation that troubled him at once. Was the woman mad? He and his brothers were well qualified to take on the positions given them. No lady needed to attend to such matters, nor would he wish her interference. What if the situation turned dangerous? The lady would not be harmed on his watch. "My brothers and I will take care of it."

Her green eyes flashed in anger. "'Tis *my* castle." Already her voice had raised a notch.

"Aye." Malcolm clenched his teeth. The woman was proving impossible to deal with, but he had every intention of taking care of her affairs as quickly as possible to assess the damage done and determine what had become of her staff members. He certainly could not have a woman, who was so easily indisposed, in harm's way if it came to that.

But if she felt comforted by the notion she was in charge—though it ground on his sense of pride to have to acquiesce—he would attempt to placate her. Word would get back to their king about how well he and his brothers had accomplished the mission. Then His Grace in all his wisdom would look favorably upon granting them the right to marry English ladies of quality.

Anice poked her spoon into her boor in brasey and pushed the pork down into the broth. Breadcrumbs, currants, and onions floated to the top.

"Can you tell me anything about these men?" It didn't hurt to begin his investigation early while she played with her food.

"They have disappeared, so I have been told." She lifted a spoonful of broth to her lips and turned to him.

He closed his gaping mouth. Was she being difficult because she had not selected his brothers and him to take over the positions? Or did having to leave the king's castle after having just arrived, disappoint her? After all, living in the royal household afforded luxuries lesser lairds' castles held not.

He rubbed his chin. No, she'd been trying to leave before she'd even learned of the calamity at her castle. What on earth had that been all about then?

"Lady Anice, earlier today you tried to take your horse from the stables and depart. I thought you had learned of the troubles at your castle, but apparently this was not the case. So that leads me to ask: why did you try to leave?"

"You have already stated the punishment you would mete out for such a rash action. Now you ask what caused that behavior?" She tsked. "A good laird finds out the extenuating circumstances before pronouncing punishment for the crime."

Malcolm quashed the irritation tightening his stomach muscles. What infuriated him most was the lass spoke the truth. He glanced at Angus, who winked at him, a smile plastered across his face. Malcolm faced Anice. "I spoke rashly before, my lady. I concede you are right. So then what extenuating circumstances caused you to attempt to leave the grounds without the king's permission and proper escort?"

She raised one brow. "Do you wish to judge me?"

The woman was maddening!

He calmed his thoughts before he spoke. "Nay, my lady. I wish to know better so I may serve you more aptly."

"Aye, I see. Methinks you are most honorable, but 'tis no' your concern."

Just her tone of voice said mockingly gave him pause. She did not think him an honorable man, rather one who should mind his own business. Infuriating! To think when first he glimpsed the lass, he'd had any interest in her! Best to leave the wench to her own secrets, and he to his. He would accomplish the job His Grace commanded him to and no more than that. He would have his English bride. The laird who took Anice for his wife would no doubt wonder whatever possessed him to ask her hand in marriage.

"My thanks, my lady, for your kind words." He wasn't sure what overcame him to say the next words out of his mouth, but as soon as he said them, he knew there'd be trouble. "Then you will not mind if I ask His Grace to allow you to stay longer. You have traveled all this way and have only been here two days. No sense in you returning so soon. My brothers and I shall—"

He quit speaking as soon as her green eyes darkened with fury, her cheeks burned bright as ripened, red tomatoes, and her mouth pursed with great restraint. He should have rested his tongue once she'd given her false compliment and he'd returned the same. So why did he not heed his own concern?

He desired to know why she'd tried to leave the castle grounds...that's why. One way or another, he'd learn the truth.

But for now, he judiciously clamped his mouth shut and waited for the explosion to follow.

CHAPTER 4

Anice glared at Malcolm MacNeill. How dare the Highlander presume to tell the king what to do concerning her disposition? How *dare* he! "Who do you think you are telling His Grace what I should do?"

"My lady," Malcolm quickly said, "I would not presume to tell His Grace anything. I only thought I would suggest—"

"If you suggested something to that effect, Laird MacNeill, you can just—"

Mai tugged at her arm.

Anice turned and scowled at her lady-in-waiting, furious with the interruption. "What, Mai? You have interrupted me when I have only just begun to speak my mind and put this hidebound Scotsman in his—"

"My lady," Mai said, her voice hushed, "do you hear how quiet the hall has become?"

Anice looked around to see the courtiers scraping their plates with spoons, and downing their tankards of wine, but the conversation had dropped to a whisper. Many an eye cast a gaze her way. Had her voice risen that much? No, some other reason caused the courtiers to speak more softly. She turned to see if the king had signaled for the staff to quiet down.

King Henry's bright eyes focused on Anice, making her feel morbidly self-conscious. He was a handsome king with black, short curly hair that covered his ears and reached down to the jeweled collar of his tunic. A mustache that curled past his lips didn't hide the grim line of his mouth, nor did the furrow of his brow go unnoticed. The queen's puzzled, but concerned look, made Anice feel as though wood ants were crawling over every inch of her naked skin. Her cheeks already burned from Laird MacNeill's words, but now the heat spread all the way to her toes. How many times would this Highlander embarrass her?

She turned her attention to her meal. The servants hurried to pass out dove on oyster shell. With no intention of speaking further to the Scotsman during the meal, Anice picked at her fowl with her fingers.

Conversation slowly renewed again to a low-pitched roar.

But the more she thought about Malcolm's words, the madder she grew. To think some Highlander she didn't know would advise the king to keep her at Arundel longer! Why here she'd presumed the Highlander could save her from the wicked lust of the king. And here instead, the Scot would help to put her at further risk? The very idea!

She ripped a wing off her bird and pointed it at Malcolm. "You may think you can do as you will where I am concerned because His Grace has made you my steward. But let me tell you something, Laird MacNeill, if you so much as hint at my staying here further—"

"My lady," Mai cautioned under her breath.

"What now, Mai? I am no' speaking verra loud."

Mai nodded her head in the direction of the head table where King Henry spoke to his steward.

The redheaded man bowed, then headed straight for Anice's table. She dropped her wing on her plate and picked up a piece of bread. The laird had no business with her so she ignored his approach.

But as his footsteps drew nearer and the hall grew quiet, her body temperature elevated again.

"Lady Anice," the steward said.

She turned to face him. "Aye, my laird?"

"His Grace wishes to know if there is some trouble here." He glanced at Malcolm as if to indicate he knew where the problem lay.

Yes, there was trouble indeed, all in the form of one brawny, dark-haired, brown-eyed Scotsman. For a moment, she took sympathy on him as Malcolm and his brother's eyes fairly pleaded with her not to speak ill of Malcolm.

The hall remained hushed while the steward waited for her answer. All eyes watched them as if Anice had become the court jester for the evening meal. If she said what she really thought, that the Highlander had no right even thinking he was taking over her castle, or that he had no business telling her or anyone else that she should remain behind, the MacNeill brothers would be thoroughly disgraced.

"Nay, my laird." She would not harm the brothers in that manner. Though she gave enough of a delay to force sweat upon the brothers' brows. 'Twas enough for now. After all, this Malcolm warred with her with his threats to tell...*advise* the king to keep her here.

Her slow response evidently troubled the steward. "Are you certain, my lady? His Grace was concerned that you were upset. He would speak with you following the meal in his solar, if—"

"Nay!" She bit her lip. Though the steward spoke softly, she did *not* and the only thing she was grateful for was that most would not have heard what she so vehemently opposed doing.

She cleared her throat hastily. "I mean, my laird, that would be most unnecessary."

"As you wish, my lady. I will tell His Grace that all is well."

"Aye, aye, my laird, that is correct."

He bowed to her, then crossed the floor to the head table. Her heart nearly stopped beating. Would the king insist on meeting with her following the meal anyway? A parting goodbye for his wife's favorite cousin? She curled her fingers into fists.

The king listened to his steward's words, though his gaze remained on her. He nodded, then a smile appeared on his lips. Had the steward told him what she had objected to? She felt as if she had been immersed into a pot of the cook's boiling stew.

When the steward retook his seat, the conversation renewed.

Malcolm said, "Thank you, my lady."

"Do not speak to me any further, Laird MacNeill."

"My lady, had I known you were concerned about—"

She glared at him. Didn't she just tell him not to speak to her? He was as bad as Mai. Then his words sank in. Did he now just realize why she had to leave Arundel? And if so, if he mentioned it here and now in front of God and everybody...

"I'm sorry, my lady. I did not know."

He didn't know what? He was going to leave it like that? Did he know about the king's interest in her or not? Men, there was no figuring them.

Still, a look of admiration flashed across his face, but then apprehension followed this.

Now what was he thinking? And why did she care? She had no reason to concern herself with anything this Highlander thought about her. If he'd had his way, he'd have taken her over his knee and paddled her for trying to leave the castle earlier, she reminded herself. And she, a grown woman.

She sipped from her tankard, wondering about his

change of attitude. Was he behaving better in light of the king's concern? Yes, that was it. He wouldn't have her steward's position, if the king didn't wish him to have it.

"I would be honored to accompany you and your lady-in-waiting for the rest of the eve, if it will help, my lady."

She set her tankard down. "Why?" Had he changed his mind about desiring an English bride? She scolded herself. Of course not. He wished only to find favor with the king. Mattered not to her whether the strapping warrior wanted to embrace an English lady tightly in his arms at night, cuddled together, naked under soft linens. To kiss her with those lips that curved up at the most inappropriate times. To...it mattered not to her, whatever he wished to do with some Englishwoman.

He cleared his throat. "I did not understand the reason for your wishing to leave here, my lady. Though if you had told me, I would have known. I will do everything in my power to keep you safe until we leave on the morrow."

He *did* understand that she feared the king's interest in her. She nodded. "Aye, my laird. I shall take you up on your offer. No one will think twice about it anyway."

His dark brows rose. "Meaning?"

"You are no' the type I would find appealing. So no one should get any ideas that might send tongues a'wagging."

Malcolm sat taller. What did she mean by *that*? He had seen the way her green eyes gazed at him and more than once had swept over the whole of him. She couldn't convince him she was not interested in a Highlander, sturdier built than most of the Normans he had seen.

If Malcolm had truly displeased her, she wouldn't have stood up for him in front of the Norman laird. She could pretend not to feel something for Malcolm, but he suspected she had a soft spot for a Highlander over that of a Norman. After all, when he offered to protect her against the king's amorous advances, she didn't dismiss his proposal, but instead had readily accepted without a hint of objection. She wouldn't spend another moment in Malcolm's company, if she didn't choose it.

No, the lass was truly intrigued with him. He knew it from the way her heart beat faster when she met his gaze, and her cheeks reddened whenever he caught her considering his physique. 'Twas a shame he had to marry an Englishwoman. He doubted any would have the same kind of temper that fired his blood like Anice did.

No, he didn't need the aggravation. The lady was best left to a Norman's care. God save him.

So why did this thought force him to clench his fists in annoyance?

He studied the smile that settled on her lips while she fingered her bird. Should he counter her words?

'Twas tempting.

He shouldn't allow the lass to get away with saying what she had, knowing full well she spoke not a wee bit of truth.

He turned to see Angus watching him, a glint of a smile tugging at the corner of his brother's mouth. Angus knew him well. It would take the best part of valor to refuse to be goaded into mincing words with the woman, concerning whether she was interested in the likes of him or not.

After sipping from his tankard, he tugged at the last of his fowl. "You are not pleased with the appearance of a Highland warrior, then, lass? I was under the impression you did not desire a Norman for a husband."

"I did not say I wouldna wish a Highland warrior for a husband, Laird MacNeill, but that *you* did not appeal. You, after all, dinna represent all Highlanders."

He smiled at her, knowing she didn't mean a word she said. But he would catch her up in her tale. "Aye. And what kind of a man would you prefer, if you do not mind saying?"

"I dinna think it any of your concern." She tilted her chin up in the way he was quickly becoming accustomed.

Her actions meant she readied for the joust once again,

her quick-tempered tongue as sharp and deadly as any lance. The only thing that concerned him was avoiding catching the king's attention further.

The flecks of golden amber seemed to darken in her green eyes and a trace of a smile touched her lips. For an instant, he wished to press his mouth against hers, to find out how she would react to a Highlander's kiss—not anyone's but his—the Highlander she said she had no interest in. If he suggested it, she would surely slap his face. Yet the idea of kissing her intrigued him.

Mayhap on their walk in the gardens later this eve. Then he could tell whether she truly had no feelings for him or not. After all, he'd kissed women before who were as stiff as wooden boards, but if Anice melted under his charms, he would know she spoke not a word of truth.

"Aye, my lady, 'tis true I have no need to know. But if a gentleman approaches you who you have no interest in, I would know this already, since you would have told me which men do not appeal. Then I would ensure the gentlemen do not bother you further."

"I see the logic in what you say, now, my laird. 'Tis most thoughtful of you to offer such assistance. The gentleman in question would have to be...younger, like your brother."

Malcolm frowned. The woman could not be speaking the truth. 'Twas him that her eyes devoured, not his younger brother.

She smiled. His physical reaction already signaled his defeat in the first round of the joust.

"Aye, younger. And the reason for this?" he asked, hoping to have another means of attack to force the truth from the foxy lass.

She raised a brow. "A younger man is quicker to please his lady suitor, dinna you agree?"

She had him there. Again he frowned, though if he'd thought the matter over first, he'd have watched his reaction, otherwise he confirmed the lady won another round.

In the case of his brother, she guessed right. He would do anything to please a lady because of his youth.

"Aye, but there is something to a man who has had more time to learn the finer aspects of what appeals to a woman, do not you agree, my lady?"

Her cheeks turned scarlet. Yes, she got his point.

"If you mean an older man has been with...with hordes of women and...and..." She folded her arms.

That did not go over well.

He cleared his throat, trying to think of another point that would pull him out of the deepening trench he'd slipped into. Though he did well in the jousts, he couldn't seem to match the lady's tactics.

Angus chuckled under his breath, heating Malcolm's blood. He had no intention of allowing the lady to say she'd prefer his younger brother to him. Somehow, he had to secure the truth from her. "Nay, I meant to say a man would know more how to woo a lady." Mayhap that sounded better than the words he spoke before. It wasn't what he'd had on his mind, but mayhap it sounded better to a lady's more delicate sensibilities.

"I see. Well, when you put it that way..."

He smiled when he won the point.

"Pray tell, my laird, how would you woo a lady in such a manner that compared to that of a younger gentleman, such as your brother, you would win her hand more quickly?"

He was back in the trenches.

Then he thought of his earlier actions that day. Did the lady know he had carried her to her bedchambers in such a heroic manner? Certainly, his brother would not have done such a thing for fear his actions would have been frowned upon by the king and courtiers.

"You seek an example, my lady?" he asked. He would win the battle this time.

"Aye, that I do."

"Earlier this day—"

She narrowed her eyes.

He would not be dissuaded from making his point. "Earlier when I had upset you so—"

"I have told you already, Laird MacNeill, that it was not your telling me, but the fact that I hadna known."

"Aye, but 'twas my folly to bring it up during the meal when I had no right."

She nodded. "Continue."

"When you fainted, servants immediately came to your aid, but I could not allow them to attend to you."

"Why not, my laird? It would have been a simple gesture on your part and perfectly acceptable."

"Aye, my lady, it would have been. Had I been Angus, I wouldna have made the effort to carry you up to your bedchamber. Not because he did not care...he was as much aghast at the situation as was I. But being a younger man, he wouldna have gone against what most consider proper protocol."

"As you had done."

"Aye. I had upset you, and I wished to make amends. I had hoped you would come to while I was still in your chamber so that I could then apologize. But you would not wake, and your lady-in-waiting warned me away, threatening to call the guards even."

Anice's mouth turned up.

Again, the desire to kiss her full lips crossed his mind. Could she deny her attraction to him if he kissed her? He could not imagine her stiffening in his embrace. In fact, soft curves and the hint of lavender would be his to hold, and he knew she'd succumb to his charms.

But then the thought occurred to him, if she had been well supervised, she might never have felt a man's lips touch hers. He smiled. The notion he would be the first pleased him.

She fingered her tankard. "I concede you have a point.

Mayhap younger men are no' as sure of themselves to act where they fear others might find folly. I thank you for assisting me as you did, my laird." She bowed her head slightly.

Walking in the garden with the lady would be a pleasure. He raised his tankard for a refill.

Then she spoke again. "Though I concede that an older man, such as yourself would do what you did for me, I must also remind you that I still have no interest in you as a prospective husband."

"Because?" He drank his wine, dying to hear why the lady found him so objectionable, when others found him just the opposite. Scottish lasses that is. English ladies kept their distance.

She squirmed slightly on the bench. Mayhap she did not have a good reply because she spoke not the truth?

The king and his queen rose from their table. The meal ended. Time for the garden walk with torches lighting their way. And the kiss he hoped he'd bestow upon her...just to show she was not so unaffected by him as she pretended to be.

But he did not wish her to avoid his question about what made him so...unworthy of being her husband. "A walk in the gardens, Lady Anice?" He motioned to the south entrance to the hall, hoping she had not changed her mind.

"Aye, a short one, and then Mai and I will retire to ensure we can rise at the break of dawn to leave here."

"Before you break your fast, my lady?"

"Aye, way before."

"As you wish." It bothered him that the king had attempted to compromise her when she wished his attentions not. If he could have done so without gaining the king's ire, he'd have taken the lady home this very eve. But the roads could be dangerous at night. Best they go at first light.

"I wished, my lady, however that you had been upfront with me before. I would have—"

"I wouldna have discussed such a thing with a man who is no relation to me."

"Aye." He thought this over as they walked outside the keep with Mai following slightly behind, and Angus and Dougald wandering some distance back. No matter what, he wished to be the one to protect her, being the chivalrous Highlander he was. "Still, I beg of you, that if such a thing does occur again with any gentleman who displeases you, you would allow me to speak on your behalf."

Though he assumed the lady could take the matter in her own hands well enough. 'Twas only the king she hadn't the ability to say no to should he have pushed his intentions farther than she cared. But any other gentleman, considering she had rank of her own, would no doubt be careful not to upset her. Particularly as she was the king's ward. Still, he wished to be the one—since she had no close living male relatives to watch out for her—to protect her while he served as her steward. "Only say the word, my lady."

"I thank you for your offer. Though I doubt I would have need of it in my own castle, I appreciate your kind proposal."

Yes, but what about the Norman fops the king sent her way? Would they try to kiss her lips as he wished to? But what if she wished the Norman laird to engage her in such a business?

He could not allow it as a kinsman of hers. Mayhap not a relative, but of Scottish blood. No Norman would kiss the woman before he was wed to her.

With that firmly in mind, he puffed out his chest, pleased with his decision. Then he had another thought. If she expressed interest in any Norman laird, he would show how incompetent the laird truly was. Should be an easy task. Not by deceit, of course, but he would prove to her that the laird was truly not the man she'd choose to wed, like she insisted Malcolm was not.

She glanced over at him as they walked in silence. She

caught the silly grin on his face and returned the smile. "You seemed pleased about something."

"Aye."

"Pray tell what about?"

He nearly laughed. Would she not like to know? If she did, she'd undoubtedly slap him. He shifted his thoughts to their earlier conversation. "You say you would not find me a suitable husband, my lady. I still wait to hear how this is so."

"Ah, why should it matter to you, my laird?"

"I have already told you why. You are stalling."

Her cheeks reddened. He had her there.

She sighed heavily. "I am ready to take my leave. In the morning we depart early."

"We will continue this conversation on the way to your castle, mayhap?"

"Mayhap."

Yes, after she experienced a good night's sleep and many hours to come up with reasons why she would not wed him. Would be well worth the wait to see what she came up with.

But what he would not have given to have a goodnight kiss. Not that he had any interest in the lass, but he just wanted to prove to her before she retired to bed that she was not above wanting him. The wiggle of her soft curves, the way she licked her lips and wrung her hands, stirred his shaft into action as if he were some randy lad. 'Twas not the way he reacted to most women, especially as coolly as the ladies of Arundel treated him. So why, when this lady espoused she was not interested in him, did his body react so interested in her?

Still, he could not just propose to kiss her without having a damned good reason. She turned and strolled back to the keep while he continued to walk beside her, trying to come up with a way to kiss her before they reached the castle doors or the prying eyes of too many of the courtiers. It would not bode well to get on the wrong side of the king again. Yet, he couldn't shake the desire to kiss her...just to prove she *did* like him...to a point.

He touched her wrist and heat seared his fingertips. The lass bewitched him like no other had done. She stopped, faced him, and waited, green eyes full of intrigue, widened, curious.

His gaze focused on her wet, full lips again. They parted slightly. He looked up. Did she want him to kiss her as much as he wanted to? If he kissed her and she screamed out in protest, King Henry would have his head.

As if her lady-in-waiting realized what he was about to do, she cleared her throat from some distance behind them.

A crimson blush rose to Anice's cheeks, and she quickly looked down at the stone path.

Damn her lady-in-waiting. He didn't want to wait until they arrived at Brecken Castle, and Anice began to see Norman lairds who wished her hand. He wanted her to think of the kiss they shared and remember how a Highlander had made her feel. Never again would she be able to think of a Highlander the same way.

She looked at him again, and before he could lean down and touch his lips to hers or fathom what she was about to do, she quickly kissed his mouth with a feather-light touch, then hurried away.

He stood dumbfounded, not being able to will his feet to move. She had kissed *him*, not the other way around. Her kiss was like a fairy's, so light 'twas almost unreal and yet it stirred his loins like no other woman had ever done. Pure magic, soft and sweet. Even now as he licked his lips, he was certain the taste of sweetened wine was from her mouth, not his. Ah, how he'd wished he had responded more quickly and shown her a Highland warrior's true kiss.

Mai brushed past him in a rush to catch up to her mistress.

He folded his arms. Anice was truly something. A paradox in silk and wool, soft with curves in all of the right places. Sweet at times, sharp tongued at others. He couldn't help but be attracted to the woman, the backbone she had to stand up to the king, the way she wished to return home to solve the problems that lay in wait for her there. Too bad he had other plans in mind for himself.

His brothers walked up beside him. Dougald punched Malcolm in the arm. "Angus has told me how ye fought with the lady at the meal. Though even from where I sat in the hall, I heard her words raised in anger. Whatever did you say to encourage her to kiss you now?"

Damned if Malcolm knew. He shook his head. "'Tis for me to know, and you to guess the reason."

Both his brothers groaned. But deep inside, so did Malcolm. The kiss she had bestowed so freely upon him was only the beginning. Now he had to show her what a kiss would truly feel like from his lips, once he had the chance to respond. A vixen was what she was.

He glanced up at her chamber window. She stood watching him, but quickly stepped away when she caught his eye. Chuckling, he shook his head.

"She said she did not like your type," Angus reminded him.

"Aye, and I believe not a word of it."

"If I did not know better, Malcolm, I would think you are pursuing the lady. But of course I know better. You wish an English bride."

"Aye."

Dougald took a deep breath and folded his arms across his broad chest. "'Tis why you did not respond to her kiss." Humor tinged his all-knowing words.

"She stunned him, do you not think, Dougald? I mean she shocked me. Never have I seen Malcolm not kiss a lady who kissed him first."

"Aye. Or either that or he was afraid of what the king might think."

Angus smiled. "Aye, that may be true."

Malcolm stalked toward the keep. "We must sleep, so that we may rise before dawn and be on our way."

"'Tis not that you have a liking for this lass, is it?" Angus persisted.

Dougald laughed. "He tells us one thing, but his actions say another."

As a servant opened the door for them, a page handed Malcolm a missive. "'Tis a missive from His Grace, my lord." He handed him another sealed letter.

"And this is from?"

"A knight I did not recognize, beg forgiveness, my lord. When he heard I had a message from the king for you, he asked if I would deliver this as well."

Malcolm nodded and shoved the other in his purse, then opened the vellum from Henry. Reading the missive to himself, he felt his brothers' breaths on his neck while they read over his shoulders.

Your Grace, Lady Anice's treasurer has been found dead in the River Arun, his head severed from his body. We have found no signs of the other men.

The news couldn't have come at a worse time. Malcolm reread the missive, hoping it would give him some clue as to what had happened.

Dougald rested his hand on his shoulder. "This is not good news, Malcolm. I worried there was foul play, but this appears to prove it so."

"Aye, mayhap this is why the king requested us to do the job. As Highland warriors we will be able to handle more than just the administrative details of the castle, should the business get physical."

"And the lady?" Angus asked, his voice worried.

Malcolm slapped his shoulder. "We will be like her kinsmen, watching out for her should anyone attempt her harm."

He glanced in the direction of her chambers and saw her standing outside her door, staring at him. Whatever was she doing, barefooted, her golden red hair hanging loosely down nearly to her knees as if she'd just fallen out of bed? His eyes shifted to the green robe she wore, and he imagined only a sheer shift beneath this, which would barely conceal her bountiful treasures. What was she doing standing there, looking like a woodland nymph in search of a man to bed her, asking for the worst kind of trouble?

Glancing down at the vellum he gripped tightly in his fist, he cleared his throat. Had she heard their words concerning the new crisis at hand?

Her eyes were round as the full moon as her gaze took in the message, and then returned to his. He had not wished to concern her before she retired to bed. Plenty of rest is what she required. On the morrow would be soon enough to tell her the news.

She stalked toward him, concern etched in the wrinkle of her brow, her eyes now narrowed.

So much for telling her on the morrow.

CHAPTER 5

Anice's heart pounded in her throat as the new premonition of ill tidings had forewarned her of further trouble at Brecken Castle. The ominous feelings had plagued her on and off all day before the Highlanders' arrival. What news had Malcolm received that prompted his and his brothers' comments? That foul play was involved? That men who had served in battle were considered necessary to fill her staff positions to protect her if need be? Now what had happened at Brecken Castle?

The look on Malcolm's face indicated he'd had no intention of telling her this eve what they had learned. Already her head pounded with fury that he thought he could withhold any information concerning her business. If it had to do with her castle, her land, her people, she had every right to know.

She warned herself that no matter the news she learned, she must not wilt again or everyone would think she had no fortitude. Which was not so! 'Twas a shock to hear the news about her staff gone missing earlier, that was all the matter. Anyone in her situation would have been just as upset, if they had any feelings concerning the situation.

Intent on getting the worry over with, she stalked toward Malcolm and his brothers. Gritting her teeth, she fought the quiver in her jaw. The men on her staff had been her uncle's favorites, and they had treated her well when he had died. She had no wish to hear ill news about any of them. That was all.

"My lady," Malcolm said, bowing low.

His voice was soothing and concerned. Did he worry she'd collapse in front of him as before? She would *not* this time. Never before had she done anything so ridiculous. This time she could handle the news because whatever word he had would not be such a surprise.

"Mayhap you should return to your chamber and rest for tomorrow's journey."

Instantly angered, she snapped, "What news have you from my castle?" She hadn't meant for her question to be so sharp, but her new steward would not coddle her. If she were to retire now without knowing what had transpired, she would fret the rest of the eve away, imagining the worst sort of things. Better to get the matter cleared up straight away.

"My lady," he tried again, "disconcerting news arrived from your castle, you are right, but I think it best if you return to your chamber and—"

She snatched the missive away from him and hastily read through the message until she got to the point of the matter. "Laird Thompson...murdered," she said under her breath. Her knees grew weak and she grabbed for Malcolm's arm, cursing herself silently before the hall grew dark and the men's frantic voices faded away.

***

When her mind cleared, Anice stared up at the blue linen canopy that cloaked the bed. The fragrance of lavender, tansy, and lady's bedstraw stirred from the mattress when she tried to rise. Mai grabbed her arm and lay her back down. "Rest, my lady."

Malcolm stood nearby, his face grave.

"Do not look at me like that, Laird MacNeill. I am no' a wilting flower."

A corner of his mouth tugged up, and his eyes sparkled with mirth.

She looked away from him, annoyed. Being a Highlander herself, she was sturdy, rugged. Not like the English ladies who swooned at the sight of their king. Not her. Mayhap it was the strain of being at Arundel. She would not react so badly were she at her own castle.

She swallowed hard. Who would do such a terrible thing to her treasurer? "We will investigate this matter fully upon our return."

"Aye, Lady Anice."

With a softened stance, she faced Malcolm. "I am sorry, Laird MacNeill. I...well, I..." She turned away from him as tears threatened to spill. Not wanting him to see she was so easily overcome with emotions, she motioned for him to leave, her throat constricting too quickly for her to choke out the words.

Mai patted her hand while Malcolm's footsteps padded out of the room.

"Is she all right?" Angus asked from the hallway.

"Aye, she is a sturdy lass," Malcolm said, which pleased her to no end.

She did not feel like a sturdy lass though. Had Malcolm said the words to make her feel better? No matter. She appreciated them just the same.

"Mayhap we should stay here, my lady, until the brigand or brigands are caught." Mai brushed Anice's hair with long, sweeping strokes.

Anice gave her an irritated look. How could Mai say that when the king proved to be such a problem?

Mai said, "I know what you are thinking, my lady, but there are worse dangers than him."

"I am no' afraid of going home."

"Aye." Mai cleared her throat. "You shouldna have

kissed Laird MacNeill, my lady."

"You have said so already several times. Do you realize you are repeating yourself overmuch lately? If I dinna know better I would say you are getting old."

Mai chuckled. "I wouldna want you thinking that. You may think to replace me with a younger lady."

"Nay. Sometimes I need be reminded of things."

Tilting her chin up, Mai cocked a brow. "Aye, like you shouldna have kissed the Highlander."

"No' that thing."

Mai shook her head. "He is your steward, my lady. It wouldna bode well if ye were kissing him in the gardens back home. The king has other marital plans for you. They dinna include marrying a stubborn Scotsman."

"Think you I would be better off with a Norman laird, Mai? Your husband was Scottish."

"Aye, that is why anything else would have to be better, dinna you see, my lady?"

Anice laughed, knowing Mai was teasing. "Your husband was a good man, as far as I remember."

"Aye, especially good with our bairn." Mai seemed to be saddened by the memory, having lost her own two children to sickness early on and then her husband on the Crusade.

Anice reached over and took hold of Mai's hand and squeezed. "Mayhap we need to find *you* a husband."

Mai laughed until tears came to her eyes.

"I jest not. It will be one of my first priorities when we return." Anice tried to lighten the darkness that surrounded them that eve, not because most of the candles had already been snuffed, but for the dangers that lay ahead. Her lady-in-waiting exhibited signs of fear, of wishing to stay at Arundel, when it would not be safe for Anice to do so. Not for the same reason as it would be dangerous to return to her castle, but Anice would rather face those dangers than hurt her cousin, if the king should want Anice's favors and she refused once too often.

***

Before the light even dawned, it was time for Anice and her escort to return home. They quickly prayed in the chapel that morn, then headed for their horses already saddled and waiting for them in the inner bailey.

Anice had said her goodbyes to her cousin earlier, and the queen's young daughter, Princess Matilda. Anice looked back one more time at the keep, then watched Malcolm take charge and handle everything so smoothly. Wouldn't someone of his character be good for Brecken Castle?

No, he wanted an Englishwoman for a bride, and when he learned Anice was cursed…she shook her head. If he knew about the problem she'd had with earlier betrothals and her second sight, she'd be doomed.

Two of the king's staff helped Anice and Mai onto their horses while Malcolm checked over his own mount.

Suddenly, Malcolm slapped his purse, and yanked out a piece of vellum as if he'd remembered an important document before they departed. The breeze caught the missive, instantly tugging it from his grasp and carrying it halfway across the bailey. Laird MacNeill dashed for it like a bounding youth after a pirate's treasure. Was it another message from the king that was so important that Malcolm feared losing?

The Highlander's face grew livid as he chased the swirling paper. Both of his brothers just stood watching, too far away to be of any service. Then the breeze shifted and the vellum landed in a washerwoman's barrel of soapy water. Had the woman been closer to the barrel she might have caught the paper, but she was hanging table linens to dry with her back turned to the scene unfolding behind her.

Red-faced, Malcolm pulled the sopping wet document from the water and gingerly opened it up. His lips moved, but she couldn't hear what he said, nor could she decipher the words he mouthed. As unhappy as his face looked, Anice assumed the ink had bled on the paper. The words were probably nothing more than a blur. When he surveyed the area, and his gazed lighted on her, his expression was one of disbelief. What now?

With haste, he returned to his brothers' sides. They both examined the vellum, and each gave her a glance that mirrored Malcolm's earlier look. All three discussed the matter, then Malcolm motioned to a man, Gunnolf, blond-haired and bearded, brilliant blue eyes, looking like one of the Viking warriors who'd landed in Scotland earlier. He was Malcolm's closest manservant, Anice had learned, and took the vellum from his laird, then began to attempt to dry it in earnest. Certain the message was about her, or her staff at Brecken, Anice assumed the news was not good.

Malcolm had not spoken a word to her while he ordered the servants to ready a wagon with everyone's trunks, gave last minute instructions to his brothers, and spoke with the king's steward, so intent was he to handle the business at hand with all due seriousness.

Mai grumbled, "'Tis no' a problem for you to ride like this back and forth from your castle to His Grace's to yours again. But you know, my lady, these bones are getting stiff in my old age."

Glad to take her mind off the message Malcolm and his brothers seemed so concerned about, Anice faced her maid and quirked a brow. "I promise you when we arrive home, we willna go anywhere else for a verra long time."

"Aye, my lady, or mayhap you can have another baron's daughter serve as your lady-in-waiting just for travel. I will rest my weary bones at home."

"Aye, I can do that, but remember, 'twas you who insisted you come with me when King Henry first summoned me to Arundel." Anice shifted her attention back to Malcolm who chanced a glance at her. He looked worried, his brow furrowed, his countenance dark like the devil had hold of his thoughts.

"Just for travel mind you," Mai added, as if she sensed trouble and tried to distract Anice before their long journey.

"Laird MacNeill has said you may ride in the wagon, if it pleases you."

Mai frowned at her. "The infirmed and prisoners ride in wagons, my lady. I am neither."

"Aye." Anice had given up on her stubborn lady-in-waiting years ago. She glanced at Malcolm when he climbed into his saddle, his eyes again shifting to her, dark, brooding, unfathomable.

"Are you ready, my lady?" he asked, his voice deeper with a hint of distrust.

"Lead the way, my laird." Anice tried to act unperturbed, though her chin rose slightly in defiance.

With piercing intensity, he studied her, but she tilted her chin even higher and pursed her lips. Whatever was the matter now?

He bowed his head to her with courtly pride, then motioned to Dougald who led the way. Angus brought up the rear, while Malcolm rode beside Anice.

To give them some privacy, Mai dropped back behind Anice, but walked her horse ahead of the wagon.

"You had another message from the king?" Anice attempted not to sound too curious, but she was dying to know what disturbed Malcolm and his brothers so.

"Nay," he said, his voice clipped.

Now it was her turn to stare at him in disbelief. "The vellum that took flight and landed in the wash barrel was not from the king?"

"Nay." He glanced at her, his eyes focusing on her veiled hair, then shifting back to her gaze.

She swallowed hard. Who else would have sent a missive that disturbed them so? "But it was about me."

Malcolm sighed deeply and looked away. "Aye."

She didn't know him well at all, but just from the little she did know of him, she didn't believe him to be the strong silent type. "And?"

"'Tis no' important."

"But it is about me," she insisted. And the reactions from his brothers definitely made her suspect it was important despite what he said.

"I was concerned about you, last eve," Malcolm said, changing the subject.

All right. She would play the game for a while. If Malcolm didn't tell her what the message said, she'd find a way to sneak a peek at it later. "I appreciate your concern, but you need not have been troubled over me."

"His Grace spoke with me later last eve. He would not force the issue, but he worried that you would return to your castle and be in some danger."

She gave a ladylike snort under her breath.

Malcolm smiled. "I believe he thought you felt you would be in less danger at home than at Arundel."

"He would think right."

"I worry though." He gave her a pointed look.

She ignored him.

***

Malcolm's thoughts shifted to the blurred missive that he and his brothers had attempted to decipher. Only three words stood out, *Anice, cursed, betrothals*. He could only guess at what it meant, and though he didn't believe in curses, Dougald and Angus did. In fact, most of their clan's people believed in rampant superstitions. Was the lady cursed and that's why some of her clansman had fallen? But that had nothing to do with betrothals. As far as he knew, the lady had never been betrothed to anyone. The manner in which some unnamed knight had passed the message off to him through a page, furthered his disquiet. Was it a ploy to discredit the lady?

Yet, he'd heard whispered rumors that the Lady Anice had strange powers. Again, he attributed it to the Englishwomen not liking that Anice was Scottish. Still, the way she appeared in the hall outside her chamber as if spirits had told her what was happening when they received the news about her treasurer, seemed odd.

He rubbed his freshly shaved face. His thoughts switched to the troubles at Brecken Castle, and though he had worried about them throughout the evening hours, he did not wish to discuss this concern with Anice. No sense in upsetting the lady with such matters. However, another issue troubled him. *The kiss*. Did the lady often kiss gentleman in such a manner? He would have to put a stop to it. Why, after saying he was not the kind of man she would be interested in, kiss him?

The horse's hooves clopped on the dirt road, the wagon's wheels squeaked as they turned, but none of these things garnered his attention like the woman who sat tall in her green woolen gown, a stray lock of hair fluttering over her cheek. Instantly, he wanted to see her tresses unbound, draping over her shoulders, silky, kissed by the rays of the sun, red and gold combined, tickling her bare breasts.

He leaned away from the pommel of his saddle when his trewes grew taut, nearly strangling him. The journey would be long indeed if he couldn't keep his thoughts about the lady's shapely attributes under better control.

Though he was sure she would not appreciate his bringing up the kiss, he had to ensure she did not avail herself to another gentleman in such a manner. Furthermore, he had to know *why* she had kissed him.

With every intention of approaching the subject with utmost caution, he straightened his posture, glanced behind him to ensure Mai was far enough away not to hear their discussion, then faced Anice. "About last eve, my lady—"

"Aye, I am sorry I fainted again. 'Tis good you have a strong back and broad shoulders if you are going to be my steward."

He smiled, gladdened to hear she was not overmuch distressed after having been indisposed for a second time that day. "'Twas to be expected, my lady, considering the ill tidings. Had not you reacted as you did, I would have found your actions disturbing."

She turned her head slightly as if conceding a point. "Aye, as if I were in on the plot."

He raised a brow. "I still worry about your safety. One of my brothers or me will accompany you at all times."

Her eyes grew round as she faced him. "Except in my bedchamber."

He couldn't help the smile that tugged at his mouth. Having already visited her bedchamber at Arundel Castle twice, the thought struck him as amusing. "Unless you have need of my services there, my lady."

She tilted her chin down and gave him a look like she thought his proposal indecent, but she seemed more intrigued than bothered by the notion. "Indeed."

"As you needed me at Arundel," he clarified, amused that she'd come to some other conclusion. The idea he'd carry the lady to her bed, then join her certainly had crossed his mind. She was a lovely lass, no doubt about it. He would not be half a man if he had not given it a thought.

Just seeing her resting in the bed as if she were waiting for her laird husband to attend to her in the manner husbands did their wives...

He shook his head. Traitorous thoughts such as these, he had no business contemplating. He would have an English bride, and the lass a Norman laird. 'Twas the way of things, and better for all concerned.

But her easy manner this morning brought on the treacherous notions. If she still had acted the lioness she had last eve, he might have been of another mind. Her disposition seemed much improved, and 'twas difficult not to enjoy the lady's company. Was it the fact she had left Arundel and King Henry behind that pleased her? If so, Malcolm was glad he had rescued the lady, though the king may not have been as content.

Her cheeks wore a bit of color from the frosty bite in the air and her lips were redder than he remembered them. She was a comely lass and any man would be proud to have the lady for his wife. He forced his thoughts from enjoying her beauty to consider her much improved demeanor. Mayhap this morning since she seemed a good deal demurer, he could question her about her staff without her being so vague and obstinate and see if she had some notion of what might have happened.

First, he had to set her straight on kissing other gentlemen.

They rode in silence for some time, then he tried broaching the subject of the kiss again. "Concerning our walk in the gardens last eve, my lady, I have a question."

She didn't look in his direction, but her cheeks grew more flushed, and her lips curved upwards a notch. She seemed to know what he wanted to ask, and it did not appear to bother her, amuse her mayhap, but not irritate her. 'Twas a good start.

"About the kiss...," he began cautiously. 'Twas not that he could not handle an outburst from her, but after all 'twas a delicate subject to discuss with the lady of a castle, particularly the one he had to serve.

"Aye." Again, she seemed tickled about the discussion, but before he could forge ahead, she continued to speak. "'Twas a sisterly peck, naught more."

Nothing about the kiss had he found sisterly. The fact she had such a quick response proved she had given the matter some thought as to what she would say if he asked.

Yet, he would know more about how often she had done such a thing with other gentlemen. He had every intention of putting a stop to such rash behavior. "Aye, and do all the men you kiss in such a *sisterly* fashion react the way I did?"

She looked at him, her eyes shining with amusement, her smile broadened. "I have not done so before, but when I do it again—"

"Only pray do such a thing with me, because if you were to kiss a gentleman as you did me, he would no doubt not resist as I did."

"Aye." She turned to watch Dougald's horse plodding along in front of them.

"I mean it, my lady," Malcolm said firmly.

"Aye." She did not look at him, instead answered so abruptly he was not sure she got his point.

"Any other man might take advantage of the situation and want more."

"Aye."

"Lady Anice," he said, his tone of voice exasperated, no longer able to contain his temper.

She faced him, innocent as a baby bird in its nest. "My laird?"

"You cannot kiss any man like that."

"You did not want me to kiss you?"

Was the woman daft? Of course he wanted her to kiss him, as much as he wanted to press his mouth against her silken lips and deepen the touch. Nearly every waking moment, he had thought of that unimposing kiss and wanted more than anything to reenact the moment to allow him the opportunity to respond. He had also worried why she had done such a thing and if she would do so again with some other gentleman, who would have no business feeling her lips against his.

Not that he should either. 'Twas only that he wished to show her she was not so immune to liking him as she espoused.

"You have naught to worry about with me, my lady. 'Tis other gentlemen who concern me who will no doubt get the wrong impression."

"Because you are like kin to me?"

He wanted to groan out loud. No way did he want her to consider him like kin. Certainly, he saw her as a woman who he would happily tangle with under the sheets—or without— not as a sister, or cousin, or any other relation, but as a bonny lass who he would love to bury himself in. Och, even now the thought of being with her naked in her bed filled him with a craving he couldn't douse. "I will not take advantage of you, is my meaning," he said hoarsely.

She gave him a strange look. "Then you will not mind if I kiss you again?"

'Twas his most fervent desire, yet he stared at her not understanding what she was getting at. Most certainly, he would love to have her kiss him, only he wanted time to react. He still was not sure why she wished to do so, unless she had some idea she wanted him for her husband. King Henry would not be pleased with such a notion if he were sending Norman lairds to court her. Still, she did express an interest in Highland lairds over Norman ones. Mayhap she liked that Malcolm had a strong back and broad shoulders and could carry her to her chambers whenever she became indisposed. Mayhap she wished he would tarry longer the next time. And damned if he didn't wish to oblige.

Before he could ask why she kissed him, she said, "I had to thank you for taking care of me earlier. After last eve, I fancied that I would have to thank you again. But if you are not agreeable…"

"You honor me, my lady." Why the hell had he said those words? He could not bring himself to tell her otherwise, though he knew he should have said she ought not kiss any but the man she wed. Dougald was the perfectly practiced man of words and actions when it came to dealing with a lady. Malcolm felt out of his league.

"I did not mean to shock you last eve," Anice said softly.

Shaking his head, he smiled. "My brothers ribbed me about it." He didn't know why he mentioned it, but she seemed in truly good humor.

"Mai scolded me…five times."

Malcolm chuckled, imagining her lady-in-waiting would do just that. "No doubt you told her it was just a sisterly kiss though."

When Anice did not answer, he looked over at her.

She ran her reins through her fingers, her cheeks cherry, her eyes averted. Vixen. 'Twas no more a sisterly kiss than he thought. She did care something for him as he suspected.

He could barely contain his amusement when he tried to get her to reveal the truth next. "We talked last eve about what you thought objectionable about me...as a prospect for marriage, my lady."

"Aye."

"I mean, you did not say. Have you some thoughts on that subject today?"

"Nay."

He smiled. Just as he suspected. She could not come up with *one* reason that she would not care for a man like him.

She took a heavy breath. "I know you are trying to talk to me about things that will not alarm me, but we must speak of the happenings at my castle."

He did not wish to distress her that was for certain, and risk having her faint while riding her mount. Could be a dangerous fall. Though, if she did become indisposed, she could ride in the wagon. The notion flashed across his mind that she could ride upon his horse with his arms wrapped around her, nestled between his legs. His shaft stiffened.

He squirmed in his saddle to attempt to relieve the building tension in his groin, yet, he still didn't wish to discuss the problems with her staff, not until they stopped for the eve. "I would not wish to upset you, my lady."

"I will not be receiving ill news. I only wish to discuss what might be the problem. Though 'tis difficult to say without checking the books and the like. Still, mayhap something I might think of could shed light on this most hideous crime."

"Aye." He moved his horse closer to hers.

Her green eyes widened.

"In case you are feeling faint, my lady. I would catch you before you fall. Or mayhap you wish to ride with me a spell."

She smiled, her face brightening like a sunshiny day, her eyes sparkling in the dim light. "I dinna think that necessary."

Not necessary, but most welcome. "Aye, go on," he prompted, but watched her carefully for signs of distress.

"Shortly before King Henry summoned me, I'd heard raised words between my uncle's treasurer, Laird Thompson, and his steward, Laird MacKnight. Now, the two didna get along and I assumed 'twas another of their rows. Each had beseeched my uncle to get rid of the other on several separate occasions. Both gentlemen were agreeable men except when it came to dealing with each other, and I couldna understand the animosity between the two."

"Did you overhear what was said?"

"Only that there was some discrepancy in the accounts. 'Twas none of my concern as the men would undoubtedly speak to my uncle about the matter. And he didna want me involved in such things. To my shock and morbid distress, my uncle died two days later."

"Do you suspect wrongful death?"

The way Anice's eyes widened so all of a sudden, her cheeks paled, and her lips parted in surprise, Malcolm feared she was about to fall from her horse in a faint. Without a moment to lose, he reached over and pulled her from her horse.

She gasped with the suddenness of his action, and Mai rode up to join them.

"What is the meaning of this?" Mai fairly shouted as if she said it loud enough Malcolm's brothers would rescue the lady from the devil's grasp.

"She grew faint," Malcolm quickly said.

"Och." Mai's facial features turned from one of disdain

to that of concern.

Dougald whipped around and headed back to them while Angus skirted the wagon to see to the matter. He grabbed Anice's horse's reins. "I will tie your horse to the back of the wagon, my lady, if it pleases you."

"I...I—"

"It pleases the lady," Malcolm said, giving her no chance to retake her mount. He told himself he did so to prevent her from injuring herself should she fall from her horse. That the day remained cold and her gloved hands like ice. For a time, he would warm her and keep her safe and secure. But her body resting against his, already heated him to dangerous levels and his trewes seemed ready to split at the seams.

Dougald's knowing smirk rested on his lips. Then he bowed his head and cantered to take the lead.

"I must apologize. I thought you might have come to the same conclusion as I had, my lady," Malcolm said, when Mai dropped back out of hearing.

"I had not." Then she frowned at him. "And I did not become faint."

He quirked a brow, admiring the lady for not wanting him to think otherwise, but he was not inclined to believe her anyway. "Your face turned as white as the cloud in yonder sky. From the cold, your cheeks were quite cheerful, and then the color drained away. 'Twas the same as the other times before."

"I didna feel dizzy like before. You shocked me with the news was all." Her back relaxed against his chest, the feel of her soft body undoing him. "However, you may verra well be correct in your assumption concerning my uncle."

"Did your uncle become sick all of a sudden?"

"For two days. He was fine before that."

Malcolm considered what might have caused her uncle's untimely death as she squirmed against his groin, trying to get comfortable in the saddle. He stifled a groan and attempted to concentrate on their conversation instead. "Mayhap someone introduced poison into the food."

"But why?"

"Who would benefit from your uncle's death?"

Anice sat quietly, then under her breath she said, "Me."

'Twas not the lady, he would stake his life on it. "You would not have killed your uncle. However, now you have inherited your uncle's properties, and should you marry a laird, he would manage them. This would not have occurred had your uncle still been alive." The idea that some Norman laird murdered her uncle to get her properties infuriated him. Would the killer do the same to the lass once he married her and had her lands and castle?

"Aye, I wouldna have received the properties until he died."

"Only Norman lairds have approached the king for your hand in marriage."

She frowned at him. "Why has His Grace not spoken of this to me?"

"Apparently, whenever you were within the sound of his voice, he had other matters on his mind."

Her cheeks flushed.

Again, the notion the king wished to bed her aggravated him, but he hadn't meant for his words to come out quite so bluntly. Quickly, he changed the subject. "So if 'tis a Norman, he must have had ties with someone on your staff. Else why would your three highest staff members vanish, then at least one end up dead?"

"Aye."

"I would think no harm would come to you as long as you are not wed."

"If the king says I must wed—"

He shook his head. "Nay, you cannot marry a Norman laird. We would not know which man murdered your uncle, but you will entertain the gentlemen the king sends to court you. Somehow, my brothers and I—"

73

"And me," Anice said, the fire burning in her eyes again.

"Aye, lass, though I wish you had no part in this, you will be the bait."

"Ahh, well see that you protect me, my laird." She snuggled against his body, and he stifled a groan. "But first you can warm me up a wee bit."

"Aye, the pleasure will be all mine." Her lithe body wriggling against his chest and groin forced him to rethink the matter of wanting an English bride.

The hint of lavender scented her hair, and resting beneath his nose, enticed him to lean his head closer to hers just to breathe in her stimulating fragrance. But 'twas the curve of her body rubbing against his rock-hard shaft when his horse took each and every step that aroused him to painful levels. Had they been alone together, he'd have loved nothing more than to relieve his tension with the bonny lass...had she been agreeable. Did she feel his arousal chafing her backside?

He glanced down at her exposed ankles as her gown rose with the way she was seated against his lap. Immediately, he thought of her gown catching on his horse's saddle during her escape from the keep at Arundel. With only the most gallant of notions, releasing her hem and rescuing her dignity, he couldn't help but enjoy the view when she fell on her arse, exposing her shapely legs. Had served her right for not letting him assist her and fighting him in every way. But now he wished her skirts would rise higher so he could get an eyeful of the lovely thigh he'd chanced to grapple that day.

He took a steadying breath and shifted his attention from the lass to the deadly business at her castle. The news concerning Anice's uncle was worse than he had suspected. Believing that the staff had absconded with the lady's monies and that was all the matter—though grave if she could not pay the king's taxes—Malcolm had not thought her life in danger. Until the king's men found Laird Thompson dead.

Still, if the three men on her staff had been in league together, the other two may have fought with him and killed him. Money and greed changed many a partnership. If her uncle had been murdered as well, this put the whole matter in a different light.

Malcolm would have sent a dispatch to the king, only he did not feel His Grace would accept his word without proof. After all, Anice and he only assumed that someone murdered her uncle. The king would not like Malcolm preferring charges that some Norman laird was responsible for her uncle's death without even knowing the man's name.

He and his brothers *had* to find proof before any laird made a proposal of marriage to her.

She rested her head against his chest. He'd not had a romp with a lass in a good long while, and the feelings Anice stirred in him were not in the least bit brotherly. When he thought she had drifted off to sleep, he wrapped his arm around her and held her close, telling himself he didn't want her to slip off his horse and injure herself. 'Twas not just her warm body that heated his own, but the craving he had for her that stirred a steady flame.

Dougald glanced back at him, smiled, then pulled his horse around and returned to Malcolm.

Riding next to him, he asked, "The lass did not get enough sleep last night? Or did you make her faint again?"

"She is sleeping."

"You could put her in the wagon, ye know."

Malcolm took a deep breath, not wanting to experience the feelings she stirred deep inside. He was protecting her, warming her, no more than that. 'Twas his job. "I do not wish to wake her now. She might not be able to get back to sleep."

Dougald chuckled. "Aye, Malcolm. Say what you will, but Angus and I know better." He kicked his horse and took the lead again.

If Malcolm were so keen to have an English bride, why was he so glad he could convince her not to accept a Norman laird's hand in marriage? 'Twas only for her safety, he reminded himself. Once they discovered who had killed her uncle, if that was indeed what had happened, he would not stand in her way to marry any she chose.

Yet, the notion she would not choose *him*, though he was not in the market for a Scottish lass, irked him. Damnable vixen. What did she not feel about him, appealing?

CHAPTER 6

Giant oaks and winsome birches shaded the way through the Forest of Dean, situated between the rivers Severn and Wye, while the sun poked through the branches late that afternoon. Geese and ducks squawked on a nearby pond, and two gray-haired sheep badgers herded their livestock through the forest, but the sound of horse's hooves headed in their direction gave Anice concern, her skin instantly crawling.

"Rider approaching," Dougald warned.

The sheep badgers quickly moved their livestock deeper into the woods, trampling fern, their sheep bleating their distress when they hurried to get out of the travelers' path.

Anice sat straighter. "Stop your horse," she said to Malcolm, not wanting any to see her riding with the Highlander. "I will ride my own."

Anice couldn't seem to stay warm, but even so, she wished to ride alone. No telling if Malcolm might need to use his sword. Her own bow and quiver of arrows were on her horse if she needed to get to them also.

"You are still cold, my lady," Malcolm objected when she squirmed in his lap. "What if you should grow—"

"How now!" a man dressed in chain mail and tunic, riding a dappled gray destrier greeted Dougald. "You are headed in the wrong direction, my good man!"

Thirty or so men dressed similarly rode up behind him. Anice assumed King Henry had called them to arms in the coming war against his brother.

Dougald replied, "Are ye joining His Grace and his men against his brother?"

"Aye. Were you with Robert Curthose during the Crusades?"

"Aye, we returned when he did."

"To take the crown?"

The knights sat stiffly upon their mounts, waiting to hear Dougald's response, their countenances grim. All Dougald had to say was they were in league with Robert, and the knights would surely slay every one of them.

"We fought during the Crusades like most of you probably did for King William. 'Twas a shame he died. We have just now come from Arundel after having an audience with King Henry."

The knight turned his attention to Anice sitting—now uncomfortably—with Malcolm still. He slipped his arm around her waist and hugged her closer to his chest. Her blood warmed. Was he worried for her safety, or...or trying to show she was his?

"You are not fighting alongside the king against his brother then?" the knight said.

"His Grace has given us other business to attend to. You seem familiar. Have we met before?" Dougald asked, his dark brow lifted.

"Aye. Robert de Beaumont, Count of Meulan. And ye, ye are the MacNeill brothers. He waved a hand at Gunnolf. "I see ye still have the Viking berserker with ye, as fearsome as ten men." He smiled. "I hope His Grace will permit me to lead a force against Robert and the Norman lords who are loyal to him."

Anice's skin prickled. Her Uncle Edgar Atheling came to mind as one of Robert's loyal lairds, though he was Saxon and not Norman. Yet, she assumed Robert would give the Saxon prince much in return for his loyalty.

The count glanced back at Anice and a smile appeared slowly. To Malcolm he said, "I can see why you would not want to leave a young bride at home alone."

Anice opened her mouth to speak, then thinking better of it, clamped her lips shut. If she let him know who she was, the count might give Henry the news of how intimate she and Malcolm had become. 'Twould not matter how innocent their actions. What if Henry sent the MacNeill brothers off to Normandy to do battle against Robert? Then where would she be? He'd undoubtedly replace her staff with loyal Norman lairds instead. Any one of them could have been in on the killing of her uncle.

"Godspeed," the count said, then he and his men continued on past Anice's party toward Arundel.

Dougald prodded his horse to a canter, and Malcolm did likewise.

For some time, they rode in silence, then finally Malcolm spoke up. "Why did you no' tell the count we were not married, lass?"

"His Grace might have received word that you and I were too intimate with one another. No matter the circumstances. You must admit our actions do look a wee bit suspicious."

"We could have mentioned your fainting."

"*I didna faint.*"

Dougald shook his head, though he still kept his distance ahead of them. She had not thought she spoke so loudly.

"I didna faint," she repeated under her breath.

"Aye, but it would have explained why you rode with me." Though he sounded serious, she detected a bit of humor in his words.

"Why did you no' offer your services to His Grace? I would think brave Highlanders such as yourselves would readily have offered your swords on his behalf."

"We'd had no word His Grace planned to fight his brother again. Once we arrived at Arundel, we learned of it and did indeed offer our services."

The notion they had, disheartened her. Would Henry call upon them to join him later in the year? Mayhap that was what worried her. She wasn't sure, but just a trickle of dread crossed her spine.

"But he said no?" she asked, hopeful that Henry hadn't intended their joining him at a later date.

"I believe he preferred Norman knights to accompany him, but the word had come to him about the troubles at your castle also. Rather than send Norman lairds to assist you who he needed in the fight, he sent us."

"Aye, and good thing, too." The words slipped out before she could stop them and in horror, she wondered how she'd explain herself without him thinking more into what she said than she wished. In fact, she could not even quite fathom herself why she wanted the Scotsman at her castle, except that surrounding herself with more of their kind pleased her.

"Why is that, lass?"

She knew he wouldn't pass up her words without further explanation.

Because she preferred Highland lairds to Norman ones. Hadn't she already said so?

'Twas not because she enjoyed the company of Malcolm and his brothers, though she could see how useful Malcolm could be, keeping her warm on a chilly night, and his brothers were certainly affable enough. 'Twas not because Malcolm stirred her blood like no man had ever done. She would rather face a mad, wild boar than marry such a man.

So why did the thought of his wiving her come to mind?

She shook her head. "I thought you were well aware that I prefer Highlanders on my staff to Englishmen or Normans."

"Aye. I thought there might be some other reason."

"And what would that be?" She couldn't help the way her voice rose with irritation at his inference.

She turned to see the smile so smugly affixed to his lips.

He was so...so intolerably arrogant!

***

After several miles with the sun finally beating down on them, she warmed up sufficiently and mounted her own horse so as not to tire Malcolm's. The loss she felt from separating from him, she hadn't expected. No one had ever held her so close, so intimately, save maybe her mother when she was a little girl. 'Twas not the same as having this burly Highlander's body so close to hers, his armed wrapped around her to keep her safe, the warmth of his body heating hers like the sun's intense rays beat down on the hard-packed earth on a summer's day. Though she smelled the leather of his saddle and the horse's sweat, his musky man-scent had cloaked her, too. She hadn't realized how much her senses were attuned to him.

As she rode beside him again, she couldn't help wishing he held her close. Did he miss the intimacy of their touch also? Or had he just been chivalrous? After all, her word to the king concerning Malcolm's good deeds could earn him the bride he so sought to have...an Englishwoman.

She tightened her hold on her reins and seethed about how he, a Highlander, could want a woman like that. Where was his sense of pride in being Scottish?

Glancing at him, she found Malcolm watching her, curiosity evident in his expression. Loosening her grip on her reins, she turned her attention to the road ahead. She'd never seen a man seem so...interested in what a woman felt or thought. Most were too busy telling the lady what was important to them. The lady in response would nod and smile sweetly, agreeing to everything he said.

Not her.

Looking over her shoulder, Gunnolf gave her a curious stare. Where had he laid the wet vellum, surely dry by now? As soon as she could manage, she'd find out just what news had shaken the MacNeill brothers so.

Turning her attention forward, she saw the majestic fortress, Godric's Castle, standing high on top of a red sandstone crag, commanding the passage of the River Wye and the wooded valley below where they now sat upon their horses. Nearby, she noticed deep ridges where once an ancient man had erected a fort, no doubt of wood, now long since gone.

Wood smoke drifted on the breeze from some distant dwelling.

"Shall we see if Laird Godric will allow us to dine with him this eve?" Malcolm asked, his words uplifted.

"Do you know the laird?" Anice only knew he owned the castle but had never met the earl.

"I have met him. He is a thane, Saxon gentry, and kept his lands despite the Norman invasion. He had a castle in the Village of Notton before this."

The party rode up to the gatehouse where soldiers roughly led two ragged men inside. "These men were poaching, I take it," the guard said, his voice hard while he combed his scraggly dark beard with dirty fingers.

"Aye, mayhap His Lordship will go easy on them today. Mayhap he will order only a hand be chopped off and not have their eyes put out or their..." The man stopped speaking as Dougald cleared his throat to get his attention.

Seeing the lady, the man offered an apology.

The gate guard motioned to the red stone keep. "Take them to the dungeon. His Lordship has court in the morn." As they hauled the men off, the guard asked Dougald, "What do you need?"

"We hoped we might share an evening meal with his

Lairdship."

"Does he know ye?"

"I'm Earl of Pembrinton," Malcolm spoke up. "He and I met at King Henry's court."

"Aye. I will send word to his Lordship. Ye are welcome to enter the bailey."

Soon Laird Godric's steward, a blond-bearded man, short and stocky with quick blue eyes, guided them into the keep. "His Lordship's game warden mentioned to me that you may have overheard his jests to the poachers, concerning their punishment." He looked over at Anice as if his words were mainly for her benefit. "I wished to dispel this notion. His Lordship requires poachers to pay a fine. Hopefully the fear of harsher punishment will deter them from poaching again." He spoke to Malcolm. "Is the lady your wife?"

Malcolm hesitated to respond, and Anice's cheeks colored beautifully. "She is Lady Anice, Countess of Brecken of Glen Affric, cousin to Queen Matilda," he said as soon as she opened her mouth to speak.

The steward's eyes widened, and his mouth curved up some. "Ah. Is the lady betrothed?"

Malcolm wondered where this bit of conversation was leading to. Did the old laird harbor some interest in Anice? "His Grace wishes one of his Norman lairds to court the lady."

"I see."

Since Lord Godric was Saxon, Malcolm figured that would be the end of the earl's interest in the lady.

Anice took a deep breath and looked decidedly relieved. It appeared he'd saved her. Would it earn him another kiss?

When they sat at the head table to share the meal, Laird Godric introduced his son, Wulfric de Croxton, who was closer to Anice's age. Though Wulfric attempted to engage Anice in conversation several times, Malcolm couldn't help interrupting him. Anice bit her bottom lip twice when he did, and he was certain she fought smiling or laughing at his actions.

His tone annoyed, Wulfric said to Malcolm, "Though you have told my lord father that you are the lady's steward, you act in some manner inconsistent with this job."

"Aye, I am like kin to her." Malcolm smiled when her lips parted in surprise. "She has none other to watch over her at the moment, and His Grace besieged me to look after the lady on his behalf. She is his ward after all, and King Alexander's cousin as well."

"I see." Wulfric leaned forward and grabbed a boar's leg. "Mayhap I should speak with His Grace and see if a Saxon nobleman could not court the lady as well as a Norman. After all, Queen Matilda is half Saxon."

'Twas the truth. And that was why the Norman king took the lady as his wife. Not only did he tie Norman kings in with the old line of Saxon kings, he bound the Scots to his wishes as well since she was King Malcolm's daughter.

"He has told me that only Norman lairds have been allowed to seek audience with Lady Anice." Malcolm couldn't help the way the hair on the nape of his neck stood on end. He didn't want either Normans or Saxons claiming the bonny lass.

"Land and power can sway many a contract." Wulfric gave him a smug smile.

Malcolm sat taller, not liking the inference. "Aye, but in the lady's case, the king wishes her to make the choice." He hoped he wouldn't be struck down by lightning upon the spot before God and everyone for lying so.

Anice shook her head and avoided looking at either of the men while she played with her bread.

Two hours later after battling with Wulfric throughout what could have been a pleasant meal, Malcolm rose to leave. Anice thanked her generous hosts and attempted to hurry their departure. But Laird Godric attempted to stay their plans.

"Will you not hunt with me in the forest tomorrow morn?"

Malcolm cleared his throat, hating to give up the hunt. He glanced at Anice who looked as though she would cut him in two if he proposed staying the night. "We must decline your generous invite, but we need travel further before nightfall if we are to arrive at a timely manner at Brecken," Malcolm sorely regretting saying.

The notion of a hunt was truly tempting. Malcolm had wanted to hunt with King Henry, as avid a hunter as the king, Malcolm, and his brothers were. But Malcolm's time there had been cut too short. He glanced at Anice. She frowned at him. If he agreed to stay to hunt in the forest, they wouldn't leave until midday after partaking of the deer they managed to kill. He hesitated. He could see Angus and Dougald hoping he'd agree and recommend them staying the night. But he knew the only reason Laird Godric offered was to give Wulfric more of a chance to woo the lady.

Malcolm should have curbed his own desire and been more considerate of Anice's needs, but wouldn't she like to sleep in a bed the night and have a hot meal the next day before they journeyed again? And Mai? What about the elderly woman? She deserved to sleep inside for the night as well.

Clearing his throat, Malcolm said, "But then again we would—"

"Need to be going," Anice finished for him.

"Mayhap if the lady does not like to hunt," Lady Godric said, "we could prepare a warm bath for her, and afterwards the ladies of my court will entertain her."

"I thought she would hunt," Wulfric said, his tone disappointed.

Obviously, he was very much interested in the lady, and why wouldn't he be? She was lovely, owned much land, and was related to the English king through marriage, and the Scottish king by blood.

"You have a bow and quivers, my lady," Malcolm said, still wanting to change her mind, "so I assumed you hunt."

"Two legged creatures should they attack." Her eyes had narrowed like a cat's that readied to pounce on a rat but hurt also reflected in their depths. Even Mai seemed more than upset that the subject was going in this direction.

"Mayhap you already hunted with His Grace, but my brothers and I did not have a chance, Lady Anice." He should have dropped the subject at that point, but Malcolm hoped he'd find some sympathy in her heart for their cause. He truly loved to have the chance at a hunt and if she chose not to participate, she would be safe in the care of Laird Godric's ladies and out of his son's reach.

"May I speak with you alone for a moment?" Anice's words bristled with the nettle sting of her tongue, not a question but a command.

"Aye." He walked her outside of the keep, while Mai followed behind. "My lady, I beg your forgiveness for asking you this, as my brothers and I would verra much like to hunt if you would but permit us to do so. Mai would have a chance to rest—"

"Leave me out of this quarrel, my laird," Mai briskly said.

Anice took a deep breath, but blush tinged her cheeks, and her eyes were on fire. When she spoke, it was with the utmost calm, yet he sensed the anger she harbored barely contained just beneath the surface. "Then you must do that which is in your heart, my laird. Mai and I will continue on our way. Once you are through with your hunt you may join us, if you can catch up."

She stalked off to her horse while Mai hurried to catch up.

Malcolm cursed under his breath more for riling her, than not getting to hunt. Her situation at home could be dire, and nothing but the need for food and rest should deter them. He dashed back into the keep.

"Laird Godric, we take our leave. Again, we thank you for your generosity." Then he ran back out of the keep while Dougald and Angus chased after him.

"She cannot mean to leave without us," Angus shouted when Anice and Mai headed through the gate.

"She is verra stubborn. I cannot see why one day to hunt..." Malcolm shook his head. He knew why, but 'twas one of the reasons he wished to be the laird of his own castle. Then he could do as he pleased.

He mounted his horse and kicked it to a gallop, soon reaching the lady cantering down the road. Mai dropped back and Dougald hurried past them to take the lead. Why couldn't the woman have argued with him further? He would have agreed with her eventually. Why did she have to bolt out of the castle on her own? The lass needed a laird who could keep her harnessed.

For at least a mile, they rode in silence. He still fumed, his blood heated, and his stomach tied in knots, unsure of how to break the silence. He wanted to thrash her for rashly leaving like she had done. Did she always behave this way? The laird who wed her would truly be in for a battle. Not one, but many. Malcolm could certainly see who'd come out on top.

He glanced at her. The woman was bewitching, her cheeks still crimson, but the fire in her eyes had simmered to a manageable glow. What had happened to her earlier in life to make her run away whenever she didn't get her way, or felt threatened? He'd never known a woman like her who would just leave the safety of a castle on a whim. 'Twas not a safe thing for a lady to do. Why had no one ever counseled the lass better while she was growing up?

Anice said over the sound of the horses' clip-clops, "You didna have to give up the hunt for us. I am certain you would have caught up with us along the way."

He gritted his teeth. She knew damned well he couldn't let her and her lady-in-waiting travel alone.

"I thank you though for saying what you did on my behalf when Wulfric was interested in seeking my hand. And I thank you for interrupting the gentleman so many times. I dinna think I have ever seen a man's face so red. Mayhap I am wrong, but I dinna think he likes you."

Malcolm couldn't help but smile. Wulfric would do battle with him if they ever met sometime on a deserted road, he was certain.

"I am sorry you missed the hunt, Malcolm."

He stared at her, not believing she had called him by his name in such a manner. Was it a slip of the tongue?

She faced front again. "I know how important the hunt is to most men, but we cannot afford losing a day when we know naught of what has happened at my castle."

He took a deep breath. "Aye, my lady. I do not know what came over me."

She turned to smile at him, and the sight of her sweet face melted any hard feelings he might have had. "You are a good man, my laird, and if it werena that we have many days travel still ahead of us, and the worry as to what we shall find when we arrive at Brecken, I would have agreed to stay. Mai could have rested up, I could have had a bath, and—"

"Wulfric would have tried to befriend you further."

"Aye, another verra good reason no' to stay, dinna you agree?"

He chuckled. "Aye, my lady. A verra good reason indeed." He shook his head. The lady was a treasure.

Before the light faded from the sky that eve, they reached Theinge Village. Anice pointed out the chapel at the end of the road. "'Twas an ancient temple of Tew, the Anglo-Saxon word meaning God of War. William destroyed it when he conquered the land, then he rebuilt it."

"Aye."

"They built it here because it sits so close to the River Mimram." She turned to Malcolm. "Mayhap we can find lodging here in a byre or such." She rubbed her arms.

"Though the day warmed up considerably, the chill is again slipping into my bones."

Dougald motioned from a distance for them to join him.

"It appears my brother has found a place for us to sleep for the night. I imagine it will not be what you are used to, my lady, but will have to do."

"I have slept in a cave before, my laird. And on the bare grass with the wind at my cheek and the stars overhead."

Malcolm stared at her for a moment. She smiled. She was not so delicate that she could not sleep somewhere other than a straw-filled mattress in a castle keep.

"You will have to tell me more about this, my lady. You have me intrigued."

Again, she was surprised he'd be interested. No laird would ever have expressed an interest in such an unimportant thing.

Dougald pointed to a wattle and daub croft. Attached to this was a byre where the occupants of the home could attend to their livestock during the winter.

They rode toward their accommodations for the night.

Anice thought having made the trip to Arundel not so very long ago, she would be more used to it. But riding all day made her ache all over. The next few days would test her resolve to get home all in one piece.

"There is a hunting lodge," Dougald said as they drew close, "but 'tis occupied with more of the king's men as they are on their way to Arundel to meet with him on the morrow. I am afraid we will have to make do with the byre."

Malcolm helped Anice down from her horse. "The lady said she has had poorer accommodations than this."

Disbelief flittered across Dougald's face. She patted his arm. "'Tis true. I was an unruly child and once ran away from Brecken and hid in a cave."

She headed for the byre.

A burst of laughter from the three brothers followed.

Mai groaned as one of them helped her from her horse.

"Aye, she was always a stubborn lass. The one who wives her will have to be verra brave."

More laughter ensued and Anice smiled to herself. 'Twas true. She was not like most Englishwomen.

She stepped onto the hard-packed clay floor littered with straw, then walked over to the ladder to the loft. The farmer's sheep slept in their corral while the weather was mild, and the byre had been recently swept clean.

"Is there enough room for all of us up there, think you, my lady?" Malcolm asked as he drew close, so close his warm breath tickled her cheek. Her whole body warmed despite the chill in the air, and she wondered if he had the same effect on all women.

"You and the other gentlemen will have to sleep elsewhere," Mai said. "The lady is a maid and cannot sleep with ye."

Anice smiled and Malcolm copied her expression. "Under the circumstances, I think we can allow it for the next few nights, Mai. No telling where we will have to sleep next. Besides, you will be with me at all times to protect me."

Malcolm's smile broadened, and his brown eyes darkened with a sinful wickedness. Mayhap she best sleep at one end of the loft with Mai between her and the gentlemen.

Gunnolf quickly said, "I will sleep with the wagon, my lady, to guard our goods."

"Aye, Gunnolf," Malcolm said.

She wondered if his brothers would also choose other places to sleep for the night.

If Malcolm hoped he'd have the loft with her alone—she shook her head at the notion—though deep inside the idea more than intrigued her. She lifted her bliaut and began to climb the ladder. Malcolm grabbed the ladder to steady it while she made her way up the rungs to the top.

"I have to take care of business and shall return, my lady. Will you be all right?" Mai asked, wringing her hands, no doubt worried what people would think of Anice being alone without a proper chaperone.

"Aye. I have three strong Highlanders to protect me. By the time you return, I shall be asleep, no doubt."

"I willna be gone *that* long, my lady." Mai gave Malcolm a rather pointed look.

"I will see to the horses." Dougald headed out of the byre with Mai.

"I will help him." Angus dashed after his brother.

Malcolm smiled up at Anice when she peered down at him. She removed her veils and wimple, then began to unwind her braids.

"I should really look after the horses, too." Malcolm's gaze fastened on her hair.

"Aye, that you should."

"But then you would be alone," he quickly added as if he were afraid she'd shoo him away.

She smiled. "Mai would be mortified."

He grabbed the ladder and hurried to the top.

Anice unplaited the rest of her hair while Malcolm sat beside her on the straw bed, his gaze fixed on her hair as she separated the woven strands. She realized how much a woman's hair did indeed fascinate a man. No wonder women had hidden their hair for the last hundred years. Only more recently had the women given up the veils because of the queen's detest of them. Yet for travel, she felt more comfortable keeping her hair covered.

She looked up at Malcolm. "You act as though you have never seen a woman's hair unbound before."

"None ever so golden as yours." He reached out to touch it. "Silky as the tassel of corn and just as golden with touches of fiery red." He pressed her lock to his face and breathed in the fragrance. "Kissed by lavender."

She smiled at him, surprised he was such a poet. "You have a romantic side, my laird."

"'Tis you who inspire it." He leaned closer and ran his

hands through her hair. "I wonder if before your lady-in-waiting returns you wished to thank me again."

"Thank you?"

"Aye, you said you wished to kiss me."

"My lady should be here with me."

He nodded. "You are right. Think naught of what I said. 'Tis folly."

He leaned back. As soon as he did, she leaned forward and kissed him, intending only the same as before, a light brush of her mouth against his. Nothing more. Not that she did not want more, but she feared she could not handle it...not the way his eyes had darkened, and his voice had turned deeper and huskier. Was it her hair that had excited him so?

Instantly, his hands reached for her face, and before she could pull away, he kissed her, not in the same manner she had kissed him, but with enthusiasm, heat and passion the likes of which she'd never before experienced.

She melted to his touch. If she hadn't already been sitting, her knees would have weakened, and she would have collapsed on the floor. Now, she wished his calloused hands to touch her breasts, to lift her bliaut and shift and touch her naked thighs like...

"My lady?" Mai called out. "I fetched ye a pail of fresh water so you may wash your face before you go to sleep."

Anice tried to pull free from Malcolm to reply to her lady-in-waiting, but he deepened his kiss. Before she realized what he was doing, he slipped his tongue between her lips, the most unbelievable thing anyone had ever done to her, and the most wickedly exciting. She touched her tongue to his, cautiously, not sure what she was supposed to do.

He groaned low, and pressed his lips against hers again, as if reassuring her actions suited him just fine, and his hands gripped her shoulders tightly in his grasp like he never wanted to let go. The heat of his fingers burned through the wool of her gown, while moist heat pooled between her legs.

"My lady?" Mai said, more hushed this time.

Malcolm leaned over the railing of the loft. "Shhh, she's sound asleep."

Anice poked Malcolm in the rib.

"Aye, she can clean up on the morrow, then." Mai set the bucket aside, then walked across the floor to the ladder, her gait slow and stiff.

Malcolm kissed Anice again before Mai caught them.

His hands dropped lower on her arms, his thumbs brushing against her breasts. She sucked in her breath, wanting him to move his hands from her arms and take her breasts in his large capable hands. Already her nipples felt tight and tingly, as did the rest of her body. God, how she wished he'd touch every bit of her, as she wanted to touch his naked skin.

"After riding all day, I am no' sure I can make it up this ladder," Mai grumbled. The first wrung on the ladder creaked with the slight woman's weight.

Anice nearly chuckled. If she could have lain all night alone in Malcolm's arms...

What was she thinking? He wished an English bride. She was only a distraction, someone available when an Englishwoman was not.

But *she* wanted a Highlander. One just like him. But what about the curse? It didn't matter about the other men, but Malcolm, she would not wish anything horrible to befall him.

Again, he tangled his tongue with hers. The ache between her legs commenced and she pulled away, not wanting Mai to catch them, nor wanting the Highlander to stir her so with a thirst she couldn't quench.

"Sleep well, Anice," Malcolm whispered in her ear, then he peered over the railing of the loft. "Are you going to make it all right, lass?"

"Aye, but you may have to toss me down in the

morning, as I am sure I will be too stiff to climb the ladder."

He reached down and gave her a hand up. In the fading light of the byre, she looked past Malcolm, but not seeing his brothers, Mai said, "Where are your kinfolk, my laird?"

"Taking care of the horses."

"Should you not have stayed down below while they were gone?"

He reclined in the hay and rested his head on his arms. "I was tired, just like your mistress."

Mai glanced back at Anice who quickly closed her eyes.

She would have given anything to curl up against Malcolm's broad chest and enjoyed his warmth all night long. Instead, Mai lay down beside her, and several minutes later Malcolm's brothers joined them. Dougald offered the ladies a couple of more blankets.

Then after more rustling, everyone lay down to sleep.

Malcolm lay still for some time pondering the sweetness of Anice's kiss. Why had the lady not already wed? King Henry said she was old enough. Why had arrangements not already been made for her?

"I wondered why the lady was not married already," he said, hoping Mai would enlighten him.

No one said a thing, but Malcolm imagined his brothers were dying to know about the cryptic message concerning Anice, the curse and betrothals.

"His Grace said she is twenty summers," he continued.

Again, there was not a word from anyone, though he only expected to hear one of the ladies respond to his question.

"It seems that the lady would have been married at a much earlier—"

"She has been betrothed four times already, my laird," Mai said, her voice coated with sleep.

Malcolm swore both his brothers chuckled under their breaths, while he barely breathed to hear the news. Four betrothals?

There was certainly more to the wee lass than he could have ever imagined. But four betrothals?

CHAPTER 7

Malcolm stared into the darkness in Anice's direction. How could the lady have been betrothed four times and never been married?

He ran his hands through his unbound hair. Why hadn't the king told him she'd been betrothed so many times? "Norman lairds?"

Mai yawned. "Two Scottish, two Norman."

He rose up on his elbow. "When was she betrothed to these nobles?"

Mai didn't reply.

Malcolm lay back trying to settle the disquiet he felt. And for what reason? He had no intention of marrying her. So why did it bother him something fierce that she'd already had four betrothals?

Worse, if his brothers were still awake, which he assumed they were, did they wonder the same as him? The lady was cursed when it came to marriage bans?

***

Early the next morning, Malcolm and the rest of the party broke their fast, eating coarse brown bread and drinking mead with the farmer, his wife, and six children.

Anice paid the farmer for their generosity, though Malcolm had offered. His brothers looked on with surprise. They were now in the lady's employ. Why would she not pay for their meal?

If he had served a laird, his brother even, he'd have thought nothing of it. But for whatever reason, he hated to think that Anice would pay for his and his brothers' meals. He'd saved money from fighting in the Crusades after all. And he'd received ample coin when he departed from his older brother's employ to carry him through several years without wanting. Still he had no properties and without, he would always work for someone else, instead of being a laird of a castle in his own right. And that's what he wanted. Not only that, but a wife who would bear his bairn, a son who would carry on his title and name.

He glanced at Anice as she washed her face and hands, singing all the while. She smiled broadly at him as Mai plaited her mistress's red gold curls. He smiled back. What would it be like to wake to such a delightful creature every morning?

Was she so cheerful because every mile they traversed brought her closer to home?

Would he be making a mistake not seeking her hand, instead of an Englishwoman's? Anice was a known quantity after all. A prickly pear at times, but sweet, sure of herself, and totally intriguing at others. Well, kind of a known quantity. He couldn't help wondering about the curse.

When she nearly danced to the chapel with them for a quick prayer before departure, his gaze gravitated toward her. He wanted to dance with her and share the delight she exhibited in her springy step.

Still, he didn't think King Henry would want him marrying his wife's cousin when His Grace already had plans for Anice to wed a Norman laird.

Malcolm straightened his shoulders. If she should wish a Highlander laird to be her husband, why shouldn't she have what her heart desired?

She glanced at him and smiled, her eyes sparkling in the low morning light.

"You had a good sleep, I see, lass."

She stretched her arms above her head and nodded. "I had never slept in a loft before. 'Twas verra agreeable."

"There was not anything else that helped you to sleep so well?"

Her lips curved up as she looked at his. "Mayhap."

He glanced back to see that Mai was following far enough behind her mistress, then he said closer to Anice's ear, "Mayhap a good eve kiss?"

"I have had many."

He frowned, the notion not boding well with him. "You said you had never kissed a gentleman." And he knew it to be so, as shy as she had been at first with him.

"Aye."

"Then which is it? You have, or you have not?"

"I have not, my laird, in the manner in which you are speaking."

Vixen. Mayhap her meaning was that she did not kiss the noblemen back. Only that they kissed her. Still, the notion struck a chord of envy deep inside him.

"Did they kiss *you*, then?"

"Aye."

He quashed the irritation rising in his stomach. How could she be so delightfully charming, and in the next instant, maddening? "Then pray tell explain your meaning as I'm at a loss to understand it."

"The gentlemen were my father and uncle."

"Ah. You are a vixen, lass. You would have me believe that—"

"You would believe what you will, my laird. I have spoken naught but the truth."

He chuckled. She had. 'Twas he who had more devious notions about the lass. Yet he knew she could not have kissed a lover, as innocent as she seemed.

But the betrothals bothered him. As much as he knew it was not his business, and as much as he assumed she would tell him so, he would ask anyway. He opened his mouth to broach the subject, but she stepped into the chapel, and that killed his questions for now.

They had a long day of travel ahead of them, and he had every intention of learning about the four men who were to be her husbands. Had her betrothed all died? Or was she a terror and the bonds hastily rescinded once the men learned of her true disposition?

The more he learned about Anice, the more curious he got. 'Twas not because she stirred his loins every time she got close to him, or that he truly wanted her for his wife. 'Twas just his business to know all about the lady he would work for.

Following services, Mai talked to Anice in private, the older woman seeming to offer advice in a somewhat aggravated fashion.

Anice caught his eye and smiled. Mai's words to her seemed to not affect her cheerful mood. For that he was glad.

Dougald slapped Malcolm on the shoulder. "I thought we would stop in Northampton for the eve."

"Aye, it would be a good stopping place."

Dougald continued, "As to the lass..."

Malcolm raised a brow.

Dougald motioned for them to walk farther from where the ladies were talking.

"What have you on your mind, Dougald?"

"If you are as interested in the lady as you appear to be, why do you not ask the king's permission to court her?"

"She does not want me...or my type, so she has said."

Angus joined them, shaking his head. "I have never seen a lass kiss you first who did not want you."

"For my title, aye."

Dougald shook his head. "You spar like lovers. You

cannot tell me you are not as fascinated with her as she is with you."

Malcolm smiled. "She is a winsome lass, I cannot deny that. But Henry wants her to marry a Norman laird. I would not think he would agree to my taking the lady to wive."

Dougald glanced back at the lady, then faced Malcolm. "You are not afraid of asking him, are you? I have never seen you fear anything before."

"'Tis the four men she nearly wed before that concerns him," Angus said, humor evident in his voice.

"Aye, what if she poisoned every one of them, or slew them with her sharp tongue?" Dougald said and laughed.

"Never know. I shall discover all I can before I would do something so rashly as ask for the lady's hand. But it would be up to her and the king to grant me such a thing. Still, mayhap the longer we get to know one another, I would find I would want naught to do with her, except serve as her steward."

"If her lady-in-waiting had not slept between you and the lass last eve, you would not be talking like this." Dougald raised his brows.

Malcolm couldn't contain a grin. The idea that he could have snuggled under the blanket with the lass...

His brothers laughed.

Dougald made a parting comment before they continued their journey. "Do not delay asking the king to court the lady. Once dandies come to seek her hand—"

"I have already warned her not to show any of them favor."

Dougald chuckled as Angus's mouth turned up.

"Because of the situation, do you not see? Whoever has killed her uncle, if this was the case, wants to take her for his wife. We do not know which laird it is."

"I see your reasoning. Though I agree with you about your logical thinking on the matter, I still believe there is an underlying reason concerning the lady you choose not to reckon with."

There was no arguing with his brothers. If they chose to believe he wished more than being the lady's steward, so be it. Who was he to spoil their delusions?

Anice approached them, the fragrance of lavender that Mai had mixed with the water Anice washed with, scenting her skin. "Shall we continue our journey?"

Malcolm led her to her horse. "Aye, 'tis time we depart. Is your lady able to make another day of riding?"

Mai said, "I am ready, my laird. I am not so old that I cannot ride for several more days."

"Aye, good Scots' blood."

"Aye." Mai smiled at him, seemingly genuinely pleased he'd say so.

The morning passed without too much trouble, though Mai grumbled a few times when they stopped to rest the horses, and her face pained when Angus helped her down from her mount.

"You can always ride in the wagon for a while," Malcolm coaxed when they watered the horses again.

"I am no infirmed."

"Aye." He couldn't help but admire the woman. He didn't know any lady who was as old as she appeared to be who was such a hardy soul.

Anice leaned over the water, careful not to dip her hem in the fast-flowing water, while she washed her face. Her blue gown caressed her rounded arse like he wanted to do. Why wouldn't she make for a bonnie bride?

He had yet to ask her about these betrothals though. When she stood and stretched, he couldn't help but admire her figure, her pert breasts stood at attention, and her slim waist—

Dougald joined him, smiled and winked, then strode across the rocky bank to the edge of the water. "My lady, you seem to be in high spirits today." He dipped his hands in the water and splashed it on the back of his neck.

"Aye, that I am. The closer we draw to the Scot's border, the happier I am."

"Aye, I know the feeling. I heard tell you were looking for a Highland laird to wed but that Malcolm did not appeal. You said you wished a younger man like Angus, however I wondered how you would feel about a man who is between the two?"

"Are you offering yourself as a prospect of marriage?" Her cheeks flushed slightly. She shifted her attention to Malcolm, who couldn't help but stare dumbfounded at his brother's actions.

When it came to women, Dougald easily won them over, but Malcolm couldn't believe he would go after Anice. The look in her green eyes seemed surprised. Did she want Malcolm to rescue her from his brother? Or was she just as astonished that his brother had approached her?

For that matter, what the hell had gotten into his brother? She was to marry the king's choice. Not a Highland nobleman. And certainly not his brother.

"The lady has *not* given any reason for my not appealing to her," Malcolm butted in. "Are you ready to ride again, my lady?"

She smiled at him. "Aye." She looked over at Mai. "Are you ready?"

"As ready as I will ever be."

Angus offered to help Mai onto her horse. She hesitated to accept his proposal when Malcolm lifted Anice onto her own.

"Is anything the matter, lass?" Angus asked Mai.

"Mayhap my horse is weary of my riding him."

Malcolm tried to hide a smile.

"Aye," Angus said, then motioned to the wagon. "I will assist you into the wagon then."

"Most kind of you, my laird. You are truly chivalrous."

Malcolm mounted his horse and glanced at Anice. She too was smiling.

The party got on their way again and this time Malcolm was determined to broach the subject of Anice's four *almost* husbands. Later, when he had time to speak to Dougald, he would also share his thoughts on his uncalled-for behavior. Whatever overcame Dougald to imply he wished to court the lady?

"I thought you had never been betrothed before, my lady." Malcolm hoped she would enlighten him without too much prodding.

"You assume much about me, my laird. Why is this so, when you are no' interested in a Scottish lady for a bride, but an Englishwoman instead? I would think your concern important for the lady you pursued, no' me."

He frowned. Why couldn't the wench just tell him what he wanted to know without making it a contest of wills always?

She said nothing further, just stared ahead at the road that crossed over rolling hill upon rolling hill.

"I was just curious."

"Aye."

Blast the woman. He took a deep breath and traveled for some distance in silence. He wasn't interested in her as his wife. Why could she not see he was just curious was all?

Mayhap he could ask Mai sometime later.

Mayhap not. He wished to know now. Patience had never been one of his virtues.

"Are you ashamed of your betrothals then? I would think you would be proud to have had so many wish your hand in marriage."

She looked at him, a smile twitching on her lips.

The wench was aggravating him to damnation. She enjoyed making him suffer to know the truth.

"Mayhap 'tis none of your business."

He knew sooner or later she'd speak those words. They seemed to be some of her favorite. Or was it just because he asked her questions she didn't want to answer more often than most?

"'Tis true, my lady, that 'tis no concern of mine." He slipped back into silence and attempted to pretend the beguiling woman didn't interest him in the least.

"The first I was betrothed to shortly after I was born, my laird."

He glanced at her, surprised she spoke on the matter without further urging. "Aye, and what happened to this laird?"

She smiled. "He died before I was six."

He frowned. Why should that have given her pleasure? "Why does this please you, my lady?"

"He was sixty-three summers when the marriage contract was signed between my father and the laird. The Norman laird could not wait long enough to be my husband. He died comfortably in his sleep, they say. I was pleased because I was to be his wife when I reached the age of twelve. He would have been ancient by then, had he lived."

"And the others?"

She shrugged. "Of little consequence. Why should it matter to you?"

The bone deep compulsion to know was his reason. "You do not have to tell me. However, I wondered why the king was seeking a husband for ye if ye were already betrothed."

"Aye. I see now your reasoning. The second was another Norman laird. I was betrothed to him when I was eight. But he was killed during the Crusades."

She didn't seem happy about his death.

"Did you love him?"

"He was fairly handsome and a young man. He was not old like the other. And very kind to me, too." She took a deep breath. "I was to join him when I was fourteen. My father at that time decided I needed some additional years of good breeding."

"Was this before or after you ran away and slept in a

cave?"

She smiled. "Before."

So what had prompted her father to wish to keep her at home longer? Malcolm would pose that question later. For now, he wished to know about the other gentlemen. "And the third gentleman?"

"Ah, now he was truly the best."

Malcolm stiffened, not wishing to hear any man would be better than him. Then he thought about the matter further and realized he must have been one of the Scottish lairds. Mayhap that was the only reason she preferred him to the others.

"He was the Scottish laird?"

"Aye, a cousin of King Edgar."

"Then he would have been related to you?"

"Aye, distantly."

Malcolm pondered the notion. "Did you prefer him to the others because he was Scottish?"

"Aye, that I did."

"And no other reason?"

Her lips and eyes smiled at him. "Why do you not give up your search for an Englishwoman and ask the king to permit you to court me? Your brothers would, I darest say, if I should ask them to."

"You wish me to court you, lass?" Malcolm asked, his voice showing his incredulity that she would say such a thing to him, especially since she told him his kind didn't appeal, though he never thought she truly spoke the truth. "The king wishes you to marry a Norman laird."

"What do you wish?"

"That you do as you desire, lass."

"Aye. But I have no Highlanders seeking my hand. How can I marry one who I would wish when there are none available?"

"So you would think me not such a bad choice then after all?" How could the woman who raised his hair in anger, lift his heart in the next instant?

"Mayhap not. But you would have to hold two jobs."

"What would they be, lass?"

"You would still have to act as my steward and help me to solve the puzzle at my castle."

"Aye."

"And you would have to court me to win my heart."

He lifted a brow, amused. "Think you I could not handle such a job?"

"Methinks you may no' be able to as you wish an English bride."

He smiled. "I would have to seek His Grace's permission."

"If he is agreeable?"

"I will put off my search for an English bride."

"Aye, and that is why you shall have difficulty wooing me." Her chin rose, but she wore a slight smile.

"Because?" The woman had no end to her riddles.

"Because I willna play second favorites. You either want me with all your heart and no other will do, or you dinna. I will no' be the one for you, just because you canna find another who wants you."

"Ah." The lady was truly to be admired. But if he should propose marriage to her, he would lose his wagers that would make him a fairly wealthy man. Even his brothers would gain a share of him. Still he could woo her, keep a closer eye on her while she was courted by whoever it was who wished her estates, and yet never propose marriage. Then he could prove to her that she was interested in him after all.

"I take you up on your offer, my lady."

"It willna be an easy task, my laird."

"The position as steward?"

"The other. I will put you through your paces."

"Of that, my lady, I am assured." Then he thought about the Scottish laird who she'd been betrothed to and the other he still hadn't learned anything about. "About the Scottish laird. What happened to him?"

"He isna dead if you are worried I am cursed and bring death to any who are bound to me by marriage contract."

He stared at her, disbelieving. That was why rumors abounded that she was cursed, but what was more of an enigma was why she would be looking for a husband, if she already had one. "If he is still alive, then what has become of him? And why would the king want a husband for you?"

She smiled sweetly. "He ran off with a Scottish lass who had no money or properties. 'Twas true love. Only if King Alexander ever gets hold of him, he will end up like the others. But in the meantime, the bans were cancelled."

"Being betrothed to you can be hazardous to a man's health."

"Aye. Keep that in mind, my laird, should you truly wish to pursue me."

She had the most devilish way of smiling at times, and this was definitely one of those times. Her challenge would not go unknown answered. She'd thrown down the gauntlet and he most heartily accepted.

Then he recalled there was one other, and she had made no mention of this Scottish laird. "And the last?"

Tears filled her eyes and she quickly turned away but didn't say a word.

"Lady Anice?"

"You wouldna wish to know about him," she said, choking on tears.

He stared at her, wondering what had happened to him. Was she cursed after all? Or did she harbor some love for her betrothed husband that would transcend all time?

Why should it matter? If Malcolm did wed her, he would have lands, a castle, and a wife to give him a bairn. What would it matter whether she could give him her heart? He never thought any Englishwoman he would wed would love him either. 'Twas the way of things. A marriage of convenience. His own mother and father had an arranged marriage, neither loving the other. His father had his favorite mistress, though he gave Malcolm's mother four sons, his duty fulfilled to leave an heir to his estates, when he wasn't drunk and tupping Isobelle. His mother had seemed content enough to raise her four sons and didn't seem to mind their father was never around.

Malcolm had always known love and marriage were not part of the arrangement.

He glanced at Anice again, wondering what the devil was wrong with him that he would even care what she felt about the other Scottish laird.

CHAPTER 8

At least a half dozen times during their journey that day, Malcolm had tried to broach the subject of the circumstances concerning Anice's final betrothal, but she seemed so distressed, he imagined he'd have to ask Mai if he were going to learn anything about the matter. Once when they had stopped and he was busy watering the horses, he spied Anice reading the washed-out missive that Gunnolf had dried, though nothing was clearer on the vellum than the three words Malcolm and his brothers had chanced to read. Her brow wrinkled and she shoved the missive back into Gunnolf's pouch resting on the wagon seat.

Then is when Malcolm attempted to speak with Mai as she stretched her arms out in front of her and groaned, weary from the travel. Before he could open his mouth, Mai turned on him and said, "Do not be asking my mistress about her last betrothal, if ye know what is good for you."

He didn't like that she seemed to read his mind, but the abrupt way she hissed the words, made him pause in questioning her. Still, Mai said nothing about asking *her* the question, just about leaving Anice alone concerning the matter.

"Then you can tell me—" But he quit his words when he saw Anice approach. She looked tired and stressed, so he said no more of the matter. Yet, he would know what happened to this fourth betrothal of Anice's before long, if he could manage.

***

Anice studied Malcolm, whose focus shifted quickly from Mai to her, and noticed he abruptly ceased speaking. 'Twas some question he had about her no doubt.

Mai avoided her look. Aye, mayhap about the curse? The vellum revealed little except it linked her with curses and betrothals. But who had given Malcolm the message was what she was dying to know.

"Are ye ready to ride again, my lady?" Malcolm asked, while his brothers stood nearby watching.

"Aye, that I am."

He helped her onto her horse. His large, gentle hands held her waist, lingering overlong, sending a sizzling blaze coursing through her. His eyes held hers and with the deep breath he took, his nostrils flared. Raking her with his hungry gaze, he cleared his throat, but didn't say what he seemed to have on his mind. Yet, he also seemed not to wish to release her.

Mai's face grew red. "Time we are off, my laird?" Mai did not oft fidget, but she wrung her hands in distress this time.

Malcolm gave her a harsh look; Gunnolf quickly helped Mai onto the wagon.

Slapping Angus on the back, Dougald smiled like an idiot, then mounted his horse. Angus's smile was smaller, but his eyes revealed his unbridled amusement as well.

Malcolm's hands brushed down Anice's thigh, the touch erotic when his fingers caressed her all the way through her gown. 'Twas indecent, and worse, everyone saw it. So why did she want him to touch her further? Around the rogue, she was shamelessly wanton.

He turned away from her, adjusted his trewes, then climbed into his saddle. With a wave of his hand, he motioned for Dougald to lead the way and hoarsely shouted, "Continue, brother!"

Throughout the day, Anice and her escort stopped where they could to water and rest the horses and partake of the salted pork and ale they carried. When they paused for the last time an hour south of Northampton, Anice skin prickled and she immediately sensed danger before a man appeared.

The stout man with beady eyes and short hair as black as coal approached on horseback, calling out, "How now, good folk. Would you have a drop o' mead for a fellow traveler?"

His hand raised in greeting, showed he carried no weapon and meant them no harm, yet the hair on her arms stood on end when the man drew nearer. The way he looked her over as if he appraised a side of beef for his master, stirred her blood.

Dougald offered the man some ale. "Where are you bound?" His words were dark, and even when he handed over the drink, he watched the man with the caution of a battle-hardened warrior.

"Northampton for the night; same as you I suspect. I am Conan," the man replied, seemingly noting the hostility in Dougald's words, but responding in a cheerful manner as if he didn't have a care in the world.

No one said anything in response for a moment, and she wondered if the other MacNeill brothers also worried about him.

"Where have you ridden from?" Malcolm finally asked, wiping his brow with a wetted cloth. Like Dougald's, his eyes remained fixed on the stranger.

"Hertford. And you?"

"Arundel."

"Aye. I have sung a tale or two there."

TERRY SPEAR

"You are a bard?" Malcolm asked, his tone edged with disbelief.

Everyone in their party watched the man, as if they suspected him, too, of being not who he said he was. Beneath his brown woolen cloak, the telltale sign of a sword hung at his hip. His horse was a destrier...a knight's warhorse, not a simple bard's. Was he a thief then? Had he stolen these things from a knight?

"Aye, a bard," Conan said, smiling, like a jester entertaining the royal family.

"You do not appear to be a bard." Anice wasn't above saying what was on everyone else's minds.

His smile broadened, not seeming to be in the least bit perturbed with her inference that he'd lied, but his black eyes pinned her with a challenge, betraying his true intentions were not what he pretended them to be. "The lady is right. I have been a knight, but I have given up the use of my sword for the time being. For now, I am a bard, and this is the only service I wish to provide. Might I join you on your travels? 'Tis better to journey with others than alone and become the victim of thieves."

Anice tucked a wayward curl of hair underneath her veil. "To Northampton?"

"Aye, and beyond with you if I may."

She narrowed her eyes at him, wondering why he would think such a thing. They had never said their destination lay beyond Northampton after all. "Think you we travel any farther than that?"

Again, the man smiled. "'Tis my folly. I would not have any idea where you were bound."

Yet, she thought his words a lie. "Why would you lay down your sword?"

"A most indelicate wound, my lady, that has not properly healed."

Before she could ask him to show her this wound, Malcolm interrupted her questioning. "'Tis only an hour to

Northampton from here. You may ride with us, if 'tis your wish." Malcolm helped Anice onto her horse, but not before she cast him a scolding look.

She would have exposed Conan for his lie, if Malcolm hadn't stopped her from seeing this man's wound, which she assumed he didn't have. No one of their party had given their names, yet this Conan seemed not to care. Why wouldn't he, as a traveling bard, be interested in who he accompanied? Would it not add to his lists of tales?

Or did he not wish to know because he already knew who they were? And if that be the case, why did he not say so in the beginning?

He was a dangerous scoundrel, that's why.

"Come ride ahead with me," Dougald said. His voice was cheerful, but the underlying tone was a command. Did he think like she that the man was a deceiver and Dougald wanted to keep the brigand away from her?

The MacNeill brothers already proved the king's trust in them was merited.

As the party got underway, Dougald and Conan distanced themselves from them and after they were well away from their hearing, Anice said, "Think you he lies?"

"Aye, lass, but you could have been a wee bit more subtle. You as much as called the man a prevaricator to his face." Malcolm cocked a dark brow.

She frowned, not one to play games with the likes of dangerous men. "Aye, because that is what he is. There is no reason to pretend that he is not."

"I did not wish you to worry that he might be a danger."

"Think you he is up to no good?"

"I am not certain. He would not lie unless he had some purpose in doing so. And I would not believe 'tis for a good cause."

"I would have asked him to show his wound to me, if you hadna stopped me."

Malcolm shook his head, his mouth tugged upwards. "I

knew that was where your questioning was headed. Would your steward have not advised you to let him speak on your behalf?"

"He would not have wasted his breath."

Malcolm chuckled. "If this Conan had refused to disrobe in front of the lady to show off his indelicate wound, I would have had to force the issue. No way did I want him to expose himself to you, my lady."

"What if he lies?"

"My brothers and I can ask to see this wound of his this verra eve without your witness."

She harrumpfed.

Again, he laughed. "My lady, your cheeks are crimson."

She tilted her chin higher. "We must do what we must to ensure the safety of all concerned, do you no' agree?"

"You are sure not like any lass I have ever met."

"Is this good or bad, my laird?"

He laughed again but wouldn't say.

She assumed it was good the way he smiled, though she wasn't positive without him saying so. "If he isna who he says he is, what reason would he have to lie?"

"There could be any number of reasons. He owes someone money, has left a troublesome wife behind, or a lady who he is not wed with bairn, and an angry father wants his head."

"Or he could be a spy for His Grace's rebellious brother."

Malcolm nodded. "Aye, and is traveling the area in disguise."

Taking a deep breath, she said, "I think he knows who we are. Or at least me."

Malcolm stared at her, worry etched in his features. "What makes you believe so, lass? Did you recognize him?"

"Nay. But he didna ask who we were, and he made my skin crawl the way he looked at me, as if he were studying me to see if I fit the description he had been given."

Malcolm turned to watch the man. "I had only assumed the man feasted his eyes on you because you are such a bonny lass. I had not suspected he might have been in search of you. But I did notice he did not ask our names. You saw how we did not offer them either."

"Aye, that's why I assumed you were suspicious of him, too."

"He rides too fine a horse and—"

"His cloak outlined his sword."

Malcolm looked at her. "You are verra observant, my lady."

"I fear our safety depends on our vigilance at all times."

"Aye." He sat taller in his saddle. "That is also why either my brothers or I will accompany you at all times."

"Even to my bedchamber?"

A slow smile turned his lips heavenward while he watched Conan. "Only I would take you there."

"If I should become indisposed."

He faced her and his smile broadened.

A trickle of heat curled into her belly. What she wouldn't give for him to join her in her bed. Then again, whatever was the matter with her to give such ideas any thought? He would truly have to have a change of heart about having a Scottish lady for his bride before she could even indulge in such notions. Though if he'd reached just a wee bit higher when he'd slid his hands up her thigh...och, she had no business thinking about that.

She wished now she had more than the ability of second sight and could instead read Malcolm's thoughts as his eyes looked sinfully seductive in the fading light while he studied her with a devilish smirk.

When they reached Northampton, Conan motioned to the walled-in town. They passed a small abbey, St. Andrews Priory on Broad Street. Merchants dealing in fine cloth displayed their linens on Mercers Row and on Woolmonger Street, the dying and weaving of wool took place. A grand castle sat watch over the town, protecting its inhabitants from any incursion.

Malcolm said, "I have met the Earl of Northampton, Simon de St. Liz, builder of this castle. He was one of William's Norman lairds during the conquest and came to have the lands and title in thus a manner—King William had Waltheof, the Norman Earl of Huntingdon, executed, some say for having been involved in a revolt with the earls against the king. William thence offered the earl's widow his own niece, Judith, as a bride to Simon. She refused, saying Simon had a halting in one leg she could not abide."

Anice quirked a brow. Was the woman so shallow so as not to please her king, or was Simon really that dreadful a lord? On the other hand, Anice had most likely displeased King Henry when she had said no to his advances. Still, the circumstances were different. One was the offer of a husband who was favored by the king. The other was an offer of a lover's tryst. Then again, his wanting her to wed Norman lairds hadn't set well with her either.

"This infuriated King William," Malcolm continued. "He seized the castle and honor of Huntingdon, which the countess held in dower. She and her daughter lived in a state of privation on the Isle of Ely. Simon was not to be deterred and though he was disappointed in not obtaining the countess of Huntington's hand, he made his addresses to her daughter, Lady Maud. She did accept and King William granted Simon both the titles of earl of Huntingdon and Northampton."

"Impressive. And you met him..."

"During the Crusades at the Battle of Antioch. I think he would welcome old comrades at arm."

"I do not know this earl. 'Tis good I brought you along then."

Malcolm chuckled, shaking his head. "You are a treasure, lass."

His words warmed her thoroughly, but she wondered

what he would think of her should she tell him about her fourth betrothed husband. Her head pounded with frustration to think she had the worst luck with gaining a husband. Malcolm would not think her a treasure if her learned of the manner in which her last betrothed died, she was certain.

Before they reached the castle, Conan quit the group. "Where is he going?" Malcolm said, drawing closer to Dougald, with Anice at his flank when the self-professed bard headed for Draper Street.

"He says he has other business to attend in town. If he can finish it quickly, he will join us and entertain the earl for a meal."

Malcolm's jaw hardened. "I suspect the earl may know him and he does not want that revealed. Did he tell you anything that might give us a clue as to what he is about?"

"He is very careful to not let secrets slip, Malcolm. I suspect it has something to do with the lady."

Malcolm frowned. "How come you by this notion?"

"I told him the lady is marrying a Highlander."

Anice gripped her reins tighter. "Why would you tell him this?" What if the word got back to Henry? She tried to quash the annoyance she felt that Dougald would say anything so foolish to a dangerous stranger.

"To flush out the quarry, my lady. His eyes grew as round as the full moon. I thought he would fade away when he did not breathe for so long. Why would he be so concerned unless he had some interest in you?"

"Mayhap because he does not like Highlanders?" she asked, wishing the man truly wasn't interested in her.

"If he does not know who you are, what difference would it make whether you marry a Highlander or no'? I believe he knows who you are and that mayhap he works for the laird who wishes your hand in marriage. The laird undoubtedly knows you are returning home. He would want you watched while you are in the company of Highlanders, do not you agree?"

"Or in the company of any but himself," Malcolm said, his voice perturbed.

"Aye."

Anice finally found her tongue. "Could you have told him something other than I would marry a Highlander? How could you? What if the word gets back to His Grace?"

"I do not think it will, my lady," Dougald said, his words even. "I believe Conan will take the message directly back to his laird."

"And then?" Malcolm asked.

"Your guess is as good as mine."

When they reached the gatehouse, a black bearded, surly gate guard met them. "What business have ye here?"

"We have come to see His Laird Earl," Malcolm said. "I am Laird MacNeill and fought with him at the Battle of Antioch."

"Aye, I will have word sent at once, my lord."

The earl was pleased to remake his acquaintance with a fellow Crusader and quickly had Malcolm and his party seated at the evening meal.

The hall grew loud with conversation as many watched the newcomers at the meal.

"Have you ever heard of a bard named Conan? He was a knight in the Crusades," Malcolm asked Simon.

He lifted his tankard and paused as if trying to recall, then shook his head. "Not a bard, but I remember Sir Conan, if it is the same man. Steely black hair and eyes. Stout in build, if I recall accurately."

"Aye, sounds like the same one. Do you know who he served?"

"Baron Harold de Fontenot."

Anice's stomach churned when she overheard Malcolm and Simon's conversation. This Conan was a spy for the same man who sought to have her hand in marriage. Malcolm reached under the table and squeezed Anice's hand clenched into a fist in her lap.

"You say he is a bard now?" the earl asked.

"Aye, to hear him tell of it, he has a wound that will not heal."

"But you do not believe him?" The earl waved at the surveyor to begin serving the meal. "I can tell from the tone of your voice you have doubts."

The surveyor waved his key to summon the pantler. The young man cut the upper crust from a round, spicy, colored loaf of bread and served the top slice for the earl.

"He said he was a bard, but he rode a destrier and carried a hidden sword." Malcolm buttered a slice of bread.

"Aye, mayhap he has caused some trouble in Lord Fontenot's court."

Anice squirmed in her seat. More likely he was still very much employed by the baron.

"You have come at the right time," the earl said, changing the subject and leaned back in his chair. "The annual fair begins tomorrow."

Anice frowned. Now 'twas her turn to be disappointed. What she wouldn't give to see all of the goods offered for sale at the fair from communities from miles around.

Malcolm's brows rose and he smiled just a wee bit at her.

She folded her arms. "I'm afraid we must continue on our way." Her voice was very small and disconcerted. She had to return to her people first thing. She stirred a mixture of plums, quince, apples, and pears, spiced with rosemary, basil and rue in a pastry tart.

But to miss the chance to see the annual fair? She groaned inwardly, knowing how much Malcolm must have hated missing out on the hunt.

"This reminds me of an earlier dilemma, my lady," Malcolm whispered to her.

"'Twas no dilemma," she said matter-of-factly. "We could not delay our trip for the hunt, nor can we postpone our journey for a day at the fair."

"Mayhap, my lady, you can wander through the stalls for an hour or two." Malcolm glanced over at Mai. "Even your lady-in-waiting seems to perk up a bit over the idea."

A sparkle appeared in her gray eyes that had not been there earlier.

Anice was disheartened to disappoint her lady-in-waiting, who needed to rest further. But the rest of her people had to be her main concern for now. "We should leave without delay."

He smiled brazenly in response. His attitude should have irritated her, but she knew she deserved it after he'd missed the love of the hunt.

After they dined on mutton and finished their wine, they thanked their host and excused themselves to take a walk around the inner bailey.

They sauntered without speaking, then Malcolm cleared his throat. "We still have a long way to go. It does not hurt for you to take some pleasure along the way."

"How can I do such a thing when I denied you and your brothers the pleasure of a hunt before?"

"That was different."

"How so, my laird? It seems the situations are verra much the same."

"If we had stayed at Hertford to hunt, we would have been delayed through to the noon meal. But a walk through the fair will not take more than an hour or two."

She studied his somber face and worried he had some concern that he was afraid to voice. "Methinks you have some darker reason for wanting to delay us."

He shuffled his shoes in the dry dirt, his eyes shifting from the ground to her gaze. "Aye. I believe Conan will be thinking we will leave at first light to make the most of our time. He will either tag along with us further on our journey, or he will meet up with us later. In any event, I believe an ambush will lay in wait for us somewhere along our path."

"Why?"

"Dougald said what he did about your marrying a Highlander for a reason. He assumed Conan works for Fontenot and now the earl has confirmed this. If Fontenot is capable of murdering your uncle, he will not stop from committing it again to ensure he has you for his wife."

"I do not understand the plan." Disconcerted, she'd known the man was dangerous.

"We cannot know for certain what he plans. But what if Lord Fontenot offers money to brigands to attack us on the road heading north? His orders would be to kill the men, but not to harm the women. Then the baron rushes in to save the ladies, only the brigands will not live to tell the truth of the tale. Fontenot no doubt would tell them he would arrive, and the men would disappear before he had the chance to kill any of them."

Anice stopped walking. "You cannot be serious."

"If I had the notion I wished your hand at any cost, I would do such a thing. That is if I were a blackguard. If he is a decent laird, he would not think of plotting such a crime. If he already killed your uncle, he will stop at naught to have your hand."

She lifted her chin, and quickly formulated a plan. "Then we will have to confuse them."

"My lady?"

"He knows how many men are in our party. He would make sure he had enough ruffians to attack ye. Probably he would not mention to them that you're battle-skilled Highlanders. Still, if there were enough of them, it could be disastrous for us. I propose we split up."

"Nay. We stay together and—"

Her blood heated and her voice elevated. She was not used to being countermanded, and she wouldn't allow her word—unless she could be proved wrong or someone had a better idea—to be discounted. "They will be looking for a wagon with two women, three men on horseback, and the driver of the wagon. If we leave the wagon behind, that will give them pause. Gunnolf can follow later. We can send some of my staff to escort him. And Mai will stay behind as well. I truly do not think she can ride another day. After a couple of week's rest, she should have recuperated."

"That leaves just the three of us men and ye."

"Aye. We can ride faster without the wagon to slow us down."

He rubbed the dark stubble covering his chin. "It might work."

"One other thing." She raised her brows with determination.

"Why do I get the notion, I will not like this one other thing one wee bit?"

"I will dress as a man."

He frowned and shook his head. "Nay."

"Hear me out. If they are looking for two women, three male riders, and a wagon driven by another, but all that passes by are four male riders, heavily armed, do you no' think they will let us pass while they wait for the real 'us' to come along? Fontenot would have their hides if they attacked the wrong party, then alerted the right one before they arrived."

"What if they attack anyway, thinking we are the four men and kill you, too? I do not like this plan of yours. And how will you be armed?"

"I will use my bow. You will wear your armor and be verra imposing, my laird. These brigands will think twice of striking such a force. I can see them now, shaking in their boots as we pass them by."

Malcolm's face was dark and filled with concern. "I do not like the plan, lass."

"Are we to just walk into an ambush then?"

"We can bypass the road we plan to take."

"It would delay us overmuch."

He began to walk with her again, his back rigid, his brow furrowed in thought. "I had thought of some kind of disguise, but...let me discuss this with my brothers. If any can come up with a better plan, we will let you know. I must say though, we could make the split during the fair."

"You dinna think they would attack there?"

"Nay. Not only will Simon's men be watching for thieves at the fair, Conan most likely suspects you would want to return home at earliest convenience and would not waste time tarrying there."

Anice nodded. "Then I believe 'tis time to retire for the eve. I will speak with Mai of our plans."

"*If* my brothers agree to it."

She tilted her chin up, not to be thwarted. "I will have no doubt a difficult time convincing her to stay behind."

"I am serious, my lady. We must all be in agreement."

"Aye." She agreed, only she was bound and determined to have her way.

They turned and crossed the bailey toward the keep.

"I must have a word with Simon, though," Malcolm said.

"What have you in mind, Malcolm?" Again, she hadn't meant to call him by his surname.

His lips rose. "I would offer to pay one of his men to send a letter to His Grace on my behalf, concerning my intentions toward you, my lady."

She couldn't help the blush that rose to her cheeks. Yet, she wouldn't make it easy on the Highlander who wished an English bride. "Aye."

"I would take you to your bedchamber, but—"

"Mai and I can manage without your assistance, my laird." Though she wished he would have escorted her anyway, but his countenance was dismal, and she assumed it was better that he take care of business. She blinked. What she wouldn't have given to have his bruising kisses again, his tongue devilishly teasing hers, hers mimicking his roguish actions, and his wayward thumbs stroking her breasts indecently. Moist heat curled between her thighs.

Och, her mind was tainted with the evilest notions. 'Twas imperative she wed a man soon before these illicit thoughts took control of her and truly turned her into a shameless woman.

When they reached the keep, Malcolm bowed low to her, his dark eyes catching her gaze, transfixing her. She curtsied. "On the morrow then, bonnie lass."

Had she not such an audience, she would kiss him good night, but she didn't want the sweet, innocent kiss that she had first bestowed upon him. She wanted the kind of passion he'd exhibited in the hayloft when they had no audience. After all, hadn't that been the reason for her having such pleasant dreams? They both hesitated to depart, then smiled at the indecision. Quickly, she pressed her lips to his, and just as rapidly, pulled away. "Again, to thank ye, my laird."

Her whole body heated, and she couldn't look him in the eye when she hurried toward the stairs. Close on her heels, Mai clucked, climbing the stairs.

"I will have to earn your thanks more often, my lady," Malcolm called after Anice, tickling her and sending another rash of heat sweeping through her.

"What did I tell ye, Angus?" Dougald said, closing the gap between them and Malcolm.

"Aye, he has lost his heart to the bonnie lass," Angus responded.

"I have not had much success at marrying a Scottish lass, you know that," Malcolm objected.

"That has nothing to do with you. God's teeth, if it hadn't been for our father's interference," Angus said.

"More than interference, drunken betrothals," Douglas inserted. "To commit you to two lassies at the same time—"

"And say you were the next earl in line of succession, when James was," Angus added, laughing.

Malcolm fisted his hands. "Aye, the drunken sot. Because of Da, the ladies' families wished to run me through. Didna help that James wanted neither of the ladies, that Da died before he could straighten out the matter and make the arrangements for James instead."

Dougald chuckled. "Aye. 'Twas a mess. But no' your fault and the ladies are both betrothed to other lairds now."

"At least you hope," Angus said, humor edging his words.

"Neither wanted you because you had no properties, so I see no reason to worry about such a thing, Malcolm. You are free to wed whom you like," Dougald insisted.

Malcolm took an exasperated breath. "If the king approves."

Angus winked at Dougald, the knowing look passed between them. "I feel it in my bones, Malcolm, the Lady Anice will be yours, God willing."

"We have more important things to discuss," Malcolm said, not wishing to talk about his marital status further. "Come, we must speak at once with his lairdship. We have many arrangements to make before the sun comes up."

"You sound as if we are in for a battle." Dougald's shoulders drew straight and he took on the posture of a great warrior as if to fight for right this very instant.

On many occasion, Dougald had watched his back, as well as he'd watched his. Though Angus was younger, they had trained him to fight like them, fearless and protective of them as they were of him. When accompanied by their older brother, James, the four of them were damned near invincible.

'Twas not the same once James had become the earl of their father's estates and left them to find new battles to fight without his leadership. Though Malcolm had to admit he was ready to lead his own people and was happy not to live under his brother's rule, despite how fond he was of him.

"A battle of wits, my brothers," Malcolm finally explained. "Be assured it is a deadly game, and we would best be on highest alert at all times."

"Does he speak of the lady, or something else?" Angus

asked.

Malcolm laughed. "Always with the lady. Let me tell you the plan before we seek audience with his lairdship, then retire for the eve."

CHAPTER 9

Early that morning, a hand touched Anice's shoulder when she snuggled against the feather-down pillow of the guest chamber. 'Twas just a dream, she told herself.

"My lady," a pretty young girl said, with midnight black eyes and black braids dangling down her bodice, trying again to stir her.

Anice bolted upright. "What is wrong?"

"Lord MacNeill wishes a word with ye, and he told me not to wake yer lady-in- waiting."

"Aye." Anice climbed out of bed and the maid quickly helped her into her shift, then her green wool bliaut.

Barefooted, Anice headed to the door.

"My lady, yer shoes."

Annoyed with herself for being so addle-minded, Anice shook her head and returned to the bed. "'Tis too early in the morn for this," she said cheerfully, being half asleep, and not wanting the maid to think she was angry with her. "Your name?"

"Catherine."

"Aye, Catherine." Anice glanced at the wall where Mai was buried under a blanket on a cot and was glad to see her lady-in-waiting sleeping so soundly.

Catherine pulled Anice's hose on, then her shoes and tied them. Anice hopped up from the bed and rushed back to the door, but the woman scurried forward to open it for her.

Malcolm held a candle in his hand in the drafty hall, his gaze instantly shifting from her eyes to her unbound hair. The look of admiration instantly pleased her, though she couldn't imagine she looked very appealing with her hair uncombed.

She grabbed his free arm and walked him away from her chamber, figuring he needed some distraction if he were to tell her what was going on.

"You sure are bonny, lass."

She smiled, appreciating the comment, though she expected her hair was tangled from tossing and turning in the bed. "I look a bit untidy, I imagine."

"You look well-loved," he said with a definite twinkle in his eye.

She glanced back to see the maid had disappeared. "You're no' a gentleman."

He chuckled under his breath, the sound echoing off the stone walls of the hallway. "You bring the devil out in me, my lady."

"Should I worry about being in your company alone?" Secretly, she hoped he'd sweep her away to some secret place in the castle and kiss her without reservation. And much more. Just thinking of his errant fingers touching her breasts made her skin heat for more of the same.

"Hmm, 'tis a shame we have no good soft place like the hayloft to discuss matters."

He did want the same as she did. "Would you be discussing matters then? I would think you would have other notions in mind, Malcolm. What say you to that?"

***

Malcolm stared at her for a moment, then realized she had not made a mistake this time in calling him by his surname. Her speaking his name endeared her to him. Not only that, she fully wished him as much as he wanted her. He set the candle down, then reached over and braced her face for the kiss he wished to plant upon her lips. She would not be permitted to kiss him and run away always without his kissing her in return.

Her lips at first curved up against his, indicating she was as willing as he. In fact, when he pressed her further, her hands slipped to his waist. He wished he could join the vixen in the hayloft again, only this time naked, writhing together in heated passion, tupping her as a ram would an ewe.

His body yearned for her, as the crotch of his trewes grew tight. He reminded himself that he had not been with a wench in a very long time and that's why Anice's tender touch nearly undid him.

He fisted his hands in her silky hair and brought it to his face, the fragrance of lavender lingering in the curls. "Bonny lass, you do not know what you do to a man."

She touched his scruffy beard. "Nor how you affect me."

"I can feel your heartbeat quicken when we are close like this. You are not afraid?"

"I have never felt anything like this for a man. Though once there was the son of the chief of the MacHeth who I felt silly over sometimes when I was much younger whenever the chief and members of his clan came to visit my da."

Quelling the urge to laugh, Malcolm wished he'd been the lad she'd so liked. Though for an instant he wondered if the MacHeth was now wed, or if he'd showed any interest in the lady. This did not bode well with him. Again, he kissed her velvet lips, and she parted them for him, begging him to plunder her. Would she offer the rest of herself so easily?

He couldn't think of such a thing. She was the cousin of the king's wife and Henry had other plans for her betrothal. With the greatest difficulty, Malcolm pulled away. "I must tell you our plan."

For a second, she seemed disconcerted, but then her eyes flashed with fire and her chin tilted up. "It better sound a lot like *my* plan."

He shook his head, smiling. "You are sure stubborn, lass. But I would have you know the earl and my brothers and I all agreed your plan has merit. What does Mai say of this?"

"She was reluctant at first because she feels it her duty to always protect me. However, she understands the dangers we face and worried she would put us more at risk. What did the earl say?"

"Simon is a bold man. He would not have it said that rogues attack nobles who pass through his shire. Therefore, he wishes for us to use part of your plan, and he has concocted one of his own."

"Aye." She folded her arms.

Malcolm curled a strand of her hair around his fingers, his gaze focused on the lock, the silky red golden strand as enticing as the rest of her.

"The plan?"

"Aye." If she thought her hair distracted him, she would be right. "Even his son Simon wishes to take part, and the earl's wife as well. You see, 'tis like a game, deadly though it is. Yet, the earl and his family are verra much agreeable to play along. Of course, I assured him we only assume this is what Conan intends, not mentioning that Laird Fontenot has any part in this without evidence. I told the earl that the knight pretended not to know you, and yet from his talk he knew just who you were. I changed the version a wee bit and said we think he may have brigands attack us so that they can ransom you to the king."

She frowned. "What if this does not happen? We only assume that this is the case."

Malcolm combed his hands through her hair, wishing he could touch the rest of her so intimately. "The earl will have played a game where the quarry cannot be found. He said he has not had to plan such a rousting good play since his fighting in the Crusades. Still, he said if naught happens, he and his men will return home and have a good laugh about the Highlanders and their wild imaginations."

She sighed deeply. "'Tis good. I would not wish harm to come to your friendship. You say when he returns home though. Does he plan to accompany us?"

"Nay. We are to attend the fair while the earl and three of his knights accompany him. They will take our wagon and all of our goods, pretending to be us. Two squires, the one his son, who are still smooth of face and about your and Mai's height and will ride as before, dressed in yer garments."

"They would be at risk—"

"They are of slighter build, my lady, as they are not yet grown men. In fact, I have met the two fine lads and they are beanpoles to be sure. But the earl assures me they shall soon be knighted, so bravely do they fight. Certainly, they will have a better chance against armed brigands than ye—"

She raised a brow.

He smiled slowly, loving the lass's tenacity. "Than Mai will."

"What about Conan? He will recognize those who ride with our wagon are no' us, do you no' think?"

"The earl has come through for us already, my lady. His men searched the town last night for Conan, the bard. He now sits in the dungeon. If Simon finds no brigands on the northerly road, he will set Conan free in a day or two."

"What reason did he give for arresting Conan?"

"'Twill be a case of mistaken identity. Of course, Laird Simon willna give the man audience because he is away on business. In the interim, Conan must wait for the earl to return."

Anice smiled. "This earl sounds like he is quite a man."

"Aye, you see now why he has two earldoms?"

"Indeed, I do. So what are we to do?"

"We will go to the fair for a couple of hours. Mai will accompany the earl's wife and enjoy shopping. Several ladies and guards will accompany them, so if someone else knows about ye, they will think you are shopping with your maid and hosts. You and my brothers and I will tour the fair as men of the cloth. We will then ride out, like the good monks that we will be."

"Monks?"

"Aye, to keep you safe. I would not have your legs exposed in men's hose, lass."

This time he tilted his chin up, waiting for her to disagree with him. Instead, she smiled.

"And underneath the pious cloth we wear our weapons, my laird?"

"That we do. Except for ye, of course. After you have shopped to your heart's desire, we will eat at the fair and leave. Does this bode well with ye?"

"Verra much. So," she said, stopping to yawn, "when do we begin our plan?"

The courtiers began to stir.

"Now, my lady. We will have prayers in chapel early, break our fast, then don our garments for the fair. After you have spent as much time as you like, we shall be on our way."

"Then I wish to thank you first for using most of my plan, before too many of the servants are up and about."

He pulled her against his body, not waiting for her to say another word. She slid her fingers lovingly over his back and pressed closer to his body, stirring his groin into action. His lips glided over hers with unrestrained need, a burning crush of her mouth that revealed a hunger not easily slaked. He struggled to quell his raging desire for her while he gripped her silken hair in bountiful bundles, and leaned against her soft, willing body. He couldn't believe how much her gentle touch and tentative kisses could light a rampant fire deep inside him. If Henry saw them now, he'd have both their heads. But Malcolm didn't want to stop, and neither did she seem to, which stoked his burning need even more.

***

Anice fought appearing too brazen and scaring her champion off, but she ran her hands over his muscled back, wishing she could feel his bare skin and press her body wantonly against his erection, hard and willing. She didn't want to quell her own lustful desires, instead wishing to have his hands lifting the hem of her gown, and his fingers rising up the sensitive skin of her inner thighs, leaving the skin sizzling in their wake, rising higher to the juncture of her legs, now aching with gusto.

She clung to him as his tongue delved into her mouth, and his fingers drew down to her breasts. Surprised, but ecstatic, she savored the experience, the feel of his large hands massaging her breasts, the nubs tight, stretching out to him and begging for relief. Shivers raced down her heated skin as she barely breathed. He growled low and nuzzled her neck with his mouth, and she moaned in blissful anticipation. The notion she was shameless briefly crossed her mind. How could she allow him to touch her in such an intimate way when he was not her husband?

With a ragged groan, he flicked his thumbs over her taut nipples, abruptly separated from her, kissed her cheek like a brother would, and stepped even further away. Her heart felt wrenched in two.

Nearly married four times, not once had she ever felt like this toward any man. She licked her lips, swollen and well-loved, but the rest of her ached for more.

Malcolm's eyes were black as midnight, and a scowl marred his now hardened face. "I beg forgiveness, my lady," he growled, his voice husky and harsh.

"There is nothing to—"

"Aye, there is," Malcolm interrupted. He appeared quite contrite and she felt queasy with his abrupt rejection. "Ye are a fine, sweet lass, and are meant to have a husband who will..." He blew out his breath. "Pray forgive me for overstepping my bounds. We break our fast, then shall be on our way."

With a deep courtly bow, he left her staring after him, wondering how he could turn from a sizzling hot man of passion into an ice-cold warrior. She pursed her lips as she watched the brawny Scotsman rush away from her. *Coward.* Or was it that he still preferred an English lady?

Her heart sank and she clenched her teeth at the thought, then twirled around to return to her room and saw Dougald watching her. Her heart leapt in her throat, while his lips curved generously upward.

"My lady." He bowed low.

How much had he witnessed? *The blackguard.*

***

Shortly after eating, the courtiers were bristling with excitement when the earl and his knights rode forth with Lady Anice's wagon and the party's goods. Then Lady Maud, Mai, several women of court, their maids, and men to watch over their purchases, headed into the main market square.

Anice's stomach tightened while she ensured the hood of her robe covered her head sufficiently one last time. When she met Malcolm and his brothers in the bailey, they all looked her over to make sure she appeared to be a monk.

"Are you satisfied?" she asked, when all Angus and Dougald did was smile.

"Aye," Malcolm said, his voice dark and his face devoid of emotions.

He'd barely spoken a word to her while they had supped, and she hated the distance he'd put between them. She had made a terrible mistake in trusting him, in acting so common with the man not her husband. She wished she could take every action back, as cold as he acted toward her now.

"We shall enjoy the fair, while these young men watch

our horses." Malcolm motioned to four squires. "They're well-armed in the event we have trouble. Also, your bow and quiver are on your saddle for later, but they are hidden under yonder blanket."

She nodded, her face feeling hot and her skin crawling with anxiety. Had Dougald told Angus what he had seen Malcolm and she doing outside her guest chamber? They must have had a good laugh between them. Stiffening her back, she vowed never to allow another man to lead her astray.

The four of them exited the castle grounds and strode toward the market square, while the young men led their horses from behind.

Delighted to see all the offerings, Anice soon forgot her distress over Malcolm's cold treatment, and hurried from one booth to the next. Not only were wool products piled on tables for examination, but produce, chicknows, even gems were offered for sale. An emerald green silk called to her from a table beneath a tent. She instantly gravitated toward it. Malcolm blocked her path and whispered, "Anice, where are you headed?"

She paused, realizing at once that a monk would have no reason to inspect the silk cloth. She hesitated.

"My lady," Malcolm again entreated under his breath.

She whipped around, ignoring him, and headed straight for one of the squires, who appeared to be too young to be a knight, but nearly the right age. "Come and help me with the purchase of some silk."

"Aye, my—"

She shook her head quickly.

"Aye." He handed her horse's reins to his companion, then walked with Anice to the silk booth.

She explained the quantity of fabric she required, slipped some money to him, then told him to give the cloth to her lady-in-waiting when he returned to the castle.

The young man did as she bid, then tucked the bound

fabric under his arm.

Anice stared at the silks from a distance, then motioned to the squire again. "Another. The paler green one beneath that royal blue. Do you see it?"

"Aye, do you wish it, too?"

She nodded. "Same amount of fabric." Again, she handed him the coin.

After the squire did as he was told, he returned to her. "Any other that you wish, my—"

"Nay, 'tis enough for now." She smiled, then turned and sauntered past a booth of wool.

Malcolm joined her and shook his head at her.

She motioned to the crowded streets. "There are so many about, no one would have noticed."

"Save the merchant and a half dozen others who were loitering nearby."

"'Tis my wedding gown."

Malcolm stifled a laugh.

Exactly what did he think so amusing about the colors of silk she'd selected for her gowns?

"Sorry, my lady, coming from a monk, the sentiment sounded curious."

She ground her teeth, still peeved at him for not wanting the likes of her for a wife. "Ah, I thought perhaps you did not like the colors—"

"Stop!" the earl's steward shouted, his face red in anger as he dashed across the square. "Stop that thief!"

The boy, wearing rags, and dirty brown hair, to match his dirty brown skin, ran straight into Anice. She nearly fell with the impact, but quickly tripped the lad instead. As soon as he sprawled out on the ground, one of the squires apprehended him, yanking him up from the street while Malcolm grabbed Anice's arm to steady her.

The nobleman tore his purse from the youth's grasp. To the squire he said, "Take him to the dungeon. His Lord Earl can deal with the likes of him."

Anice hurried to speak with Baron Crichton in private. "Sir, you have your purse back. If the young man agrees to travel with me to Brecken Castle, he will be no more trouble to ye. If he doesna, he is your laird's problem."

"My lady, why would you want such a blackguard as the lad? Would he not be more trouble than you already have?" the baron asked, his voice hushed.

"A young boy in our service would make it look less likely that I am the Lady Anice and that I travel with the Highland warriors."

The baron glared at the boy. "If he gives you any more trouble, I will have him locked up."

"'Tis a fair bargain. If he leaves with me, he will no longer be a problem in your shire."

"Aye."

She returned to Malcolm and offered her proposal.

"You cannot be serious."

She folded her arms intent on having her way. The lad would solve two problems at once.

"You *are* serious."

"They willna expect us to travel with a child, do you no' agree?"

Malcolm frowned at her. "Who will rob us blind while will sleep."

"I will leave it up to ye, Malcolm." She figured he might know better of what he spoke of though. If Malcolm thought they could manage the boy, then they'd take him. "Speak to him. Think you he canna be trusted, we will leave him here for the Laird Earl to deal with."

He took a heavy breath, then walked over to speak with the lad. "Brother John has acted on your behalf to have you released to us, if you will join us on our journey. If not, you will be turned over to the Laird Earl who will have one of your hands cut off for the act of thievery."

The boy stood on his tippy toes, cupped his mouth, and whispered to Malcolm.

She was dying to know what the boy had to say.

Malcolm turned to look at Anice. Now she had to know even more so what the boy had said. Malcolm faced the boy again, but this time spoke under his breath. The lad looked back at Anice, his bright blue eyes wide. Then he nodded. "Aye I will serve ye." He bowed low.

"You will be Brother Angus's charge."

"Aye."

Malcolm joined Anice but before she questioned him as to what the boy had said, she asked, "What is his name?"

"Scoundrel."

She tilted her head down. "He has to have a name."

"And you wish to know it?"

Of course. He would be a member of their party. Why wouldn't she wish to know the lad's name? Would seem odd to call him boy. "Aye, Malcolm, I do."

He shook his head and returned to the lad. "Brother John wishes to know your name."

The boy, who couldn't have been any older than ten, straightened his back, seemingly proud that Anice would want to know his name. "Kemp."

"Have you a family?"

"Nay, they have all died. I live on the streets now. No one will hire me as they say I am too small to be of much use. But I will show ye I am strong."

"Aye." Malcolm nodded at Angus who came to stand by the boy.

Angus glared at the lad. "No doing anything wrong, Kemp. You will be under my watchful eye."

Malcolm walked back to Anice and the two continued to stroll through the market.

Now, Anice had to know what the boy whispered to Malcolm. "What did he say to you in private?"

"He said that the lady was no more a monk than he was king."

Anice nearly laughed, but quickly stifled the urge. "'Tis

good we are taking the lad with us, is it no'? If he had been locked in the dungeon with Conan, and the youngster spoke of what he ken, Conan would have told Fontenot when he is released."

"We shall see. If he steals one of our horses in the middle of the night, then no, I will not think it was a good idea. What will you do with him when you get him to Brecken, *if* you manage?"

"His name means warrior. Mayhap I shall make him a groom in my stables, and he can learn to fight like you when he is no' tending my horses."

"You are too kindhearted to take the scoundrel in."

"Nay, he will suit our purpose."

The smile on Malcolm's face indicated he thought she was softhearted despite her words. The boy would have to work hard in her service, just like everyone else did to earn his or her keep. Yet, it was more of a chance at a better life than he had in the village here with no way to earn a meal.

Malcolm's face lit up when he spied a booth filled with knives, swords and shields, many used, a few new.

"You have no reason to look over weapons of war," Anice reminded him under her breath. She couldn't help but be amused that the weapons drew him in just like the fabrics had done her.

"Aye." He motioned to one of the squires. "Check on that dagger, yonder. The one over there. See if it has a good weight to it and ask the price."

Within a few minutes, the squire returned. "'Tis a fine weapon, my lord. But he is asking too much for it."

"Offer him half the price. Tell him that you are on the way to Nottingham where you have heard there is an armorer who makes the best weapons of war at half the price he asks."

"Aye."

The squire spoke to the merchant who eyed Malcolm with suspicion. He responded, then the squire returned to

Malcolm. "My lord, he wants to know why you wish a dagger?"

Malcolm stalked into the booth, then lifted the blade and examined it. "You best not want the answer to your question. Do you wish to sell for the aforementioned price or not?"

"I would not make a farthing on a sale like that. So no."

"As you wish." Malcolm laid the dagger down, then stalked out of the booth. He walked at a quickened pace toward a booth where roasted chicknows were being sold while Anice hurried to catch up. "Time to eat, my lady, then we must be on our way."

"Could you not have bargained a wee bit higher, Malcolm?"

"Nay, he will come around."

"But we leave after we eat."

"Aye, you never want to appear too anxious."

They paid for their fowl and shared with his brothers, the squires and the lad, Kemp.

Out of the corner of her eye, Anice noticed the weapon's merchant watching them. "He does appear to be growing more anxious if you shall return."

"Did you want me to snatch it for ye?" Kemp asked.

"Nay," both Anice and Malcolm said at once.

The lad was determined to prove his worth, but not in any way that Anice would wish him to. She had to admire him for wanting to please his mistress, though. 'Twas fate that the boy should run into her, and she should stick her foot out and trip him. She smiled to herself. Despite Malcolm's misgivings in taking the boy with them, she was certain Kemp would be as much of a help to them as they would be to him.

After eating their meal, the party headed away from the market square to a more deserted side street. One of the squires assisted Anice onto her horse while the MacNeill brothers mounted their own. Angus pulled Kemp into the saddle behind him.

Before they left, the sound of hurried boots clomping on the cobblestone path caught their attention. Two of the squires drew their swords. A red, puffy-faced weapon's merchant hastened toward them with the dagger clutched tightly in his fist. "I know not who ye are, my lord," he said, addressing Malcolm, "but if ye have to pose as ye are, and ye have the Lord Earl's squires attending ye, ye must be on an important errand. I would lay awake in bed this eve, praying that I had not done ye an injustice by refusing to drop the price on the dagger."

"To half the price you first offered, my good man?" Malcolm asked.

The merchant wavered as his brow furrowed, evident that having to part with the weapon at such a bargain, pained him. "Aye."

"I will tell everyone I chance to meet what an honorable armorer you are."

He bowed his head slightly. "Aye, thank ye, my lord."

"Call me brother, would ye?"

"Aye."

Malcolm exchanged money for the weapon, then secured it under his robe. "You have guessed we are on a dangerous mission. You must speak of this to no one."

"Aye, no one, my...brother."

"God be with ye."

"Aye, and with ye."

Anice smiled. Malcolm seemed to like this cloak and dagger ruse. The squires bid them safe passage, and then Anice and her party road out of Northampton. As before, Dougald took the lead, Angus dropped back to the rear and Malcolm and Anice rode in between.

"You see, my lady, the gentleman indeed did wish to sell the dagger."

She sighed deeply. "To think a monk would dupe him out of so much money."

"'Twas too high a price, my lady."

When she frowned at him, he said, "Truly, my lady. I would have bargained for your cloth had you not paid for it so hastily."

"'Twas a good price already."

"It would have been even a better price had you let me bargain with the merchant."

"Next time, my laird, I will put you to the test."

He smiled at her. "I love it when you challenge me, did you know that?"

"I noticed. And I love it when you accept the challenge." She still couldn't fathom his earlier actions, though she wondered if again, he'd come to the conclusion he wished an English bride and Anice had distracted him momentarily. She clenched her teeth in annoyance.

Two hours on the road out of Northampton, they came across what looked like a battlefield, dead men and some who lay dying in the road, all badly clothed. Daggers and knives lay by the attackers, yet the blades of nary a one of them was stained with even a hint of blood. The tracks of a wagon had recently passed through the area, but there was no sign of the earl or his men.

"Think you we somehow missed them when they returned home?" Anice whispered, her heartbeat quickened. She'd seen men killed before when she was little, thieves who'd attacked her mother and her escort on a visit to see her uncle, but their escort had struck the men down like this, leaving the bloody carnage strewn across the dirt road. The raw cold seeped into her bones like it had done that day, and she shivered. What if the baron was close by and suspected Malcolm and his party had done the killing? Then they'd be in the same bind as before.

"The earl would have disposed of the bodies. Nay, I think they have taken chase up ahead," Malcolm assured her.

They listened for signs of any threat from the path that lay ahead of them.

"Do you want me to scout it out for ye?" Kemp asked, his voice enthusiastic.

"You might try to run away, fearing the path we take too dangerous for ye," Angus replied.

"I am not afraid. Nobody will notice a small lad spying over the hilltop."

"It would not be safe," Anice said. "I need you to be my groom and learn to be a braw Highlander warrior. I do not want to lose you this soon."

The boy stared at her, his blue eyes round. "Ye want me to tend horses and be a warrior?"

"Aye. You will have to work hard, but I think you have it in ye."

The boy jumped off Angus's horse and ran to Anice. Kneeling on one knee, he bowed his head. "I will serve ye well, my lady."

"I think you shall. Rise and rejoin Brother Angus."

"He is no more a brother than I am a—"

She glanced over at Malcolm who raised a brow. "King, aye I ken, Kemp. For now, we are monks. It will be safer for all of us that way."

He glanced at Angus and Malcolm, then turned to Dougald. "But they are Highland warriors, are they not, my lady?"

"Aye, and good ones, too. Sometimes different steps must be taken. You must learn to use your wits, rather than only brute strength."

"Oh, aye, my lady. I know just what ye mean."

He reached for Angus who pulled him back into the saddle.

"What about these brigands?" Anice asked.

"Those that are still alive will be dead before morning. Naught can be done for them." Malcolm motioned to Dougald. "Ride up the hill and see what you can see."

Dougald nodded and kicked his horse to a gallop. After he reached the top of the hill, he sat and watched, then he rode back to them. "All clear. If the earl and his men took chase after more brigands or even the baron and his men, they are either way ahead, or they are off the road somewhere."

"Aye, let us continue on our way. We have spent enough time delaying our journey," Malcolm said.

Again, they headed out, but Anice's heart thundered with anxiety. Expecting to see the earl and his men safe and sound, she couldn't believe there was no sign of them. What if they were ambushed somewhere? Injured or dying like the brigands on the road? Yet, she had a premonition of another danger ahead.

But she couldn't speak a word of her concern. Did Malcolm worry also? If so, he didn't let on. He was probably used to going into battle. One more wouldn't bother him. She didn't want him to know she was scared though, or that she could sometimes sense future danger. He had enough on his mind without being concerned with how she felt or that she had this strange ability of second sight. What if he thought her a witch? She was no more a witch than Kemp was the king, but she couldn't chance anyone thinking she was cursed.

A mile ahead on the road, two men stood, neither of them knights from the earl's party, both of them wearing ragged clothing. Dougald approached with caution.

Danger, Anice's mind shouted.

"How now, brother," the slightest of the men said, with a jerk of a bow.

"Good day to ye, good man," Dougald said.

The bigger, burly man stared at Angus. "Who have you with ye, brother?"

Kemp was trying to hide behind Angus's back.

"Kemp, is that ye?"

Anice's heart sank. She'd imagined the boy had no living relatives like he had said. Now she assumed he had lied.

"Tell him nay," the boy said, his voice cowed. "He is my uncle and nearly beat me to death last summer."

She sensed the angry, red-faced man was dangerous and cruel hearted.

"The Earl of Northampton has given this boy into my care, or else he would be locked away in the dungeon," Angus said, his voice firm.

"What have you been doing, boy? Stealing again?" The man advanced on Angus.

"He taught me how to steal. He is one of the biggest thieves there is!" Kemp said, his tone frantic, his slight body struggling to slide further away from the threat.

Before the man reached Angus, Anice notched an arrow to her bow.

"Brother John," Angus said, motioning to Anice, "wants you to leave the boy to us."

The man stared at her with such hatred, she was certain everyone would be better off if the man were dead. Yet, without his raising a hand to her, she couldn't kill him.

The other man said suddenly, "The earl and his men are coming!"

Had these two men been in on the plot to kill Malcolm and his brothers?

"I will get you for this!" the burly man shouted at Kemp, then ran with the other across the rolling hillside.

The earl and his four knights chased after the two men and struck them down. Anice shuddered, her stomach growing queasy, and she quickly looked away. Only then did she realize the wagon was no longer with them.

The earl galloped back to them. "I suspect you have seen what happened to the others."

"Aye," Malcolm said. "Have you seen the baron's men?"

"No. If he planned on coming to the lady's rescue...," the earl said, then motioned to the two squires who smiled back at him, "he gave up on the idea once we attacked the brigands. In all seriousness, I apologize for this happening in my shire. We could not make any of them reveal who hired them. They said the man was well-dressed, which supports your claim that Conan had hired them to take..." He paused as he glanced at the boy.

"He will be my groom," Anice said, tilting her chin up. She was not handing the boy over to anyone in the shire so that any more relatives could attempt to lay claim to him and brutalize him further.

"The road is clear, but we will ride with you until you reach Leicester."

"Thank ye, my Laird Earl, we appreciate your services," Anice said.

"Then let us away, shall we?" Simon asked.

"The wagon, my laird, what has become of it?"

"Another man hiding in the back, returned home with it once the fighting began. He must have reached Northampton before you began your journey."

The party continued on their way and when they reached Leicester, the earl and his men returned home. Anice and her party continued on to Nottingham.

"Why say you that you have no living relatives?" Angus asked Kemp in a gruff voice.

"Who would want to say my uncle was their only living relative?"

"Are you sure that you have no more?" Anice did not want to find out later that he had others who might be looking for him.

"Nay, my lady."

Anice was even more glad that she had taken the boy under her wing, but she still wondered if he didn't have other relatives that might want to skin the poor lad's hide. She doubted any would ever come for him at Brecken though. Too deep in the Highlands for the English ruffians to venture for one wee lad.

Dougald motioned to the clouds in the sky that amassed

into mountains of blue-black vengeance. "It will not hold off long."

"Nay, the air has grown colder by the hour, and the air heavy with moisture. We will have to find shelter soon."

Anice sensed they'd find more trouble than they bargained for just up ahead. She couldn't shake loose of the fear that gripped her and knew that whatever they faced would change her life forever.

Malcolm glanced at her. "You look most stricken, Anice. What ails you, my lady?"

She shook her head and avoided looking at his searching gaze. How could she reveal to him how she sensed things about the future that no God-fearing man or woman should ever know? 'Twas unnatural and best to keep her secret from the world as much as possible. Only Mai knew the truth about her, and her uncle, mother, and father, all now deceased.

They rode on but could find no farm or byre, nothing to shelter them if the rains should pelt them mercilessly. She glanced at the darkening sky, the weather growing more ominous by the hour. Anice pulled her cloak tighter as the winds whipped around her, chilling her to the bone.

Dougald shouted from a rise in the next hill, "A farm's ahead!"

Anice and the others galloped to catch up. The news should have cheered her, but the impending doom cloaked her with a sense of dread that she could not dispel.

"Aye, let us get the lady out of this weather, and quickly," Malcolm said, his voice anxious.

They approached the small house, but soon spied six knights' horses tethered on the backside. Were these men honorable knights, or Fontenot's?

A man stalked out of the house, though he had his back to them, causing her to catch her breath. He glanced up at the sky for a minute as Anice and her party sat deathly still, no more than a hundred yards behind him.

If just one of their horses made a sound...Anice's whinnied and her heart sank, but not before she whipped her bow out and notched an arrow.

CHAPTER 10

To Anice's profound relief, the knight never looked to see whose horse just whinnied. Still, she held her breath, and assumed he'd thought it was one of their own tethered nearby. Despite his neglectful actions benefiting them, she couldn't help feeling the man should have been more alert. Nor could she douse the suspicion she had that the man was not to be trusted.

For an instant, fear snaked down her spine when the notion crossed her mind that these men may not be Fontenot's, but knights who backed Robert and his rebellion.

Once he disappeared inside the house, Malcolm waved for the party to continue on past. To her astonishment and trepidation, Kemp jumped off Angus's horse and ran to the farmhouse before anyone could stop him. They pulled farther away from the house, watching to see what he was up to. He stood on tiptoes and listened at a window, already shuttered to keep out the wind and coming rain. Then he dashed back for the tethered horses and gathered their reins.

Angus rode to where the boy was and helped him onto the horse, then the party rode north again.

"I hope you are no' planning on stealing the knights'

horses," Angus said.

"Nay, Brother Angus. I thought we would give them some more exercise. Then we will let them go."

"Who were the men?" Anice asked, concerned that they should have let the horses be. "They could have served some laird around here and were perfectly honest. Or they might have been on their way to aid King Henry."

"Aye, my lady, but I did not think so when they asked if the farmer and his family had seen two ladies and four gentlemen pass through this way with a wagon."

Anice took a deep breath. "So they are the baron's men and they do not know about the massacre of their mercenaries."

"Nay," Kemp said. "Now if they try to follow, they will have a nice long walk." He smiled at her.

She laughed. "I knew you would make a good addition to our party."

"This means we cannot stop now until we are a good distance from the farmhouse," Malcolm said, "but I doubt the weather will cooperate for verra much longer."

They rode another hour before the raindrops began, few and far between at first then in such a downpour that the road turned to a slippery, sliding torrent of mud.

Anice's woolen monk's robe kept the water out for a while, but the constant rain finally seeped through to her gowns, then to the skin. Though she felt frozen to the bone, she was more concerned with her horse's footing when the water rushed down the hill, nearly sweeping them away. Already she had lost sight of Dougald who had maintained his scouting post some distance ahead. She glanced back into the driving rain to see Angus was no longer with them either. Her heart thundered with concern for Malcolm's brothers and the boy.

"Malcolm!" she screamed over the wind and rain to get his attention. "We have lost Angus and the boy."

He reached over and grasped her reins. "Aye...I do not

want to lose you, too."

Just as he spoke, his horse stumbled, and he lost his connection to her.

"Malcolm!"

***

Malcolm's heart wrenched when he lost hold of Anice's reins. The river of water swept him and his horse away. In the blinding rain, he could see no sign of her, nor could he make out the elevation of the land. "Anice!" he shouted repeatedly, attempting at the same time to move to higher ground. With the land turning to knee-high muck no way that he turned seemed less treacherous. In the low visibility and wind-driven rain, he couldn't see or hear any sign of her when he attempted to get his bearings. "Anice!"

His own body shook with the cold, and he doubted any of them could stay out in this weather for very much longer without dying from a chill.

He shouted until his voice grew hoarse while attempting to retrace his steps. Then a sheet of lightning illuminated the area shrouded in a ghostly white mist. Instantly, he spied a shadow of something solid against the skyline beyond the curtain of rain. A dwelling? It had to be. His spirits lifted, hoping beyond hope Anice and his brothers had found it, too. He inched his way through the storm while lightning forked a wicked streak into the ground a mile away. A crack of thunder followed, adding to the noise of the deafening wind and downpour.

After what seemed like hours, he drew close to the byre of the house, and hurried his horse inside. Disheartened, he found neither Anice nor his brother's horses inside.

He pushed the door open to the house from the attached byre, and called out, "How now? Is anybody here?" No one answered in the darkness of the croft. Were the inhabitants cowering in the dark?

He searched for the hearth, and finding it, discovered deadwood ready to burn. After several tries, he lighted a fire, and trembled so hard he could barely stand. With every intent of building a fire, providing a beacon in the storm, he then planned to scour the area for Anice again.

After managing the beginning of a fire, a noise in the byre cut his efforts short. He grabbed his sword and rushed through the doorway. The sight of Anice huddled on her horse, filled him with joy, but she shivered so hard he feared she wouldn't make it. "Anice!"

"S—so, c—c—cold," she said when he pulled her off her horse.

He lifted her in his arms, his own skin icy and further chilled by the touch of her wet clothes. He hurried her into the room where the fire began to catch and the flames grew higher.

"I have to remove your clothes," he said firmly, expecting her to argue.

"A—aye," she said, raising her hands to unfasten her wimple and veil. "Wh—where are y—your brothers and the—the lad?"

"There was no sign of anyone here."

Gladdened she wouldn't fight him on this issue, he helped her to sit, then removed her shoes, but he didn't want to think about his brothers. He assumed as battle hardened as they were, they'd make it all right. Kemp was a sturdy lad, who'd had to endure a hard life, no doubt. Anice was the one who worried him most. Reaching under her skirt, he grasped her wet hose, unfastened the garter, and pulled one down, then the other. Her skin felt like ice and her whole body shook so hard, her teeth rattled, but she stared blankly at his chest and said naught more.

"Anice, talk to me while I help you out of your clothes." He worried she was going to die on him, like men on the battlefield who'd grown too cold to utter a word. Their skin would be as frosty, and if they weren't warmed up fast enough, they'd slip away into a sleep and never wake up. He wouldn't let her die, if he had anything to say about it. His heart pounded while he attempted to help her as quickly as he could. Even now, her lips were blue and her skin colorless.

He helped her to stand then pulled her arms from the monk's robe. He peeled off her drenched bliaut next, his own fingers numb and struggling with the effort. "Anice, are you feeling a little warmer?" He had to get her to respond. If she fell asleep now, she might never wake. "Anice—"

"C—c—cold."

"Aye, that you are, lass." He dropped her bliaut on the floor, then grabbed the shift that clung to her body like a translucent, second skin. Nothing was left to the imagination, as her extended pink nipples poked against the wet fabric, and the triangular patch of golden red curls at the apex of her thighs caught his eye. Yet, his only concern was removing the icy garments, then getting her tucked into blankets and onto a straw bed. He yanked the shift off, then pulled his own monk's robe off, and his shirt. Though his skin was wet, he held her close for a moment, trying to warm her body with his own, his hands rubbing her arms vigorously.

"Y—you are sh—sh—shivering, too," she bit out between shudders.

"Aye, lass, we took a wee bit of a chill." As much as he didn't want to stop holding her tight, their bodies warming each other, he had to find something dry to wrap around them. He helped her to sit down before the fire. "Rub your arms and legs. I will be right back as soon as I find some blankets."

Much relieved, he found three woolen blankets and straw tucked away in a corner of the house, stored there until it was needed for nighttime. After grabbing the blankets, he hurried back to Anice who clutched her legs with her arms and lay her head on her knees, her face turned toward the fire. He wrapped all three of the blankets around her and rubbed her back and arms. "Anice, speak to me. Are you getting warmer?"

She lay down on the floor and closed her eyes.

'Twas not a good sign and his heart plummeted to think he might still lose her. "I will make us a straw bed." He stalked across the room to retrieve the straw. "Anice, lass, talk to me." He had to keep her awake until he warmed her up enough. With haste, he seized an armload of straw and hauled it back to the fire, hoping that between the blankets, fire and him, he could revive her enough.

After grabbing the remaining straw, he fashioned a bed out of it, then yanked off his wet trewes. "Anice, lass, tell me what you are feeling. Can you feel your fingers? Toes?" She didn't respond, her eyes still shut tight. Not what he wanted to see. He removed one of her blankets and laid it on the straw. Then he lifted her off the bare wooden floor and rested her on the bed. She shivered violently, though it wasn't a good sign, he preferred it to her being deathly still. Though he desired more than anything to join her and warm her body with his own, he piled more wood on the fire to keep it going while the storm raged outside. The wind swept through the walls and shuttered windows, howling like a wounded animal while intermittent flashes of light poked through the cracks and thunder followed.

Once he was satisfied the fire would last a while, he laid out their clothes to dry the best he could, climbed under the blankets, and pulled her into his arms.

He rubbed her back, trying to get her warmed, though his hands were as cold as her silky skin. "Anice, talk to me," he whispered against her cheek, hoping she was reviving.

She murmured something inaudible.

'Twas not a good sign. "Anice." He lay her on her back and covered her with his body. "Do not leave me now, lass. I cannot pursue you if you are gone." Though he said it half in jest to force any kind of reaction, he couldn't help feeling he was losing the lass. No matter what, he couldn't. Not the way he had felt about her from the moment she slid down the rope from the tower keep into his grasp. She was his to protect always.

She mumbled incoherently again.

"Speak to me, lass." He nuzzled his face against hers, fighting the reaction his body had as he lay on top of her. 'Twas not chivalrous. Yet, how could he not feel something for her, as wonderful as she felt beneath him? Her lack of response sent another trickle of dread down his spine.

For what seemed an eternity, he held her close, rubbing her arms to warm her and speaking to her with encouraging words. Her shivers lessened, and her temperature seemed to rise, but she was still incoherent whenever muffled words escaped her lips. Though he couldn't help but notice her soft body beneath his, nor the curve of her breasts against his chest, nor the way his staff hardened against her stomach with an ache he couldn't fulfill, he attempted to keep his mind on ensuring she lived.

He realized he'd truly fallen for the lass, from the moment he'd first seen her at Arundel. No matter the wager he lost, his brothers were right, he wanted her for his own. Not because she had property and money, but because she was Anice, a woman who inspired, amused, and pleased him and when he least expected it, tantalized him with her quick-witted, tongue-lashing swordplay. Yet, he still didn't know what had become of her fourth betrothed husband. Was the lass truly cursed?

When the fire grew low, he left the warmth of their makeshift bed and threw some more timber on the hearth.

Anice stirred and mumbled some more nonsensical words.

Her incoherent words tugged at his heart. She had to be all right. He had to ensure she made it through this. He quickly returned to the bed and she moaned when he lifted the blanket to climb back in with her. The sound tore at him.

"Anice, lass, you have to be all right. You have a young boy counting on you to make him a groom and a Highland warrior. And you have me who wants to wive ye. No one else but ye. Please believe me."

The cold had taken its toll on him, too. Exhausted, he slept with his arms wrapped securely around her, her back fitting against his chest as she drew her legs up, sitting against his thighs while he attempted to keep her as warm as physically possible.

Later, the sound of men's voices stirred him from his ragged sleep. For a moment, he lay muddle-headed trying to discern what it was he'd heard. Was it his brothers? Then they spoke again. He bolted upright. 'Twas not his brothers' voices. Instantly, his body went on high alert. Was it the owner of the croft then? If so, would he be angry to find they'd used his dry wood for the fire and used his blankets, too?

Malcolm covered Anice's face with the blanket, then grabbed his damp trewes and shoved them on when four men stepped out of the byre into the house.

They appeared to be knights, not a farmer and his family, bearded, wet, and bedraggled, scabbards hanging from their belts. The situation couldn't be worse.

"How now," Malcolm said in greeting, but edged in the direction of his sword.

"We got caught in this storm and beg your charity, good man," a black-haired man said, his voice dark, but attempting cheerfulness, his blue eyes icy. He pulled off his rain-soaked cloak, handed it to a stockier man, then glanced at the body buried underneath the blanket.

"Aye, the fire can warm ye." Malcolm motioned to the hearth, trying to be cordial, though he felt less than charitable if they were some of the baron's men.

The other three men began to pull off their wet clothes, hanging them around the room to dry.

The first said, "If those are your horses in the byre, methinks you are not the owner of this farm."

"Aye, the owner was not here when my wife, and I came upon the place in the storm."

"Wife?" The man's thin lips turned up slightly, but his eyes remained hard. He cast another glance at Anice. "I am Baron Harold de Fountenot. You must be a knight to own such a fine horse, and the lady a daughter of a knight, perchance?"

Malcolm's heartbeat pounded fiercely to hear that this was the very baron who wished to marry Anice. "Aye, Laird MacNeill." But he couldn't give away Anices's identity. If they knew who she was, they'd kill him, just as they'd planned to do using their mercenaries earlier on their travels.

"We will take the place by the hearth," the baron said, stripping out of his clothes.

The baron was shaking, undoubtedly chilled to the bone like he and Anice had been. Too bad he wouldn't die from a chill. Mayhap he would still. "My wife is still sick from the chill she had taken."

The baron's mouth turned up. "Then I will warm her. 'Tis the only way, do you not agree?"

Malcolm grabbed up his claymore. He would kill all of them if any laid a hand on Anice. The men were half naked and trembling from the cold so hard, he assumed he could easily kill all four of them. A part of him wanted to, to protect Anice from this murderer. But how would he explain his actions to the king if he should act on his feelings? That he had killed the king's first choice of a husband for Anice because the baron had found them bedded together naked?

His dark beard dripping of water, and his blue eyes like ice, hard and chilly, the baron motioned to Anice. "Move her then but leave the blankets and bedding."

Malcolm curbed the anger sizzling in his blood. Best to remain calm and in charge of his senses. "Nay, laird, the lady stays where she is. If you want to stand, sit or lay by the fire, so be it. But the lady moves not a hair."

"I can be a hard man when I do not get what I want."

Malcolm readied his sword, determined to show how hard he could be in return. He would not move Anice from the fire for anybody. Even the king. If he moved her now to another part of the room where it was colder, without a blanket and the fire to warm her, she'd surely die. Besides, he would not expose Anices's naked beauty to this man and his men.

"Aye, no doubt. But I will not lose my wife to the sickness because of you or anyone else. Some rags are in that chest over there. Mayhap you can use them to dry off a wee bit."

One of the three other men, Malcolm assumed all were knights by the look of their fine woolen garments and the swords they carried, retrieved the cloths. If the men slept, Malcolm would have to sneak Anice out of the house, except he worried taking her into the bad weather could only harm her further. They'd be better off killing Fontenot and his men and waiting out the storm.

Two of the men returned to the byre and dragged in more straw for additional bedding.

The men finished making their beds, then huddled on the straw next to the fire and Anice, which did not please Malcolm. Yet, he could do nothing about it, or begin the battle.

The baron waved at Anice. "Join your wife. Keep her warm. We will not begrudge you too much."

Keeping Anice warm with his body heat was preferable to leaving her to sleep on her own, but watching their backs was his primary concern at the moment. Having to make that choice though, soured him toward the baron even further. "I will keep the fire going."

"Good fellow," the baron said, then lay down on the straw.

Good fellow, my arse. Malcolm knew the baron figured he didn't trust him and his men. Malcolm tested Anice's and his clothes and was glad to find her shift and hose dry. But her woolen bliaut and monk's robe were still damp, as were their leather shoes.

Outside, the rain hadn't let up. He moved closer to the fire to dry his trewes and plot his next move.

***

Fearful that the baron would discover who she really was, Anice lay deathly quiet, though her body still shivered slightly from time to time. The constant shuddering had finally lessened, and her teeth no longer chattered while she attempted to keep them gritted tightly together, but her whole body ached from the cold and shivering and riding. How could their luck grow any worse? But she'd envisioned trouble would find them, and this was the worst kind of trouble indeed.

Where was Malcolm? She'd heard him speak with Fontenot, then everything grew quiet. She feared moving from her blanket, lest the men were still awake. All she could think of was getting dressed and fleeing from the croft before they caught her and Malcolm in their deception. What was he doing? Her heart beat too fast, but at least she'd warmed up considerably, and her fingers and toes were no longer so stiff.

When some of the men began to snore, she raised the blanket slightly. Quickly, a hand covered her mouth. Malcolm leaned over her and held his finger to his lips. Relief flooded through her to see him. He leaned over and whispered, "We have to leave."

She nodded, knowing at least one of the bodies lying close to her was the man the king wished her to marry. He wanted Malcolm dead anyway, but if he found that she was naked with the Highlander, the baron would have felt justified. She shuddered. Malcolm was truly her Highland hero, and she wished no harm to come to him ever.

Malcolm helped her up while she held the blankets tightly around her. She glanced in the men's direction, worried they may wake, and curious as to what the baron looked like, but the sight of their naked bodies shocked her, and she gasped. She hadn't realized...

Malcolm pulled her toward the byre with her clothes draped over his arm. When they entered the cold room, he whispered, "I'm sorry you have to dress out here, but I'm afraid they may see you and—"

"Aye," she said, already beginning to chill.

She lifted her arms so he could pull her shift down her body, then she dropped the blankets. As quickly as they could, she donned her bliaut, and then she tried to braid her hair. "I have a maid always who does it for me," she whispered, exasperation lacing her words.

"Does not matter." He helped her on with the monk's robe and a cloak. "Sit, lass, and I will help you with your hose and shoes."

Once she was dressed, she felt much warmer, thrilled their clothes had dried sufficiently.

He seated her on her horse. "The rain has stopped. As Kemp did with the baron's men's horses earlier, we shall take these horses for a wee bit more exercise also."

"Did you feed and water ours already?"

"Aye. I removed their saddles and brushed them down later in the night, then readied them for our journey again early this morn."

He was truly worthy of being her husband. With a hurry to their efforts, they headed out of the byre, trailing the baron's horses behind them.

When they had ridden some distance from the croft, Anice took a deep breath. "Malcolm, you told the baron we were married."

"Aye, I had to, lass. They caught us together naked, alone in the house. We had a verra good reason for it, but I doubt the baron would appreciate I had to keep you warm so that you would live. He will not believe I did not have my way with ye, as bonny as you are."

"We slept together? Without...without..." She knew he'd removed her clothes. She'd been naked when she woke, for heaven's sakes. But she didn't want to think about what

Malcolm had seen or what he'd thought. Or...or that he'd touched her with his naked body. She couldn't fathom he'd lain with her. Why couldn't she remember any of it?

"We were both soaking wet, lass. We had to get dry and warmed up as quickly as possible."

"Did we...we—"

"We did not make love, if that is what you are worried about."

"I dinna remember." She looked over at him, hoping he didn't remember what he'd seen either.

"'Twas the cold. If you get too cold, you go to sleep, and never wake. I worried you were dying, Anice. You spoke incoherently. You had the talk of death."

"What about ye? Do you remember?"

His lips rose slightly. "I only worried about your health, lass. But, aye, I was more fully aware of what was going on than ye."

She shuddered, not from the biting cold, but from the worry that he'd seen her naked. More than that, he'd touched her with his own unclothed body. Och, and now the baron, when he discovered Malcolm was her steward and he had no wife...

"What are we going to do, Malcolm? When the baron realizes you serve as my steward and you have no wife and we were traveling alone together—"

"He did not see ye."

For some time, they rode in silence. Mayhap that *was* the best solution after all. If she pretended to be his wife, the baron would find Lady Anice not at Brecken after all. She straightened her back. "I will be your wife."

Malcolm's mouth dropped slightly. "But the king has not approved my courting you yet."

Was he disappointed in the idea? She only meant to pretend for heaven's sakes. Did he think she was going to force him to marry her for compromising her like he did, though through no fault of his own? She frowned at him.

"Nay, I will be your wife and you will be Brecken Castle's steward."

He stared at her as if he disbelieved what she was saying. "You mean you would pretend not to be Lady Anice?"

Aye, do not worry. I wouldna force you to really marry me. She couched the growing annoyance that festered in her stomach. "Aye. The baron can come to wed me, but the lady will never arrive. When he gets tired of waiting for her, he will leave. In the meantime, we can find evidence that he is the one who was behind my uncle's and Laird Thompson's death and it will provide us time to make a case against the baron. It will allow the king time to consent to your pursuing me."

"But your people—"

"If we arrive before the baron and his men do, my people will go along with it. All they have to know is that the baron most likely killed my uncle. He was well-liked by my people."

"And our sleeping arrangements?"

Now he was interested in being her husband? All because he might get to lay with her again? "I will be one of Lady Anice's ladies-in-waiting, and I will sleep in her chambers, like I always do."

"But I will have to have time with my wife."

"We will spend plenty of time together. Any kind of evidence we gather, even just the everyday workings of the castle. I am verra much involved in everything that goes on in the management of my lands, especially since my uncle's death."

"That is not what I mean."

She raised a brow. "Aye, I know what you mean. I am ignoring that meaning."

He chuckled. "I thought you meant at first you wished me to marry you for having slept with you like I did."

Aye, that's just what she thought. He feared she

intended to force him to marry her. She shook her head in annoyance. "There would go your chance at having an English bride."

"I would not need an Englishwoman, Anice, if I had ye."

She ran her reins through her fingers, wanting to change the subject. She still didn't trust that Malcolm wanted her for herself, and not from some sense of duty now, or as a poor substitute when he couldn't have an English lady for his wife. "Malcolm what of your brothers and the boy?"

"Like us, they will search for a dwelling to get out of the weather. The first village we come to, we will begin our search."

"Like right there," she said pointing to a village in the distance.

"Aye. That is just what I mean." He released the baron and his knights' horses.

"He will want your head over stealing his horses, do you no' think?"

Malcolm smiled. "The byre door blew open in the violent storm. Too bad his horses got away."

"He will not be happy about it, and since I will not be the Lady Anice, I canna protect you from his wrath when we meet with him again."

"I will not need protecting from the likes of him."

When they reached the village, they first visited an inn and proceeded to tether their horses out front. "They will not serve a woman inside, so you will have to remain hidden beneath that hood of yours, Anice."

"Aye. You just didna want anyone to see your blushing bride."

He smiled at her, and as soon as he did, the heat rose from her toes to the top of her head. Forgetting he'd lain with her naked wasn't going to be easy.

"You have probably been with many a woman, but I have never been with a man like that before." She furrowed her brow at him.

He donned his most serious face, which wasn't genuine in the least. "You are troubled by our having been together in the raw, but you have naught to worry about, lass."

She wanted to know how she compared to other women, but he wasn't cooperating. She ran her fingers over her horse's mane. "What I meant to say is you are so used to seeing a woman without...without..." She pursed her lips, hating not to just be able to come out with what she wanted to ask. "'Tis no big deal to ye. I mean, one is much the same as another and...well, you know what I mean."

He rubbed his whiskered chin. "I think I know your meaning. You wonder how you compare with the others, do ye?"

CHAPTER 11

Anice was dying to know how Malcolm compared her to other women he'd lain with, but when he came to the point like that, it sounded so coarse. "Nay, of course not. You are not getting my meaning at all." She couldn't help the anger coating her words.

He chuckled softly under his breath, then drew close to her and took her hands in his. His touch was warm and gentle, and she wished she'd remembered feeling his body resting with hers. "I worried you were going to die on me, and so I tried to keep my mind on warming you before you left me for good. I cannot deny I saw the most beautiful woman in the firelight's soft glow, nor that I did not desire that same woman who lay so cold beneath me. As a gentleman, I put aside such notions and concentrated on keeping you alive."

His darkened gaze at first focused on her eyes, but they shifted to her lips, and she assumed he wanted to kiss her.

She smiled, glad he had been so heroic, but did still desire her. "I would thank you for saving me, but it would be queer that two brothers of the cloth would kiss one another outside of a tavern, do you no' think?"

He smiled broadly. "Aye, let us see if we can find my brothers and the wee lad."

As soon as they opened the door to the tavern, stares from eight men sitting at two tables greeted them. In a corner of the room, two monks and a boy sat supping porridge.

Elated to see them, she said, "Oh, Malcolm—"

"Brother John, you must keep your voice low."

She instantly clamped her mouth shut, forgetting that she served as a monk...a man of the cloth...not a woman. He moved with her to the table where his brothers sat, leaving a wide berth around the ones that were already occupied. She avoided looking at the men, lest they wonder why she had smaller features than the other men.

Kemp saw Anice and Malcolm first and dashed to greet them. He grabbed Anice's hand and pulled her with him, warming her heart. Dougald tugged another two chairs over to their table.

"Thank God you are all right," Dougald said as Angus nodded his head in greeting, his face filled with relief.

"Did you make it here then and stay the night during the storm?" Malcolm asked.

Dougald motioned for a wench to serve them. "Aye. Half dead and half frozen. But we thawed out during the night. And ye?"

Anice couldn't help the blush that heated her cheeks again.

"We found a farmhouse," Malcolm quickly said, but didn't offer anything more in explanation, though both his brothers looked from her to him as if they thought something more had gone on that Malcolm was not wishing to speak of.

A buxom wench leaned over the table to show off ample cleavage. "Aye, what will it be brothers?"

Malcolm ordered. "Porridge, same as the others are having and mead."

When she returned to the kitchen, Dougald said, "We must have missed the farmhouse. I lost the whole lot of ye, then finally found the village. An hour later, old Angus and the boy dragged in." He reached over and tussled Kemp's hair. "He has been wanting to search for you ever since he woke this morn. Said he had to save his lady, who is going to make him a Highland warrior. I'm thinking he's forgotten about the tending to your horses part of the bargain."

She smiled at Kemp, tickled at his enthusiasm and good heartedness. "You will make a fine groom and a great warrior, lad."

"So," Angus said, his dark brows pinched together, "tell us about this farmhouse."

Afraid he'd ask more about their whereabouts, her

stomach flip-flopped with anxiety that Malcolm would say too much.

Malcolm cleared his throat, looked at each brother with a stern eye and said, "We ran into trouble."

Angus motioned with his head to the two occupied tables. "There is more trouble. Fontenot's men we learned, searching to find the Lady Anice for their laird. Apparently, she and her escort have vanished."

"'Tis no' good. We ran into the baron himself."

Dougald sucked in a breath. Angus shook his head.

"Aye, I was tempted to run him and his knights through with my claymore."

"He saw her? With ye?" Angus asked, worry etched in the wrinkle of his forehead.

"She was buried under a couple of blankets. They never got a peek at her."

The brothers both looked at Anice, and she knew they realized what had to have happened. She'd been with Malcolm, naked.

She looked down at the wooden table, her face burning as if it were on fire.

"What happened?" Dougald asked, the dark concern in his voice evident.

"We were in a real bind. Soaked to the skin, and the lady was near death, incoherent and shaking so hard, I knew she could not last long."

Dougald ran his hand over his stubbled chin and again cast a glance in Anice's direction, then faced Malcolm. "Aye. And the farmer and his wife? Could not they confirm that—"

"The house had been abandoned for some reason. Mayhap the family was attending a funeral or wedding. There was no one there."

Both Angus's and Dougald's jaws tightened while Kemp's eyes grew round.

Before anyone could say anything further, the serving

wench returned with steaming bowls of porridge and two mugs of mead. When she left, Anice tried to spoon out her porridge, but her hand shook too badly. She quickly set the spoon down, then rubbed her hands together in her lap under the table to calm herself. Did his brothers have to know all this? Best if nobody did.

Malcolm reached under the table and squeezed her hand. "The baron asked about her, and I had to tell him she was my wife."

Dougald cursed under his breath. Angus's eyes grew wide.

Kemp smiled, obviously intrigued. "And I thought I made up a lot o' tales."

"When he arrives at Brecken and finds you there and you have no wife...," Dougald said.

"I will be his wife." Anice tilted her chin up, daring anyone to contradict her. Then she grabbed her mead and drank a goodly sum of it.

The brothers stared at her, then Dougald said to Malcolm, "You have not even received word from the king that you may seek the lady's hand in marriage."

"Aye, we will only pretend she is my wife."

Dougald shook his head. "You cannot be with her as husband and wife. This baron already wants us dead. He will kill the lady, too, do you not think?"

"I willna really be his wife," Anice said, frowning. "For heaven's sakes. I will only pretend so that the baron will get tired of searching for the Lady Anice and leave. By then, Malcolm can have permission to court me and all will be well. I willna need to marry then. Just bide my time until some other Highland gentleman seeks my hand."

The brothers looked at Malcolm to see his response.

He ignored Anice's jab. "If we can get to her castle before the baron and his men do, she intends to let her courtiers know the plan, then we will all be bound by it. In the meantime, we will uncover the plot that the baron killed her uncle."

"And if someone makes a slip?" Angus asked.

"We will have to hope no one does."

Dougald finished his mead. "I do not like any of this."

"It could not be helped, Dougald. No one could have been more shocked than I when they arrived at the farmhouse, half-drowned like a crew on a sinking ship. The baron would have asked who she was. I could not say who she truly was. Then for pity's sake he told me he would warm her, when I refused to lay with her."

Anice quickly downed the rest of her drink.

"I understand," Dougald said.

Did he really? Both Malcolm's brothers watched her. They knew. She'd slept naked with a man not her husband. Scandalous, particularly when she was the king's ward and promised to a Norman laird.

Chairs scraped the wooden floor when they scooted away from a table on the other side of the room.

Dougald warned, "One of his men is coming. They have already questioned us about whether we had seen the lady and her companions."

Boots clomped in their direction and Malcolm whispered to Anice, "Let me do the talking."

She hadn't planned on speaking, afraid her voice would give her away.

"How now," the burly, dark-haired man said as he maneuvered in between Malcolm and Anice. Her blood grew cold when the man stood so close to her. "Your brothers said they have not seen two woman and four men on their journey. Since you must have been separated from your brethren, I wish a word with ye."

Malcolm shook his head. "Nay, we have not seen any sign of these people. Then again, the weather was verra bad there, and we even lost our own brethren in it."

"Did you come across our lord, mayhap? Baron Harold de Fontenot? We became separated from him during the storm also."

Malcolm glanced at the man's sword. "You have lost quite a considerable number of people, Sir Knight."

The knight's response was harsh. "Ye have not answered my question."

Anice wrung her hands in her lap. If Malcolm said no they hadn't met up with the baron, and the knight met them later and the baron said yes...but then again, Malcolm wasn't dressed as a monk. Heaven's have mercy, he wasn't dressed at all.

All of a sudden, her stomach grew queasy.

Angus reached over and grabbed her arm, gruffly, as a man would another man, not a woman. "Are you ill, brother?"

Malcolm said, "Mayhap we should get you a room, Brother John. The storm has taken a wee bit out of ye."

She shook her head, but kept her face averted from the knight.

"You did not answer my question," the knight said again, his voice rising with impatience. "Did ye, or did ye not see his lordship?"

"Sorry, sir. We saw no one during our travels. Like I said, 'twas a devil of a storm. I even lost Brother John for a time."

The knight waited and Anice feared he looked her over. "You appear young to be a monk, lad."

Was he talking to Kemp or to her? Though she wanted to shrink in her seat to disappear from the man's interrogation, she sat up taller and straightened her shoulders, trying to make herself appear larger.

The telltale sound of a sword sliding out of its sheath startled her. She opened her mouth to speak.

"Brother John cannot speak," Kemp quickly said. "He was beaten by his family when he was little, and he cannot talk."

Angus and Dougald reached under their robes for their

swords. Wouldn't the knights be surprised to find well-armed men of the cloth? But this was not the time to fight.

"Come on, James," one of the men shouted. "They know nothing. Their damned Scots."

"And so is the lady we are searching for." The man scowled, then the sword slid back into its sheath with a whoosh, and he stormed off.

"Are you all right?" Malcolm reached under the table and took Anice's hand in his. His fingers were warm and reassuring, and she wished he'd pull her close and squeeze her tightly against his chest.

"Aye," she whispered. "Let us finish our porridge and be on our way."

"Are you sure you do not want to rest a bit longer? You look awfully pale."

"Nay, our horses were well rested. We should tarry no more. I fear the longer we delay, the better chance we have at getting caught." She couldn't help but feel they were quickly sinking deeper into a quagmire of quicksand with no way to get out. Physically and emotionally she was drained. But she couldn't show the strain. The best thing for all concerned was to push on.

After they finished their meal, they headed outside and found the knights examining their horses to her dismay. She'd hoped they'd left the area already. They were sure to wonder why monks, if that's who owned the horses, had such fine mounts.

"Walk on past to the chapel down there," Malcolm said under his breath.

She tugged at her cowl. "They will think the horses ours, will they no'?"

"There may be some others sleeping—"

"They would have stabled their horses for the night, like we had done," Dougald warned.

"Shhh, just keep moving," Malcolm said. He knew as well as she did, the men would suspect the monks, and already they were some suspicious of her.

Kemp ran back toward the men. Anice jerked her head around to see where he was off to.

"Anice, do not look back. Just keep moving. The boy will be fine. He is a canny young lad."

"I fear for him, Malcolm."

He glanced back at Kemp. "He is asking about their swords, distracting them."

"What if they question him about us?"

"You heard him. He tells tales all of the time. He knows what we said. He will be careful."

Before they reached the chapel, small footsteps pounded the muddy road behind them.

"Kemp," Anice scolded, "you shouldna have run off to speak with those men."

He smiled at her. "I told them I would much rather be a knight like them and asked if the baron would be interested in having another page."

"What did he say?"

"He just laughed, but they stopped looking your horses over, and headed down the street." Kemp glanced back. "They are gone."

Malcolm pulled Anice into a butcher's shop. "Dougald, you and Angus get your horses and meet us at the inn. Then we will be on our way."

"How now, my lord. How can I help ye?" the baldheaded butcher asked as Malcolm's brothers hurried off with Kemp.

"We wish to purchase salted pork if you have any."

After they'd made the purchase, they hurried back outside.

The baron's knights rode south in the direction Malcolm and Anice had come from, which gladdened her. If they had ridden in Anice and her escort's northerly direction, no telling when they might have run across the men again and this time when they saw all of the monk's fine horses, more questions might be asked.

"I wonder how long it will be before they discover the baron's horses and the baron himself." She hoped bandits would rid them of all of the baron and his knights. But as armed as the men were, 'twas wishful thinking.

"Probably not a whole long while to locate the baron, but it might take a while to round up all of the horses. Luckily, he did not see our monks' robes in the farmhouse. I had laid them in a corner of the room where the firelight did not reach them after they dried."

"Your brothers seemed upset that we were in a farmhouse alone together."

He helped her to mount. "They worry I will lose my head. The baron deserved to walk for saying he would warm you like he did. And here I had told him you were my wife already."

"Aye, he deserves worse than that."

The sound of hooves pounding in the mud forced them to turn to see the brothers joining them with Kemp once again riding behind Angus.

"We're in for a bit of trouble, lass," Malcolm said to Anice as they took their usual positions on the road.

"Aye, Malcolm. But I have been getting in trouble for years."

"You never said why you slept under the stars all on your own one night."

She smiled at the memory. "My uncle was going to battle with the Campbells. I wanted to watch our brave men fight."

Malcolm's brow furrowed. "You did not, did ye?

"Nay. I ran for three miles but lost them. By the time I returned home, the gate was locked for the night. Since I had dressed as a lad, the gate guard thought I was a beggar boy and wouldna let me in."

Malcolm who watched her with a strange expression she couldn't quite fathom. "What?"

"Is that why you took the boy with us?"

"Aye. My mother had always said I took in too many strays. When I have so much to give, I canna help but want to assist someone who has no way to improve himself. Granted, if the person does not appreciate this and work hard in return, I wouldna give him another chance."

His lips curved up slowly.

"What?"

"Methinks, Anice, that if you like a lad enough, you will give him all the chances he needs."

"Kemp is a good lad, do you no' think?"

"Aye. Even if he does not work out as a groom, he will be one of the most loyal men you can trust in your employ. I bet my life on it. He is utterly devoted to you already."

They fell into silence, then Anice said, "Your brothers didna seem pleased that I am going to pretend to be your wife."

"They are concerned for your safety. And mine."

"Aye, you might lose your head." She smiled.

"You do not seem upset over the prospect."

"Aye, I have had so many betrothals over the years, what is another?"

"This one has kissed ye, for one."

She turned her attention straight ahead but couldn't help smiling.

"If he were truly married to ye, he would do more than just warm you when you are cold."

"You shouldna talk like that." Her tone was scolding, but a hint of amusement laced her words. 'Twas not fair that he spied every bit of her, when she was too ill to get a glimpse of him.

"You brought it up, lass. I was just trying to explain how this man would be more of a husband you would wish to keep than your others. He would kiss every inch of your creamy, soft skin and—"

"Rider up ahead," Dougald shouted in warning. "Make

174

that four."

As the four men approached, Dougald greeted them.

"If you wish to use this road, you will have to pay a toll," the closest of the men said.

"We are men of God and have little more than the clothes on our backs," Dougald remarked, but his hand reached for his sword.

"Stay here, Anice," Malcolm ordered, his voice firm and concerned. He galloped off to join his brother. When he reached him, he said to the man, "Do you work for a laird here, or for yourselves?"

He was determining whether these men were brigands, in which case he could kill them. If they worked for a laird, they would have to pay the fine. She tried to relax her tense muscles and loosened her grip on her reins. If they needed her help, she'd be ready to use her bow.

"We cannot kill monks," one of the men entreated. "We will all be damned."

"We work for Lord Trussot. But because you are clergy, we will let you pass."

"God be with ye, my son," Malcolm said.

"We will include you in our prayers," Dougald added.

"Pass then and be quick about it. We do not want the word to get out that we did not charge you the toll."

The party continued on their way, though one of the men commented that Anice looked to be too small to be a monk, and then said something about the boy. But Anice and her escort continued on their way without further incident, to her relief.

"I was looking forward to removing this robe but appears it might come in handy every once in a while," she said to Malcolm as he returned to her side.

"Aye, lass. And if we run into any more of the baron's men, they will not know if it is us, either."

The rest of the day's journey was slow and tedious, but that eve Anice was looking forward to a stay in a castle.

As soon as they saw the towers in the distance, she smiled. "Do you know the laird here?"

"Aye."

She quirked a brow at him.

"I was in the English royal court for a time, during William's reign. I met several of these Norman lairds."

"Then he will no doubt remember you."

"Aye."

"Then we shall have to remove our disguises."

"Aye. And this time you shall be my wife."

"We do not need to play the role this early on."

"Aye, but we must." His lips curved into a broad smile and his eyes sparkled with devilment. "You see, lass, if the baron stops here sometime after we leave to see if you have stayed here the eve, it will be better if Laird Whitehaven says, 'Nay, she has not been through here, but Laird MacNeill has just visited us with his lovely bride.' The baron will recognize us for what we pretended to be at the farmhouse. If we did not profess to be husband and wife when we stay with Whitehaven, and we said I was accompanying you as your steward, and now there are three Highlanders with ye, then the baron might begin to think the woman hiding under the blanket was none other than Lady Anice."

She worried her lower lip, thinking the situation at the farmhouse over further. "Aye. But you ken, Malcolm, the baron never saw me naked."

He frowned at her.

"Well, he didna, did he? Not unless he peeked like you did."

Malcolm chuckled. "I did not peek."

Her face heated. "You ogled me?"

"Nay, lass, but 'twas hard not to see you when I was removing all your wet clothes. To answer your other question, he saw every one of your garments hanging out to dry. It would not take a brilliant man to figure the curvaceous, petite body lying underneath the blanket was a naked woman."

The notion they had been so close to a deadly confrontation forced a shudder down her spine. Had the men wanted to press the issue as to who she was, Malcolm would have undoubtedly used his sword. She considered Whitehaven and the problem she might face if she were called Malcolm's bride. "What if the laird here wants to put us together for the night?"

"I will ask that he allow you to sleep with his other ladies."

"Are you certain this will work?" A growing sense of disquiet filled her. Again, a premonition that all would not be well.

"Aye." Malcolm glanced over at her, his look serious. "I dinna want to upset you, my lady, but ye have not told me what happened to your fourth betrothed husband."

Anice looked at her horse, unable to lift her face, unable to look at Malcolm. 'Twas a despicable thing she'd had to do, necessary for her defense, yet she would never forgive herself. "I killed him."

Only the sound of their horses' hooves clip-clopping on the road filled the air, otherwise dead silence reigned. She tucked an errant curl inside her wimple, her fingers icy against her skin and she shivered.

"Are you all right?" Malcolm asked, his voice comforting, but she wanted it not.

"He was a Robertson of Glenorchie," she said, softly, hating to relieve the pain of that day, ignoring Malcolm's question.

Of course, she was not all right, but she would tell him her past, and be done with it. If he decided he wished her not, so be it. She couldn't hide from her past forever, though she was still unwilling to tell him about her premonitions. He'd think her a witch.

Sighing deeply, she continued. "He was a descendent of

the Celtic Earls of Atholl, who were descended from the line of kings of Dalriada, hotheaded, arrogant, but he—like others of his ilk—had King Alexander's favor. He was the laird's son, and though he appreciated that I was King Alexander's cousin, he did not like the dowry offered. But his da forced him to take me, saying my uncle had no other living relative to hand down his title and lands to, and these would be his someday if Robertson wed me."

She swallowed hard, her eyes misting to her annoyance. "He was a drunkard and mean-hearted. I begged Alexander to reconsider." Tears streaked down her cheeks, which she quickly brushed away.

"My lady…"

She motioned for his silence but could not look at him. "'Twas my sixteenth birthday, and my uncle had a grand feast to celebrate. I was to wed Robertson on the morrow, but my uncle wished to have a hunt later that afternoon to provide more meat for the wedding feast. Robertson was well into his cups, and tried to get me to drink, but I wished no part of him, or his crude actions. I was praying for a miracle, that he would die before I had to wed the beast." She paused, unable to go on.

Sniffling, she finally said, "Don't ever pray for something that badly, or you may get your wish. I refused to go on the hunt, yet somehow, I was goaded into it, between Robertson and his brothers insisting, and even some of my uncle's drunken staff, who pushed me. I wish I could say that Robertson was truly an evil man, but he had some good in him. He had a small son, whom he loved dearly for one, and…"

She shook her head. "He had a sister that he'd rescued who'd been abused by a previous husband. But there was something about Robertson and me, something that was wrong between us. From the moment he saw me, he despised me, and I never knew why. Whenever my uncle was around, Robertson pretended to care for me, but when my uncle was not, Robertson played his true self, cruel and bitter. I always thought there was another woman, that he intended to take me for his bride, but as soon as he could take my uncle's estates to call his own, he would have murdered me and married this other woman. There were times I thought I saw them rendezvous in the woods, or near the loch. Still, many a husband takes a mistress and the poor wife has naught to say about it. But I transgress.

"We soon became separated from the others on the hunt, and I saw the look in Robertson's brothers' eyes, cold and calculating, as if they were in league with the devil late that afternoon. I sensed..." She paused, realizing she almost revealed her abilities of second sight. "I tried to stay with the others, but his brothers and he had cut me off from my people. Within the hour, or even less time than that, I found myself with the hulking, brawny Scotsman, his harsh blue eyes demonic, his lips curved up in a sinister smirk. He had no intention of hunting deer or any other quarry. He planned to bed me before our wedding vows could be exchanged. What I say to you, I have never told a soul, though Mai suspected as much. I killed him in self-defense, but I told everyone it was an accident, that I thought he was a deer, and I turned and shot the animal. In truth, I shot him right after he tore at my gown and tried to have his way with me. I'd managed to scramble away from the drunken brute, except I feared he wanted to kill me as well. Though I killed him in self-defense, I always felt it was my fault."

"Nay, Anice—"

"I wished him dead, Malcolm. I wanted it! I prayed for it! And I killed him." She hung her head low.

"You would no' have done such a thing if he had not tried to violate you."

"His kinsmen did not believe me and wished me put to death for killing their brethren. But my clansman and King Alexander put a stop to their cry for vengeance. My uncle did not try to marry me off again, and when he died,

Alexander hustled me off to his sister, hoping King Henry would have better success at finding me a husband."

Anice looked over at Malcolm. "I am cursed when it comes to betrothals, just like the missive said that Gunnolf had in his possession."

"Ah, lass, 'tis no such thing as a curse."

"For years the ugly rumors have followed me."

"Anice, mayhap…" He thought for a moment, then smiled. "Mayhap your kissing me broke the curse."

"Och." She frowned at him, disbelieving he would say such a thing.

"You'd never kissed one of your betrothed before. Mayhap by…showing your gratitude to me, you ended the spell." Malcolm had nearly said choosing him for her own may have broken the curse, but he figured he'd have a joust on his hands if he even intimated such a thing.

"Mayhap," she said, her gaze focused on her hands, as if she were considering the matter favorably.

"Aye, lass, think naught more of it." At least he truly didn't believe in a curse, only that the lady had a horrible case of bad luck when it came to her family choosing husbands for her.

As they approached Whitehaven's castle in the fading light, they removed their monk garb and hid them under their bedrolls. Then they proceeded to the gatehouse, where the guard permitted them entrance to the inner bailey.

Once they'd dismounted, Whitehaven's steward hastened to greet them. "Lord Whitehaven is pleased you are here, Laird MacNeill. He says you finally caught an English lady to wive, and I must say she is lovely." The steward winked at Malcolm, but Anice fumed. For how long had Malcolm been searching for some English lady? How many of his friends had he confided this plan of his?

She knew he couldn't be trusted. Malcolm didn't correct the gentleman and avoided looking at Anice's scowl.

Laird Whitehaven greeted them in the hall where the

evening meal was already in progress. Tall, and dark-haired, he was a stately gentleman. "Come, sit with me." He smiled broadly at Anice. "And this is your lovely bride, Lady MacNeill. 'Tis truly a pleasure to meet ye."

"Aye." Malcolm wrapped his arm around her waist. "But the lady is Scottish, not English as your good steward had presumed."

She wanted to scream.

"Honest mistake as the last time I heard, you were still seeking an English wife. So where are you headed?"

"Glen Affric, to her estates."

The laird raised his brows. "The lass has properties?"

"Aye."

She glared at Malcolm. What happened to the plan to say he was the new steward at Brecken, and he was her husband? Not a lady who owned a castle.

They took their seats and Malcolm reached for Anice's hand clenched in her lap, but she pulled away from him. He patted her thigh instead, and her blood heated. She did not like this plan of his to pretend they were married. 'Twas all right at her castle, because her people would know it was not so, but she did not like the ruse they played in front of the earl and his people.

"I will make sure you have the privacy you need with your lovely new wife, Malcolm."

Malcolm didn't object. Was he afraid to have the laird think there was something amiss between Malcolm and his wife?

There was! They weren't married! She punched Malcolm in the leg. He grabbed her hand and uncurled her clenched fist, then held her hand securely to keep her from hitting him again.

"Mayhap for the eve since we are in a strange new place, it would be best if the lady slept with some of your ladies," Malcolm suggested.

She held her breath, ready to release it when the earl

TERRY SPEAR

agreed.

"Nonsense. I would not think of it. The two of you would be sneaking around the castle to have some treasured moments alone together. This way you will be assured of having the whole night with your lovely wife without interruption."

Och, she wanted to scream. She tried to jerk her hand free from Malcolm to poke him again, to encourage him to change the laird's mind. Instead, Malcolm twitched his mouth as if he were deep in thought. "Would it be possible for the lady to have a bath after the meal?"

Now she could really scream. Did he want her cleaned up so she could smell nice for him on their bed of straw?

"Aye, and for you, too. It would bode ill if your fair lady smelled of lavender and you of your horse."

Malcolm laughed. "You are right, of course. I cannot thank you enough for sharing your feast and hospitality with us."

"You took an arrow for me once. I will always be indebted to ye."

Anice frowned at Malcolm. He said he'd met the laird at the king's court. When did the arrow incident happen? And why hadn't Malcolm told her he'd saved his life? No wonder the laird wanted to ensure Malcolm and his new wife had a night of marital bliss.

"I wonder, have you come across a Lady Anice and her escort on your travels?"

The wine Anice attempted to swallow slipped down the wrong way. She sputtered and coughed, and Malcolm patted her back. "Are you all right, lass?"

With watery eyes, she nodded, then coughed some more.

When she'd settled down, Malcolm said to the earl, "Where was the lady coming from and where was she headed?"

"She had been at Arundel and was headed for Brecken

Castle."

"Nay, I cannot say as I recall anyone like that. Have you any idea what she may look like?"

"Nay, the baron said only that His Grace remarked she was a fair lady who would be any man's pride and joy."

"Aye." Malcolm turned and smiled at Anice. She scowled back, still furious with him over the bath and bed arrangements.

"She travels with a lady companion and four gentlemen, but the baron fears some harm may have come to her and her escort."

Malcolm cut up his beef. "Why would he come to that conclusion? Has there been evidence of foul play?"

"He thought he should have met up with her by now."

"You know women. They can be a bit slow at times."

Anice sat taller on the bench. "Aye, and who wanted to go on a hunt and delay our journey for a whole eve and a half a day?" she asked, infuriated he'd blame her for slowing them down.

The earl smiled at her. "I like this lass of yours."

"Aye, she is a verra good catch."

Was she a fish now? "You are treading on verra swampy ground," she whispered in warning to Malcolm.

He responded by kissing her cheek. "I love ye, too, lass."

She stabbed her beef with her knife, lest she do what she had the urge to do. Slap him for his impertinence. If he thought he was sleeping with her that eve, he was gravely mistaken.

CHAPTER 12

"I have a special surprise for you and your wife," Lord Whitehaven told Malcolm. Then he motioned to a servant following the meal. "Take Lord and Lady MacNeill to their quarters off the kitchen."

He turned to Malcolm. "The kitchen heat warms the room we use for storage and there is ample space to take a bath and sleep. I oft use it for special guests."

A maid waited quietly until Laird Whitehaven nodded to her.

"We cannot do this, Malcolm," Anice whispered to him. "He and all of his staff will know we slept together, unwedded, when he learns who I truly am."

Malcolm rubbed his whiskered chin. "I cannot think of a way to get out of it."

"'Tis because you dinna want to."

He smiled. She frowned back at him. How could he not see how much trouble they were buying with their actions?

They walked into the room where the servants were filling the half-barrel tub with water. The tub looked oversized and owing to the surprised expression Anice must have exhibited, the maid smiled. "'Tis the lord's pleasure to bathe with his wife."

Ladies sometimes bathed together in a tub off their kitchen, but never had she heard the laird and lady would do such a thing. Anice's cheeks grew hot and she turned to Malcolm almost in a panic. "You will have to wait outside."

"The earl will think I do not appreciate my wife verra much." His lips were curved up slightly like a rogue's would, who was about to steal the lady's jewels, and his eyes darkened with intrigue. He was enjoying her discomfort entirely too much.

"If you dinna wait outside, I will tell the earl the whole story."

Malcolm glanced back at the tub and smiled. "We will have to have one of these larger ones made for us, lass."

When he returned to the kitchen, the earl walked in. "Have you seen a tub like that before?"

"Nay, I was just telling my wife we need to commission one. I can see the advantage of bathing together. Saves water and time."

The earl laughed. "You always did have a sense of humor."

Anice folded her arms, watching the servants fill the tub.

"The servants will help you to undress, and after that, they can stay to wash ye, or—"

"Laird MacNeill will bathe after I do," Anice said, her chin tilted up and her voice raised with determination.

Malcolm shook his head. "'Tis no' that she does not appreciate the offer, but that she is shy around your people."

"Aye. The servants will be dismissed then, and you shall be left alone with your lovely bride."

Anice's blood couldn't have boiled any hotter. Now what was she to do?

After the servants added lilacs to the water, they left.

Malcolm moved toward the room, but Anice held her hand out. "You willna join me, Malcolm MacNeill."

"But, lass, we will have our privacy."

She was certain he would turn his back and wouldn't watch her bathe, but that wasn't the problem. 'Twas the fact everyone else in the castle would think they had bathed together. If the word ever got out that she was Lady Anice and not married to Malcolm...it would be a disaster.

"I will let you haggle this one out between yourselves," the earl said, smiling.

As he turned to walk away, Anice said, "We are not married, and I am the Lady Anice." She slammed the door closed and proceeded to struggle with her gowns. After she removed her wimple and veils, she opened the door to find both men staring at her with their mouths agape. "Beg your pardon, my laird, but if one of your maids could assist me with my gowns, I would appreciate the assistance."

She closed the door again, only gentler this time.

"A word with ye, my lord," the earl said gruffly to Malcolm. "And, Elizabeth, attend to Lady MacNeill like a good girl, if you would."

***

After Anice's actions, the king would have to give Malcolm a dukedom to marry such a woman. Of all the gall. Hadn't they been in perfect agreement that she would pretend to be his wife? Hell, she was the one who suggested it in the first place! He walked with the earl to his solar, and they sat down at a gaming table.

"Fetch us some wine," the earl said to a servant. Then he turned to Malcolm. "What is this all about? I have given you my hospitality, and this is how you repay me?"

Malcolm explained how they had come to believe the baron had killed her uncle. The evidence was only circumstantial, though, as they could not prove the baron had paid the mercenaries to murder what they thought to be Lady Anice's escort. The only way they had escaped detection was by wearing monks' garments while the baron and his men searched the countryside for them.

The earl waved for a word. "I do not understand why you would tell me the lady is your wife."

Malcolm took a deep breath, realizing if he didn't tell the truth, not only would the baron undoubtedly soon learn about his staying with Anice alone, Laird Whitehaven would also. The secret was slowly getting out, and soon he feared, the king would hear of it, too, the way news traveled. He could think of no other reason for lying to his friend.

"'Tis a delicate matter, my laird, and I would not wish to ruin the lady's honor, as there is no basis for it. We ran into foul weather and were not only separated from my brothers, but from each other for a time. I discovered a farmhouse, but the occupants had left for some unknown reason. Chilled to the bone, I began a fire. Then to my heartfelt relief, the lady arrived, but sick with cold. You must believe me when I say I had only her health in mind. She was near death, and I warmed her in every way I could."

Lord Whitehaven took a deep breath. "Yet this secret of yours never need have been told. Which means something else happened. You made love to the woman?"

"Nay. She was verra ill. I only wished to warm her so that she would not die."

"Again, I say you need never have told me this unless something else occurred."

"The baron arrived with some of his knights."

The earl stared at him, his face lined with concern. "They saw the lady and you together?"

"Nay. I had donned my trewes, and she was buried underneath the blankets. I feared the baron would ask, and so I said she was my wife. They planned to kill me before when I was Lady Anice's escort. If he had known I was alone with Lady Anice like she was, he'd have felt justified in killing me on the spot. No one would have questioned his actions. I would have killed him and his men before he did me, but then where would I have been with His Grace? We have to prove the baron's guilt. Should the men have killed me instead by some luck, then the lady would have been in the murderer's hands."

The earl stared at the table, then opened his mouth to speak, but his butler returned to serve him wine, and the earl waited. He motioned for the man to leave after their tankards were full. When the man left the solar, the earl faced Malcolm. "You must marry the lady then."

"I have sent word to His Grace that I wish to ask her hand in marriage."

"We have no time for that if the baron has killed her uncle like you believe, and from the sounds of it this is truly the case. If you are married to the lady, you can still uncover the baron's plot and you will not be in danger of the baron killing you for having lain with the woman, as innocent as the situation might have been."

"She is the king's ward. I do not believe he would be pleased if I married her without his permission."

The earl stroked his beard. "Is the lady agreeable to marrying ye?"

Not at the moment, Malcolm didn't believe. "Aye, she wishes a Highland laird to wed."

"Then I will have you married in my chapel here this very eve. The word will not reach His Grace of the news for a good long while. I have heard the lady is his wife's favorite cousin. I would think he would allow Lady Anice this transgression."

"I would hate for you to be involved if His Grace should take offence to your aiding us."

"If the Earl of Northumberland can aid ye, and think naught of the consequences, I can also."

"If the lady is agreeable," Malcolm muttered under his breath. Then again, they could always have the marriage annulled. He straightened his back. Surely, she would be amenable to that. Even if he had no intention of having the marriage annulled.

A maid approached the door. "My Lord Earl, the lady

has finished her bath and says if Lord MacNeill wishes to use the tub, he may do so."

"Aye," Malcolm said jumping up. "I will propose your plan to the lady and let you know how it goes."

"Aye. Good luck with the lady. She seems to suit ye."

If that were the case, why was Malcolm already contemplating how to talk her out of an annulment?

When he strode into the kitchen, Anice was sipping from a tankard. She glanced up at him and frowned. "I'm sorry, Malcolm. I could not live the lie. Is the Lord Earl ready to throw us out for our deceitfulness?"

"Nay, I explained what had happened."

Her eyes grew big. "Not all of it."

"*Ye* gave me no choice, lass. I had to tell him why we lied."

She rubbed her temple. "Och, Malcolm, you should not."

"He says the only way he can see around this is to have us married this verra eve."

"Nay, we cannot without His Grace's permission."

Did that mean she didn't disagree with his marrying her, except on the grounds the king might disapprove? His heart soared upon hearing her words. "The earl is a verra good friend of the king. He even said he would put in a good word for us." 'Twas a little lie, but the longer he enjoyed Anice's company, the more he desired the Scottish lass for his own, despite her shifting temper...mayhap because of it. She certainly added spice to his life. He couldn't see being married to a woman who had little spirit.

Anice's bottom lip quivered and her eyes widened.

Malcolm furrowed his brow, not liking the way Anice reacted to the idea. "You do not think being married to me will be all that bad, do ye?"

"The baron will kill you for sure."

Then she was concerned about his health, which pleased him. He could handle that. "Ah, lass, the baron would kill

TERRY SPEAR

me once he realizes who you are, and that you were naked with me at the farmhouse anyway."

"Malcolm, what have we done?"

"Naught we cannot fix by getting married."

She ran her fingers over the tankard, then faced him. "We can have it annulled once we expose the baron for the murderer he is."

The notion irritated him, and he gritted his teeth. He was the one who meant to say it could be annulled if she fought him over it. The fact she brought it up first didn't bode well with him. What was there about him that didn't appeal?

"Aye," he belatedly admitted. Now he really didn't want to lose her. Somehow, he had to convince her of all of the husbands she'd almost had, he was the only one she'd learn to truly love. Once he wed her, he had every intention of earning that love and keeping her for good.

Tonight was only the beginning.

Still she seemed worried as she chewed her bottom lip. Then she nodded. "Aye, but if you die, do not blame me."

The curse. She was still worried about the curse.

Malcolm hid his smile. His brothers had been right. He had wanted her from the moment he'd tried to rescue her while she was climbing down the rope outside her chamber at Arundel. He hoped the king wouldn't have his head and prove the curse true.

Malcolm took his bath and after the earl's wife had one of her ladies-in-waiting loan a gown to Anice, she was led to the chapel where Malcolm already waited. He tapped his foot on the floor, more impatient than he'd ever been.

The impromptu wedding astounded the earl's courtiers as Malcolm overheard whispered sentiments concerning this, and the fact the lady was not his bride already, but the Lady Anice who had vanished with her escort. Malcolm's brothers both smiled at him, all knowing like. He'd lost the wager this time. They'd been right. He'd ask the lady to marry him, only not quite under any circumstances any of them could ever have imagined.

Yet, even if she had regrets, he had none. He'd never thought it would turn out this way either. Marrying a woman for her property was just something that had to be done. He would have given the woman children, 'twas a natural state of affairs, and his first son would inherit his title. He never thought he'd fall in love with the lady he was to wed. Not like this.

Though the ceremony wasn't as grand as if they had planned it at her castle, nor was she able to wear the pretty silk cloth she wished for her bridal gown, the lady was as bonny as ever in her borrowed purple gown. The garment was slightly big for her, but still framed her curves beautifully and the bodice gaped slightly at the neck, being a little too big so that when he drew close to her, he could see the cleavage between her ivory breasts. When he kissed her at the end of their nuptials, loving the feel of her silky lips against his, she didn't return the affection, and he knew the road ahead remained stormy.

Still, he attempted to reassure himself 'twas her shyness in front of a chapel full of courtiers whom she didn't know. At least that's what he told himself.

When they retired to the room off the kitchen, his brothers, the earl and several of his courtiers hung around to cheer them on.

The earl said in good humor, "Though 'tis our custom to see that you our well pleased with each other before you consummate the marriage, since the Lady MacNeill is so bashful, we will leave you to your own devices."

He bade a maid shut the door, while several joked and laughed in the kitchen as tankards were undoubtedly refilled to celebrate the occasion.

Malcolm touched Anice's cheek. "Lass, I love ye, truly, I do. I would want to consummate this marriage and make it lasting, just as I affirmed in my wedding vow to ye. But if you would rather wait—"

She nodded vigorously.

Not the response he wished. He began to remove his shoes and hose, sure that she was reluctant to have him help with hers. What he wouldn't have given for the butler to have left wine for them to drink to help calm the lady.

Then he spied two tankards of wine sitting on a table against a wall. He smiled. "Wine, to smooth away the jitters, my bride."

He crossed the floor and seized the tankards, but when he turned, Anice was already buried underneath the blanket. He glanced around the room, but saw no sign of her gowns. "Did you not need help with your gowns?"

"Nay. I'm exhausted, Malcolm. Hurry and extinguish the candles so that we may sleep."

"You cannot mean to sleep in your bridal gown."

"'Tis *not* my bridal gown."

He sensed the distress in her voice, and set the tankards back on the table, then joined her. "Lass, I know you wanted to wear the silk you purchased at the fair in Northumberland. You would have been fetching in the gowns made from such a lovely cloth, but you're beautiful in anything you wear, whether 'tis a monk's robe or the silk gown you wore tonight. If you wish, we can be married again at Brecken when we reach there—"

"We should not have done this, Malcolm. I fear for your safety, both where the baron is concerned when he learns of what we have done, and His Grace, who will surely be displeased."

Again, he was relieved to know the lady feared for his safety and it was not that she abhorred the idea of being his wife overmuch. "Aye, you worry for me. But I have fought many a battle for matters that hardly concerned me. Not this time. Whether you believe me or no' I want you for my wife, lass. I will fight for that right, if I have to, with every bit of my strength until my dying day."

She smiled at him, kind of a soulful smile. 'Twas better than her scowling at him for the moment. He grabbed the tankards and returned to their straw bed. "Here, lass, drink some. I do not intend to ravish ye, though the notion certainly appeals."

This time her smile broadened, and she reached for the tankard. He swallowed a couple of gulps, then set his wine down, and lifted the blanket to expose her shoes. He chuckled and a blush rose to her cheeks. "You are going to wear your shoes to bed even? Nay, this will never do."

He crouched at her feet, and untied the laces on the one, then slipped the leather off. Then he reached for the other. Looking up to see her expression, he was well pleased to see her watching with a smile still teasing her lips.

He massaged her hose-covered feet, and she purred in response. Immediately his groin tightened. If he could only touch other parts of her body this very eve and show how much better a husband in the flesh was compared to one on paper...

Though that luscious body of hers hidden under the gowns and blanket took his attention, he attempted to engage her in lighthearted conversation to ease her mind.

"The earl said he would send one of his ladies with us to accompany you home, if you would like, Anice."

"Nay, I would worry about her safety." She leaned back, seeming more relaxed. "Besides I have you to help me with my gowns. Why would I need a maid?"

He chuckled under his breath, pleased no end with the way things were turning out. "Aye, why indeed?" He slipped his hand up her gown, removed her garters, peeled down the hose on one leg, then did the same to the other.

She remained so still he grew worried she had fainted or fallen asleep.

"My lady, are ye all right?"

She bent her leg, placed her arms beneath her head, and rocked her elevated knee back and forth. "Uh-huh."

Had she too much wine? He glanced over at her tankard, but couldn't see how much she'd consumed, though then he'd recalled while he was speaking to the earl, she was drinking from a tankard after her bath. "Did you need more wine?" He pulled away the blanket.

"The wine is done."

'Twas what he worried about. She motioned to the container that held more. "You can fetch me some more."

"Aye." But just a wee dab. He didn't want her passing out on him.

He refilled her tankard, but when she sat up and reached for the vessel, he set it aside and lifted her from the floor. "Will be easier to remove your gowns if you stand, lass."

Before she had a chance to object, he slipped her bliaut over her head with ease because it was designed for a slightly larger woman. Now his bride stood before him in her chemise shift. Though he could not see through it as well as when she wore it soaking wet, the fabric translucent and clinging to all her curves, he could still make out the rosy crowns of her breasts, already perfectly aroused.

Her breathing became rapid and her heart beat at a quickened pace.

"You're not going to faint on me, are ye, Anice?" he asked, worried that she would.

"Nay, my laird, why would you worry about that?"

He smiled. "Aye, why indeed." He rested his hands on her face and kissed her lips, lightly at first, but when she rested her hands on his hips, he deepened his kiss.

She moaned and though he wanted to lift her shift off her at once, he feared frightening her with moving too quickly. He hadn't even removed his own clothes yet. He yanked at his shirt while continuing to kiss her, hoping she wouldn't change her mind.

"Malcolm," she said breathlessly.

"Aye, love." He threw his shirt down on the floor, then took her hands and held them against his chest. "You feel the way you make my heart beat faster?"

She ran her fingers through the light smattering of hair covering his chest, and touched his scars, feeling the muscles beneath the skin. He grabbed his belt and began to remove it, expectation of bedding the lass, setting his body afire.

"You have been wounded many times."

"Aye."

He could barely think of anything except making love to her, but when she ran her finger down one scar that ran beneath his nipple to his hip and asked where he got that one, he figured anything that would help her to relax was worthy of conversation. "During the Crusades, love."

He dropped his belt, then slid his trewes down. They stood so close together, she couldn't see his body. Would she be frightened to see his eagerness to have her for his own? Already his shaft was hard as his lance, ready to penetrate her untried sheath.

"Did you suffer much?" she asked, avoiding looking lower than his chest.

Not like he did right this very minute. "For some days. My brothers did not think I would live. I ran a high fever." That didn't sound very heroic. He only wanted her to think of him as the Highlander who would always protect her. "It would not keep me down for long."

"Aye, you are a Highlander, verra brave and strong."

Her words filled him with pride to think she felt that way about him. He pressed her close to enjoy the feel of her soft curves against his hard body. Only her thin chemise rested between him and what he wished to conquer. Delaying the inevitable was driving him insane.

Again, he kissed her lips and she kissed him in return this time, sweeping her fingers over his back. "You have scars on your back, too."

Her exploration of his muscles triggered another rush of blood straight to his groin. "Aye." He ran his hand down her side then cupped her bottom and pressed his erection hard against her stomach.

She moaned in response, eliciting a groan deep inside him when her soft body pressed against his arousal. His ache for her intensified tenfold. Did she feel the same for him?

He grasped her shift and began to draw it up, praying she would not stop him.

"I am afraid, Malcolm," she said when he lifted the gown higher. She trembled.

"Of what are you afraid, lass? I will be gentle with ye."

"You are kind to me, Malcolm. I...I only worry what will happen when—"

He kissed her lips to silence her words. He had no need to hear anything more spoken about the baron he already hated. As long as the lady did not fear Malcolm's making love to her, he would proceed.

When he removed her gown, she shivered again.

"I do not want you getting chilled." He helped her to lie down and that's when she saw him naked for the first time.

Her gaze focused on his arousal, her lips dropped open and her green eyes grew big. "'Tis nearly as big as a horse's."

He laughed with gusto. If the lady had wished to give him a compliment, she could not have thought of a better one.

She looked up at him, her face concerned. "Have I offended ye?"

Joining her on the bedding, he shook his head. "Nay, love, I was just surprised to hear you say so."

"We will just sleep, is not that so, Malcolm?"

Sleep? What made the lass think they only would sleep?

"You are only removing our clothes because we do not sleep in them, but you dinna mean to make love to me, because we can still annul the marriage if the king wishes it."

"*I* do not wish it, love." He pulled the blanket over them, then wrapped his arms around her. He repressed the worry that she'd insist on remaining a virgin until they had the king's blessing. "I thought you understood that I do not want to annul the marriage. I want you to be my wife."

She touched his chest with her fingers, tracing the longest of his scars again. "Nay, you can keep me warm as before."

Her touch forced more urgent cravings into his groin again. He might not make love to her as husband and wife this eve if she was dead set against it, but he planned on warming his wee bride up just fine, only not quite the way she had in mind.

CHAPTER 13

Malcolm kissed Anice's cheek and it was more than she could bear not to allow him to make love to her. Every time he grew close, she ached between her legs and the feeling was agonizing. Would his making love to her, relieve the throbbing?

"Aye, love," he said. "I will warm you up. Did you like it when I rubbed your feet?"

"Aye, 'twas verra nice."

The way he cared for her truly touched her, but she couldn't allow him to be harmed because he married her to keep her honor intact. 'Twas best that they plan for an annulment should the king request it of them and, too, if Malcolm changed his mind about wanting her for his wife.

The notion the baron would marry her solely for her properties was bad enough, especially since she was certain he had murdered her uncle. 'Twas equally wrong for Malcolm to feel forced to marry her when he wanted an English bride. And for what? To protect her from the tongue-waggings that would commence once 'twas discovered she and Malcolm had been alone together as man and wife, only not having had the nuptials to make it such. He was being kind to say he wanted her was all. He'd had no intention of marrying her or any other Scottish lass before that.

"Good. You seem tense. Would you like me to rub your back?"

She hesitated, wanting his touch, but realized he would be concerned that others knew that he had not consummated their marriage. Would they think there was something wrong with him? Or with her? She took a deep breath, trying to crush the worries that flittered through her mind. "I would not want you to work so hard to please me when I willna allow you to make love to me."

"'Tis no' work but all pleasure, if it makes you feel good."

"Aye. I will do the same for you afterward."

She was sure he said something about taking a cold bath afterward if she did, which could give him a chill, so she couldn't believe he truly said such a thing. "Malcolm, what say you?"

"I would feel honored."

She was sure those were not the words he spoke, but when he rolled her onto her stomach and started to knead her shoulders like he was a skilled baker kneading a roll of dough, she hummed in ecstasy.

"Remember, you promised to massage my muscles, Anice." His voice was dark and husky, nearly groveling.

She smiled. "Think you I willna?"

"I think you might become so relaxed, you will fall asleep before you can give me a massage."

"Then if that happens, I will give you one tomorrow eve. Well, mayhap no' as we shall not sleep together tomorrow eve. I will try no'...hmmm, that feels sooo good."

Every bit of her neck and shoulders began to relax, but then he moved her arms. "Rest your head on them, so I can get all of your back muscles."

When she readjusted her arms, she felt her breasts somewhat exposed, though his hands continued to knead her back with finesse, and she assumed he was too busy to peek. He shifted, drawing his fingers over her sides, sweeping up and down, the tips of his fingers touching the fullness of her breasts with an insistent stroke.

The area between her legs grew wet. She squeezed her thighs together, trying to stop the ache.

His hands drew lower to the tip of her spine and around her hips. "You are tensing when you are supposed to be relaxing."

"Aye, I am trying."

She swore he chuckled under his breath.

Then he touched her bottom. She stiffened.

"Relax, Anice. If you do not relax, I will feel I have done a poor job." He massaged her bottom, lifting and stroking until her insides burned.

"I think I am coming down with a fever," she whispered.

Again, she thought she heard him chuckle to himself.

"Nay, lass, your skin feels just right. You have no fever."

He slid his hand between her legs, touching her where she ached so badly and moved her legs apart.

"Malcolm," she scolded.

"Aye, lass. I am working on your legs, then you can give me the same kind of rub."

She bit her bottom lip when he massaged the upper part of her thigh, bumping into her aching center with each stroke. She wanted to open her legs further and let him stroke the ache. Would it relieve the tension there, too? Then she scolded herself. No decent lady would think such a thing.

It seemed he worked on her upper thigh overmuch, making it almost numb, but then he switched to her other and applied the same sensual strokes. 'Twas not the massaging of her leg that garnered her attention, but the area between her legs.

"Malcolm," she entreated.

"Aye, lass?"

"You are doing a verra good job, but you have created a new tension that aches something awful."

Again, she thought she heard him chuckle. "Tell me where and I will aid you in getting rid of it."

She hesitated. "Nay, I was mistaken. If you are almost done with me, I will give you a rub next."

He worked lower on her legs down to her feet, but much more quickly this time. Then he ran his hand over her back. "I can help the ache between your legs, if you wish me, too."

She knew his meaning then. "We cannot make love."

"There are other ways."

She frowned. "I have never heard of other ways. The ladies newly married tell of what happens, but none of them said anything about other ways."

"Mayhap their husbands do not rub their backs either."

"Nay, you are right. I do not remember any of them saying their husbands did that with them. 'Tis verra nice between a husband and wife." Though she instantly felt guilty that they were truly not husband and wife.

"Aye, love. Before you rub my back, did you want me to ease your other ache?"

Again, she hesitated. "Would it take verra long? I would not want to fall asleep before I give you a massage."

He smiled. "Roll over and let me rub away the ache."

"Can I be covered up?"

"It will be harder to see what I'm doing, but if it pleases ye, aye, lass."

"It does, Malcolm."

She rolled onto her back, but before he pulled the blanket over her, he touched her breast.

"That is not where the ache is," she objected.

He tried to contain a smile, but failed, then circled the tip of her breast with his finger, leaned over and licked it.

"Aye, lass. I will get to it."

His touch sent burning heat streaking through her.

Moaning out loud, she touched his hair, dangling against her skin, tickling it. "You are making the ache worse, no' better, Malcolm."

He took the bud of her breast in his mouth and swirled his tongue around it, forcing a groan of ecstasy from her lips.

His hand moved down and touched her between her legs. 'Twas nothing like she'd ever experienced before, and the pleasure and pain of it wasn't like his removing the tension from her muscles. "I think you were wrong," she breathed out between strokes.

"What is that, lass?" He shifted his leg between hers and leaned over to caress the other nipple.

"You are making it worse."

"Takes a little time, but it will get better."

She dug her nails into his shoulders when his fingers dipped deep inside her, and then once moistened, he slid them out and stroked her nub with renewed enthusiasm. Arching her back, she wanted to feel more and at the same time wanted him to stop before he drove her to madness.

She realized he was rubbing his manhood against her, and it was throbbing as much as she was. It would be so easy to relieve both their aches by allowing him to make love to her, would it not? That's what he wanted. Why couldn't she allow him to bed her after all he had done for her?

Because she didn't want to anger the king and bind Malcolm to her, that's why. He would be free to marry any lady he wanted. He only wanted her like any man would who lay naked with her like this. She had no doubt even a man as old as her first betrothed would have wanted her if she gave herself to him willingly.

She gripped Malcolm's shoulders tighter and moaned with delight when he pulled her into the sea where waves of heat washed through her and the ache was replaced with a new kind of throbbing, but one of satisfaction. He inserted his fingers into her again and penetrated deeply.

"Has the ache lessened, love?" he whispered against her breast.

"Aye."

"Would you not reconsider letting me love you then?"

"You would be bound to me, Malcolm. I cannot permit it."

"I wish to be bound to ye, forever, Anice." He reached up and held her face. "What are you thinking, love? Do you no' believe me when I say I want you for my very own?"

"You feel obligated. You are a braw and dutiful Highlander. But I cannot force this on ye."

His brow furrowed. "You are forcing naught on me. I wish this marriage more than anything."

"You have never wanted anyone but an English bride."

"I was mistaken, love. Ye are the one I want."

"Any man would say that about a woman who is laying naked under him in a bed of straw."

Malcolm's eyes instantly grew stormy, and he shook his head, his face hard. "There is no making you believe me. I should have known you did not want me. For whatever reason—and you have withheld the truth from me before— you believe I am not good enough for ye."

He rose from the bed and tossed the blanket to her. "I will sleep with my brothers tonight like I have done for many a night in the past, before I sleep with a woman who thinks I would ravage her just because she is a naked woman beneath me."

He threw on his clothes as quickly as humanly possible, then stormed out the door.

She was so shocked at his actions, she hadn't expected them at all, and she didn't know how to rectify the situation one bit. Mortified that she'd not only hurt his pride, but would cause him further embarrassment when the rest of the staff at the castle discovered her husband favored sleeping with her brothers to her...

Damnation. She was the one who'd be unable to face the courtiers in the morning.

She grabbed up her clothes that she'd traveled in, dressed with the most difficulty, then pulled the monk's robe over that. No one would touch her, being that she was a man of the cloth. She had no need of traveling with Malcolm and his brothers. Best they leave things as they were.

Grabbing a candle, she hastened through the kitchen, then outside into the kitchen garden. The fragrance of lavender stirred on the chilly breeze. After stalking between rows of herbs, she ended up in an expansive area where buckets of soapy water waited for the washerwomen the next day, and the blacksmith's anvil sat ready for the strike of his hammer.

All was quiet except for men-at-arms who walked their posts on guard duty along the castle walls. Each of them looked beyond the castle grounds for signs of trouble and not toward the inner bailey. Still, how could she convince the gate guard to let her leave?

Mayhap being that she was a monk, he'd feel obligated. If that didn't work—she jingled her coin in her purse. A little money might do the trick.

She hurried into the stable and searched for her horse. He whinnied softly as she reached her hand out to his gray muzzle. "Come on, Mystic, time to take a little walk again."

The notion of riding one more hour didn't appeal and traveling alone without companionship would be lonely. Better than dealing with an angry, almost husband.

Thank God she'd been a willful child and had left home on her own more than once. She fumbled with her saddle though, not from not knowing how to affix it to her horse, but from the worry she would soon be caught. The sky was still dark, but she couldn't see any stars, and she assumed stormy clouds still stalked them.

Once she had saddled Mystic, she climbed onto a bale of hay, slipped her leg over the horse and rode out of the stable. So far, so good. Though the chill in the air and the worry she would not be allowed to leave sent shivers hurtling through her whole body.

She walked Mystic toward the gatehouse where the portcullis had been shut tight for the eve. Already several of the men on watch turned their attention to the bailey to see who would ride out this early in the morn before any had arisen.

One of them hurried for the stairs. 'Twas not a good sign. Her skin prickled and she straightened her back.

The gate guard was nowhere in sight, but when she neared the gatehouse, he lumbered out, his mouth turned down into a scowl, and his bushy black brows furrowed. "You cannot mean to be leaving at this time of morn, Brother. The bell won't ring for another three hours or so to wake the staff."

"'Tis the will of God." Anice spoke as low and commanding as she could manage.

The knight from the wall walk, who'd run down the stairs when he'd spied her, stalked toward her. "Remove your hood."

"You would not talk to a man of God like that," Anice said, her voice as harsh and manly as she could make it. Though it sounded fine to her ears, she worried it sounded too high-pitched to the men.

"We have no Scottish monks here, and the only ones I know of who are Scots born, are the Lady Anice and her escort. Now, being you are not as big as any of the men, I assume you are the wee lad they brought with them...but that would not be right either as he is not Scottish. Which leads me to believe you are the lady herself."

Wee lad? She was much taller than the boy.

"My lady, is it ye? His Earl Lord would have my head if I let you out without an escort. What could you be thinking, my lady?" the gate guard asked, his voice full of concern.

"Come," the knight said, "I will take you back to the

keep and return your horse to the stable."

"Let go of my horse!" she snapped, irritated that some knight would tell her what to do. She faced the gate guard. "Open the gate. You have no right keeping me here against my will."

"Lady MacNeill," the knight said again, "you will come with me, or—"

She whipped out her bow and before any realized what she was doing, she notched an arrow. "Open the gate before I get angry."

"Kill me if you must." The guard folded his arms in obstinacy. "His Earl Lord would give me a more painful death if I should let you go."

The knight stormed off toward the keep.

She cursed inwardly. Then she figured now that the knight was gone, she could bribe the gate guard. She lifted a bag of money from beneath her monk's robe. "How much would it take my good man?"

"No amount of money, my lady. His Earl Lord would know you bribed me to get me to open the gate. You can put your money away. You are not getting by me this morn."

The sound of several men running toward them forced a chill up her spine. Not because she was afraid, but because she was furious not to get her way. She retied her money pouch to her belt.

She wished not to travel with a man who got mad at her when she only spoke the truth. Heavens knows if she stripped off her clothes in front of the gate guard, he wouldn't hesitate to ravage her, would he? Or the knight who'd been on watch or any man. The point of the matter was Malcolm was just like any other man. They couldn't help themselves when it came to wanting a woman who was naked and willing. It didn't mean he wanted her forever. Once he had a chance to have a good English woman, he'd regret he'd lain with the Scottish wench.

"Last chance," she threatened, renotching her arrow.

"Take your best shot, my lady."

"Anice!" Malcolm shouted as he ran toward her.

"Tell him to open the gate. My horse needs a ride," she shouted over her shoulder, but kept one eye on the guard lest he duck.

"Quit this foolishness!"

Her cheeks flamed. Who was foolish? The man who left her bed, or she who wanted to return to her castle as quickly as possible to right the wrongs there?

"Can you truly use that bow?" he asked as he reached her horse's flank.

"Aye, that I can." She glowered at him. "Were you no' listening to my tale earlier?"

His brothers moved around to her horse's other flank.

"Traitor," she said to the knight, who'd run there and back and was huffing a bit.

"Then shoot me because 'tis me you are angry with," Malcolm ordered.

"My husband? Nay, I have already lost too many of my betrothed. It would be a shame to lose another so quickly."

A murmur of conversation swept through the five other men who'd joined the brothers to see if they could help. Probably the most excitement the courtiers had had in a good long while. Several more watched from the wall walk, leaning over the stone wall and speaking low with one another. 'Twas probably good she could not make out their conversation.

"Anice!"

She lowered her weapon to turn and face Malcolm who so rudely stood slightly behind her. Why didn't he face her like a man?

As soon as she lowered her weapon, the guard lunged forward and grabbed her bow, Dougald, seized her reins, and Malcolm pulled her from her mount.

She cried out, not from fright, but from surprise, then tried to wrench free. He hoisted her over his shoulder. "We have another three hours of sleep before we go to mass, break our fast, and continue our journey."

"Let me down, you brute!"

"But if you cannot sleep, you can give me a backrub like you promised."

How could he be so infuriating? "I will do no such thing."

"Then I will give you another."

The men followed them back to the keep and laughed, then shared some comments she couldn't quite make out, but she was sure it was not in her best interest to hear what they said. Already her body was on fire, his actions humiliating her so. What did he think she was? A sack of wheat?

A woman hurried to greet Malcolm as he stormed back through the keep to the kitchen. "His Lord Earl asked me to see if you wanted me to stay with you and the lady the rest of the morn."

"Nay, the lady and I will be fine, but if we do not wake on time to break our fast, do not allow any to disturb us."

"Aye, my lord."

The lady hurried away and Malcolm stalked into the storage room. "I wanted a woman with spice, love. But you would try the devil's patience." He pulled her off his shoulder, then set her on the bed. "Stay!"

He slammed the door closed as several milled around to see what happened next and shoved a table against the door. "You are staying put, until I say so."

She scowled at him just every bit as good as he scowled at her. "You did not want me. I see no point in this." She lay down and yanked the blanket over her.

"We are going around in circles on this, Anice. I do want ye, but you cannot get that through your head." He shrugged out of his clothes, then stalked across the floor and yanked the blanket off her. "I am only going to do this one more time tonight."

She crossed her arms, not wanting to expose herself to a

man who did not love her. "I am fine."

"My wife will not be dressed in monk's clothes when she sleeps with me. It would be sinful." He pulled her up and quickly dispensed with all her clothes. "I would leave your shift on, lass, but I mean to show you that no matter how much I desire to make love to ye, I will not. We will sleep together as before, like you suggested in the first place. Naught more. I am no such an animal that I could not sleep with ye, as provocative as you are, naked against me. If that were so, I would have given in to my baser needs when you were sick."

He was right to an extent, though he couldn't seem to recognize like she did that he didn't really want her.

He pulled her onto the blanket on the straw, then wrapped it around them. Though she thought he intended to sleep beside her, with as little touching as possible, he slipped his arm around her back and pulled her against his body. No matter how much she resisted the notion he truly wanted her, a Scottish lass, his touch undid her. She nestled her head against his chest and listened to his quickened heartbeat.

"I am sorry, Malcolm."

"Aye, lass." He kissed the top of her head.

She wrapped her arm around his waist and took a deep breath, loving the feel of his hard body beneath her.

He stroked her back. "You are much softer to sleep with than my brothers, and you smell a whole lot better."

She couldn't help but smile. "They did not have a bath like we did."

Again, he kissed her head. "Nay, lass. Sleep. Everything will look better on the morrow."

She was sure the battle of words would renew sometime on the morrow. If the baron caught up with them, it would be a battle of swords and a fight to the death.

Would she lose her fifth of her betrothed husbands then, too? She would kill any man who attempted to harm him, and then she would release him to find the kind of woman he truly wished to wed.

CHAPTER 14

Anice and the MacNeill brothers had barely eaten more than a couple of bites of their bread with Laird Whitehaven that morn when one of the earl's men charged into the hall with a scowl on his face. Instantly, Anice grew alarmed. 'Twas probably only a problem the earl had to deal with concerning his own estates, but the way the man quickly glanced at her convinced her otherwise. She'd had no premonition that anything was amiss, not until the man arrived so all of a sudden. Now her heartbeat quickened, and the same kind of panic filled her as it usually did when she knew there was danger, but she couldn't fathom its source, and worse, she couldn't stop it from happening.

The hall grew quiet while everyone watched the man stalk toward the head table and Laird Whitehaven. Before this, she'd heard bits and pieces of conversation about how the Lady Anice had threatened to shoot the gate guard and was hauled back into the castle over her husband's shoulder. Had the laird bedded the lass and shown her who was in charge? 'Twas what she had heard whispered wherever she walked in the castle and grounds this morn.

The man spoke in private to the earl, who listened

intently, then nodded.

The earl rose from his seat. "Lords and ladies, I must have your cooperation in a matter most grave. You know how events have changed so rapidly concerning the Lady Anice and her hasty marriage to Lord MacNeill, but you know not the reason for this matter."

Anice's cheeks grew hot. He couldn't mean to tell his courtiers what had happened between she and Malcolm the night of the storm.

"They are attempting to uncover the murder of her uncle, and much evidence points to the murderer being a former suitor of hers, Baron Harold de Fontenot. He is now at my gatehouse."

Her heart sank. She'd so hoped they'd be well on their way before the baron ever caught up with them. She was certain the earl would take great pains to keep the baron at his castle as long as he could to give Anice and her party a good head start.

A pronounced stirring of conversation rushed through the hall.

The earl waved his hand for silence. "We aid these young lovers in their quest to uncover enough evidence to support their case. Until then, naught of these matters will be spoken to any. In the interim, the Lady Anice is only the Lady MacNeill. As far as we know, the Lady Anice has disappeared with her escort."

The earl was truly a friend in their time of need, and she was gladdened to know that Malcolm had made so many acquaintances among the Norman lairds. Especially when they had to fight the baron, also a Norman laird.

Many nodded in agreement.

Malcolm rose. "I wish to thank ye, Laird Earl, and ladies and gentlemen of his court. We will now be on our way, if we can slip past the baron and his knights."

The earl turned to Malcolm. "Gather your belongings and go to the kitchen. Once I have word you are safely there,

I will send for the baron and his men. You can leave by the kitchen gardens, find your way to the stables, and leave before the baron knows you were here."

He turned again to his people. "No one is to mention to the baron or his men that Lord MacNeill and his party were here." Then he said to Malcolm, "Go, and keep your wife safe."

"Aye, that I will. Thank you kindly for your generosity."

"Thank ye, my laird," Anice said before Malcolm hurried her out of the great hall.

Not long after they entered the kitchen, Malcolm's brothers and Kemp followed with their belongings. Anice couldn't help but feel they were in a race, but no matter their tactics, they could never stay much more than a footstep ahead. Though they couldn't kill the baron and his men without just cause, the notion often crossed her mind.

The maid Elizabeth said to them, "I will inform my Lord Earl that you are safely here. Once the baron and his men are seated in the great hall, I will return and take you to the stables."

Before anyone could say a word to the young woman, she slipped back into the great hall.

Anice paced, hating to wait, hoping not to get caught. Though she knew the earl would not allow the baron to harm any of them while they remained at his castle, she wanted to deal with this matter on her own, once and for all. If the baron and his men left for Brecken with them, might the baron still try to kill Malcolm and his brothers? When she arrived at Brecken, her own men and the MacNeills would be a force to reckon with. But the three MacNeills would be no match for an overwhelming number of the baron's men on the road there.

Malcolm said, "Anice—"

"I am fine."

He smiled. "Aye, that you are."

"I would feel even better if I had my bow and quiver of arrows."

Dougald chuckled.

She turned to frown at him.

He gave her a devilish smirk. "The baron is not only the one who had better watch out for you and your bow and arrow. The gate guard this morning warned Malcolm to be careful how he treated you in the future. The word is that you must have been awfully hard on your last four betrothals."

"Aye," she said. "Mayhap if the baron knew this, he would reconsider wanting to marry me."

The maid scurried back into the kitchen, her cheeks flushed. "There are fourteen men, including the baron, my lord, lady."

"Fourteen." Too many for the brothers to handle by themselves—well, and for her, of course also. But still too large a number to consider fighting. Her stomach clenched when she headed toward the kitchen garden entrance, but the maid halted her. "I'll show you the way, my lady."

"'Tis not necessary, good woman. I used this verra path only several hours earlier—"

The maid bolted ahead of her. "Oh, no, my lady, I will be able to tell all the courtiers what happened. *I* would be part of your adventure then."

Anice smiled at the poor, deluded girl. Their adventure was far too dangerous to romanticize. Anice knew the baron wouldn't recognize her as the Lady Anice, but he would know Malcolm as being the laird who stole his horses. She'd love to hear the tale he told the earl about this horse-stealing Scottish laird. Between she, Malcolm and the baron, the earl's courtiers were being well entertained. Except she preferred the entertainment to be less dangerous.

When they reached the stable, the maid told the man in charge, "The word must be given that Lady Anice has not been here, nor has Lord MacNeill. I will inform the soldiers on guard duty."

"Also," Malcolm said as several stablemen began saddling their horses, "Baron Fontenot wishes his horses taken into the village to be reshod."

Anice stifled the urge to laugh.

"But, my lord, he gave orders to have the horses fed and watered and—"

"Tell him when they come to gather their horses that a man who says he was one of the baron's knights was ordered to take the horses to be reshod. He will find them in the village."

The man glanced at the maid who nodded. "Aye, His Earl Lord wishes to help Lord MacNeill and his lady. Lord MacNeill saved the Earl Lord's life, you know."

"Aye. Very well then. We have removed their saddles and gear to wipe them down."

"They will not need their saddles."

The party rode out of the bailey and the maid hurried after them shouting well wishes, then spoke to the gate guard.

Anice glanced back at the baron's horses, wondering what the baron would say when he found out. The earl would not allow him to harm his marshal of the stables. "Will His Laird Earl be upset with us for taking the baron's horses?"

"Nay, lass. The earl has a great sense of humor. If the roles were reversed, he would have done the same."

"The baron will get tired of walking, dinna you agree?"

He chuckled. "Aye."

But it would not help them verra much to leave them in the village so close by. "You are really no' going to leave them in town are ye?"

"Nay, somewhere along the way to Carlisle. But far enough that he will not have an easy time of it."

"When he sees you at Brecken—"

"He will not know I released his horses here. He will

only know I let them go at the farmhouse. It will be easy to explain as the winds were blowing so hard, and we did not close the byre's door tight enough."

Tickled by his explanation, she chuckled. "You have the devil in ye."

"Actually, I have never had the opportunity to do such a thing. Young Kemp has taught us a thing or two already...that there are more ways to win a battle than causing bloodshed, though I am certain it will get to that. The baron will not like it that I have taken you for my bride once he learns you are the Lady Anice."

She took a deep breath. "Let us hope he doesna learn this, until after we have proof of his murdering my uncle, and then the king can deal with him."

Malcolm smiled, seemingly in good spirits this morn, despite the troubles they'd had that eve. Though she'd been disconcerted to see he'd left the kitchen storage room before she rose for early mass. She'd wondered then if he were angry with her still over her not allowing him to make love to her, or for trying to leave the castle on her own that morn. Confused about her feelings for him, and his for her, she was torn between talking to him or letting the subject be.

Twice she'd awakened in the middle of the morning to find him stroking her arm. What went on in that head of his? As tired as she'd been, she'd fallen asleep again shortly afterward and not given it another thought.

But now she wanted to ask him if he were angry with her for last night. Then she thought about his saving the Laird Earl's life and decided to talk to Malcolm about this less volatile subject instead. "Were you in a verra terrible battle when you saved the earl from an arrow?"

"Nay, lass. 'Twas only a hunt. A young laird nearly hit him by accident. I galloped in front of the earl but was not sure why I did so afterward. It hurt like the devil."

"You are a verra brave man, my laird. That's why. Where did the arrow strike ye?"

"My left arm. 'Twas good, too, as I could still wield my sword with my right. But I was no good at the hunt for a long while." He studied her for a second. "Do you hunt often?"

"Aye, with both my bird and bow. Though I enjoy the bow more."

"To show your skill?"

"Some say I'm no' too bad."

He shook his head. "Then the gate guard was in serious trouble this morning."

"Certainly. Though as close as he was to me, I could not have missed."

He laughed. "Mayhap we could have an archery contest."

"A contest?"

"Aye. Of course you being a lass, I would have to make allowances."

"You are a gentleman to be sure."

"I have my reason, lass." His smile broadened and his eyes glittered with intrigue.

The devilish look in his eyes fascinated her. "What have you in mind, Malcolm?"

"A goodly wager. To sweeten the pot, you see?"

"Money?" She raised her brows. She wasn't used to making wagers. But she knew others who did and that was usually the bargain.

"Nay, lass. You is what I want."

The idea he wanted her thrilled her, but she couldn't succumb to his devilish charms. Was he like her king? Because she said no to allowing his having her fully, he desired her even more?

She turned to study Dougald some distance ahead of them, keeping a vigilant lookout for danger. She would not agree to consummate the marriage if that was what Malcolm had in mind. Not until the king approved and she was certain Malcolm truly wanted her and no other. "What exactly do you wish from me?"

"You have said you will play the role of my wife, and pretend no' to be the Lady Anice. But your people must be made aware that we are indeed married."

That was easy enough. She sighed. "Aye, I will tell them this. Is this the bargain you have in mind?"

"Nay, this must be done anyway."

She frowned at him, not sure she was going to like this wager of his. "Why?"

"Because it is so. If for some reason we have to 'pretend' to be married, I want your people to know we truly our wed."

"In what way?"

"If I have to kiss ye or show some affection toward you in some other way to prove to the baron and his men that we are indeed married, I want your courtiers to know that we really are married and 'tis acceptable."

"Aye, I see your meaning. So what is it you wish of me in this wager of yours?"

"You have already said you would sleep in Lady Anice's bedchamber but would no' allow me to. I wish to be able to come to you and share your bed."

She ran her reins through her fingers as she thought of his request, not liking the idea. Not that she didn't want his arms around her, the feel of his hard body against hers, but the baron concerned her. "What if the baron is in residence and he discovers you are visiting me in the mistress's chamber? It would no' be allowed."

"Would not cause much speculation. We are husband and wife already. The lady herself should no' mind because she is the Lady Anice and not in residence at the moment." He turned away from her, but the smile still lighted his face. "Besides, she owes me."

"Owes you?"

He turned to her. "Aye. A backrub."

She couldn't help smiling, the memory of his massaging

her muscles and...and so much more. Even now, the ache renewed between her legs, the thought of his fingers penetrating her womanly folds, making the blood rush to her face. "If I win the match?"

"Anything you wish to ask of me."

"I will think on it."

He glanced at her, a brow raised. "I wish to know what I am getting myself into."

Taking a deep breath, she considered the matter further. "An English lady is one of my ladies-in-waiting, a baron's daughter who intended to marry my uncle's former steward, only he died before they wed. She stayed to serve me because she was unhappy with her da, but her grandfather on her mother's side intends to leave the lass his estates." Anice tilted her head to the side. "She will have her own castle near Westminster and would make a lovely bride." An English bride, Anice wanted to emphasize. "You will dance with her after the evening meal."

The smile left Malcolm's face. "Think you the lady would change my mind about you because she is English?"

"She is verra agreeable. No' like me."

He shook his head. "'Tis a deal. If I should lose, I will dance with the lady."

"For every dance that eve."

He glowered at her. "I have never danced with ye, and you are my wife now. It would no' be proper if I danced all the dances with another maid to exclusion."

"'Tis the wager. Just dancing one dance with her wouldna be like my taking you to my bed." Tilting her chin up, she waited for him to agree.

"Verra well, then I shall have to win." He rubbed his beard. "Though had I known the wager, I wouldna have agreed to giving you allowances."

She loved the way he was. "You are a good man, my laird. You would have done so anyway."

"No' under the circumstances, lass. I mean to bed ye."

This time he waggled his dark brows at her.

She chuckled, knowing she had a very good chance at beating him. "I am verra good with a bow. Even without allowances made, you might no' have won."

"Then mayhap we should have the same target placement, no allowances."

"Nay, you have already given me your promise." She laughed to see his humor return and the notion he would want to best her no matter what to be able to sleep with her again.

Three hours after they began their journey, they released the baron's horses at the River Eden, watered their own horses, and took a break.

When they arrived at the timber castle of Carlisle, Anice was gladdened they had less than ten miles to travel before they reached Scotland.

"I know you want to travel on to your home, my lady, but we should rest the horses a bit and mayhap eat with the laird who runs the place."

"You do not know him?"

"Nay. I know that William Rufus built the castle and Henry had to rebuild it, but no' who is running it at present."

"I do not wish to bother this laird then. I want to reach my home before long. We will eat salted pork as before and continue on our way."

***

'Twas only another couple of hours into their journey when the worst kind of concern plagued Anice. Even Malcolm noticed her anxiety and turned to study her.

How could she let him know she could sense the future, that in the worst way she wanted to run and hide, that if they did not, he and his brothers could die by the sword, and only God knew what would become of her?

"Anice, lass, are ye feeling ill?"

"Malcolm, we must…" She faced forward again and stared at the hills that hid the view of the threat ahead. "I…"

How could she tell him they must find a place to hide without revealing her ability? He would think her a witch for certain.

"Lass," Malcolm said, pulling his horse closer to hers. "Ye have lost the color in your face. What ails you?"

***

Malcolm's heart was wrenched in two when he saw how scared Anice had become. Her lips trembled and her wide green eyes searched the horizon for signs of danger. Was she capable of seeing danger unseen by others? He'd noticed on other occasions she seemed to have an uncanny ability to recognize a threat before there truly was one. He'd seen the same thing with soldiers on the battlefield who'd had an eerie ability to see peril before it presented itself. Even his three brothers and he had a pretty good awareness of threatening situations. But this went beyond seeing a hazard and recognizing it for what it was. She often predicted one before it was even in sight.

Now, she pursed her lips and said not a word, yet she'd pulled back on her horse's reins and slowed to a walk.

"Dougald, wait up!" Malcolm hollered, bound to find out what frightened Anice before they ventured any further.

Dougald pulled his horse to a stop, then turned to see the matter.

Angus continued to follow behind them with the boy trying to see around him to find out what was going on.

"Anice," Malcolm said again, trying to curb his annoyance that she seemed afraid to tell him what concerned her. "What is it, lass?"

"There is...is danger up ahead."

"Aye, I sensed that was what concerned ye, but pray tell, what see you?"

"Edgar Atheling's men-at-arms. Mayhap thirty." Her eyes filled with tears. "My uncle intends to fight alongside Robert Curthose. They hide Edgar's standard, but 'tis them. His steward, Laird Robertson, rides with the men. There

TERRY SPEAR

would be no fighting between us, if we ken no' what they were up to. But Torq Robertson, brother to the man I killed, would recognize me at once. He would realize I would know he sided with Henry's brother. They would slay us all to keep their whereabouts secret. Some of the lowlanders would hide Edgar's men, many of them being Saxon lairds who fled when William of Normandy invaded. King Malcolm gave them safe haven, including Matilda's mother, Princess Margaret, whom he wed. Some of the lowlanders are Normans who would be loyal to Robert Curthose."

Malcolm stared at Anice, disbelieving she could know the men were her uncle's without even seeing them. "How…" Tears spilled down her cheeks, and he quickly dismissed the question. "They may not wish to kill ye, my lady, but take you hostage and use you for ransom."

She shook her head. "Laird Robertson hated me for the death of his brother. Without my uncle to stop him, he may seek revenge."

Malcolm would let no harm come to the lady, but before he could speak, Dougald whipped his horse around and rode back to them, his countenance highly agitated.

Looking from Anice to Malcolm, Dougald said, "What is the problem, Malcolm?"

"Trouble lays up ahead."

"I see nor hear anyone," Dougald argued.

Malcolm looked steadily into Dougald's eyes, his brother's doubts noted. "Nevertheless, we will have to ride—"

"Farther east to avoid the men," Anice quickly said.

"What men?" Dougald asked, shifting his gaze from Malcolm to Anice.

"Men who align themselves with Robert Curthose." Anice stiffened her back, as if she were readying for the joust.

"You ken this how?" Dougald asked, his voice filled with disbelief.

She glanced at Malcolm, then raised her chin higher and spoke to Dougald. "I saw Edgar Atheling's standard, flown by his steward, Laird Robertson, and Robertson and his clansmen are headed in this direction."

Malcolm stared at her. Had not she just said the standard was hidden? She had not seen the men at all, or Dougald, who had been riding farther ahead, would have spied it.

"I saw no sign of anyone up ahead, my lady. Ye must be mistaken," Dougald argued.

"Ye cannot fight them, Dougald. There are too many of them."

"Why would they fight us, my lady? They would have no idea we are loyal to King Henry, nor would they wish to begin a battle here in Scotland, at least I wouldna think."

"I ken Laird Robertson. He kens me. If he sees me, what think you will become of us? Queen Matilda and I are Edgar's nieces, but I am the only one who is unmarried."

Malcolm cleared his throat.

Dougald's knowing look exchanged between the brothers. Now everyone would know their marriage had not been consummated. They were married, all right, but the marriage could easily be annulled if Malcolm didn't bed her.

Anice's cheeks turned brilliant red and Malcolm frowned at her. 'Twas not his brothers' business, and a situation he meant to rectify as soon as he was able.

"I mean to say, my uncle might want to ransom me to Henry because he wishes to marry me to a loyal Norman laird. Then again, Edgar might wish to give me away to someone loyal to himself. But you see, I killed Laird Robertson's brother, and he has always wanted revenge."

Again, Dougald looked at Malcolm as if seeking confirmation that the lass spoke the truth.

"We travel east, Dougald, well away from these men," Malcolm ordered.

"It will add hours onto our destination when we dinna

know if what the lass says is true."

"We cannot risk a confrontation if the lady is correct." In his heart, he was certain Anice spoke the truth, yet he didn't want his brothers to concern themselves with how she knew, at least not at present. If she said so, the danger moved in their direction. Best be concerned with moving out of its path.

When they continued in their usual configuration with Dougald well in the lead, Malcolm took a deep breath and said what was on his mind. "Lass, I ken you knew what you were talking about. What I have to know is how you knew this."

"Thank ye for believing in me, my laird. 'Tis naught."

"Ye said they were hiding Edgar's standard, which would be prudent in case others who did not support his cause, fought them. Then you said you saw the standard. I venture to guess you did not see any sign of them. In that case, how did you know they were beyond the hills, out of sight, and heading in our direction?"

"Mayhap I overheard someone telling someone else of Laird Robertson's movements?" she asked, her green eyes wide, expressive, endearing.

"Mayhap not, my lady. Ye are gifted?"

She stared ahead and didn't say a word.

"How oft do ye see things like this?"

"I dinna know what you mean."

His jaw tightened. If he was to be her husband, he had to know everything there was about the lady. He would not allow her to put his concerns asunder. "Anice, ye need not worry how I feel about this. I am verra open-minded, not like some of my kinsmen."

She looked at him, and his heart nearly gave out. She looked so fearful. Why? Thinking he would cast her aside if she had such a gift?

"Lass, whatever ye think, I treasure you for being you. If you wish no' to tell me—"

"And your brothers?" she asked.

How could he keep such a thing from his brothers? They never kept secrets from one another, except for his not mentioning that he had failed to bed the lass, but 'twas not any of their concern for now. Still, they would suspect something was not as it should be, the way she sensed danger before any of them did.

When he hesitated overlong to speak, she nodded. "I suspected as much. You will tell your brothers."

Which meant she did possess some uncanny ability.

"Exactly what can ye see, lass?"

"Sometimes danger, but not always. I didna see that Laird Robertson wished me ill..." She quit speaking abruptly and her face paled.

"Anice?"

"Nay, I sensed the danger long beforehand. Robertson loved another and I 'heard' him and the woman he rendezvoused with making plans. They knew the only way I could inherit my uncle's estates was if he died. Laird Dunstan was healthy and robust. He would have lived forever, had someone not murdered him. But Robertson planned to wed me, kill my uncle, and then me. He would have had my estates and the woman's hand in marriage. When he tried to take me before our wedding, I killed him. There was a madness in his eyes, and I could never understand why he wished to do the thing he did, though I suspected 'twas because he'd had too much to drink. Had he not, I might not have had a chance to thwart him where my uncle's life was concerned once I was wed to the beast."

"Do you see anything about us?"

She looked over at him, her eyes misted.

Malcolm's heart plummeted. "Anice, what is it that ye see?"

"I fear we will have much trouble when we return to Brecken, yet we must go home. I cannot delay returning there no matter what I feel."

He ran the reins through his fingers, then asked, "Did ye see Henry's response to my request to seek your hand?"

She looked away, tears spilling down her cheeks.

"Anice, lass?"

"Aye."

"What do you see?"

"He and many of his men will come. 'Tis no' good, Malcolm. He is angry and wants your head."

Malcolm considered her words, unruffled, then sat taller in the saddle. "But he does not get it, does he?"

"Och, Malcolm, how can ye even jest about a thing like this?"

"I am no' jesting, my lady," he responded, semi-seriously.

"I cannot see the outcome of things, only the danger present itself, sometimes, no' all the time. 'Tis frustratingly annoying." Anice shoved a loose curl back inside her veil.

To change the darkness of the subject, he asked, "Pray tell, will I win the archery contest, or will ye?"

She furrowed her golden brows at him. "I canna see everything that is ever going to happen in my life."

"Like ye dinna see if we have children?"

Clenching her teeth, she responded. "Nay. If the king has your head, I doubt we will have children."

Malcolm pondered the notion further, then smiled. Mayhap he might lose his head, but he had every intention of bedding the lady, and leaving her with a child of his making. Just the way she took in Kemp, the homeless urchin, showed Malcolm she was the kind of woman who would love a child of her own verra much. If he did nothing else for her, and nothing else with his life, he had every intention of giving her a bairn.

CHAPTER 15

Though Malcolm suspected Anice's mood would improve the closer they rode toward Brecken, she became even more fretful, which did not bode well with him. Though he'd managed to avoid answering his brothers' questioning glances, he knew before long he'd have to tell them about the lass's abilities.

Both were more superstitious than him, so he wasn't certain how they might take the news. Certainly, even for him, the notion she would see things in the future made his blood chill.

Most nights, they'd slept under the stars, separated, because he knew he would have wanted to bury himself deep inside her, not just hold her close to keep the chill out. Even now, his trewes grew uncomfortably tight. His reluctance to sleep with her did not go unnoticed by his brothers, and from time to time he caught them speaking to each other out of his and Kemp's hearing. Did they know he kept secrets from them, and they were now keeping secrets from him?

He hadn't realized the lass would come between his brothers and him and the thought unsettled him.

"I must take care of business," Anice said, motioning to

the ancient Caledonian Forest, the floor cushioned in fragrant pine needles, a light chilly breeze stirring the dark green needles of the Scots pine. The whooshing of the breeze through the branches, added to the pleasant sound of the gurgle of the rush of a stream nearby, the cold waters bubbling over rounded moss-blanketed rocks.

"Stray not too far, lass."

"'Tis my home," Anice said, motioning to Glen Affric. "Naught would harm me here."

'Twas too late to continue their journey with still several hours to travel and the horses dead tired. They'd pushed too far this day, yet he'd worried about them not getting the lady tucked safely inside her fortress. He would not argue with her about how safe the place was, but thieves and other disreputable men lived everywhere. If any knew she was King Malcolm's cousin, and the cousin to King Henry's wife, Anice might very well be taken hostage for ransom.

He paced with his sword in hand, waiting for the lady to reemerge.

The sound of crunching on the pine-needle floor, made him whip around. Relieved, he found Dougald before him. "Where is the lady?"

Malcolm waved at the trees behind him.

"Angus and I want to ken what the lady knows about..." Shaking his head, Dougald folded his arms. "Tell me she isna a witch."

"She is not, Dougald," Malcolm said, his words harsher than he had intended.

"She sees things God hadna intended," Dougald insisted.

"Have ye ever felt something was going to happen before it did?"

Dougald narrowed his eyes. "Ye cannot say that what I might have felt is the same as what she sees."

Malcolm shrugged a shoulder. "When the MacTaggart

tried to split your skull in two, ye whipped around and killed him first. Both James and I had started in your direction, trying to warn ye. There was too much fighting, too much noise for you to hear the man coming up behind ye, particularly when you were fighting one of his kin in front of you. Do you remember what ye said when we were partaking of a fine draught of whiskey once the battle ended later that night?"

Dougald's lips remained sealed in a thin gloomy line.

"Ye said, as I recall, that ye sensed the man behind ye. You did not hear him, did not see him, only felt he was there with a claymore raised to split your skull in two."

"'Tis no' the same," Dougald insisted.

"'Tis the same. What about the time James knew Angus was tupping a chambermaid? None of us heard a thing in the stables that morn, yet James somehow knew."

Dougald smiled, then quickly wiped the smile from his face.

"And Angus, too. He warned that our da intended to betroth me to two lasses at the same time. We looked for our da at every tavern we could think of that he oft frequented to put an end to his madness. No' knowing which ladies he meant to wed me to, we had no way of knowing where else he might have gone. Yet, by that next afternoon, all hell broke loose when the word spread I was to marry two women who thought I was the next MacNeill chief. Angus had never overhead our da speak of the matter, so how did he know? We never did figure out how."

Dougald blew out his breath. "I concede ye have a point, Malcolm. So, does she foresee something is the matter up ahead? I have seen the way she is, frightened, uneasy, and your furtive glances at her, just as concerned. What does she see?"

"Trouble. She cannot tell what it is, only that it exists." Malcolm didn't dare mention the king wanted his head, too. His brother would insist he not consummate the marriage, but Malcolm had every intention of doing so. If Henry wasn't happy about the marriage, he'd have it quickly annulled. But if Malcolm bedded Anice, Henry might have a change of heart.

"Where is the lass?" Angus asked, joining them.

Malcolm glanced back at the woods. Anice never took this much time to take care of personal business. He turned around and headed in the direction she had taken, his hands clammy, gripping his sword tightly in his fist, his heart thundering against his ribs.

"Anice?" he called out, his brothers stalking beside him, fanning out to help locate her.

***

Anice removed her wimple and veil and washed her face in the cold stream, but a red deer bolted across the water, promptly startling her, and she slipped into the frothing stream with a squeal. 'Twas annoying to let the deer scare her so, yet her blood chilled even more when she felt someone watched her, than from the wet gowns that now clung to her skin, or from struggling to regain her footing.

Chill bumps covered every inch of her skin. 'Twas not easy, as slippery as the moss-covered rocks were, to climb out of the swiftly moving water. Grasping for the multi-trunk rowan trees that lined the banks, all she could grab were handfuls of red berries. Her fingers were becoming numb while she fought being pulled downstream.

Even over the muffled roar of the water, she heard men crashing through the underbrush to reach her. With all her heart, she hoped to see Malcolm and his brothers. 'Twas not to be. The four men she saw wore short cut hair and English clothes. She didn't recognize any of them, though instantly she worried they were some of Edgar Atheling's men.

"Mistress, reach out your hand," one of the black bearded men said, stepping into the swift current. Immediately, he slipped on the rocks, landed on his butt in the rush of water, and swore out loud.

The others laughed. One of these tried to get to her, this one slighter of build, his hair also dark. This time, the man managed to grasp her hand and pulled her toward the bank, while the other two stood there waiting to grab her.

'Twas more than embarrassing, but what's more, she didn't trust their leering gazes as they took in her appearance, her hair dripping wet to her knees, her gowns plastered tightly against her skin.

"You will need to remove your clothes before you catch a death, mistress," the man said, still gripping her arm. The others chuckled.

"Thank ye, gentlemen." She attempted to sound confident and unafraid, yet the tremble in her voice both from the chill and panic, betrayed her.

Malcolm rushed forth with his brothers. "Thank ye for taking care of the lady."

The man who held her arm, tightened his hold, while the others swiftly moved in front of her, unsheathing their swords.

"She is with us." Dougald readied his sword. "The lady is my brother's wife."

The man's grip on her arm lessened for a moment, but when she tried to pull away, he tightened his hold again. "So say you."

She wondered then whether these men intended to kill Malcolm and his brothers and keep her for sport.

"Are ye from around here?" Malcolm asked.

She quickly shook her head.

The black bearded man, just as wet as she, gave a wicked smile. "We are from here. But you are not."

"I am the steward of Brecken." Malcolm's brows rose, challenging the man's response.

The men's faces fell. Which meant what? Anice's mind was failing her, mayhap because of the cold. She truly couldn't understand what their responses meant.

"Release my wife," Malcolm said, his eyes as black as

the deepest loch, his sword readied to run every last man through, his voice commanding, brooking no argument.

"What say you, Thomas?" one of the men said to the black bearded man.

"The steward of Brecken is gone and another takes his place," the man responded, his black beady eyes so small Anice didn't think they could narrow any further, but her heart nearly stopped when the man announced someone else had taken her steward's place without her permission.

"Aye, in the interim, mayhap, but he doesna have the king's blessing," Malcolm replied, taking a step forward.

The men kept their eyes focused on the threat before them, but Thomas shifted nervously. "Which king, pray tell?"

Were they Robert Curthose's men then? If Malcolm said he was under King Henry's orders, would the men attempt to slay them?

"King Alexander," Anice quickly said, though she wasn't sure why. If all went as planned, her cousin intended to marry Henry's illegitimate daughter, so he would not be backing Robert's rebellion either.

"And King Henry's orders," Malcolm said, his tone menacing.

The man holding her backed away, while the others lunged forth and attacked. She struggled to get away from the one, but no matter how much she kicked, yanked, and pulled, she could not break loose. Swords clanged against swords, men's words shouted in anger, the MacNeill brothers in Gaelic, the others in English. Then in surprise, the man who held her grunted and fell backwards, pulling her down on top of him.

"Run, my lady," Kemp shouted, slamming a tree branch against the brigand's head. Somehow, the lad had managed to trip the man, and sent him sprawling.

With another bash of the sturdy limb against the man's skull, Kemp's actions caused the man to release Anice, yet she could not run away. Only when Malcolm and his brothers had dispensed of the brigands, did she feel somewhat relieved.

"Anice," Malcolm said, sheathing his sword, then rushed to grab her up in his arms. Quickly he stalked back through the woods to their campfire in the clearing. "Ye are shivering overmuch, lass."

"We have no farmhouse this time, Malcolm," she said in warning.

"We are wed this time, lass. 'Tis no' the same as before."

She groaned. "What about your brothers? And Kemp?"

"If they were wed to ye, they would give no thought about it, and do the same as I will with ye."

That sent another trickle of shivers through her.

"I will only warm, ye lass, naught more. Ye will catch your death this verra eve if I do not warm you."

"But the others, we have no shelter for me to remove my clothes."

"They will busy themselves in burying the dead men first, lass. They will give us our much needed privacy."

Malcolm hurriedly helped her strip out of her clothes beside the flickering flames of the campfire, then once he'd covered her in his wool blanket, he pulled off his clothes, dampened by her own. Was it the cold that made his manhood stand out like a thick lance readied for the joust, or his touching her that made him so ready to have her?

He smiled when he caught her looking at his magnificent body. 'Twas oft said that women had bodies that were uncommonly beautiful, but gazing at his, she could see at least as far as he looked, some men were exceedingly beautiful, too.

"We should no' be together like this, Malcolm, unless we intend to consummate the marriage."

"I await only your word, Anice, to make it so."

He climbed under the blanket and settled on top of her

to warm her. She stilled his hands on her cheeks as an image came to her, horrifyingly clear. 'Twas Henry's physician who examined her to see if her maidenhead was still intact or not. If not, then what? She couldn't see any more than that. Would the king forgive them, or have Malcolm executed for it? If not, she still feared Henry would annul the marriage if they had not consummated it, and he would marry her to someone of his own choosing.

She stared into his eyes, full of longing and lust. "What about the curse?"

His mouth curved up.

She frowned. "'Tis no' amusing."

"Mayhap if I make love to you, the curse will be broken."

"You said that about the kiss."

"Aye. I wish to give Henry no reason to annul our marriage." Malcolm kissed her forehead.

She combed her fingers through his long hair. "I love my people."

"Aye, lass, I ken this."

"If Henry doesna approve our marriage, he could take Brecken from me."

Malcolm said nothing in response, just touched her face with a gentle stroke.

"You wanted land and property. If you remained married to me, and King Henry took these away from me, you would lose the chance to have a wife who owned thus."

"Aye."

Aye? 'Twas all he could say? Aye? "If...if we dinna consummate the marriage, King Henry will have his physicians examine me. When they discover you havena bedded me, he will have my marriage annulled and marry me off to someone else."

He sighed deeply and kissed her cheek. "We do not know this for certain."

"Aye, I do."

His gaze met hers. "Because ye know him so well?"

Not wanting to tell him how she knew, she said instead, "Malcolm, we have a choice—consummate the marriage and hope Henry will be reasonable, or if he takes away my lands, we will have to move elsewhere and may end up owning naught but the clothes on our backs. Or he may want you dead, in which case we will have to leave our home anyway."

"I love you, Anice, and dinna want to give you up for any man. Ye only have to say the word, and I will love you like a man does his wife."

She wasn't sure whether it was the notion Malcolm truly was her husband and she wanted him to make love to her despite where they were at present, or if her mind was so cold and numbed, she wasn't thinking properly. Or mayhap the threat of what she knew King Henry would have his physician do to her once he arrived at Brecken spurred her on, but in that instant, she made the decision, rash though it was.

She wrapped her arms around Malcolm's neck and in the most unthinkably brazen way, shifted underneath him until she'd spread her legs for him. Without being able to stop himself, he fell between her legs, his heated body pressed against her mound, sending an instant pang of need through her. At first, he seemed surprised, his brows arched in question, his mouth slightly parted, but when she lifted her pelvis slightly, encouraging him to take her, he didn't hesitate to respond.

His mouth settled over hers with heated passion, almost desperation, as if he were afraid she'd try to stop him in his quest. She had no intention of stopping him, not this time. King Henry would attempt to annul the marriage, she knew that now. If she were still a virgin, she'd have no choice. But she had wanted Malcolm from the moment she spied him astride his destrier, holding his hands outstretched to catch her, a brawny Highlander with no equal.

His hands held her face, while his tongue tangled with hers, brashly plundering her mouth, conquering her, claiming her, but 'twas only the beginning. His hands quickly slid down her arms, caressing, touching, memorizing the feel of her, as she explored the muscles in his arms and back, rippling with his actions. She moaned into his mouth, her body no longer chilled but heated deep inside, the area between her legs aching for relief.

"Och, Malcolm, make love to me before the others return."

"'Tis what ye desire?" Malcolm asked, his voice husky, his eyes heavily lidded, his hands stilled on her shoulders.

"Aye, do as ye will."

Smiling, his look was pure wickedness.

"That the church allows," she quickly added.

He chuckled, but the deep, sensual sound sent another rash of hot liquid heat streaking through her body. No married lady had ever told her how feverish a man's touches could be. Mayhap their husbands didn't do it right.

He lifted off her and at once she felt dejected. He couldn't mean to stop, could he?

His lips moved down her jaw, his whiskered chin scratching her sensitive flesh, then he moved further down, his hands cupping her breast while she raked her fingers through his wild unkempt hair.

Before she knew what he was about, his lips latched onto her taut nipple, sending a sweet tingling throughout her, but increasing the ache between her legs. "Malcolm," she pleaded breathlessly, "make love to me."

"Aye, that I am."

"Before your brothers return," she urgently scolded.

He tugged gently on her nipple, then suckled with passion, ignoring her wishes. 'Twas unlike anything she'd ever experienced. She reached down to touch his shaft, teasing her, rubbing against her thigh.

Before she could reach him, he slid his hand lower,

between her legs, cupped her mound, and slipped his fingers deep inside her. She bit back a moan, concerned even her people at Brecken several miles away would hear her animal-like growls of pleasure.

He moved his fingers to her swollen nub, stroking while her body climbed higher and higher, toward the peak of Aonach Shasuinn, reaching for the black sky, sprinkled with stars and the full orange moon. Her body shivered with exquisite fulfillment, her fingers gripping his broad shoulders, unable to concentrate on anything, but the wave of heat and pleasure that washed over her.

"Ye are sure bonny, sweeting," Malcolm whispered against her ear, then nibbled on the sensitive lobe. "Ye truly wish me to make love to ye?"

She was certain, surer of anything she'd ever decided in her life. "Aye, Malcolm, 'tis your turn."

***

Malcolm smiled at the winsome lass, her soft body still shuddering with the tremors he'd brought about. Shifting, he centered himself between her legs, but to his surprise, she wrapped her legs around him, her heels pressing against his arse. God's teeth, he hadn't expected that from the vixen and her action nearly made him spill his seed.

Returning his mouth to hers, he hoped to take her mind off the pain he knew she'd experience the first time they made love. His fingers tangled with her silky hair, but he feared his brothers would return soon now, though he knew they'd try to give them ample time to mate. He impaled her slowly, but she held her breath, and tightened her muscles, making it almost impossible to bury himself deep.

He moved his hands to her face and dove his tongue deeply into her mouth, taking her mind off what he was attempting to do between her legs. 'Twas the right move, because instantly she concentrated on his mouth, kissing him back like a woman well loved, and with a thrust of his staff between her legs, he penetrated her virgin territory. A muffled cry escaped her lips, and he quickly pulled out.

"Nay," she said, her hands clutching at his arse, which did nothing but stir his loins even further. "Dinna leave me yet."

"Are ye all right, Anice?"

"Aye, it…it hurt for a minute, but…but I dinna want you to leave me…yet."

He had no intention to as much as he wanted the lass. Sliding into her slowly, he quickly built up the pressure, encouraged by her heels digging into his arse, her fingers gripping his shoulders with passion. No woman had ever made him feel so complete, so loved, so satisfied. Her body rocked with his, and mews of pleasure escaped her swollen red lips, while her golden lashes hid her emerald eyes.

"Ye are breathing, lass?" he asked when he sensed she barely breathed.

She nodded vigorously. "Dinna…ask…me…questions, Malcolm."

He smiled and thrust deeper, wanting to draw out the pleasure, wanting it to last forever. 'Twas the sound of a twig cracking on the forest floor, that spurred him to release.

"Oh, Malcolm," she murmured against his head, her body clenching his staff with renewed spasms. His seed expended, he quickly glanced toward the woods and saw Dougald motion to him that all was well.

Malcolm knew Dougald would never have intruded, but they must have finished burying the men and figured he would have bedded Anice by now, if he was to do the deed at all. But having alerted him someone was in the woods, Dougald had to signal that it was only he, and not some brigand.

Malcolm rolled off her, and pulled her into his arms, showing his brothers that he was done with the most pleasurable of business, making the lady his wife. Thankfully, Anice was so spent she never noticed the intrusion. Instead, she sighed deeply against his chest and snuggled closer. "'Twas verra, verra good, my laird. Verra good."

He smiled and kissed her head, his groin already stirring with her touch. It would be a verra long night indeed.

***

Early the next morn, Malcolm stirred. He realized then, no one had disturbed his sleep so that he could pull guard duty. He unwrapped himself from Anice's warm, soft body, recovered her, and hurried to dress. Kemp stirred the fire and watched Malcolm when he pulled on his shoes. Dougald came out of the woods and nodded, his face unreadable.

Angus soon followed, his gaze shifting from Malcolm to Anice.

Malcolm knew what his brothers were thinking. He should have waited for King Henry's approval. Even when Anice and he had difficulties on their wedding night and Malcolm had joined his brothers, they had been relieved. Then again after Malcolm had rejoined Anice, and because of her own admission, they'd learned he and Anice had still not consummated the marriage. He assumed whatever Dougald had spied last eve had convinced them the lady was now his wife forevermore.

'Twas what he wanted, no matter the consequences. He would take her to France, or Italy, any place to keep his lady safe if the King was so inclined to disallow their marriage.

"Ye did not wake me," Malcolm said, sipping his mead, his look pointed. Had any tired because he had not relieved them, they would all have been at more risk.

His brothers both looked at the lady buried in his blankets.

"Ye should not have pulled extra duty," Malcolm insisted.

Dougald slapped him on the shoulder and handed him a piece of stale bread. "'Tis only because we figured ye needed to keep the lady warm." He motioned to the fire where her gowns were laid out to dry. "Without a stitch of clothes on, and I am certain her hair was still wet, she needed ye to keep her warm."

Anice stirred and everyone looked her way.

The lady was lovely, no doubt about it. Her golden red curls shimmered in the firelight; her green eyes stared at the men's shoes, but she did not raise her gaze to look at them. Instead, she licked her lips nervously and sent desire coursing straight to Malcolm's groin. Stifling a groan, he glanced at his brothers. Dougald shook his head at Malcolm, a perceptive smile tugging at his lips.

Angus stared at Anice, his gaze transfixed on her.

Dougald punched their youngest brother in the shoulder. "Go get the horses."

"Aye," Angus said, then stalked off.

"And ye, Kemp, go with him."

Kemp grumbled something under his breath but hurried to join Angus.

"Ye might want to accompany the lady into the woods today, Malcolm," Dougald suggested, though Malcolm didn't need the warning.

He had no intention of letting his lady out of his sight this time.

"Aye." He crossed to where her clothes were, grabbed them, then gave his brother a critical look.

Dougald nodded and turned his back.

"Come, Anice. I will accompany ye in the woods where you can dress."

"Aye, Malcolm." She attempted to rise without showing any bare skin, but the blanket dropped, exposing a creamy white breast, the rosy nipple, exposed to the chill in the air, grew taut.

His trewes instantly tightening, he was glad he'd made Dougald turn away. Grabbing Anice still wrapped in the blanket up in his arms, Malcolm carried her into the woods.

Sighing deeply, she rested her head against his chest. "Do your brothers know about us?"

"Aye, Anice."

She looked up at him, her eyes widened. "Ye told them?"

"Nay, lass. But 'tis naught to be ashamed of, nor naught that would have been easy to hide."

"They saw?" Her voice elevated, upset.

"Nay, lass," he lied to protect her fine sensibilities. "'Tis only for them to see the blush in your cheeks to know."

"Och, Malcolm, why did ye not tell me? I could have hidden my face until the coloring went away."

Chuckling under his breath, he set her down in the woods, then helped her to dress. "My brothers will say naught to anyone about it until ye are ready to let your people know the truth." He paused after pulling her shift over her head, and the hem fell to her ankles. "Ye are no' regretting last night, are ye?" He hoped that the cold had not affected her mind overmuch, and she had not truly wanted to consummate their marriage.

"Nay, Malcolm, ye are verra beautiful."

Again, he laughed. "'Tis ye who are beautiful, sweeting." He hurried to help her finish dressing, hiding her again in the monk's garment, then walked her back out of the woods.

"We should make it to Brecken today," she said to Malcolm, his brothers, and Kemp. "But I have to warn ye, I sense trouble ahead."

CHAPTER 16

Despite the disquiet plaguing her, Anice was gladdened that Malcolm and his brothers didn't denounce her for being a witch for sensing trouble ahead while they continued on their journey. After traveling for several hours, they arrived late afternoon across the loch from Brecken Castle, the six rounded towers, topped with blue banners, fluttering in the breeze a welcome sight. Thick stone walls covered in a fresh sheen of bright green moss, surrounded the palatial castle, elevated on the remains of a Roman motte, perched on an islet of the Loch Affric, and everything looked peaceful and quiet. In fact, too quiet.

To the north, the peak of Sgurr na Lapaich rose into the blue sky dotted with fluffy white clouds, while to the south Aonach Shasuinn watched over Glen Affric. Westward, the stunning view of the Five Sisters of Kintail could be seen. 'Twas a fine sunny day, though the sun was dropping out of sight beyond the craggy mountains and the air was beginning to cool. The breeze stirred the pine needles lining the loch's banks with a whispered whoosh and rippled the deep blue waters of the loch. A golden eagle soared high above while a red deer drinking from the water's edge caught sight of them and dashed off.

Stopping in the stand of pines and enjoying the view of her home from across the loch, overwhelming panic skittered across her bones, overshadowing her delight. Though naught appeared out of the ordinary, she sensed all was not as tranquil as appeared. No one from the village nearby fished in the river feeding the loch, nor was anyone gathering timber for their dwellings.

Malcolm rested his hand on her shoulder. "Anice, what think you?"

Dougald and Angus watched her with guarded expectancy. Kemp was crouched at the base of a tree, examining creeping ladies tresses among the mosses, pine needles, and heather—the small row of orchids resembling ladies' neatly braided hair.

The earth smelled sweet and damp after a summer's rain, while the pine fragrance and the smell of peat burning in a dwelling some distance away scented the air.

Nothing seemed amiss, except for the lack of people.

Glancing up at Malcolm, she wished she could assure him naught was wrong. But it would have been a lie.

Knowing only that she had to enter the castle and face whatever danger lay within, she ran her hands over Malcolm's bearded cheeks. "'Tis danger, but I know not from what."

"But we survive," Malcolm whispered, leaning closer to her ear, the warmth of his breath tickling her cheek, "because Henry will come seeking my head. Unless, 'tis him that is in yonder castle already."

She shifted her gaze from his liquid brown eyes full of love and life, and looked again at her castle, ignoring his attempt at humor to cheer her, unable to shake the cold in her bones. "'Tis time I returned without any further delay."

Malcolm helped Anice into her saddle. Kemp reached up and handed her a handful of creeping ladies tresses; the creamy white flowers looked ice white against his muddy fingers. She smiled, thinking to have her staff give him a bath as soon as they arrived at Brecken.

"Thanks be to thee, Kemp. 'Tis a lovely gesture." She lifted the flowers to her nose and smelled the sweet scent. She was home.

Pulling the monk's hood over her head to disguise that she was the Lady Anice in the event her concern that trouble lay ahead was warranted, the five travelers rode for Brecken's main entrance. They spied several men atop the wall walk watching their arrival, but she could not make out whether they were her men or someone else's. The metal portcullis was up and a gate guard, wearing brown wool trewes and a jacket, his brown hair cut short, hurried out to speak to them. "Who are ye, brothers, and what are you doing here?"

Malcolm looked to Anice, but she quickly shook her head, hoping he realized she didn't know who the man was, and feared foul play.

Malcolm drew taller in his saddle. "We have come here as Lady Anice's staff."

"Monks? She's not here," the man said tartly. "You will have to come back once she has returned."

"You dinna work for the lady," Anice said in her deepest, most threatening voice, trying to rein in her rage that she was not even welcome in her own castle, and that this usurper would turn her men away. "Who are you to give orders when she isna here?"

The gate guard stared curiously at her. Had her voice given away that she was a woman? Angus and Dougald exchanged glances.

A man dressed in chain mail standing nearby hurried for the keep, while another came off the wall walk and planted himself behind the gate guard. None of the men were on her staff.

"Lord Rousseau, the new steward, gives the orders," the gate guard replied brusquely.

"By whose authority?" Malcolm quickly asked before Anice exploded.

She clenched her teeth as her body heated. Malcolm's handling the man's arrogance at the moment was best for all concerned, unless she revealed she was Lady Anice. Certainly, as Malcolm's wife, and just a lady-in-waiting to Anice, she had no authority to tell this man where he could go...like she truly wished to.

"Baron Harold de Fontenot gave the order. He is taking Lady Anice to wive as soon as he returns here."

If he can find the lady. Anice gave a smug smile.

Malcolm yanked off his monk's robe. "I am Earl of Pembrinton, and by the power vested in me by Henry, King of England, I am the Lady Anice's new steward. My brothers are the new chamberlain and treasurer."

"And I am her new groom," Kemp proudly piped in.

"I take orders only from the baron and his steward. So you will have to take this up with him when he returns."

Dougald and Angus both pulled off their robes, making it easier to get to their weapons.

A tall grim, black bearded man with a scar cutting across his brow, giving him a perpetual scowl, stalked toward them with the knight from the wall walk at his side. "I am Lord Rousseau. What is the trouble here?" With a dark look, the baron's appointed steward regarded the MacNeill brothers' show of force with disdain, then turned to Anice.

She pulled the brown woolen hood back and motioned to Malcolm. "Lady Anice's new steward, Earl of Pembrinton." She quickly added for the benefit of a man who'd just joined the group who was on her own staff, "And I am Countess Pembrinton and lady-in-waiting to Lady Anice."

The knight's brown eyes widened, though he spoke not a word. Thomas, only five years her senior and when he'd been the former marshal's son, the lad she'd liked to tease most, one of her uncle's most faithful staff, a man she'd oft admired, and she suspected had a wee bit of interest in her, too. "I ken, Thomas, the marriage is a surprise. Do tell everyone you can, will ye?"

"Aye, my lady," he said quickly, his eyes shifting from her to Malcolm, then he made an expeditious bow and stormed up the stone stairs to the wall walk.

"My laird," Anice said, facing Malcolm, "mayhap you can handle this matter with the baron's laird. I wish to wash some of the dust off before Lady Anice arrives." In truth she wished to make it known at once that her people were not to reveal her identity at any cost.

Malcolm turned to Dougald. "You and Angus speak with Lord Rousseau and spread the word concerning our appointments. I will meet you in the hall shortly."

"Aye," they both said.

"Can I go with ye, my lady?" Kemp asked, sliding from Angus's horse, and hitting the ground in his tattered leather shoes with a small thump.

"You are my groom, so of course, Kemp. I have many things for you to do. I wish you to take special care of my horse, Mystic. But also, I must have a new set of clothes made for ye." After she ensured he had a bath.

The captain of her guard approached, his dark hair hanging loosely at his shoulders, his icy blue eyes ominous, but otherwise his emotions were tightly guarded. "My lady—"

"Aye, MacTavish. So good to see ye again. Spread the word to any that work here Laird MacNeill and his brothers serve Lady Anice, so they should be granted access to come and go as they please. Also, they are investigating the death of Laird Thompson and the disappearance of our other staff." She cleared her throat, knowing the captain of her guard would be shocked to hear the next news from her lips. "I have married Laird MacNeill."

MacTavish stared at Malcolm, then shifted his gaze to Anice.

Smiling, she said, "Aye, 'tis true. I am wed. Ye thought it would never come about?"

MacTavish didn't say a word, but she could just imagine him wondering what would happen now that they had a new laird to govern the place, when her poor people must have believed the baron was taking over.

"It would seem, Lord MacNeill, that your lady thinks she runs the place," Rousseau sarcastically said, his scarred brow raised.

"The lady has lived here all her life. She knows these people better than any of us." Malcolm smiled at Anice, then gave the guard a stern look. "Lady Anice's men will be manning the guard post from now on. You are relieved of your duty at once." To MacTavish he said, "See to it that my orders are carried out."

"Aye, my laird," MacTavish said with a curt bow, then he took command of the situation.

Malcolm faced Anice. "Are you ready for your bath, my lady?"

"Aye, before the evening meal."

They rode toward the stables where the marshal hurried to greet them. "My lady," Heath said, running his hand over her horse's muzzle. His dark green eyes were troubled. "We worried something terrible had happened to ye. The baron's men said Fontenot was searching for ye, but that ye and your escort had vanished without a trace."

She explained as much as she could to the laird in charge of the stables and told him to pass the information to all who he could that she was Lady MacNeill and she would do the same.

"'Tis a dangerous game you play, my lady."

"I am sure the baron had my uncle killed, Heath. I will no' marry a man who is a murderer."

"Aye, my lady. We will do the best we can."

"Do ye ken how many of the baron's men have settled inside the castle and grounds?" Malcolm asked.

Heath shook his head, his windswept blond hair sweeping his shoulders. "Nay, my laird. They come and go at will. Though had we known the circumstances, we would have fought to keep them out."

"Tell the others there will be trouble," Malcolm warned.

Then she, Malcolm, and Kemp walked into the keep where five of the baron's men were speaking with ten of her men. Spreading the word to her people wasn't going to be as easy as she'd hoped.

Instantly, her men's expressions turned from surprise to bridled relief to see her. Before they could greet her, she hurriedly said, "I have returned ahead of the Lady Anice." She ignored their bewildered expressions and continued, "As her lady-in-waiting, I wished to get her room ready for her. But I am no longer Lady Agnes. I have married Laird MacNeill, Earl of Pembrinton, our new steward, by order of His Grace, Henry, King of England. I am now Lady MacNeill. Laird MacNeill's brothers, Dougald and Angus are our treasurer and chamberlain."

Several of the men exchanged looks and she knew they were not happy that the baron had first sent his men to take over her castle, and now King Henry sent others to do the same thing.

"They are also investigating the death of Laird Thompson and the disappearances of our other men. So I..." She paused, cleared her throat, and started again. "The Lady Anice has ordered that all cooperate with these men to discover the truth of what has happened as quickly as possible."

"Aye, Lady MacNeill," Ewen said. The others bowed to her and she curtsied in return.

"The word must be spread to the rest of our people at once. I wish no mistake in being called Lady Agnes, as I will now be referred to as Lady MacNeill."

"Aye, my lady."

One of her ladies-in-waiting hurried to speak with her,

but Anice spoke first, "I wish a bath at once, Nola, before Lady Anice returns."

Nola flipped her red braid over her shoulder and glanced behind her. Her green eyes widened to see the Highlander stranger. She whispered to Anice, "I overheard what was said, my lady. Some of the other ladies are spreading the word. But where is Mai?"

"We ran into trouble and had to leave her behind. I'll send a party to get her at as soon as we've ensured the castle is free of vermin." Anice tousled Kemp's dusty brown hair. "This is my new groom, Kemp. I want him cleaned up and a new set of clothes made for him. Then he'll work for Heath."

Another of her ladies came forward and quickly curtsied to her. "I will see to the young man."

"Aye, Mary, and make sure he has a good scrubbing."

"Nay," Kemp quickly objected.

"If ye wish to work for me, you will have to bathe from time to time."

Mary tenderly wrapped her arm around Kemp. The poor lady had lost her husband and son to a fever earlier in the year, and she seemed at once to take a liking to the lad.

Anice headed for the wide stairs leading to the second floor and her chamber.

"Are you truly wed to Laird MacNeill?" Nola asked, her brow wrinkled, her green eyes narrowed.

"Aye, that she is," Malcolm said, below them on the stairs, amusement lacing his words. Anice looked behind her, surprised to see Malcolm following them. He winked and added, "I stay with ye, or one of my brothers does at all times, remember?"

She gave him a barbed look. "I am taking my *bath*."

"Aye, and until this deadly business is uncovered, you will always be accompanied."

Trying to conceal her embarrassment in front of her ladies, she pursed her lips. "Verra well, you can stand outside my chamber while I bathe."

TERRY SPEAR

***

Malcolm smiled at Anice, loving the way she twisted her hands together, the way her cheeks colored beautifully even underneath a coat of dust. He had no plan to stand outside her chamber while his bonny bride bathed. In fact, he had every intention of washing the grime off her soft skin.

When they reached the second floor, five ladies hurried into Anice's chamber, carrying buckets of cold water while others waited for water to be warmed over the kitchen fire on the first floor of the keep.

He watched Anice take a deep satisfying breath to see her chambers again, most likely thankful to God that she was no longer in the king's guest chambers within his reach. She turned her attention to the pale blue curtains left open to allow the cool air from the narrow windows to refresh the blue bedding. She glanced at him when he shifted his gaze back from the bed to her. Her cheeks grew red. 'Twas not the same to make love to him in the wide-open spaces, as contemplating such a thing in her verra own bed with all her staff knowing, he imagined.

The women glanced at Malcolm, seemingly not sure what to do with the lady now that she was a married woman, which made him believe none of the lasses were married. Finally, the striking redheaded Nola said, "Did you wish us to undress ye, my lady?"

"Aye. Laird MacNeill will leave the chamber."

He crossed his arms, spreading his legs farther apart as if bracing himself for battle and to show he was here to stay. 'Twas not the same as it had been at Arundel when he'd had to leave Anice in the chambers alone at Mae's insistence. He had no intention of granting Anice's wish.

"He is no' doing as you say, my lady," Nola said, her voice terse, her look at Malcolm, piercing.

"He will." Anice sat down on a cushioned bench and the ladies began to remove her shoes, hose, veils, and wimple.

250

Malcolm sat on her bed, the ropes holding the mattress groaned slightly. "You may remove my shoes and hose also."

The ladies' eyes grew big.

Anice smiled. "If he doesna do a good job as a steward, he can be our court jester."

The ladies smiled, but none dared to laugh.

Malcolm smiled, not one to take offense at Anice's jabs. He wanted to prove to her and her ladies that he was now the lady's husband and laird. "Hurry, ladies, I am waiting for more of my wife's garments to come off."

The ladies giggled, all but Nola. She took a hard stance and turned to Anice. "Are ye truly husband and wife, my lady? Ye are no' pretending to protect yourself from Baron Fontenot's men and are providing a ruse?"

Anice took a deep breath. "Aye, we are truly wed."

Nola quickly glanced back at Malcolm, her look concerned. Had she worried her hostilities toward him would cause her trouble now that she knew he was the laird of the manor?

"Ye married at Arundel?" Nola asked Anice, her voice confused.

"Nay, on the way here."

The ladies began to unbraid Anice's hair.

"But...did King Henry approve?" Nola persisted.

Anice patted Nola's hand and said to Malcolm, "She is my half-cousin, my laird, and overmuch concerned for me, if ye didna ken."

Malcolm noted the resemblance, the green eyes, bright and sensual, the full, naturally red lips, and the red in their hair, though Anice's was like shafts of satiny gold light tinged red, whereas Nola's was red with highlights of spun gold.

"Aye, ye are drowning in the loch of troubles from time to time, my lady, and if Mai is no' here to watch over ye like a mother hen, 'twill be my responsibility." Nola's eyes darted back to Malcolm.

She had the same kind of fierce determination to protect her mistress like Mai did, but the lady appeared to be more Anice's age. Mayhap, a year or two older.

"You need not worry, Nola. All will be well once we prove Laird Fontenot is the criminal we are sure he is. What has happened to the widow Lady Thompson?"

"She returned to her brother in Fife with her three young bairns."

Anice stared at the floor for a moment, then nodded. "'Tis a shame, but understandable. What about Laird MacKnight's wife?"

The ladies remained silent.

Anice frowned and stood. "What has happened?"

"She died, my lady," Nola said, her face grief stricken.

Anice swallowed hard and Malcolm rose from the bed, worried Anice would faint. "When?"

One of the ladies wrung her hands. "The night Laird MacKnight vanished, my lady. Everyone was so concerned that your staff had disappeared, no one noticed that the lady had failed to appear at evening meal, too."

Anice sat hard on the bench. "How had she died?" her voice was hollow and faint.

"'Twas like your uncle, my lady. We found her sleeping in the chamber already, only she was not sleeping," Nola said.

"Poison?"

"No one could say. It did not appear that she had had anything to eat or drink before she lay down."

"It had to be poison." Anice looked up at Malcolm, hovering over her.

"Are you going to be all right, Anice?" he asked, rubbing her arm, his tone concerned.

"Aye, thank you for your thoughtfulness. But you ken, you are supposed to call me Agnes."

He shook his head, then took her hand and kissed it. "It

will take a bit of getting used to."

She turned to her ladies. "What of Laird Iverson's mistress?"

"Left, my lady. Went home to her father."

Anice rose to her feet and raised her hands so they could remove her dusty bliaut. "What is being said about Laird Thompson's murder?"

Nola cleared her throat. "That Laird MacKnight did it, my lady, as much as the two hated one another."

"Aye. And there has been no sign of either him or Laird Iverson?"

"Nay, my lady."

Suddenly, the door was thrown open, and it banged against the wall. Instantly, Malcolm unsheathed his sword. The woman who burst into the room screamed at the sight of him, half of her dark brown tresses loose from her plaited hair, her brown eyes wide with fright. "Oh, my lady," she said with her hand to her breast. "Tell me 'tis no' true."

"Morrigan," Anice said, giving her a hug. "If ye are asking if I am wed to his lairdship," she motioned to Malcolm and continued, "aye 'tis true."

Morrigan stared at Malcolm for a minute, then looked back at Anice. "But Baron Fontenot has told us he will wed ye."

"Nay."

Malcolm resheathed his sword, and removed his belt, hoping to stir the ladies to work faster on Anice's clothes. The ladies waited for Anice to tell them what to do next when she stood in her translucent shift.

Her tone firm, Anice said, "Laird MacNeill, you canna stay."

"The ladies will have to get used to us being man and wife." Though he suspected it would be easier for them to get used to it than Anice. He pulled off his shirt and smiled as the ladies considered his broad, bare chest.

"You are supposed to be investigating—"

"I am supposed to protect ye, too. We will investigate later, after we have had our bath, evening meal, and a good long rest."

She folded her arms.

He yanked off a shoe, and then the other. "Ladies, you may leave now. I will help your ladyship take her bath."

The ladies didn't move an inch and looked to Anice to see her response.

"Laird MacNeill...," Anice said, her tone more pleading now.

He took her shoulders in his hands and kissed her mouth with pent-up passion, trying to ignore Nola and Morrigan's gasps and the other ladies' giggles.

Anice closed her eyes and tangled her fingers in his hair, grabbing handfuls and holding on with dear life. 'Twas what he'd wanted to do for many a mile. The lady was now his and he would not have her say otherwise. She leaned against his chest, bracing her soft body against his arousal and moaned softly when he nibbled on her ear. 'Twas only the beginning before the evening meal.

When he released her, he smiled to see her cheeks beautifully colored.

Flustered, Anice motioned to her ladies to leave.

"Remember," Malcolm said, "she is my wife and lady-in-waiting to Lady Anice. Spread the word to all you can for her safety sake."

Nola frowned at him, then quit the room, while Morrigan gave him one more long look before she exited behind her.

"Aye, my laird," one of the older ladies said, humor reflecting in her voice, then hurried out of the chamber, shutting the door behind them.

"You ken, my laird, they are my ladies to dismiss, no' yours."

"Aye, but if you do not have them do as I want, I will."

She tilted her chin up and crossed her arms. "And what

exactly do you want?"

He smiled at her and unfolded her arms. "Ye, my lady. Every bit of ye."

CHAPTER 17

Malcolm pulled up Anice's chemise shift and dropped it on the bench, then lifted her, and set her in the bath, splashing water on the floor. He admired Anice's creamy skin, and soft curves, a patch of golden curls at the joining of her thighs, her rosy nipples already peaked and ready for his touch. And he, like a randy lad, was ready to take the lady, dust covered or no'.

"What have you in mind, Malcolm?" Anice asked, her lips and eyes smiling, her gaze shifting from his to his shaft pressing hard at his trewes, throbbing with need.

"Bathing with ye, though it might be a wee bit tight. I will order a larger tub made on the morrow."

"And embarrass me?"

He yanked off his hose and dropped his trewes, then climbed into the tub behind her, and slid his legs on either side of hers. The feel of her soft thighs resting against his muscular ones, heated his blood. She leaned against his steel hard shaft, and he stifled a groan. "When you're swelling with child, you will need a bigger tub."

Chuckling, she shook her head. "Nay, I would no'."

He pulled her long hair aside and kissed her cheek.

"You do not know what you do to me, Malcolm."

"I do, lass."

"I cannot help worrying that if His Grace disapproves of our having married—"

"You worry more than even my brother, Angus, does."

She smiled. "No' that much."

He grabbed two cloths and a bar of soap on a table beside the tub. Lifting the soap to his nose, he sniffed the aromatic herbs, attempting to get his mind off what he wished to do with Anice next—lift her onto his lap and bury himself deep inside her. "I have never seen a solid bar of soap before, only the soft soap made of mutton fat, wood ash, and natural soda. What is this made of, lass?" He handed her a cloth, then pulled her hair aside and ran the other wet one over her back.

"'Tis a gift from my cousin, Her Grace, from a knight who traveled to Spain. 'Tis made of olive oil, soda, and a little lime. Some kind of sweet-smelling herbs were added, but I know not what. Does it please you?"

He wetted it and ran it over her back. "Aye, lass, it smells fine. But 'tis you sitting between my legs, that smells even better."

"Shush, Malcolm. You shouldna speak like that."

He gave a short bark of laughter.

"You gave me a nice back rub before. I shall give you one this eve in return."

The thought of her bent over him, her skin brushing against his, her tender strokes, sent a thrill straight to his loin. "Seems we willna be having the archery competition after all. Mayhap we will have to come up with another challenge."

"Aye, that we will."

"Think ye love me, Anice?" He knew she did, but he wanted her to say it repeatedly, to assure him it was truly so. 'Twas fate that she should escape from the Arundel chambers and slip into his hands, then fall in love with him the way she did.

She ran the wet cloth over his knee and down his leg. 'Twas not the warm water that heated his flesh, but the way her hands touched him with a gentle caress. Never had he delighted in having a bath like this eve. "Aye, Malcolm. I love ye because you keep me safe, you see?"

"You feel safe in my arms?" He couldn't contain his amusement that she would mention this, and not that giving her pleasure when he ravished her had anything to do with it. He wrapped his arms around her, giving her a hearty embrace. Leaning forward, he nuzzled his face against her neck, and ran the slippery bar of soap over her breasts.

"Aye, I feel safe in your arms, my braw Highlander," she purred.

The sound of her mews nearly did him in.

"What if I just post myself outside your chambers wearing my chain mail? Would this no' make you feel safer?"

"Nay."

"Why no'? I would keep you safe." His voice grew huskier while his shaft throbbed with needed release as he ran the cloth over her satiny shoulders. "'Tis no' because there is something else I do that pleases ye, is there?"

"Malcolm—"

"Aye, 'tis easy to say if you truly love me."

She laughed. "I have already told ye I love you. Think you I do not?"

"Nay, I just need to hear you say it, lass." He dipped the cloth lower. She leaned against him, but he quickly shifted to ease the agony.

"From the moment I saw ye, I knew you to be the one. Then I worried you were married." She switched the cloth to his other knee, stirring his loins with her affectionate touch.

"No' like ye, four times betrothed, lass."

She chuckled. "Only on paper. Queen Matilda said you wouldna be satisfied unless you had an English bride."

He groaned, irritated that her cousin had infected her with this idea. "Is that where you have had this notion all along?"

"Do not you say you have no' wanted one, Malcolm MacNeill."

He reached around her arms and ran the cloth over her breasts. Her blushing nipples begged for his kisses, as he wondered how in the world he'd ever come to the notion he'd wanted an English bride.

"The Earl of Northampton mentioned it as well. Even his steward made the mistake of thinking me English. Dinna tell me you havena been trying to find one."

He sighed deeply. "Aye, you are right, but you should have heard my brothers when we were at Arundel. As soon as I saw ye, they knew I had fallen for ye, no matter how I tried to tell myself it was not so."

"Why did you tell yourself that?"

"Foolishness, pure and simple, Anice. When it came to the meal, though, I had already had an audience with the king and was told the circumstances of your plight at Brecken, I did not have to sit by ye. But I wanted to. When I caused you to faint and you came down for the evening meal, you do not know how anxious I was when you hesitated to sit by me."

"There were no other seats for me."

He squeezed her breasts playfully, the soft mounds filling his large hands, the urge to quit the bath as quickly as he could, consuming him. Yet, he reigned in the notion, wanting to enjoy every new experience with her to the fullest. Leaning forward, he nibbled her ear. "There were plenty of seats, but you chose to sit by me. Had you no' I would have moved to sit by ye."

"If there were no seats by me?"

He growled. "I would have forced someone to move. So, Anice, ye have no regrets?"

"I love ye, Malcolm. But I worry about the—"

He lifted her legs on top of his. When he ran his cloth between her legs, she squealed. "What are you doing, Malcolm?"

"Washing ye." He swept the soft fabric up and down. But not being able to feel her folds like he wished, he dispensed with the cloth. Stroking her swollen nub with his fingers, he elicited a deep-throated moan from her. His own body ached to enter her.

She leaned back against him, attempting to arch toward his hand. His erection throbbed against her back. Didn't she realize how much agony he was in?

"Anice, lass, do you no' know how much a man pains when he cannot fulfill his commitment to the lady he loves?"

She started to pull away from him. "Then we must stop this at once so you will not be in pain."

He held her tightly. 'Twas not the reaction he expected. "Nay, lass. I will suffer."

She chuckled. "I would not wish you to."

Trying not to send the water splashing overmuch, or seem too eager, he climbed out of the tub, grabbed a towel, and offered his hand to pull Anice from the water. "Time for ye to fulfill your promise."

"A back rub."

He'd never last.

"Afterward, love," he said, drying every curve of her body, his hands lingering overlong on her breasts.

She touched his cheek, and smiling said, "They are dry, my laird."

He smiled, towel dried her hair, then dropped the wet towel on the floor. 'Twas her turn next, and in her teasing vixen way, she dried his chest, letting the edge of the towel dangle against his erection. Gritting his teeth, he ran his fingers through her damp hair, trying to ignore the way her touch sizzled against his skin. "Enough!" he growled when she tried to dry his shaft.

He would lose his seed if he allowed her to touch him

any further.

Lifting her in his arms, he stalked toward the bed, the bonny lass the greatest victory he'd ever won. Her pink skin shimmered in the soft glow of candlelight, and she smelled like a bit of flowery heaven.

She'd never need look any further for her Highland hero, and he was damned pleased she'd chosen him. Though he still couldn't believe he'd have considered anyone else, once he'd caught the vixen dangling from the Arundel keep.

Easing her onto the bed, he kissed her forehead, her eyelids, her blushing cheeks, and full red lips. She grabbed handfuls of his tangled hair and held on tight when he deepened his kiss, her tongue mating with his in a nubile dance, teasing, caressing, commanding him. He smiled, loving the way his wife felt, the sweetness of her kisses, the way her body arched, seeking fulfillment, the way her eyes gazed at him with adoration.

She sighed, the sound music to his ears. Her fingers released his hair, and drifted over his shoulders, down his arms, heating the skin wherever she touched.

Leaning over, he brushed kisses along her jaw, down to the hollow of her neck, lower still to the fullness of her breast. He ran his tongue over her taut nipple, took it in his mouth, and gently suckled.

"Make love to me," she pleaded.

He smiled. "I am, lass. Ye are much too impatient." Moving his hand to the juncture between her legs, he felt the heated moisture pooled there, dampening her curls. Rubbing her swollen nub, he brought her panting and arching, her fingers dug into his shoulders, her legs parting further, inviting him in.

Crying out his name, the sound of her voice echoed off the stone walls. She clamped her hand over her mouth, her eyes wide.

Malcolm laughed out loud. Before she came down from her peak, he penetrated her heated sheath and did her bidding, made love to her as a Highland husband would, with deep, thorough thrusts, filling her narrow chasm, stretching her to take his size.

'Twas not the same as making love to the lass in the Caledonian Forest with the smell of pine needles scenting the air with only blankets to cover the spongy forest floor. But the fragrance of flowers scattered in the bedding and of the lass's soap-scented skin, made for just as wondrous an experience as he loved her against the straw mattress.

Anice wrapped her legs around him again, digging her heels against his arse, spurring him to thrust harder, deeper. Her body trembled again with completion, her body clenching his shaft with fine tremors, and he quickly followed, releasing his warm seed deep inside her. She was like no other woman, his bonny lass, and he would give her up to no man.

When he kissed her lips, swollen and well-loved already, he felt her tense. "Lass?"

A pounding at the door forced his heart to jump. He covered Anice with the blanket and assumed it was trouble or no one would interrupt them at a time like this. Had Anice sensed the difficulty already? "Aye?" he called out, his voice irritated.

"We have trouble, Malcolm," Dougald said.

"I'll send your maids in to help you to dress," Malcolm said to Anice, then grabbed his trewes. "What's happening, Dougald?"

"Fontenot is here, blazing mad."

Malcolm hastened to dress, then hurried out of the chamber, shutting the door behind him.

Anice grabbed her bliaut, threw it on, then dashed out of the chamber after Malcolm. "Malcolm!"

He was halfway down the stairs with Dougald but whipped around and stalked back toward her. "You need to be more dressed, lass," he said, his voice lighthearted. He cupped her face in his hands and kissed her lips with tenderness. "More tonight, love."

**

"Be careful, Malcolm." Anice couldn't help worrying things could get out of hand as quickly as an arrow sought its mark.

"Aye, lass." He glanced down at her feet and tsked. "Where are you hose and shoes?"

She wiggled her toes. "By the bath where I left them."

"Do you even have your shift on?"

Her cheeks grew hot and his eyes rounded. He gathered her in his arms and carried her back to her chamber. "I will send your maids to ye. Do not leave here until you are properly dressed. No' unless we are alone together. Then the less you wear the better." He kissed her lips again. "Dinna worry about me. We will be fine."

"I dinna want to lose my first real husband."

"I have more unfinished business with ye. You will no' get rid of me that easily."

"Malcolm, make the baron wait." She touched his shirt. "Let me dress before you go down."

Nola hurried into the room. "Beg your pardon, my laird, my lady, but Laird Dougald wished me to help my lady dress."

"Aye. She is missing a few articles of clothing." He swept his finger down Anice's cheek. "I will see you at the meal shortly, and we will retire early." He kissed her cheek and hurried out of the room.

"Hurry, Nola, and help me. Where are my other ladies?"

"You have no shift on, my lady?" Nola asked, when she saw the shift lying on the bench.

"I need a clean one from the trunk. But do hurry. You are getting to be like Mai."

"Kemp told us Mai stayed behind because you worried about her safety," Nola said, but the way she spoke and the look she had, made Anice believe her half-cousin wanted to know the details.

"Aye, I worried about her." Despite how close she was to her, Anice had no intention of telling her the half of what had happened. Like Mai, Nola would be telling her what she should not have done when there was naught she and Malcolm could have done differently.

Mary hurried into the chamber. "Wynne is taking care of the boy. Laird MacNeill asked me to help you dress."

"Thank ye. I must hurry down at once."

"Your hair is still wet," Nola said, lifting the damp strands.

"Aye, just plait it. After the meal I can dry it by the fire."

Nolan reached for Anice's bliaut and began to pull it up.

"We are supposed to be dressing her, no' undressing her," Mary said. She gasped when the gown was around Anice's thighs and she wore no shift.

"Where's your shift, my lady? And your hose and shoes?" she asked, her voice filled with surprise.

Anice pointed to her trunk. "I hadna time to dress. Hurry, ladies. I worry about Laird MacNeill."

"Kemp told us the laird took the baron's horses and scattered them to the wind."

The ladies both giggled.

"Aye, I hope the baron will no' be to upset with my laird."

Nola pulled a shift over Anice's head, then helped Mary with a blue bliaut. Afterward, they secured a pale blue silk girdle.

"He told us all about the baron trying to find ye," Nola said.

"That is why he must not know who I am."

"Ye are twirling your hair between your fingers like ye always do when you dinna want me to know something." Nola hurried to help Anice with her hose and shoes. "What are you no' telling me, my lady?"

She had no intention of revealing the way of things. "Naught that need concern you."

Nola shook her head, her green eyes studying Anice's. "Then I ken I do. I'm no' sure everyone in the castle realizes you have wed the laird. I fear someone will make a mistake."

Mary didn't say a word, just watched Anice to see what she would reveal.

Anice took a deep breath and patted Nola's shoulder. "We will do the best we can."

After she was dressed and her hair plaited, she hurried out of the chamber with her ladies following behind.

Most of the courtiers had already gathered for the evening meal as sconces lighted the great hall.

As soon as she walked into the hall, everyone grew quiet. Not good. She was being treated like she was the lady of the manor. What would the baron think?

Quickly the conversation renewed to a dull roar when her people realized their mistake.

Nola whispered, "It will be difficult for everyone to play this ruse, my lady."

"Aye. My laird is not here. I dinna see the baron either."

"Have you seen him before, then? Will he no' recognize you, too?"

She saw him all right...naked at the farmhouse. She couldn't let her ladies-in-waiting or anyone else know it, lest they discover she'd been naked with Malcolm before she was wed. "I saw him but was lucky he didna see me in return."

About sixty men that she didn't recognize stood at the tables. Most likely they served as the baron's retinue.

Then her gaze rested on Canon, short cropped, black hair, black eyed, stockily built, speaking with another of the baron's men, the faux bard. How in God's teeth had he been released from the earl's dungeon?

Quickly she turned, but not before he caught her eye. She bolted out of the great hall.

"My lady, what's the matter?" Nola asked, as she and Mary hurried after her.

"A man who knows me on the baron's staff just saw me."

"Then be the Lady Anice and—"

"Nay, no' yet. We must prove the baron..." She stopped walking when she spied Malcolm, his brothers, and the baron headed straight toward her while they made their way to the hall.

Malcolm and his brothers saw her, but the baron had his head turned toward Malcolm as he spoke.

She quickly ducked into the kitchen with her ladies. Would Malcolm realize there was something wrong?

"What are we to do, my lady?"

"I must exchange clothes with someone. He cannot discover I am here. If only we could throw this Conan into the dungeon." She wrung her hands, then turned to Nola. "Were any of the baron's men here the night Lady Thompson died?"

"Nay, my lady."

Anice began to pace, deep in thought. "If that is the case, someone on our staff is working for the baron. He would know I am pretending to be Lady MacNeill." She cursed inwardly.

Angus hastened into the kitchen, his brown eyes darkened with concern. "What is wrong? Malcolm says you are troubled about some—"

"Conan! Did you no' see him in the great hall?"

Angus's brown eyes darkened. "Nay, he must have left the hall after you did. Probably in search of ye."

"We have another problem."

"What is that, my lady?"

"A traitor is amongst my people. Whoever he is, he knows I am pretending to be Lady MacNeill."

"But, my lady, you truly are Lady MacNeill," Angus gently reminded her.

"I ken, Angus," she said, exasperated. "I mean, just that I am the steward's wife and that he is no' the laird of the manor and I, the lady."

"I have to tell Malcolm about this, but he wanted me to find out what was wrong and escort you to the table."

Anice swept a loose curl away from her face. "My plan has gone awry. Escort me then, as Lady MacNeill, lady of Brecken Castle."

Angus smiled. "'Tis about time." He held out his arm to her.

"Why? Now your brother can be laird of the manor?"

"Aye, my lady."

She shook her head. "He better no' plan to make too many changes."

"He will have to find a steward."

"Most likely he will wish to elevate Dougald to the position."

"Aye, my lady, as the older brother of the two of us. So he will have to find a new treasurer."

Angus walked into the hall with Anice's hand lightly touching his sleeve. Everyone grew quiet.

She crossed the hall to the head table, glancing over where Conan had stood, but he and some of the other men were missing. Looking for her?

Baron Fontenot impressed her no more naked than now fully clothed. She curtsied to Malcolm, and he bowed to her, but the look on his face showed his concern.

Before Malcolm could ask her what was going on, she raised her tankard. "To Laird MacNeill, our new laird of the manor."

Everyone stood holding their tankards in surprise, but no one responded. She smiled.

"And to the Lady Anice, now Lady MacNeill," Angus added to help to explain the situation.

Everyone from Anice's court cheered and drank to the newly married couple.

But the baron and his men did not.

Anice and Malcolm sat and everyone else did, too.

"I do not know what you are trying to pull, but His Grace gave me permission to have your hand in marriage," Fontenot said gruffly to Anice.

"Actually," Malcolm said as he took Anice's hand in his, then kissed it, "the king was considering five other Norman lairds for her hand as well."

"*You* are not Norman."

"Nay. My people descend from the Irish king, Niall of the Nine Hostages, therefore, I am a true Scot. When King Henry learned that one of his Norman lairds murdered Anice's uncle to obtain her hand in marriage and her properties, His Grace agreed to allow me to wed her."

The baron stared at Malcolm with cold hatred. "Why could it not have been you and not a Norman lord who murdered her uncle?"

"Because, as the king verra well knows, I did not ask for the lady's hand in marriage."

"Nay," Anice said, her chin tilted up to make a point, "Laird MacNeill didna. He asked the king for an English bride and was verra sincere about it. Malcolm didna know me, wasna interested in marrying me—"

"Yet he did. Why?" the baron asked, his tone icy.

"Why we fell in love, Baron Fontenot. He saved me from a fall from a verra high place and from then on, we couldna be separated."

Malcolm took her hand in her lap and squeezed it. Was he thinking of how he'd slipped his hand up her gown to her bare thigh at Arundel? She was.

The baron stared at the table for a moment, then looked at Malcolm, his voice dark. "You were with her in the farmhouse." He rose from his chair. "I should have run you through when you told me—"

"That he wouldna move his wife who was sick from the cold away from the fire? What kind of a husband would you be if you allowed another laird to speak to you like that?" Anice asked, and tsked.

The courtiers' conversation ceased.

"You had not been married," the baron said, outraged.

"Aye, that we had. His brothers and my groom witnessed the wedding even. We are verra much married."

The baron sat back down.

To her surprise, he didn't make a move to leave yet. She was certain he was thinking if he could kill her uncle, he could kill the MacNeill brothers, too. The difference this time was her people knew. However, he must have figured they didn't have the proof to convict him of the crime or the king would have already sent for him.

Still, not only did they have to prove the baron was behind the murders, somehow, she had to find the traitor in their midst.

Conan and the men returned to the keep and when he saw her sitting at the head table, he looked over at the baron who motioned for him to take his seat.

Malcolm leaned over to her and whispered in her ear, "Think you your people will mind if I cut the meal short?"

She smiled at him, and with a hushed voice responded, "You have a mind to ravish me, do ye?"

"Aye, lass. Just what I have in mind to do."

The bread was cut, with the top of the crust served to Malcolm. He looked at Anice as if to see if she wished the first piece. She motioned for him to give it to the baron.

When an omelet of eggs mixed with almonds, currant, saffron and honey was served, Anice considered it. Turning to Malcolm, she whispered, "Share my meal with me, my laird."

He stared at her for a moment, then getting her meaning, nodded. "Aye, and your drink, lass, if you dinna mind too much." He set aside his tankard.

"Nay, 'tis safer that way, my husband," she whispered back.

"Is something wrong with your meal?" the baron asked.

CHAPTER 18

Anice knew Baron Fontenot would mention the fact Malcolm wouldn't eat his meal. Did it perturb the baron that he couldn't kill her husband so easily? If she could, she'd force the baron to drink and eat Malcolm's portions. When he refused, their case against him would be more assured.

"Nay," Malcolm said to the baron, "there is naught wrong with my food. The lass and I grew used to sharing our meals on the trip here. It's romantic, dinna you think?" He shoved his eggs to the baron. "But do have mine. You must be ravenous from your travels and no sense in wasting the food."

Anice tried to stifle a smile.

The baron pushed the omelet away. "One is enough for me. Two would appear glutinous. You may give it to the poor, if you desire."

Malcolm motioned to the young man serving them. "Give my omelet and all of those foods prepared for me to Sir Conan." He pointed the baron's knight out. "He is a good stout man and no doubt needs more to eat."

"Aye, my laird," the curly, redheaded man said, then quickly carried the omelet to Conan's table.

Conan glanced at the baron, who made no response. The knight nodded at the redhead, then the young man returned to the kitchen.

Anice watched Conan glance at her, his look pure menace. Would he eat the meal that had been served to Malcolm? Or would he find some way to dispose of it?

Malcolm leaned over and kissed Anice's lips. 'Twas not just a simple kiss either, but one of feeling that forced a slow burn to sizzle deep inside her. She kissed him back, too, forgetting for the moment that her people watched her every move. Her hands slid to his waist while his held onto hers. 'Twas not for the baron's benefit that she touched Malcolm's tongue with her own, nor pressed her lips against his with as much enthusiasm as he did with her. She loved him with all her heart and would give him up for no one.

When they separated, her breathing was fast and her heart beat way out of bounds.

Hearty laughter and cheers filled the hall. Her cheeks burned and the area between her legs ached with renewed gusto.

Malcolm slid his hand over her thigh. In a hushed voice he said, "You are entertaining your courtiers in good spirits this eve."

"They have never seen me kiss a husband of mine before. 'Tis a new experience for them."

"Aye, one they will soon get used to." He finished drinking the wine from her tankard and waved for the butler to refill it.

After they shared the omelet, a man served a pie filled with pork, beef, honey and peas. Only this time the portion was nearly double the size. The redheaded Gavin MacNair who had been serving them, bowed low to Malcolm when he raised a brow in question. Then he came around the long table between Malcolm and Anice and spoke to him in private so the baron would not hear. "My laird, I did as you bid me, only I did not say that your food was being served to

Sir Conan."

"Aye."

"And the double portions I said you requested for the lady as she is with child."

Malcolm's eyes sparkled and a smile split his face. "Aye," he said heartily, and slapped the young man on the back. "Think you that you can discover the cook—"

The man nodded vigorously. "I have my suspicions, my laird. But I would no' wish to arrest the wrong woman."

Malcolm's mouth dropped open.

Anice had never considered one of her women could have been in on the crimes. The notion both sickened and infuriated her.

"Aye," Malcolm said aloud, "a special treat for my lady will be most welcome."

MacNair bowed to Malcolm, then to Anice, and headed out of the hall.

Malcolm's mind didn't seem to be on the food when he ran his hand over Anice's thigh again, sliding her gown up and down her leg. She smiled at him. "If you are trying to warm me up before we retire to bed, you have already done so, my laird."

He chuckled. "I will warm you further when we retire, but this will have to do for now."

She stilled his hand when his fingers tickled her, and she suppressed the laugh that rose in her throat. "What about your brothers' food? I worry that someone may wish to poison them, too."

"They are eating with the ladies who sit beside them."

Anice glanced over at his brothers. "Who chose those ladies to sit with them?"

"Your Mistress Nora did. Does this displease ye?"

"Nay, I just wondered how they had found two of my most eligible unwed ladies-in-waiting so quickly. Though Nora is also unwed. Do your brothers no longer want English brides? I wouldna wish the ladies to be hopeful where there is no hope for them."

He glanced over at the lasses. "It seems you might have changed my brothers' minds."

She laughed. "Nay, 'tis only a bonny lass that will change men's minds. All of a sudden, no one else seems to exist." She looked over at the dark-haired woman, whose dark brown eyes sparkled, while a smile stirred her lips. Indeed, Morrigan appeared to be pleased with Dougald's attentions. She was relieved as angry as Morrigan had seemed about her marrying Malcolm. "You ken, Malcolm, Morrigan was named that by her mother, because she kicked so hard in the womb."

Malcolm raised a brow while he observed the lady. "After the war goddess?"

"Aye. She is also as good an archer as me, even beats me sometimes."

He lifted the tankard. "'Tis good to know. A man should always be on the lookout for a woman both comely and brave who could protect her husband when need be."

"You are so funny, Malcolm. 'Tis one of the things I love most about ye."

His smile turned wicked. "Mayhap there are other things you love about me." He looked at the other woman sitting beside Angus. "What of the other lady?"

"Venetia? She is blessed with a large dowry and heart. She came to serve me two years ago, but there are many who vie for her hand. She will no' be so easily won over."

"Angus looks to be doing no' so bad a job of it."

"Aye," Anice said as the petite, fair-haired girl leaned over and whispered something to Angus. He smiled, then nodded.

Anice tsked. "I hope your brothers are investigating these crimes, and not just chasing after my ladies-in-waiting."

Malcolm shook his head. "This ugly business no doubt is verra much on their minds. What better way to win your people's confidence than to befriend two lovely ladies of your court while they begin their duties?"

Up until now, the baron silently stewed, then he said to Malcolm, "Why did you not tell me the lady was Anice, Countess of Brecken, buried beneath the blanket at the croft?"

Anice set the tankard down and listened to what the baron had to say, her stomach tightening with apprehension.

"Why should I have? She was my wife, you were half frozen, and so were we. We had lost our escort in the storm on top of that so we were no' in the best of moods. Lengthy conversation was not what any of us had on our minds."

The baron glared at him, then nodded. "Aye." Then he smiled, a kind of wicked look. "I see why you objected to my sleeping with her and drew your sword."

"Any man worth his salt would have done the same."

"I still cannot believe the byre door flew open and allowed my horse, as well as my men's, to escape. And why did you not wake us in the morn when you left? We could have traveled together. Safer in a group."

"I had no idea where you were bound. Your men and you needed rest more than anything after the weather had turned so foul. As for the horses, 'tis one of those things. I had found the door open when I woke in the morn. It must have happened only after a mighty gust, and no' long before I stepped into the byre. Though I did close it after we departed, the wind must have banged it open again. Even when we first arrived, the door was swinging open in the wind. The owners need to do some repair work, I venture to say."

The baron stared at him for a moment, then finished off his tankard. "You knew I was the king's choice to wed the lady. Why did you no' tell me she was the one sleeping beneath the blanket?"

The baron couldn't seem to get over that she had been laying naked beside him, when she knew he would have killed Malcolm had he known.

"Nay, I only knew the king had five Norman lairds waiting in line to see her. I hadna idea who they were," Malcolm said, buttering a slice of bread.

Anice was torn between being amused that it bothered the baron so much that she lay beside him for the rest of the night and he had never known, and worried that his hatred for Malcolm was growing by the moment. Though she wasn't sure he could dislike Malcolm any more than he already did.

The baron poked his knife into his pastry and stabbed a piece of beef. "Where did you marry?"

'Twas a question she dreaded he'd ask, and one she hoped Malcolm had a good quick response for, though she was certain it would not matter what Malcolm said, the baron wouldn't be pleased. If Malcolm said they married after the farmhouse incident, then what?

Suddenly, Dougald jumped up from his seat and stalked out of the room with Gavin MacNair. Her marshal hurried after him.

She could feel the tension in Malcolm's posture and knew he wanted to investigate, but being the lord of the castle, his position was to sit and wait for his men to inform him what was going on.

Everyone grew quiet, hushed conversations here and there, and furtive glances at the head table and the entrance to the hall were shared.

Malcolm tapped his foot on the floor, watching the entrance where the men had stormed out.

Then Anice had an idea to change the subject both of what was going on in the hall, and the baron's question concerning their marriage that Malcolm had avoided answering. She leaned around Malcolm to speak to the baron, but thought better of it, and whispered to Malcolm instead. "Conan told us he was a bard. Have him entertain us for the meal."

Malcolm smiled. "Aye, lass, you are clever indeed."

He rose from his seat and raised his tankard. Everyone stood. "Because we have so recently arrived and had no' the time to plan for entertainment, the Lady Anice would ask that a man who traveled with us who put down his sword because of an indelicate wound that still ails him, is now a bard and has entertained even for our king. Let us greet Sir Conan as he entertains us this eve. A treat for my bonny bride."

Conan looked stricken and glanced at the baron as if he waited for his master to rescue him. Two of the baron's men closest to the knight chuckled.

The entertainment had already begun.

When Malcolm took his seat, everyone else did, their attention now resting on the knight, whose face drained of color.

Malcolm wrapped his fingers around Anice's hand and kissed it. "You are such a treasure, lass."

She smiled at him. "We must outwit them all we can."

"Aye."

Two servants came forth with a lyre and lute to accompany him, but Conan waved them away.

"No' a singing man," Malcolm whispered to Anice.

She smiled. "And I suspect he has no indelicate wound either."

Conan cleared his throat and looked directly at Malcolm with murder in his eyes. "I ask a riddle of ye, good people. I, a lonely wanderer, wounded with the sharp edge of steel, smitten with war blades, worn with the sword-edge, have seen many battles, much horrendous fighting, fearing evermore I shall perish and fall in the fighting of men. The pounding of hammers, the bursting of flame, batter and bite me, hard-edged and sharp; the brunt of the battle I am doomed to endure. There are no herbs or rags to heal or bind my wounds, as day and night with the deadly blows of the war-blades, they double and deepen."

Everyone allowed Laird Malcolm the first chance at guessing the riddle as he was laird of the manor. He whispered to Anice, "'Tis a shield. Did you know it?"

"Aye, 'tis too easy. I am sure everyone has heard it."

"A warrior's trusted shield, but surely, Sir Knight, you know something more difficult."

"Aye, even a wee bairn would know that one," Angus called out.

Laughter filled the hall.

Anice glanced at Angus. She'd never heard him so rowdy before. Had the wine loosened his tongue, or was he trying to impress the lass at his side, or get back at the knight who was not a bard?

"Another riddle!" MacTavish shouted. "You must stump our new laird of the castle this time."

Cheers followed and Malcolm raised the tankard. "Aye, impress me."

Conan stiffened his back, his face now red. "A strange thing hangs by a man's thigh, hidden by a garment. 'Tis stiff and strong with a hole in its head. When the man hitches his clothing high above his knee, he grasps the head of that hanging thing and pokes the hole of fitting size it oft has filled before. Its firm bearing reaps reward."

Giggles erupted amongst the ladies while several men discussed the matter with good humor.

"Do you know the answer, Anice?"

She shook her head and her cheeks grew hot. "I know 'tis no' what it sounds like," she said, smiling. "Do you know what it is?"

"Think you what it sounds like but is not?" he whispered in her ear.

Her whole body heated. "That which you prod me with when you have kissed me overmuch."

He broke into laughter. Under his breath he said to her, "I promise I will not poke you with the thing he speaks of when we retire to our chamber." Then he faced Conan. "'Tis a key to unlock the treasury."

She laughed with many of the courtiers.

"Aye, milord," Conan said, but he seemed pleased that his riddle intrigued the crowd better.

"'Twas a good riddle, do you no' think?" he asked the courtiers.

Most everyone cheered. But the baron sullenly waved his tankard for a refill of wine.

Servants served a custard-type dish of a paste of chicken, blended with rice boiled in almond milk, seasoned with sugar, cooked until very thick, and garnished with fried almonds and anise next.

Malcolm waved to Conan. "Another riddle."

The squire placed the double portion of food before Anice, then spoke to Malcolm and Anice in private. "Laird Dougald has taken the cook into custody and wishes you to know he would return to the meal momentarily."

"Has he found out who hired her?"

"Nay, no' yet. But the Laird Marshal will guard her until we can ensure someone loyal to the murderers doesna silence her."

"Aye."

He looked up to see Conan waiting for him to conclude his business with the squire. Before Gavin MacNair left, Anice grabbed the young man's arm. "Who is she?"

"A new girl, my lady. She was hired about the time of his laird's death."

She nodded. As soon as the meal was over, she had every intention of speaking with the woman who'd murdered her uncle. Though she never considered herself a violent woman, she'd wring the cook's neck if she had to get the truth out of her that way.

When the squire left, Conan said, "See if you can guess this riddle then if you may. I am scratched by the shin bones of the horse and deer, poked with wooden poles on sunny days, glisten in the sunlight, become bone once more at sunset."

"Anice?" Malcolm asked.

She'd had many a day ice skating in such a manner on Loch Affric. "Aye, frozen water."

"The lady has guessed correctly."

Everyone cheered.

Malcolm rose from his seat to conclude the feast. He'd been anxious to end the feast before it had even begun, but the reason had been to get Anice alone with him. Now that a clue to the murder of Anice's uncle had come to light, he wanted to find out more about that at once.

Still, with the way Anice acted, he was certain that she wished a word with the cook, but he wanted his bride nowhere near anyone who could have done anything so evil. Yet he suspected he was in for another battle if he tried to deny her right to question the woman.

He straightened his shoulders. He was the lord of the manor now and his word was law.

He raised his arm to escort Anice out of the hall, so that those of the head table could leave afterwards and everyone else quit the room after that.

Turning to Angus who followed behind him, he said, "Play a board game with the baron, will ye? I will join you after a bit."

The disappointment in Angus's face shown. He wanted to see what had occurred with Dougald, too. But Angus also knew that Malcolm was his laird for now, and that he had just as important a mission to perform. Keep the baron under their watchful eye, and from causing more trouble.

Malcolm motioned to two of Anice's men. "Join Laird Angus and the baron and have the butler ensure the men are well served."

"Aye, my laird."

He had no intention of leaving his youngest brother in the baron's sights without having men-at-arms to watch his back.

Malcolm spoke to Nola when she joined them. "Lady MacNeill will retire to her chamber. See that she is ready for me when I return."

"You may pull down the coverlet and sprinkle the bed with lily and roses. I will join you in a little while," Anice countermanded.

"Aye, my lady." She looked from Anice to Malcolm.

"You cannot come with me, Anice," Malcolm said firmly.

"I want to speak with the woman, too, my laird. I have every—"

"I wish it not. 'Tis bound to get brutal and I dinna wish you to see or hear what is said. Please, do as I ask."

She hesitated, then in a huff, she stormed for the stairs.

He sighed deeply when her ladies hurried after her. Anice was bound to be a terror when he retired with her later that eve. So much for getting her in the mood for what was to come. Yet if she saw their interrogation of the cook, how would that make her feel? Certainly not in the mood for lovemaking either.

He strode toward the stairs and started down them. Gavin MacNair joined him. "You have sent Cawley to watch over the baron, and he told me to watch over ye, my laird."

Malcolm smiled. "The man is a fine Scotsman."

"Aye, he says he is glad the lady found a Scot to wed and no' a Norman."

Pray the king felt as reassured when he learned of their marriage.

***

Anice only went as far as the entrance to her chamber, then as soon as the ladies stepped into the room, she turned and hurried back toward the stairs.

"My lady!" Nola said, chasing after her, with the other women gaining ground.

"I have some business I must take care of. One of you may come with me, but no more than that."

"You cannot go to the dungeon after Laird MacNeill told you to wait for him in your chamber," Nola warned.

Anice wondered if Nola had been too long under the influence of Mai. "I have no intention of going to the dungeon. 'Tis a dank, dark, horrifying place." She shuddered.

Though she wished to speak to the cook, she knew it was best left to men this time, but she wasn't about to give up the investigation to them. With everyone so preoccupied, she'd just investigate elsewhere.

"With the baron's men here, you cannot have just one lady with ye. 'Tis too dangerous, kenning Fontenot wants you for his own," Nola said.

"Aye, two ladies then."

"Where are you off to, my lady?"

Anice stopped at the bottom of the steps. "Mary and Venetia, return to my chamber and prepare it as his laird has asked. Morrigan and Nola, come with me, but if you dinna be quiet and you get in the way, I will send you to my chamber also."

The two women nodded, wide-eyed. She knew they'd rather join her on her adventure and find out what she was up to. Though Nola was too much like Mai, and might try to stop her, she had the heart of a feral cat, courageous and curious. But Venetia was too sweet to deal with matters as grave as this. Mary would have been fine, but Anice really wanted to do the investigation alone. Too many she feared would scare any away who might confess something to her. Morrigan would watch her back without a word of complaint and do a fine business of it. The lady would have made a braw warrior had she been born a man.

Anice continued to the kitchen and when she reached there, she found the kitchen staff sitting at the long table, eating leftovers from the meal. Everyone hurried to rise.

She motioned for them to take their seats, then she spoke to the head cook. "Tell me, Robina, what was said during the meal when the girl was found to have poisoned my uncle."

The robust woman paled. "My lady, I didna hire the girl."

"Nay, I ken that," Anice hurried to reassure her. The middle-aged woman had sneaked honeyed cakes to Anice when she was a wee lass, well, even when she was older. Robina would never have harmed her uncle. "Did our steward, Laird MacKnight, hire the cook?"

"Aye, my lady." Robina nodded her head vigorously.

Anice had never considered that possibility. She had assumed Laird MacKnight was in on the killing of Laird Thompson. Then she'd thought mayhap the baron's men had murdered both he and her chamberlain, Laird Iverson. If the steward had hired the girl, had he been in on the plot all along? Easily, he would have wanted Laird Thompson dead. He'd always hated him. Had he been angry with her uncle for not discharging the man? When the baron schemed to get rid of her uncle to have her and the properties for his own, did Laird MacKnight greedily go along with it so that he could keep his place as steward?

What of his wife? Did he conveniently dispose of her, too? Anice had never heard him speak ill of his wife though.

"What was said to the girl?"

"Gavin MacNair, who was serving ye and His Lairdship, asked who was preparing the meals for His Lairdship. He said that Laird MacNeill was extremely pleased with the fine quality of the food's presentation and wanted to thank whoever it was properly with a gift of coin."

The woman glowered at one of the male cooks, then turned back to Anice. "Any would have been tempted to say they had prepared the meal to win extra wages and praise from his lairdship. Froman said he had prepared the meal, at which time I knocked him upside the head for lying and pointed to Gertunia. Why would she no' speak up for herself, I wondered. Anytime the laird of the manor praises a servant's work is naught to be ashamed of. She paled as if she were going to faint, and her eyes grew as round as my cakes. MacNair dashed for her before she bolted into the kitchen garden. I had no idea what the matter was. In fact, none of us did. We thought the young man had gone quite mad."

The cook took a deep breath. "The MacNair's face was ten times redder than I have ever seen it when he yanked the girl back into the kitchen. Here we still had to get the next course of the meal out to ye, and we were frozen by what was taking place."

"You did a fine job. None of us knew what was happening."

"Thank ye, my lady. I made everyone continue with their work as the squire pinned Gertunia to the floor and asked her who paid her to poison your uncle, my lady. Of course that brought us all to a dead halt. Froman took his knife and approached the girl, threatening to cut off her ears if she didna tell."

Froman gave a satisfied look and folded his arms.

"Your uncle very much liked us and rewarded us verra well from time to time. So Froman was pretty hot that this slip of a girl might have killed your uncle."

Anice nodded, trying to keep the tears in abeyance.

"She confessed. The wicked thing."

"Who paid her?"

"She said she did not ken. That a man had given her the money."

Anice groaned, wondering how many more of her staff were involved in the hideous crimes against her uncle and the other courtiers. "One of our staff?" she asked, her voice shaky, hating to hear that it was so.

"Aye, it had to be. No others were here at the time visiting."

"Had she tried to poison Laird MacNeill this verra eve?"

"Aye, she was paid again, this time to murder him. Only MacNair must have worried that one of the cooks had poisoned your uncle and would do the same thing to the new laird of the manor."

Anice held onto the table.

Froman jumped up and offered her his seat.

She shook her head and tried to settle her queasy stomach, straightening her back. "Did she give any description of the man?"

"Nay, my lady, but the men will get it out of her."

Anice didn't even want to envision what that would entail. She'd seen a murderer beaten half to death when the villagers were trying to get a confession out of him before her uncle condemned him to death. For a year, she'd had nightmares over it. 'Twas a horrible thing and she knew the men would not be gentle when getting the truth out of the woman who helped to murder the laird they'd served and loved.

"Do any of you remember a man speaking to this girl at any time that seemed odd, out of place?"

Froman spoke, "No' before as I am certain she was paid when none of us were aware she had poisoned your uncle, but a man approached her just before we began the evening meal. I didna think a whole lot of it because she is young and bonny and some of the men..." He stopped speaking as his cheeks grew red. "Beg your pardon for speaking so frankly—"

"These times warrant the truth and every bit of it. Continue."

"Some of the lads oft visit three of the ladies here, so I dinna think it verra odd."

Anice glanced at the ladies who all blushed. "Except?"

"That Gertunia was not one of them. She kept to herself the whole time she has been here. Like she was scared to death of all of us. We have never mistreated her, and really are like a family. So why did she act so strangely? Before preparations of the evening meal, the squire came to her, and they disappeared into the kitchen garden. Cook was going to beat her if she left her duties just when we needed her, when here she planned a quick roll in the hay, beg your pardon, my lady, with the man. She suddenly burst into the kitchen, naught amiss with her gowns or veils, and we assumed he had wanted her, and she said no. But now it seems he told her to poison His Lairdship."

Anice asked through clenched teeth, "You ken the man's name?"

CHAPTER 19

Anice both dreaded and longed to know who the man was who paid to have the girl kill her uncle. How could any of her staff have done anything so hideous?

"Firth MacKnight," the cook said.

"Laird MacKnight's nephew?" Her throat grew dry. Who else on her staff was related to the laird? Would his nephew have had a hand in murdering his own aunt as well?

"Aye, my lady," Froman said, his voice shaky as if he worried the laird's nephew would get him next once he learned the cook had told on him.

Anice swallowed hard, then nodded. "Thank ye. Laird MacNeill did indeed enjoy the meal. Who was so thoughtful to prepare the double portions for us?"

Froman smiled. "I did, my lady. When Gavin MacNair said you were with child, I wanted to make sure you and the bairn had plenty to eat."

Anice opened her mouth to speak, felt her face heat, then the warmth spread all the way to her toes. She remembered that Gavin had mentioned such a thing to them at the meal, but now the notion truly hit her. She glanced at her ladies whose eyes had grown wide. The cooks, too, seemed to wait with great expectancy for her to say more about her condition.

"Thank ye, kindly, Froman, Robina. Please eat your meals."

She hurried out of the room with her ladies following on her heel. She would get the truth out of MacKnight's nephew before her husband found out what she was up to and stopped her.

"My lady, are you truly with child?" Nola asked.

"Of course no'. We only just got married for heaven's sakes. Gavin MacNair only said so to avoid the cooks becoming suspicious of why Laird MacNeill wouldna eat his own food."

"But you could be with child," Morrigan said. "They say it can happen even if you have only made love once."

Anice shook her head. "I am no' with child." She hastened outside of the keep and targeted the wooden barracks that housed both her men and the baron's for now.

"My lady, you must have the men deal with the MacKnight," Nola attempted to appeal to her just like Mai would have done.

"And he will be thrown in the dungeon, if he hasna already escaped," Anice said. "Then I will not have a chance to know what is going on."

Forging ahead, she would not be deterred by her ladies or anyone else.

As soon as she approached the entryway to the barracks, one of her men rushed out to greet her. "Lady MacNeill. You shouldna be here. Half the men are in a state of undress while they prepare for bed."

"Eanruig, I come for Firth MacKnight. If he is here still, send him out to speak to me," she demanded, her tone caustic. She would not be thwarted.

Eanruig narrowed his gray eyes disapprovingly, his black bushy brows furrowed, his black hair shaggy about his shoulders. A man who excelled on the battlefield, and with the ladies in bed, she'd heard tell. "Does Laird MacNeill know you are here?"

For a second she hesitated, then she succeeded in doing what she did best, took the matter into her own hands and stormed past him into the barracks. She would have none of her staff barring her investigation just because she had a husband who would disapprove of her actions. Her ladies followed her inside and instantly, Nora gasped and Morrigan giggled. Anice felt the blush return to her cheeks when the naked men covered their exposed privates. "I wish to speak to Firth MacKnight about his poor uncle. At once."

"Aye, my lady," Thomas said, who wore his shirt resting mid-thigh, and a smile. "I will get him for ye."

When she turned to see what had happened to Eanruig, she was surprised to find he wasn't behind her. She hurried outside and saw him entering the keep. Damnation. He'd tell Malcolm.

She stepped back inside. "Thomas, I apologize for inconveniencing ye, but would you stay with me while I talk to the young man?"

"Aye, my lady." He hurried to the end of the barracks and spoke to a man already buried in his blankets.

"Come on, lad, Lady Anice herself is here to see ye."

The blond man sat up on the straw cot, looking half dazed.

"Firth MacKnight," Thomas said, raising his voice to stir him. "Hurry. Dinna tarry any longer. Her Ladyship is waiting on ye."

The man was twenty and was the son Laird MacKnight hadn't had. Some day he would have had his uncle's title, but not now. How could he have done such a thing? Mayhap to get in good with the new laird, but Baron Fontenot would never be his laird.

He scrambled out of bed. "What does she want with me?" he whispered, but his words echoed off the walls as the other men watched to see what happened next.

"She has news of your poor uncle."

"My uncle?" He sounded confused, his voice not as deep as a man's yet. Was he in league with his uncle or not? Aye, he had to be if he paid the girl in the kitchen.

"You best get dressed. The lady is waiting for you at the end of the barracks."

He turned to see her standing there at the entryway, and she swore he looked like he was going to faint.

Though she should have moved outside with her ladies, she dared not in case the man bolted. But if she told them what her purpose was in coming there, they wouldn't have allowed her to talk to him. Instead, they would have turned him over to Laird MacNeill and again she wouldn't find out what had happened.

When he had dressed, he walked toward her like a man who would soon be beheaded, which would soon be his fate. But not before he indicted those who had bribed him to do this evil deed. His defeated posture instantly condemned him.

She commended him for not running like she thought he would, though. Did he think what he had done had been for everyone's benefit? Or only his own and his uncle's? But why had Lady MacKnight also been murdered?

When they stood outside, MacTavish, the captain of the guard joined them, but soon after this, six more men drifted outside, four of hers, and two of the baron's. She said to the baron's men, "This is a private matter between my people and me. You will have to leave us."

The two stalked in the direction of the keep, not back to the barracks. Now the baron would be told his plans were quickly crumbling.

"Stop those men!" Anice shouted. Four of her men raced after them, forcing them to turn back, while the baron's men loudly protested.

MacTavish said, "My lady, what is this all about?" Already her men seemed worried something terrible was the matter, and she was certain they figured they'd better turn the matter over to Laird MacNeil.

"I do not wish the baron to learn we have this young man in custody."

"But the lad serves you, no' the…" Seeing the exasperation on her face, MacTavish ordered the four men, "Stay with them in the barracks." He grabbed Firth MacKnight's arm. "Why do we have the young man in custody, my lady?"

She said to MacKnight, "Who paid you to poison my uncle?"

MacTavish looked at MacKnight with disbelief.

"I did not poison your uncle, my lady, you must believe that."

"You paid the kitchen maid to do it, I ken. But who gave you the money to pay her?"

MacTavish cleared his throat, his eyes hard, though she was certain he was angry at the man and not her. "My lady, Laird MacNeill should be taking care of this matter, if Laird MacKnight's nephew has done something so heinous."

She ignored him, wanting to question MacKnight as much as possible before her husband stopped her. "Who, MacKnight?"

"My uncle."

She let out her breath, knowing the truth of the matter even before his nephew revealed it. "Did you do it willingly?"

The man looked at the ground.

Through clenched teeth, she asked again, "Did ye?"

"Aye, my lady."

Her head spun with frustration. Why would any on her staff have killed her good-hearted uncle? "Where is Laird MacKnight?"

He shrugged. "I dinna ken. Mayhap in the village."

"And Laird Iverson?"

"Dead." The squire's tone was wooden, his brown eyes

dull.

Her heart quickened at the news. She'd prayed her chamberlain hadn't been guilty of any crime and would still be alive. "Who killed him?"

"My uncle."

"By whose authority?"

"He is a powerful man and will marry ye whether you want it or no'."

"*Baron Fontenot.*"

"The Norman lairds will rule this land, and we might as well get used to the fact. The sooner we ally with them the better off those of us will be who recognize it and be in good stead with Robert Curthose."

The two MacKnights were the damnable rebels in their midst, siding with her Uncle Edgar Atheling and Robert Curthose! God's teeth, if Henry found out and thought the rest of her people were in league with his rebellious brother...

"Lady MacNeill!" Malcolm's voice was deep and threatening.

She attempted to ignore him, but her skin grew clammy, and she spoke more quickly. "Why was Laird Iverson murdered?"

"He discovered that my uncle killed Laird Thompson."

"And Lady MacKnight? Your aunt? Why her?"

Firth MacKnight glared at her. "She wouldn't go along with his plans. No' only that he had a verra agreeable mistress, and she was all for whatever he intended."

What else did she and her uncle not know about their staff? "Who was his mistress?"

The sound of Malcolm's rapid footsteps and the others drew closer, yet she persisted, her heart thundering with urgency. "Who?"

The squire looked down at the ground, then up at Anice. "The marshal's daughter."

She wanted to scream. "Was the marshal also

involved?"

"Nay."

Thank God for small miracles. She couldn't bear it if one more of her higher staff members were involved in this deadly mess.

"Did his daughter know that your uncle was going to kill his wife?"

"Aye, that she did. She helped make the poison."

The dreadful girl made her own bed and would lay in it for all eternity. Anice didn't pity her for what would happen to her one wee bit.

"Lady MacNeill!"

She whipped around to see Malcolm stalking toward her with his brother, Dougald, Eanruig—the man who had told on her—and four more of her men. Malcolm's dark brows were furrowed, and she knew he was about to hang her with the rest of the vermin who'd committed the crimes.

Not one to be intimidated, she tilted her chin up. "Aye, Laird MacNeill, I was just finishing my walk before I retired to bed. Firth MacKnight may have something to say to you though."

"Interrogate the lad," he said to Dougald. "I have matters to discuss with Lady MacNeill."

"Oh, and two of the baron's knights are being detained so they will not tell him what we have uncovered concerning this plot of theirs." She headed back to the keep with her ladies.

Malcolm seized her arm and stormed back to the castle with her. "You would try the devil's patience, Anice."

She frowned at him, not liking that he wouldn't permit her to help. "You said you would let me help with the investigation. You said I would be the bait."

"I did not mean it. You are the lady of the manor, and I dinna want a precious hair on that bonny head of yours harmed." He glanced back at the men. "And why was one of your men half dressed in front of you?"

She shrugged, amused that he would have noticed. "Getting ready to retire for the night, dinna you suppose?"

"As you should have been doing. The man who came to warn me about what you were doing said you stalked into the barracks. Did you do things like this often before I wed ye?"

"Why nay, my laird. I think you have brought the devil out in me, more so than usual."

He shook his head. "You are never to venture into the barracks. If you wish to see a naked man, you can see me all you like."

The ladies giggled behind him.

"So what did you learn from the man?" he asked.

"Had the cook told you his name?"

"Nay, she did not know it." He looked down at her. Anice smiled. He frowned at her. "Do not give me that look. We would have learned it before long."

"Aye."

"You are a vixen, lass. So what did you learn from the MacKnight?"

"The baron did hire the men to kill my uncle and the others. Also, he is working for Robert Curthose."

He stopped her at the entrance to the keep. "My God, Anice. He has sixty men at various places in the castle and the surrounding grounds."

"You will have to arrest him then. You can do it. After all, you are laird here now."

"I have to get you somewhere safe. A battle is bound to erupt."

"Arrest him first. Mayhap his men will leave peaceably with no one to lead them."

"Take the lady to her chamber," Malcolm ordered her ladies. "I will send men to guard ye."

He kissed her cheek, then hurried back to the barracks.

Anice turned toward the stables.

"Where are you going, my lady? Laird MacNeill told us

to take you to your chamber," Nola said, her voice raised in disbelief.

Morrigan on the other hand remained with Anice, desiring to do anything she bid.

"Aye, and that he would send someone to protect me. But I can protect myself in the interim. My bow and quivers are still there." Anice walked into the stable where she heard men talking, sending fear skittering across her skin.

She and her ladies quickly slipped into one of the empty stalls.

"The baron says we are to take her tonight, kill the MacNeill and the rest of these people, and slip her away from here. When the king gets word of it, he'll be told the border clans killed the whole lot of them, and the baron came too late, but was only able to save the lady."

"Aye, and the time?"

"The baron will motion with a light from the third-floor window."

"He is still fuming about her being in the farmhouse with us, sleeping right next to him, and none of us knowing. That MacNeill has the tenacity of a bull."

"Not after tonight he will not. She was naked, evidenced by her wet gowns hanging to dry. Think you the lady and the MacNeill were already wed? Not I."

Anice nearly died to hear their words. She couldn't bear to see the looks on her ladies' faces. She whispered to them, "There are only the two of them."

"Aye, my lady," Morrigan said.

"There are three of us."

Morrigan smiled and pulled a dagger from beneath her bliaut. Anice raised a brow. "When the baron's men arrived, I began to wear it, my lady."

Anice looked at Nola. She shook her head, but motioned to a pitchfork behind them.

"They will not want to kill me, so I will go first. Morrigan, you give the dagger to Nola."

"But my lady—"

"You are as good as I am with a bow. 'Tis the next stall over. When we rush the men, you get the bow."

"Aye, my lady."

"Are you ready, Nola?"

"Aye, my lady. I am ready."

Anice walked out of the stall and toward where she'd heard the men speaking, her leather shoes crunching on the straw. The men were quiet now and she worried they'd exited the stable through the rear door.

Then a man stepped out of a stall at the other end of the building and asked, "Who goes there?"

"Lady Anice." She hoped using her unmarried name would bode better with them. "Who are ye?"

"Two of the baron's knights. What are you doing out here?"

"I oft come out to feed my horse." She walked toward the two men with the pitchfork. "He likes it when I speak to him before I retire."

The knight smiled, then he said to the other, "The timing could not be more perfect. Do not you think?"

"Aye."

"Mayhap we can help ye, my lady. If ye will just hand me the fork."

"Nay, I like to do my own work"

"The baron would not like to see ye doing such menial labor, my lady."

"'Tis Laird MacNeill that I would concern myself with pleasing, no' Baron Fontenot."

The man smiled. "Well, you see, my lady, the baron still wants your hand in marriage."

"Aye, 'tis true, I ken, but he cannot have it as I am already wed." She continued to move toward the men using caution, waiting for Morrigan to reach her bow. It would not do well for Nola to get hurt if Anice moved too quickly and Morrigan wasn't ready.

The telltale sound of an arrow whooshing through the air met her ears, then the weapon hit its mark with a whap. The man grabbed his chest and dropped to his knees and fell on his face. The other pulled his sword from his scabbard. Anice thrust the pitchfork at him, but he knocked the prongs aside with his sword. Before she could swing it around to strike at him again, Morrigan let loose another arrow and hit him in between the eyes. He collapsed, dead like the other without making a sound.

"Come, ladies, we must tell Laird MacNeill their plan," Anice said as Nola stared at the two dead bodies. She grabbed her wrist. "Come, Nola. They planned to kill everyone in the castle." Anice dropped her pitchfork. "Where is your bow and quiver, Morrigan?"

"Over there. Here, you take yours, I'll get mine."

More men's voices haunted them. Theirs? Or the baron's?

The ladies grabbed one of the dead men and pulled him into the stall, then hurried to get the other.

Footsteps sounded in the stable as someone, no, two people walked one after the other farther into the building. "Stafford? Morrisay?"

More of the baron's men.

Anice readied her weapon. Morrigan did the same with hers.

"What is wrong?" the other man said.

"They were supposed to be waiting for us here. The baron was to have given them word as to when to begin the siege."

Anice giggled. "Oh, my you are so big, my laird. Oh, oh, aye."

The men stormed toward her. "Morrisay? Stafford? Damn we have work to—"

Morrigan's arrow met its mark first. Anice sent her arrow flying next and dispatched the last of the baron's men. "Come, ladies, let us hide the bodies and return to my chambers. We can fight—"

"Lady Anice?" Gavin MacNair called out.

"Aye, help us."

He hurried into the stable and his mouth dropped wide open when he saw the baron's men dead. "What have ye done?"

"They are planning to kill everyone in the castle. We must get word to—"

"Anice, if that is your voice I hear in there...," Malcolm said, his tone dark.

She let go of the body and straightened her back. "Aye."

"The ladies have killed four of their men already, my laird," Gavin said proudly.

"Come, we will get the ladies to my wife's chamber. You and my brother, Dougald, will see that they stay there."

"We came to get our bows." Anice stalked out of the stable. "With no one to protect us, we had to find our own way. The baron intends to raise a light in the third tower window when he wants his men to kill all of our staff."

Malcolm nodded, his look dark and brooding like a building thunderstorm. "Tell my brother, Gavin MacNair, that he is needed at the lady's chamber. And tell him about the warning signal. I would have you take the lady to her chamber, but I do not trust she will get there."

"You didna expect us to go to the chamber unarmed, did ye?"

"I expect you to do as I tell ye."

Anice smiled. Then he had a lot to learn about his new wife.

He hurried her to the keep, his sword drawn while she held her bow and a notched arrow at the ready. The four found no one, save a servant who quickly joined them. "What is the trouble, my laird?" he whispered.

"The baron and his men plan to lay siege to the place. Have everyone armed that can be. Have the women and children take refuge in the ladies' chambers."

"Aye, my laird, at once."

Malcolm rushed Anice up the stairs and to her chamber. Inside, she found Venetia and Mary wringing their hands. "Oh, my lady, what has happened?"

"Keep the door bolted," Malcolm said, then kissed Anice's lips. "I love ye, lass. I cannot lose you at any cost."

"Oh, Malcolm, what about Angus? He is with the baron."

Venetia hurried out of the chamber.

"Venetia!" Anice cried out.

"Beg your pardon, my lady, but I will speak to Angus in private and warn him about what has occurred." Venetia ran up the stairs.

"Let me go with her," Anice begged Malcolm.

"Nay, lass, if she goes alone, she should be fine. If you go, the baron may take you hostage. You stay put. I will remain outside the chamber until Dougald relieves me."

She laid her bow and quivers down and wrapped her arms around Malcolm. "'Tis no' the way I wished to spend the night with ye, my husband."

"Aye, lass. We will find the time soon." He kissed her lips, leaned his forehead against hers as if not wanting to leave her alone, then pulled away. "Bolt the door."

He barely made it out of the room before he swung his sword at an armed knight.

Morrigan and Anice swept out of the room with their weapons readied.

Two more of the baron's men dashed up the stairs, and Anice let her arrow fly, then Morrigan.

Had Venetia made it up the stairs to the room where the baron and Angus had played the board game?

"You stay here and protect the ladies," Anice said, then ran up the stairs.

Malcolm clanged his sword against the knight's and shouted, "Anice!"

She should have stayed put and let Morrigan go, but she couldn't. Not with worrying what had become of Venetia and Angus.

She slowed her step when she heard Venetia speaking softly to Angus in the hall.

Angus had no sword to protect him from the baron's men. It would have looked too obvious if he'd worn one to play a game with the baron.

When a knight ran up behind her, she whipped around and readied her arrow. She stopped to see MacTavish.

"My lady," he whispered. "You need to—"

"See to Angus."

"If you return to your chamber."

She nodded and took two steps down the stairs.

MacTavish ran up to the top and Anice waited. She would return when Venetia came back down. Instead, she heard the sound of swords striking metal and against the stone walls. She dashed up the steps. Venetia stood watching, horrified, as Angus fought a swordsman with the sword MacTavish had armed him with.

Anice couldn't strike any with her weapon, so instead, she grabbed Venetia's wrist. The lady cried out in fright. "Come, let the men fight. We will return to my chamber."

They headed down the stairs, encountering three more of the baron's men running up it.

"'Tis the Lady Anice," the one said.

"We will not harm you or your lady," another said. "Just lay down your weapon."

"Forgive me if I do not believe ye."

They tried to shorten the distance so they could strike at her bow. She shot the first man and sent him tumbling backward into the other two. Again, she readied her weapon, only winging the second man. But the third man she killed outright. The second one tried to get to his feet, but Malcolm suddenly appeared, blood dripping from his shoulder. "Malcolm!"

He slew the last man and motioned for her to return to her chamber.

She hurried past him with Venetia, while he followed behind.

"Neither Dougald nor the lad have come to relieve me."

"So Morrigan and I will aid ye."

"Aye, she has killed a goodly number already. If you help me, I shall feel well protected," Malcolm said sarcastically.

Anice smiled, but then quickly frowned. "While we wait for the next batch, I will take care of your wound."

"'Tis only a scratch."

Nola rushed out of the room. "I will take care of our laird while you ladies defend us."

"Where is Mary?" Anice asked, peeking into her chamber.

"She has fainted."

"Och," Anice said, shaking her head, thinking Venetia would have been the one to faint instead. "'Tis good we havena such weak stomachs."

Malcolm kissed her cheek. "Have I told you how much I love ye, lass?"

"You will have to prove it, my laird. With Gavin MacNair telling folks I'm with bairn, you will have to make sure he tells no lie."

"Are you challenging me, Anice?"

She wrapped a cloth around his arm. "Aye, my laird. I know how you like a good challenge. Now if you are unable to do anything about it because of your wound..."

He chuckled. "You know how I am when you challenge me, lass. I'll take you up on it."

Tying the cloth securely around the wound, she asked, "Aye, why think you I challenged ye?"

"Malcolm!" Dougald shouted from the third floor. "Fontenot's got Angus!"

CHAPTER 20

Malcolm's head pounded as he tried to think of a way to save his youngest brother. Mayhap if he offered himself as a hostage instead, he could get the better of the baron.

When he reached the solar, the baron had a dagger at Angus's throat, sending a shard of ice hurtling down Malcolm's spine. MacTavish had his sword readied but couldn't get any closer for fear of the baron slitting Angus's throat.

"I want your word you will give me and the rest of my men safe passage from here," the baron said.

"And in return?"

"I will let your brother live."

"Aye, you are free to go."

The baron released Angus. "I know you are a man of your word."

"Aye, you have my word." As much as Malcolm did not wish to give it to a murderer like Fontenot. But the king would seek the man's head for having killed Anice's uncle, and for siding with Robert Curthose. And that would be the end of it.

"How many are left of the baron's men?" Malcolm

asked Dougald.

"Five, maybe six." Dougald rounded the men up and corralled them into the courtyard.

"Our horses," the baron said as they moved them toward the outer bailey.

"You have lost the battle. Just as in the joust, you have given them up to the winners." The baron and his men should have all died, and if it hadn't been for Angus, every last one of the baron's men would have. "How many of our men were killed or wounded?" Malcolm asked.

"Five killed," MacTavish said, "ten wounded. None seriously. The women are taking care of them."

Angus walked with them, his head hung low. "I'm sorry, Malcolm."

"Nay, Angus. I left you the most dangerous of jobs. You were unarmed with three of his knights and the devil himself. You did well."

"If you like, my laird, you can return to Lady MacNeill while we clean up around here," MacTavish said.

"There is naught more that I would like to do."

Angus said, "You are no' hurt verra much, are ye?"

"Nay, just a scratch. It will no' stop me from finding pleasure with the lady tonight."

"Aye, good Scots' blood," Dougald said. "Go, tend to that sweet lass of yours. We have been through enough of these skirmishes to know how to deal with it."

The gate guard and his men closed the portcullis once the baron and his men had passed beyond the gate. "They will no' be coming back inside here any time soon."

"Make sure there are none of them left skulking about the place," Malcolm said. Though his body was weary from all of the fighting, his step was instantly invigorated by the notion he would join his lady and bed her again.

When he reached the top step, servants were dragging the bodies of the baron's men down them. "My laird," the men said in greeting.

"Good work, men."

"Aye, and ye, my laird. Had the baron and his men won, none of us would have been left alive."

"Aye."

Malcolm hurried down the hall and found the door to Anice's chambers shut. He listened, but not hearing any voices, he knocked. "Anice?"

"Come in, Lord MacNeill," she said.

He hesitated to hear her call him lord in the English way. She wouldn't have addressed him so formally either. Was she warning him that something was amiss? "Anice, I will return."

He motioned to one of the servants and whispered, "Get three of my men at once."

"Aye, my laird." The servant ran down the hallway and scooted down the stairs.

After what seemed like an eternity, Dougald, Angus, and MacTavish bolted up the stairs. Malcolm motioned them to tread lightly.

When they reached him, he said in a hushed voice, "I fear one or more of the baron's men is with Anice."

"What about her ladies-in-waiting?" Dougald asked.

Malcolm bit back his anger. "I dinna ken. I told Anice I was leaving. Mayhap you can ask to speak to Morrigan and see what happens."

"Aye." Dougald stepped up to the door and knocked. "'Tis me, Dougald MacNeill, my lady. May I have a word with Mistress Morrigan?"

"She...she is not here, my lord."

Dougald frowned, then whispered to Malcolm, "Is the lady trying to speak in the English manner?"

"Aye. And she wouldna. No' unless she was trying to warn us something was not right."

Dougald spoke to the door again. "Angus would like to speak to Venetia. Is she there? He cannot find her anywhere."

"No. No one is in here. Where is Malcolm? I wait for him."

"His wound is bleeding something fierce. One of the servants is taking care of it. I think 'tis worse than he thought before, my lady."

"I will not sleep until he lays down with me."

Malcolm whispered, "How can we get her to tell us how many men are in the room with her?"

"My lady, how many arrows are left in your quiver?"

"Four."

Angus whispered, "Then whoever is in there could try to use them on us when we enter the room."

Dougald said, "Then if he uses it on us, we will know he will run out when he has finished the four."

Malcolm clenched his fists, trying to keep a clear head and not go charging in and slaughtering the brigands, however many there were, like he wanted to do. "Morrigan has a quiver also."

"Och," Dougald said, under his breath.

Malcolm said to MacTavish. "Do you have a ladder that will reach her room?"

"Aye."

"Get it. Nay, do you have two?"

"Aye, my laird. I will get them right away."

Dougald spoke through the door. "How many arrows are left in Morrigon's quiver?"

"I would not know."

Her voice sounded harried and tight. Malcolm was certain he heard whimpering from another corner of the chambers, like the soft crying of one of the women.

He said to Angus, "Have someone count all of the bodies of the baron's men. There were sixty to begin with. The baron and six of his men left. We need to know how many remain."

"Aye." Angus hurried down the hall.

"I will leave ye, Dougald, and MacTavish to storm the

door, and I will send some other men up this way."

"You are coming up the ladder?"

"Aye."

"But your arm."

"Of no consequence." The burning sensation had completely vanished when he had discovered the lady in harm's way.

Dougald gave him a sly smile. "You will wait until all the arrows have been fired."

Malcolm nodded. "Ye are right, brother. And that is why I am the laird of the castle." He slapped him on the back. "We will let you know when to storm the chamber."

"Watch yourself, Malcolm. If you go and get yourself killed, I will have to marry the lady. With her record of betrothals, I am no' sure I wish to do so."

Malcolm rubbed his chin. "I have no intention of leaving her a widow." He hastened to the stairs. 'Twas no big a deal to draw the arrows in his direction, then call for his brother to storm the chamber from the hallway. He only hoped the baron's men were lousy shots.

Before he reached the exterior of the keep, Angus grabbed his arm. "The ladders are ready. I want to be the first on one of them."

"Nay, Angus."

"Venetia is up there, too."

Malcolm stalked toward the ladders. "I dinna want to tell James I got you killed when I am to protect ye."

"I can do this, Malcolm."

He stopped in his footsteps. "You wait until I give the signal to enter the windows."

"Aye."

He nodded, not wishing his youngest brother to be hurt, but knowing his pride was more of an issue than anything. Before he ascended the ladder, he sent five of Anice's men upstairs to join Dougald. After waiting a few minutes for the men to get into place, he motioned to Angus, and they began the thirty-foot or so climb. Two more men followed after each of them and when Malcolm and Angus reached the stone sill, they both paused and listened.

Dougald shouted through the door, "My lady, you must come at once as His Lairdship has taken a turn for the worse."

"He is not coming to me?" The tears in her voice shook Malcolm to the core.

"Nay, lass. He could not make the stairs. He is lying by the fire in the kitchen, barely conscious."

A man cursed inside the room in the direction of the bed. Hushed male voices spoke all at once in a corner away from the door.

"What will we do, Conan?" one of the men asked.

Conan. Malcolm would gut him once he got hold of the false bard.

"Tell his other brother to come in, that you have sprained your ankle."

"Dougald," Anice called out from the bed, her voice nearly weeping, "you must come to me as I have sprained my ankle and need help to be with my husband."

"Aye." He pushed on the door slightly.

As soon as he did, Anice shouted, "'Tis a trap! There are—" A slap followed and Anice cried out.

All at once bedlam reigned. Malcolm motioned for Angus to enter through the window. Dougald stormed into the chamber with the men. Arrows flew at them, while Angus charged the men with his sword as they stood in front of the women.

Malcolm challenged Conan and dove at him with his sword. "Your wound is not so bothersome these days I see."

"Nay, 'tis much improved."

"What do you and your men hope to accomplish? You will all die here this verra eve and for what? The baron has tucked tail like a whimpering dog and abandoned ye."

"He will return."

"Nay this eve. Nay to save your neck."

One of the baron's knights grabbed Morrigan, and she let out a startled scream. Venetia thrust a dagger into his back, and he quickly released the lady.

Conan thrust again at Malcolm, but he blocked the blow with his sword, metal striking metal, ringing like an echo in the air. "How did you escape Northampton?"

"Pretended to be dying."

"Aye, well this time," Malcolm said, slashing his sword at Conan's chest, "'twill not be a pretense."

Conan groaned as the claymore struck him with such force, his ribs cracked and penetrated his lungs. Gasping for air, he collapsed on the floor. "The baron will...return."

"Aye, no doubt, and meet the same fate."

He glanced over at the other of the baron's men who'd all been killed. "Remove them."

"Aye, my laird," MacTavish said.

"And for God's sake, ensure there are no more of them on the grounds or in the keep."

"Aye," several of the men said.

Dougald motioned to the women. "Let us allow the laird and his lady to get some sleep." He winked at Malcolm.

Anice touched Malcolm's shoulder. "I worried Dougald was telling the truth. That you were hurting overmuch."

Dougald waited until the last, ensuring all the bodies were removed, then led Morrigan out after the others left. "You might want to bar the door in the unlikely event some of the staff may wish to intrude on your privacy."

"Aye." Malcolm barred the door upon his brother's retreat. He turned to see Anice drop her bliaut to the floor. He stared at her for a moment dressed only in her shift, her breasts already peaked and the rosy tips showing through the nearly transparent cloth. "Are you all right, lass?"

She shivered. He crossed the floor to her.

"'Tis you who have been injured, my laird." She touched his bloodied sleeve. "You dinna want to wait because of your shoulder, do ye?"

"'Tis only a scratch." He touched the redness on her cheek where one of the baron's men had slapped her. Then he combed his fingers through her unbound hair, taking a deep breath of the lavender-scented satiny strands scented. "You are a vision, love."

A smile stirred on her lips while she traced his chest with her fingertips, tantalizing him, stirring him up. "I want ye, my laird husband, but only if you are no' hurting."

"I ache something fierce, but no' in the arm." He raised his brows to punctuate his remark.

"I promised you a back rub." She leaned over and kissed his cheek.

How such a soft, unimposing kiss could tantalize him so, he couldn't fathom. But he restrained the urge to rip off the rest of his clothes and hers also to fulfill his randy desire. A back rub was not what he had in mind for now. "A back rub?"

She reached down and pulled his shirt over his head. "Only I wouldna wish you to fall asleep on me before you pleasure me, my husband."

"Nay, I wouldna do that to my bonny bride."

She started to lift her shift, but he hurried to help her.

As soon as the gown lay on the floor, he covered her breasts with his hands and lifted and fondled the soft mounds.

"You are sure bonny. You ken, you never told me why you were climbing out of the second story window at Arundel, my lady."

"I wished to walk in the gardens."

"Aye. Taking the stairs inside the keep was too inconvenient for ye?" He studied the sparkle in her green eyes and the smile that played on her full lips.

"Mayhap I saw a Highlander upon his fine destrier and wished to catch his eye."

He chuckled. "You caught my eye, lass. You nearly

gave my brothers and me a stroke. Had you left the castle before in that manner?"

"No' there. Here, many a time."

He shook his head, then ran his hands down her naked skin. "I will not allow my lady wife to endanger herself in such a manner in the future. But I will submit to a backrub, after attending to…other business."

CHAPTER 21

Early the next morning after a night of sexual delight with the lady of his dreams, Malcolm and his brothers and a select group of men-at-arms prepared to leave the castle in the direction of a village north of Brecken intent on taking Lord MacKnight, Anice's former steward, into custody. 'Twas good the marshal's daughter had overheard MacKnight's nephew say where his uncle was hiding.

Dougald said to Malcolm, "Lady Anice will not be pleased ye go to capture Laird MacKnight without taking her with ye."

"She's had a long hard ride already."

"Are ye talking about the travel we took to get here, or your activities last night?"

Malcolm smiled. "She may not be able to sit on a saddle on either account for a couple of days."

Dougald shook his head. "No annulment, eh, Malcolm?"

"No' now." Which pleased Malcolm no end. Only he still had to deal with King Henry.

The party rode beyond the gatehouse and the portcullis was dropped back into place.

Angus said, "Ye are sure the marshal's daughter was correct in believing he is at this particular village?"

"We can only hope. But we will search any hovel along the way, just to be sure."

"Lady Anice will be a handful when you return," Angus said, smiling. "She did not want to be left at the castle when you track down her steward."

"Aye, she will have to learn that I am laird of Brecken Castle now."

Angus glanced at Dougald and smiled. "It will be entertaining when we return, dinna you think?"

"Aye, the lass and Malcolm have been a great source of entertainment for the last few days."

"Och, ye will see the lass will be so pleased we have returned with the vermin, she will think naught of the fact we left her safely behind." Malcolm's scowl was meant to silence his brothers, but both burst out laughing instead.

***

Anice swept her hands over the mattress beside her, trying to locate her husband after a night of steamy sexual encounters, but when she found him not, she bolted upright. If he left the castle grounds to capture MacKnight without her, she'd strangle him!

Fuming, she untangled herself from the bed linens and jumped from the high bed. Once she'd lit a candle, she yanked her shift off the floor where Malcolm had thrown it the night before.

How dare he leave without her? Mayhap he hadn't left yet, and she could still catch up to him.

A light tap on the door preceded her half-cousin's appearance, then Nola entered the chamber. "I saw the candle's soft glow underneath the door but thought you might sleep a wee bit longer after your long tiresome journey."

"Where is Laird MacNeill?" Anice snapped, unable to control her temper.

Nola helped her on with her blue woolen overgown, unruffled by Anice's outburst. "He has gone with his brothers and fifteen of our clansmen to take Laird MacKnight into custody. But I have to tell ye the good news."

Anice frowned at her, not believing any news could be good under the circumstances. Malcolm knew very well she wanted to help arrest the man who was instrumental in the death of her uncle and other staff. "Aye?"

"Mai and Laird MacNeill's bodyguard, Gunnolf, came in this morning."

"Mai?" Anice's mouth dropped open in astonishment. She couldn't believe her lady-in-waiting had gone ahead and traveled anyway.

"Aye. After a day of rest, she said she couldna stand the thought that ye were alone with the MacNeill laird and his brothers. So she convinced Gunnolf, who apparently was also of a mind to rejoin Laird MacNeill, to go with her."

"All alone?"

"Nay, the earl sent some men with them. They are still asleep as I thought ye would be." Nola plaited Anice's hair, though she could barely sit still to allow it.

"Where did His Lairdship go?"

"They would not tell me. I think they had some notion ye would try to follow them."

"Who told them where MacKnight was headed?"

Nola hesitated to speak which increased Anice's ire.

Anice folded her arms. "Tell me, Nola. 'Tis only a matter of time before I should find out and then..."

Nola finished with her hose and shoes. "His Lairdship will be angry with me, but I overheard him mention the marshal's daughter."

Anice's stomach vaulted. God's teeth. In all the excitement, she'd forgotten about the girl's duplicity. "Who did Laird MacNeill leave..." She shook her head. "Never mind." She stormed out of the chamber.

"My lady," Nola said, running after her.

Anice stalked down the hall, and motioned to a male servant, who instantly looked alarmed as his black brows pinched together, and he quickly bowed to her. "Is MacTavish still here?"

"My lady, I overheard Laird MacNeill tell him he was to stay and protect ye."

She noted the quaver in his voice, and she suspected her husband had already made it clear she was to be kept at home like a good lady of the castle. "'Tis most urgent. Tell him I wish to see him at once."

"Aye, my lady." He quickly bowed again and hurried off.

"What is wrong, Lady Anice?" Nola asked.

"The marshal's daughter poisoned my uncle."

Nola gasped.

"Aye," Anice said, lifting her gowns, then ran down the stairs. "She poisoned MacKnight's wife, too, because she was his mistress. I dinna believe she would reveal his hiding place except possibly under threat of death."

"My lady, whatever shall we do?"

"Where is Mistress Morganna?"

"She was practicing archery this morn."

"Fetch her for me, will ye?"

Nola clasped her hands together. "My lady, Laird MacNeill has given strict orders that ye are no' to leave the castle unless he gives his express permission."

"Is that so?" Anice smiled, but she was certain the look was pure evil. "His Lairdship doesna know me verra well, does he now?"

"Aye, my lady. I shall fetch Morrigan, but I can see my head will be separated from my body when His Lairdship returns."

"He is not that bad a tyrant, most of the time."

MacTavish stalked into the keep, his blue eyes hard, his jaw tight. She knew the look, when he was determined to say no to her, but she was even more determined than him. Though he was but twenty and six years old, he'd earned his position as captain of the guard for his prowess in fighting on the battlefield. Of all her uncle's staff, she'd always found him the most difficult to get around when she wanted her way and it was against her uncle's wishes. This time she would not be thwarted.

"My lady, you wished to speak to me about something most urgent?"

"Aye. The marshal's daughter poisoned my uncle. She told Laird MacNeill where to find my former steward, yet she was his mistress. Do ye think the devil would tell him the truth about Laird MacKnight's hiding place?"

MacTavish's eyes grew round. "I will have the woman arrested at once."

"And assemble fifteen men as my escort. We'll need to warn Laird MacNeill he is on a wild boar chase."

"Ye cannot go, my lady, by order of Laird MacNeill himself." MacTavish's jaw was set, like always when he attempted to countermand her wishes.

Despite himself, she liked the man. The only one she'd ever known who could stand up to her. Well, like Malcolm could.

She knew Malcolm only wished to keep her safe, but she wasn't about to sit back and wait for Malcolm's return like the dutiful wife she should be when he was not headed in the right direction, she was certain. Now, she had every intention of going after him, informing of his error, and accompanying him in his quest.

"Go!" Anice said, unable to contain her irritation. "Arrest the girl."

For a moment, MacTavish moved not a foot to do her bidding. Then deciding otherwise, he said, "Aye, my lady."

When he hurried outside the keep, Morrigan rushed inside, carrying her bow and arrow, her brown hair loosened from the braids by the breeze, her brown eyes wide, her face flushed. "Nola says ye are going to leave here to capture MacKnight."

"Aye."

"And ye wish to take me?"

"Aye. Mai will insist I have a lady accompany me, but I need one who can use a bow as well as me."

"We are not going alone, are we?"

"Nay. Fifteen of our men will escort us."

"I heard tell Laird MacNeill gave orders to detain you."

"Did he now?" Anice shook her head. "That is like telling the sun not to rise when the day arrives."

***

As soon as all the men were armed, the party rode in the direction Malcolm and his men had taken, but on the way there, like so many times before, Anice sensed trouble, only this time in the village of Carr, in an easterly direction not north where Malcolm and his men had gone.

"Och," Anice said, the vision as clear as if she saw the scene played out before her now.

"What is the matter, my lady?" Morrigan asked.

"Laird MacKnight is in the village of Carr, hiding out until he can secure reinforcements."

MacTavish heard her words and turned his horse to rejoin hers. "My lady, are ye sure?" he asked, his face a mask of disbelief.

"Aye," she lied, not wanting to reveal how she knew, "the marshal's daughter oft went there on business, but when I questioned her about it, she had seemed uneasy about something. I thought she was secretly meeting with a man her da did not approve. Now I know it was MacKnight."

"Ye said you wished to locate Laird MacNeill first, my lady." He sounded hopeful Anice would go along with her earlier plan. In fact, she assumed it was the only reason he finally agreed to it.

"Aye, that was before I realized where MacKnight would be hiding and it takes us east instead of north where

316

Laird MacNeill was headed."

"Will ye return with an escort, my lady? The rest of us will go to the village and arrest MacKnight." 'Twas not a question, but more of a command.

"Nay, your numbers would be reduced. Lead the way, sir."

He shook his head. "I was rather fond of Laird MacNeill. He will now have my head over this."

"I will speak on your behalf, MacTavish. I have His Lairdship's ear."

For a second, MacTavish stared at Anice, then he smiled and barked out a laugh. "Ye have much more than that, my lady." He kicked his horse to a canter and spoke to several men about the change of plans.

Anice's whole body heated with chagrin. Took a man to see something sexual in a lady's comment when there was none intended.

"Did ye see MacKnight in a…a vision, my lady," Morrigan asked, her words hushed, her eyes big.

"Think you I have visions?" Anice had no idea anyone other than Mai was aware of it. She hoped her ladies didn't think her a witch.

Morrigan's gaze did not shift. Finally, she nodded. "Aye, my lady."

"Who else thinks such a thing?"

"Nola, my lady. And Mary. Well, and Venetia. We suspect Mai does, but she wouldna say."

"You have discussed this behind my back?" Anice raised a brow, annoyed.

Morrigan nodded. "Beg pardon, but Mai said we should never bring this up if we knew what was good for us. So can you? See the future, I mean?"

"Sometimes," Anice admitted, hoping her ladies would understand and judge her not harshly. "But no' everything." Not everything, but she could see a battle in the village, and there was no stopping it from happening.

Worse, Laird Robertson was there with some of his men. If he caught sight of her, he'd kill her for certain to avenge his brother's death.

***

Malcolm and his men searched the village but found nothing amiss.

"Think you the marshal's daughter had the wrong place?" Dougald asked, joining him after searching a croft.

"Methinks the wench might have been protecting MacKnight."

Angus grunted. "How many more traitors are at Brecken?"

"My laird!" Kemp shouted, galloping into the village, sending the dust flying, his small size dwarfed by the horse he'd commandeered.

Malcolm started to spit out, "What the devil are ye—"

"'Tis Lady Anice."

"What has happened?" Malcolm said through clenched teeth, his heart thundering against his ribs.

"She has led a party to the village Carr—"

"What?" He couldn't curb his anger.

"I followed behind them, until I kenned what direction they were headed. Then I heard the men tell one another where they were going. Ye have to protect her, my laird. They say MacKnight and more of his men are there."

Malcolm and his men were already mounting their horses. They headed out at a gallop, and Malcolm turned to Kemp. "How does she know MacKnight is at this village?"

"I do not know, milord."

Had she had one of her uncanny premonitions? 'Twas the only reason he assumed she'd have left the safety of Brecken Castle. The next time he gave an order, he would have the lady locked in the tower to ensure she didn't talk her people into allowing her to do whatever she had a mind to do. *Willful lass.*

He and his men headed across Glen Affric, hoping they

would reach the village in time to protect Anice and the men she rode with. That sent a new plague of concern washing over him.

"How many were with her?" he asked Kemp.

"The Mistress Morrigan."

"And?"

"Oh, aye, I get your meaning. Fifteen like ye have here. But she also has a lady with her."

Malcolm glanced at Dougald who responded with a shake of his head. "Did we no' tell ye, Malcolm?"

"Say naught a word, brother, as I am sorely vexed with the lass."

The only sense of relief he had in the matter was that she said Henry would have his physician examine her, and if she knew this for certain, she had to live.

When they arrived at the village, his heart sank. Anice's men were fighting hand to hand in the village square against armed men, and some of the farmers were aiding the lady's men, swinging pitchforks and scythes.

Malcolm and his men charged into the fray, but he saw no sign of Anice. Seeing MacTavish, he headed in his direction, slashing at MacKnight's men as he made his way.

"MacTavish! Where is Lady Anice?"

"My laird!" MacTavish motioned with his sword toward the tavern. "Safely inside."

"Which of these men is MacKnight?"

"I havena seen him, my laird. As soon as we came into the village, armed men began attacking us. I warn ye, the men over there are Baron Fontenot's men I recognize as three of the six we freed last eve. Worse, Laird Robertson is here also. He has always threatened to take revenge for Lady Anice killing his brother."

Malcolm cursed, his cut arm throbbing as he cut down another of MacKnight's men. They were outnumbered two to one, yet Malcolm and his men were quickly evening up the odds, fighting skills he and his brothers learned in the

Crusades.

He'd no more than sliced a man's chest with his claymore when he heard Anice scream and saw her run into the square with her bow and arrow readied.

Dodging men to get to her, his blood rushed in his ears. "Anice!"

She didn't hear him above the noise of angry Gaelic shouts and clashing swords.

She let her arrow fly, just as he reached her. Grabbing her up, he ran her back inside the tavern.

"Malcolm, Kemp! A man nearly killed him!"

"Damn, woman, stay here, will ye? I'll get the lad safely to ye."

She nodded emphatically, tears streaking her cheeks, washing away the dust in rivulets.

His heart in his throat, he gave her a quick hug, then dashed outside and ran for Kemp, who wielded a sword too heavy for him. He probably had found one lying about, the owner no longer needing it.

"Kemp!" Malcolm shouted. "Get yourself to the tavern and protect the women!"

"Aye," the lad shouted back, his youthful voice tugging at Malcolm's heart.

No lad should be as young as he, fighting his first battle. Though he recalled Angus doing the very same thing at his age in a skirmish with the Campbells.

Malcolm fought the men around Kemp, clearing a path for the lad to retreat to the tavern.

A man raised a sword to strike the lad, but an arrow hit the man in the neck, killing him instantly.

Malcolm looked back to see Morrigan notching an arrow from the doorway of the tavern and Anice doing the same.

More men poured into the square, and Malcolm dodged the sword's sharp blade of one of the baron's men.

"Where is your laird, mon?" Malcolm taunted, the

blood coursing hot in his veins. "Where is Fontenot? Left ye to fend for yourselves?"

The Norman swung his sword, cutting Malcolm's shirt.

Malcolm heard a lady's scream. Anice? Morrigan?

With a sharp decisive thrust, Malcolm stabbed the baron's man, then swung around.

Morrigan lay in front of the tavern still as death. Anice was nowhere in sight.

His heart couldn't beat any harder. "Anice!" Considering the swarm of new men, Malcolm feared he and his brothers would not survive this battle. Then Anice's words came to mind. The king would want his head. He would survive.

Fighting his way back to the tavern, he saw Fontenot thrusting his sword at Angus.

His brother's sword arm dripped with blood, and he struggled against Fontenot's blows, no doubt because the coward had waited until Malcolm's men were half worn out. Malcolm barreled through the men and slashed at Fontenot's flank.

Startled to see Malcolm, Fontenot jumped back, but not before Malcolm's blade cut Fontenot's shoulder. "All of your vermin will die at Robert Curthose's hand," Fontenot said. "Except ye will be mine."

Angus struck at Fontenot, the baron's eyes sparked with fury, but he deflected Angus's sword with a clank. Another of his men threatened Angus, and Malcolm again took the lead against the baron.

Thinking to unsettle the baron, Malcolm gave him a thin smile and goaded, "Ye wondered if Lady Anice and I were wed before or after the incident of the croft."

As he assumed, Fontenot swung blindly out of rage, but Malcolm easily outmaneuvered him, sweeping aside Fontenot's ineffectual thrusts. Fontenot struck again, this time Malcolm forcing his sword down. Malcolm lunged in attack; Fontenot countered but fell back. Malcolm swung, slicing through Fontenot's sleeve, the baron lumbering backwards, attempting to regain his footing. Malcolm directed the battle, and all Fontenot could do was block and retreat, losing ground again and again.

"Ye were not man and wife," Fontenot accused, his words full of hate, the sweat pouring from his brow. He bumped into another man fighting with Dougald, then quickly gave them space.

Malcolm thrust his sword at Fontenot, who fell, landing square on his back with an oof, the hard-packed earth knocking the breath from him. Malcolm slammed his boot on his chest and held his sword tip at his breast. "The lady was sick with the cold, and ye would have tossed her from the bedding with no concern to her well-being. Or ye had it in mind to bed the lass, had I no' kept my sword readied the rest of the night to gut you if you had tried, ye whoreson. Give me a reason I should let ye live."

Fontenot's chest heaved, his eyes narrowed. "I am the king's choice for the lady, and he will have your head for taking her innocence."

"Ye are a traitor to the king and have stolen the life of the lady's beloved uncle." Malcolm plunged his sword into the baron's heart, for Anice, for her uncle, for the others the baron had ordered murdered.

Fontenot cried out, his eyes glazed over, and he grunted, "Ye were not married."

Thinking of what Anice so oft said, Malcolm replied with a sneer, "'Tis no concern of yours, Fontenot. 'Tis no' your concern."

Fontenot's eyes held death, no longer blinking; the baron no longer a threat to Malcolm's beloved lass. Malcolm swung around, seeing Angus still managing to fend off the hoard and his brother fighting as if he were a Viking berserker possessed. But he couldn't believe his eyes when he spied Gunnolf, the blond bearded Norseman who served as his bodyguard, swinging his ax at the enemy. When had he arrived, and what had become of Mai?

'Twas not anything he could deal with now.

Malcolm bolted for the tavern, and when he reached Morrigan, he touched her moon-pale cheek, then felt her neck, finding a faint pulse. Blood pooled on her temple from where someone had struck her. He shoved his sword in its scabbard and grabbed the lady up. Carrying her into the tavern, he knew it would be safer than were she'd lain in the square, but his mind focused on Anice and what had happened to the lass.

Upon entering the tavern, he saw her tied to a chair in the corner of the room, her mouth gagged, and her eyes wild with fear. His heart nearly stopped. Kemp lay on the floor near her feet, his eyes closed, a knot as big as his fist on the side of the lad's temple.

On the other side of the tavern, a redheaded man waved a sword in the air and shouted in Gaelic, "Ye will grant me safe passage or the lady dies." He worked his way back toward Anice maneuvering around wooden tables and chairs, as Malcolm lay Morrigan on a table.

"Ye be MacKnight?" Malcolm asked, advancing on the man and withdrew his sword from its scabbard. "Ye be the one who killed the lady's uncle?"

MacKnight tried to maneuver in Anice's direction, his sword hand shaking, his cheeks blazing red, his green eyes fearful.

Not about to let the brigand get any closer to his wife, Malcolm lunged forward like a lion intent on killing the threat. The dull ache in his arm dissipated, the weariness he'd felt from battling so many, faded until all he saw was the man who would die before he murdered another soul.

MacKnight tried to run for Anice, but Malcolm jumped into his path, his unbound hair bristling with tension, anger filling every pore. "Ye had your wife poisoned, aye? And Laird Dunstan as well? A woman's way, ye cowardly son of a whore. And Thompson, did ye cut him down in a fair fight or have your men take care of him, too? Ye are nothing but a cur."

MacKnight slashed at Malcolm, clearly rattled.

"Have ye been the steward of the castle too long? Havena fought your own battles for overlong, mon?" Malcolm knocked MacKnight's sword aside. "As the new laird of Brecken Castle, I condemn ye for the death of Laird Dunstan." With a violent thrust, Malcolm pinned MacKnight to the wooden wall, then yanked his sword out and wiped the blood off on MacKnight's shirt.

The laird collapsed to the floor, dead.

"Malcolm!" Dougald hollered, running into the tavern, only pausing to see Morrigan unconscious and Anice bound to the chair.

"What news?" Malcolm shouted, waving his sword at the village square, knowing if Dougald was no longer fighting, the battle had to have ceased. Though how they could have come out on top was a mystery to him. He hurried to cut Anice's ropes.

"Ye will never believe who came to our aid."

Malcolm pulled the dirty rag from Anice's mouth and she cried out, "Henry is here!"

Malcolm stared at her, then looked out to the square. "Think you he knows that I have wed ye, Anice?" Without a second guess, he gathered her into his arms, squeezing her against his chest, grateful she was unharmed. He would not give her up to any man.

She returned a loving embrace, but then hurriedly pulled away to check on Kemp. With the lad's head cradled in her lap, she said with tears in her eyes, "He is alive, and Morrigan?"

"She is stirring, my lady," Dougald said, wrapping a cloth around Morrigan's wound. "As for King Henry, he is verra angry. I wouldna want to be his new relation by marriage about now who hadna permission to wed his ward."

***

Once the wounded men were taken care of, and Morrigan and Kemp were resting comfortably back at Brecken Castle, Anice changed her dirty gowns for clean ones, and hurried to make King Henry welcome, but Malcolm intercepted her with a grim look before she entered the hall.

"What is wrong, Malcolm?" Anice asked, her heart already pounding with fresh anxiety.

He took her hand in his and kissed it, then pulled a missive out, tucked in his belt. "My brother, James, needs our help. Trouble with another clan at his border."

Anice's throat constricted, her heart sinking. "You...you are leaving?"

"Nay, love. King Henry says he learned Laird Robertson was gathering troops for Robert Curthose but was unable to apprehend him in the village this morn. Since Robertson is still a threat in the area, I wouldna leave ye to your own defenses."

She raised a brow, wondering if he did not think she could defend her castle.

Smiling, he kissed her cheek. "No' that you would not do a fine job, lass, but I would be useless to my brother when my thoughts would be about ye."

"Aye, I understand your meaning, and I am thankful ye will not be going, but your brothers—"

"Dougald, aye, but Angus's wounds need mending. Gunnolf will accompany Dougald, and I will send thirty men, if you approve."

Anice sighed deeply. 'Twas Malcolm's call to do as he pleased now that he was laird of the castle, but she appreciated that he wished her approval. "Aye, and thank ye for asking me, Malcolm, but the lasses will surely miss your brother."

"Aye, lass." He winked, then motioned to the hall. "The king awaits us."

With dreaded expectancy, she rested her hand on Malcolm's sleeve, trying to calm her rapidly beating heart and her trembling legs when she and Malcolm joined the king in the hall.

He spoke not a word to her or Malcolm until they sat down to the meal. Henry raised a tankard of wine to his mouth, took a healthy swig, then set it down on the table. "My advisor tells me Baron Fontenot sided with Robert Curthose."

"Aye, Your Grace," Malcolm said, watching the king.

Henry looked at Anice, his countenance grim. She quickly nodded her head, more concerned about how he felt about her marriage to Malcolm, than the fact Malcolm had slain the man Henry wanted Anice to wed.

"My advisor also tells me Lord MacKnight was the one who killed your uncle, Lady Anice, and had several others murdered, including his own wife."

"Aye, Your Grace," Malcolm said again, answering for Anice, which was fine with her.

She couldn't seem to find her tongue, afraid Henry would force Malcolm to give her up. Anice felt the tension crackling in the air, while her people ate in morbid silence.

Buttering a piece of bread, Henry continued, "He said Baron Fontenot was the one behind Lord MacKnight's despicable acts."

"Aye, Your Grace."

"This is all very well indeed, and you and your brothers are to be commended for a job well done. What I do not understand is the part about your marriage to Lady Anice."

"I had to wed her to protect her from Baron Fontenot," Malcolm hastily said.

"Then the marriage can be annulled at once since ye no longer need to protect her. I shall have another Norman lord sent to court the lady." Henry lifted a black brow.

"Nay!" Malcolm quickly added, "*Your Grace*. I love the lady, and she me. We wish no annulment. I intend to protect her forever."

Henry's face remained hard, and Anice knew what the king had on his mind, though she prayed he would not mention it at the meal.

"Has this marriage been consummated?" Henry asked Malcolm, with a sly glance at Anice.

She swore everyone in the castle heard the king's question. She quit breathing, and every inch of her body melted under the pressure.

Malcolm reached under the table and squeezed her hand. "Aye, Your Grace."

Henry ground his teeth, then looked at Anice. "Queen Matilda asked that I allow ye this transgression. But I will not, if ye have not consummated the marriage. My physician will see to ye after the meal. And, Lord MacNeill, when ye ask me if ye can court one of my wards, ye are to give me time to say aye or nay, not take it upon yourself to do as you please."

"Aye, Your Grace," Malcolm said, this time with a definite lift to his voice.

Anice still wasn't happy. Malcolm wasn't going to be the one the king's physician examined to prove she and Malcolm were telling the truth. On the other hand, unless the king's physician lied about Anice's condition, it verra much sounded like Henry would permit her marriage to Malcolm after all.

"One other thing," Henry said with a glint in his eye, "do not allow the lady to have access to ropes. Rumors abound that she climbs out windows of a keep too many stories above the ground should she wish your company not."

Malcolm smiled, and drank his fill. "Aye, Your Grace. I will remember that."

Henry shook his purse. "I understand ye will be paying off a wager soon, which will make me a richer man."

The king was one of those who had bet Malcolm would

wed her?

She shook her head. There was no understanding the English, or the Normans. She kissed Malcolm's hand. 'Twas a good thing then, that she ended up with her Highlander.

Henry began talking to Dougald about the battle, leaving her and Malcolm to speak in private.

"Love me, lass?" Malcolm asked Anice.

"Ye know I do, my braw Highlander." She kissed his lips without reserve, loving the taste of wine on his velvety mouth and tongue.

"Bonny lass," he whispered against her cheek, "'ye are a treasure. And all mine to keep."

"Aye, forever, my laird, as ye are mine."

"Now, if we can only get our good king to retire early," Malcolm said, one brow cocked in a devilish way.

"We can retire to our chambers for a much-needed sleep."

He chuckled, the sound darkly sensual. "I have no intention of sleeping with ye this eve, lass. And I wager I will have to nap during the day to keep up my strength at night."

"No more wagers, my husband. From the sounds of the last one, ye lost money. Think I you are not a betting man."

"'Tis I who won the bet, lass."

"And I, love." Sitting beside the brawniest of Highlanders, her husband, her love, her life, Anice glanced at her people. King Henry's making her his ward had turned out well after all, no' a curse as she feared.

Malcolm ran his hand over her thigh in a sensual caress. No' a curse at all.

ABOUT THE AUTHOR

Bestselling and award-winning author **Terry Spear** has written over sixty paranormal romance novels and seven medieval Highland historical romances. Her first werewolf romance, *Heart of the Wolf,* was named a 2008 *Publishers Weekly*'s Best Book of the Year, and her subsequent titles have garnered high praise and hit the *USA Today* bestseller list. A retired officer of the U.S. Army Reserves, Terry lives in Spring, Texas, where she is working on her next werewolf romance, continuing her new series about shapeshifting jaguars, writing Highland medieval romance, and having fun with her young adult novels. When she's not writing, she's photographing everything that catches her eye, making teddy bears, and playing with her Havanese puppies. For more information, please visit www.terryspear.com, or follow her on Twitter, @TerrySpear. She is also on Facebook at http://www.facebook.com/terry.spear. And on Wordpress at:

Terry Spear's Shifters

http://terryspear.wordpress.com/

ALSO BY TERRY SPEAR

Heart of the Cougar Series:
Cougar's Mate, Book 1
Call of the Cougar, Book 2
Taming the Wild Cougar, Book 3
Covert Cougar Christmas (Novella)
Double Cougar Trouble, Book 4
Cougar Undercover, Book 5
Cougar Magic, Book 6

Heart of the Bear Series
Loving the White Bear, Book 1
Claiming the White Bear, Book 2

The Highlanders Series: Winning the Highlander's Heart, The
Accidental Highland Hero, Highland Rake, Taming the Wild
Highlander, The Highlander, Her Highland Hero, The Viking's
Highland Lass, His Wild Highland Lass (novella), Vexing the
Highlander (novella), My Highlander
Other historical romances: Lady Caroline & the Egotistical
Earl, A Ghost of a Chance at Love

Heart of the Wolf Series: Heart of the Wolf, Destiny of the
Wolf, To Tempt the Wolf, Legend of the White Wolf,
Seduced by the Wolf, Wolf Fever, Heart of the Highland
Wolf, Dreaming of the Wolf, A SEAL in Wolf's Clothing, A
Howl for a Highlander, A Highland Werewolf Wedding, A
SEAL Wolf Christmas, Silence of the Wolf, Hero of a
Highland Wolf, A Highland Wolf Christmas, A SEAL Wolf
Hunting; A Silver Wolf Christmas, A SEAL Wolf in Too
Deep, Alpha Wolf Need Not Apply, Billionaire in Wolf's

Clothing, Between a Rock and a Hard Place, SEAL Wolf
Undercover, Dreaming of a White Wolf Christmas, Flight of
the White Wolf, A Billionaire Wolf for Christmas, All's Fair
in Love and Wolf, Wolff Brothers: You Had Me at Wolf,
Night of the Billionaire Wolf, Red Wolf Christmas
SEAL Wolves: To Tempt the Wolf, A SEAL in Wolf's
Clothing, A SEAL Wolf Christmas, A SEAL Wolf Hunting,
A SEAL Wolf in Too Deep, SEAL Wolf Undercover, SEAL
Wolf Surrender
Silver Town Wolves: Destiny of the Wolf, Wolf Fever,
Dreaming of the Wolf, Silence of the Wolf, A Silver Wolf
Christmas, Alpha Wolf Need Not Apply, Between a Rock
and a Hard Place, All's Fair in Love and Wolf, Silver Town
Wolf: Home for the Holidays
Wolff Brothers (New to Silver Town): You Had Me at
Wolf
White Wolves: Legend of the White Wolf, Dreaming of a
White Wolf Christmas, Flight of the White Wolf
Billionaire Wolves: Billionaire in Wolf's Clothing, A
Billionaire Wolf for Christmas, Night of the Billionaire Wolf
Highland Wolves: Heart of the Highland Wolf, A Howl for
a Highlander, A Highland Werewolf Wedding, Hero of a
Highland Wolf, A Highland Wolf Christmas
Red Wolves: Seduced by the Wolf, Red Wolf Christmas
Heart of the Jaguar Series: Savage Hunger, Jaguar Fever,
Jaguar Hunt, Jaguar Pride, A Very Jaguar Christmas, You
Had Me at Jaguar
Jaguar Novella: The Witch and the Jaguar
Romantic Suspense: Deadly Fortunes, In the Dead of the
Night, Relative Danger, Bound by Danger
Vampire romances: Killing the Bloodlust, Deadly Liaisons,
Huntress for Hire, Forbidden Love
Vampire Novellas: Vampiric Calling, The Siren's Lure,
Seducing the Huntress
Other Romance: Exchanging Grooms, Marriage, Las Vegas
Style

Science Fiction Romance: Galaxy Warrior
Teen/Young Adult/Fantasy Books The World of Fae:
The Dark Fae, Book 1, The Deadly Fae, Book 2, The
Winged Fae, Book 3, The Ancient Fae, Book 4, Dragon Fae,
Book 5, Hawk Fae, Book 6, Phantom Fae, Book 7, Golden
Fae, Book 8, Falcon Fae, Book 9, Woodland Fae, Book 10
The World of Elf:
The Shadow Elf, The Darkland Elf
Blood Moon Series:
Kiss of the Vampire, The Vampire...In My Dreams
Demon Guardian Series:
The Trouble with Demons; Demon Trouble, Too; Demon
Hunter
Non-Series for Now:
Ghostly Liaisons, The Beast Within, Courtly Masquerade
Deidre's Secret
The Magic of Inherian:
The Scepter of Salvation, The Mage of Monrovia, Emerald
Isle of Mists (TBA)